FROM
MIND TO MIND:
Tales of Communication from analog

ANTHOLOGY #9

FROM
MIND TO MIND:
Tales of Communication from analog

Edited by Stanley Schmidt

Davis Publications, Inc.
380 Lexington Avenue
New York, NY 10017

COPYRIGHT NOTICES AND ACKNOWLEDGMENTS

Grateful acknowledgment is hereby made for permission to reprint the following:

Barrier by Anthony Boucher; copyright © 1942 by Street & Smith Publications, Inc.; renewed 1969 by The Conde Nast Publications, Inc.; reprinted by permission of Curtis Brown, Ltd.

The Signals by Francis A. Cartier; copyright © 1966 by The Conde Nast Publications, Inc.; reprinted by permission of the author.

The Gift of Gab by Jack Vance; copyright 1955 by Street & Smith Publications, Inc.; renewed 1983 by Davis Publications, Inc.; reprinted by permission of Kirby McCauley, Ltd.

Top Secret by Eric Frank Russell; © 1956 by Street & Smith Publications, Inc., renewed 1984 by Davis Publications, Inc.; reprinted by permission of Scott Meredith Literary Agency, Inc.

Meihem in ce Klasrum by Dolton Edwards; copyright 1946 by Street & Smith Publications, Inc.; renewed 1973 by the Conde Nast Publications, Inc.; reprinted by permission of the author.

Omnilingual by H. Beam Piper; © 1957 by Street & Smith Publications, Inc.; reprinted by permission of Berkley Publishing Group.

Minds Meet by Paul Ash; copyright © 1966 by The Conde Nast Publications, Inc.; reprinted by permission of the author.

Two-Way Communication by Christopher Anvil; copyright © 1966 by The Conde Nast Publications, Inc.; reprinted by permission of Scott Meredith Literary Agency, Inc.

Duplex by Verge Foray; copyright © 1968 by The Conde Nast Publications, Inc.; reprinted by permission of Scott Meredith Literary Agency, Inc.

Sailing, Through Program Management by Al Charmatz; copyright © 1980 by Davis Publications, Inc.; reprinted by permission of the author.

Beam Pirate by George O. Smith; copyright 1944 by George O. Smith, renewed; reprinted by permission of Blassingame, McCauley & Wood.

From Time to Time by Bruce Stanley Burdick; copyright © 1983 by Davis Publications, Inc.; reprinted by permission of the author.

Shapes to Come by Edward Wellen; copyright © 1969 by The Conde Nast Publications, Inc.; reprinted by permission of the author.

The Piper's Son by Lewis Padgett; copyright © 1944 by Street & Smith Publications, Inc.; renewed 1971 by The Conde Nast Publications, Inc.; reprinted by permission of Don Congdon Associates, Inc.

Babel II by Christopher Anvil; copyright © 1967 by The Conde Nast Publications, Inc.; reprinted by permission of Scott Meredith Literary Agency, Inc.

Collaboration by Mark C. Jarvis; copyright © 1982 by Davis Publications, Inc.; reprinted by permission of the author.

Cover by Joe Burleson

CONTENTS

Introduction
Stanley Schmidt

Minds are, in a sense, islands—but many of the ones we know about have an irresistible compulsion to build bridges. Lacking direct mind-to-mind contact—telepathy—we humans have developed all manner of devices to get ideas and feelings from one mind to another. The oldest and most fundamental, of course, are spoken and written language; but we have greatly extended those basic capabilities by such technological means as printing, telephones, radio, and now computer links.

Problems of communication lie at the root of all interactions among intelligent beings and the growth and maintenance of civilizations, so they have provided a fertile field for the probing imaginations of science fiction writers. Their speculations have expanded outward from familiar questions like how to get anything done when "communication" is conducted by bureaucratic memos, to larger ones like how human languages might evolve in the future and how messages might be transmitted across interplanetary or interstellar distances. If there are other intelligences, either here on Earth or elsewhere, what radically different forms might their communications take? Could we even recognize them? Could we learn to read a dead alien language without a "Rosetta stone"? If we did have telepathy, would it be more help or handicap? For that matter, to what extent do we depend on communication *inside* our own minds, and what might happen if those internal networks were "rewired"?

For more than fifty years, much of the best of such speculation has appeared in *Analog Science Fiction/Science Fact* (formerly called Astounding Science Fiction). In this book you'll find a wide range of those stories, providing entertainment at its best while grappling with questions like those above. Even the wildest of them may someday be a problem we must face in reality—but in the meantime, you're invited to enjoy them both here and in every new issue of *Analog*. ■

BARRIER
Anthony Boucher

THE FIRST DIFFICULTY was with language.

That is only to be expected when you jump five hundred years; but it is none the less perplexing to have your first casual query of: "What city is this?" answered by the sentence: "Stappers will get you. Or be you Slanduch?"

It was significant that the first word John Brent heard in the State was "Stappers." But Brent could not know that then. It was only some hours later and fifty years earlier that he learned the details of the Stapper system. At the moment all that concerned him was food and plausibility.

His appearance was plausible enough. Following Derringer's advice he had traveled naked—"the one costume common to all ages," the scientist had boomed; "which would astonish you more, lad: a naked man, or an Elizabethan courtier in full apparel?"—and commenced his life in the twenty-fifth century by burglary and the theft of a complete outfit of clothing. Iridescent woven plastics tailored in a half-clinging, half-flowing style that looked precious to Brent, but seemed both comfortable and functional.

No man alive in 2473 would have bestowed a second glance on the feloniously clad Brent, but in his speech, he realized at once, lay the danger. He pondered the alternatives presented by the stranger. The Stappers would get him, unless he was a Slanduch. Whatever the Stappers were, things that Get You sound menacing. "Slanduch," he replied.

The stranger nodded. "That bees OK," he said, and Brent wondered what he had committed himself to. "So what city is this?" he repeated.

"*Bees*," the stranger chided. "Stappers be more severe now since Edict of 2470. Before they doed pardon some irregularities, but now none even from Slanduch."

"I be sorry," said Brent humbly, making a mental note that irregular verbs were for some reason perilous. "But for the third time—"

He had thought the wall beside them was solid. He realized now that part of it, at least, was only a deceptive glasslike curtain that parted to let forth a tall and vigorous man, followed by two shorter aides. All three of these wore robes similar to the iridescent garments of Brent and his companion, but of pure white.

The leader halted and barked out, "George Starvel?"

Brent saw a quiet sort of terror begin to grow on his companion's face. He nodded and held out his wrist.

The man in white glanced at what Brent decided must be an identification plaque. "Starvel," he announced, "you speaked against Barrier."

Starvel trembled. "Cosmos knows I doed not."

"Five mans know that you doed."

"Never. I only sayed—"

"You only! Enough!"

The rod appeared in the man's hand only for an instant. Brent saw no flame or discharge, but Starvel was stretched out on the ground and the two aides were picking him up as callously as though he were a log.

The man turned toward Brent, who was taking no chances. He flexed his legs and sprang into the air. His fingertips grasped the rim of the balcony above them, and his feet shot out into the white-robed man's face. His arm and shoulder muscles tensed to their utmost. The smooth plastic surface was hell to keep a grip on. Beneath, he could see his adversary struggling blindly to his feet and groping for the rod. At last, desperately, Brent swung himself up and over the edge.

There was no time to contemplate the beauties of the orderly terrace garden. There was only time to note that there was but one door, and to make for it. It was open and led to a long corridor. Brent turned to the nearest door. Once you've damned yourself with Authority, any private citizen chosen at random is preferable to meeting your nemesis. He started at the door, and it opened before him. He hurried into an empty room.

He looked back at the door. It was shut now, and no one was near to have touched it. He peered into the two adjoining rooms, whose doors were equally obliging. Bathroom and bedroom. No kitchen. And no exit but the door he had come through.

He forced himself to sit down and think. Anything might happen before the Stapper caught up with him, for he had no doubt that was what the white-robed man must be. What had he learned about the twenty-fifty century in this brief encounter?

You must wear an identification plaque. (Memo. How to get one?) You must not use irregular verbs (or nouns; the Stapper had said "mans"). You must not speak against Barrier, whoever or whatever that meant. You must beware white-robed men who lurk behind false walls. You must watch out for rods that kill (query: or merely stun?). Doors open by selenium cells (query: how do they lock?). You must—

The door opened. But it was not the Stapper who stood there, but a tall and majestic woman of, at a guess, sixty. A noble figure—"Roman matron" were the words that flashed into Brent's mind.

The presence of a total stranger in her apartment seemed nowise disconcerting. She opened her arms in a broad gesture of welcome. "John Brent!" she exclaimed in delighted recognition. "It has beed so long!".

"I don't want a brilliant young scientific genius!" Derringer had roared when Brent answered his cryptically worded ad. "I've got 'em here in the laboratory. They've done grand work on the machine. I couldn't live without 'em, and there's not a one

Anthony Boucher

of 'em I'd trust out of this century. Not out of this decade. What I want is four things: A knowledge of history, for a background of analogy to understand what's been going on; linguistic ability, to adjust yourself as rapidly as possible to the changes in language; physical strength and dexterity, to get yourself out of the scrapes that are bound to come up; and social adaptability. A chimpanzee of reasonably sub-human intelligence could operate the machine. What counts is what you'll be able to do and learn after you get there.''

The knowledge of history and the physical qualities had been easy to demonstrate. The linguistic ability was a bit more complex; Derringer had contrived an intricate series of tests involving adjustment to phonetic changes and the capacity to assimilate the principles of a totally fictitious language invented for the occasion. The social adaptability was measured partly by an aptitude test, but largely, Brent guessed, by Derringer's own observation during the weeks of preparation after his probationary hiring.

He had passed all four requirements with flying colors. At least Derringer had grinned at him through the black beard and grunted the reluctant, ''Good man!'' that was his equivalent of rhapsodic praise. His physical agility had already stood him in good stead, and his linguistic mind was rapidly assimilating the new aspects of the language (there were phonetic alterations as well as the changes in vocabulary and inflection—he was particularly struck by the fact that the vowels *a* and *o* no longer possessed the diphthongal off-glide so characteristic of English, but were pure vowels like the Italian *e* and *o*) but his social adaptability was just now hitting a terrific snag.

What the hell do you do when a Roman matron whom you have never seen, born five hundred years after you, welcomes you by name and exclaims that it has beed a long time? (This regular past participle of *be*, Brent reflected, gives the speaker something of the quality of a Bostonian with a cold in the nose.)

For a moment he toyed with the rash notion that she might likewise be a time traveler, someone whom he had known in 1942. Derringer had been positive that this was the first such trip ever attempted; but someone leaving the twentieth century later might still be an earlier arrival in the twenty-fifth. He experimented with the idea hesitantly.

''I suppose,'' Brent ventured, ''you could call five hundred years a long time, in its relative way.''

The Roman matron frowned. ''Do not jest, John. Fifty years be not five hundred. I will confess that first five years seemed at times like five centuries, but after fifty—one does not feel so sharply.''

Does was of course promounced *dooze*. All r's, even terminal, were lightly trilled. These facts Brent noted in the back of his mind, but the fore part was concerned with the immediate situation. If this woman chose to accept him as an acquaintance—it was nowise unlikely that his double should be wandering about in this century—it meant probable protection from the Stapper. His logical mind protested, ''Could this double have your name?'' but he shushed it.

"Did you," he began, and caught himself. "Doed you see anyone in the hall—a man in white?"

The Roman Matron moaned. "Oh, John! Do Stappers seek you again? But of course. If you have comed to destroy Barrier, they must destroy you."

"Whoa there!" Brent had seen what happened to one person who had 'speaked against Barrier.' "I didn't . . . doedn't . . . say anything against Barrier. Not me."

The friendliness began to die from her clear blue eyes. "And I believed you," she said sorrowfully. "You told us of this second Barrier and sweared to destroy it. We think you beed one of us. And now—"

No amount of social adaptability can resist a sympathetic and dignified woman on the verge of tears. Besides, this apartment was for the moment a valuable haven, and if she thought he was a traitor of some sort—

"Look," said Brent. "You see, I am—there isn't any use at this moment trying to be regular—I am not whoever you think I am. I never saw you before. I couldn't have conceivably. Because this is the first instant I've ever been in your time."

"If you wish to lie to me, John—"

"I'm not lying. And I'm not John—at least not the one you're thinking of. I'm John Brent, I'm twenty-eight years old, and I was born in 1914—a good five and a half centuries ago."

You'd think a remark like that would have some effect. It sounds like an impressive curtain line. There should at least be a tableau of stunned reaction. But the Roman matron simply stared at him sadly and murmured, "I know, John, I know. Then why do you deny me and all our plans? What will Stephen think?"

The amazement turned out to be Brent's. "You . . . you know that I'm a time traveler?"

"John, my dear, why be you so foolish? You be safe from Stappers here. Stephen has treated walls against listening. And you know that to admit to being time traveler is as dangerous as to admit your plans against Barrier. Trust me, John."

"For some unknown reason, madam, I do trust you. That's why I'm telling you everything. I'm asking you to be my ally. And you persist in—"

The door opened. The man who entered was as tall as the Stapper, but wore the civilian's iridescent robes. His long beard seemed to have caught a little of their rainbow influence; it was predominantly red, but brown and black and white glinted in it. The hair on his head was graying. He might have been anywhere from forty-five to a vigorous and well-preserved seventy.

"We have a guest, sister?" he asked politely.

The Roman matron made a despairing gesture. "You don't recognize him? And John—you don't know Stephen?"

Stephen slapped his thigh and barked—a sound that seemed to represent a laugh of pleasure. "Cosmos!" he cried. "John Brent! I told you, Martha. I knew he wouldn't fail us."

Anthony Boucher

"Stephen!" she exclaimed in shocked tones.

"Hang the irregularities! Can't I greet John with the old words that comed—no, by Cosmos—came from the same past he came from? See, John—don't I talk the old language well? I even use article—pardon me, *the* article."

Brent's automatic mental notebook recorded the fact, which he had already suspected, that an article was as taboo as an irregular verb. But around this self-governing notation system swirled utter confusion. It might possibly have been just his luck to run into a madwoman. But two mad brains in succession with identical delusions were too much. And Stephen had known he was from the past, with no cue given him.

"I'm afraid," he said simply, "this is too much for me. Suppose we all sit down and have a drink of something and talk this over."

Stephen smiled. "You remember our bond, eh? And not many places in State you'll find it. Even fewer than before." He crossed to a cabinet and returned with three glasses of colorless liquid.

Brent seized his eagerly and downed it. A drink might help the swirling. It might—The drink had gone down smoothly and tastelessly. Now, however, some imp began dissecting atoms in his stomach and shooting off a bombardment stream of particles that zoomed up through his throat into his brain, where they set off a charge of explosive of hitherto unknown power. Brent let out a strangled yelp.

Stephen barked again. "Good bond, eh, John?"

Brent managed to focus his host through the blurring lens of his tears. "Sure," he nodded feebly. "Swell. And now let me try to explain—"

The woman looked sadly at her brother. "He denies us, Stephen. He sayes that he haves never seed me before. He forgets all that he ever sweared about Barrier."

A curious look of speculation came into Stephen's brown eyes. "Bees this true, John? You have never seed us before in your life?"

"But, Stephen, you know—"

"Hush, Martha. I say in *his* life. Bees it true, John?"

"It bees. God knows it bees. I have never seen . . . seed either of you in my life."

"But, Stephen—"

"I understand now, Martha. Remember when he told us of Barrier and his resolve?"

"Can I forget?"

"How doed he know of Barrier? Tell me that."

"I don't know," Martha confessed. "I have wondered—"

"He knowed of Barrier then because he bees here now. He told me then just what we must now tell him."

"Then for Heaven's sake," Brent groaned, "tell me."

"Your pardon, John. My sister bees not so quick to grasp source of these temporal confusions. More bond?" He had the bottle in his hand when he suddenly stopped, thrust it back in the cabinet, and murmured, "Go into bedroom."

Brent obeyed. This was no time for displaying initiative. And no sooner had the bedroom door closed behind him than he heard the voice of the Stapper. (The mental notebook recorded that apartment buildings must be large, if it had taken this long for the search to reach here.)

"No," Stephen was saying. "My sister and I have beed here for past half-hour. We seed no one."

"State thanks you," the Stapper muttered so casually that the phrase must have been an official formula. His steps sounded receding. Then they stopped, and there was the noise of loud sniffs.

"Dear God," thought Brent, "have they crossed the bulls with bloodhounds?"

"Bond," the Stapper announced.

"Dear me," came Martha's voice. "Who haves beed in here today, Stephen?"

"I'm a homeopath," said the Stapper. "Like cures like. A little bond might make me forget I smelled it."

There was a bark from Stephen and a clink of glasses. No noise from either of them as they downed the liquor. Those, sir, were men. (Memo: Find out why such unbelievable rotgut is called *bond*, of all things.)

"State thanks you," said the Stapper, and laughed. "You know George Starvel, don't you?"

A slightly hesitant "Yes" from Stephen.

"When you see him again, I think you'll find he haves changed his mind. About many things."

There was silence. Then Stephen opened the bedroom door and beckoned Brent back into the living room. He handed the time traveler a glass of bond and said, "I will try to be brief."

Brent, now forewarned, sipped gingerly at the liquor and found it cheerfully warming as he assimilated the new facts.

In the middle of the twenty-fourth century, he learned, civilization had reached a high point of comfort, satisfaction, achievement—and stagnation. The combination of atomic power and De Bainville's revolutionary formulation of the principles of labor and finance had seemed to solve all economic problems. The astounding development of synthetics had destroyed the urgent need for raw materials and colonies and abolished the distinction between haves and have-nots among nations. Schwarz-walder's "Compendium" had achieved the dream of the early Encyclopaedists—the complete systematization of human knowledge. Farthing had regularized the English language, an achievement paralleled by the work of Zinsmeister, Timofeov, and Tamayo y Sárate in their respective tongues. (These four languages now dominated the earth. French and Italian had become corrupt dialects of German, and the Oriental languages occupied in their own countries something the position of Greek and Latin in nineteenth-century Europe, and doomed soon to the complete oblivion which swallowed up those classic tongues in the twenty-first.)

There was nothing more to be achieved. All was known, all was accomplished.

Anthony Boucher

Nakamura's Law of Spacial Acceleration had proved interplanetary travel to be impossible for all time. Charnwood's Law of Temporal Metabolism had done the same for time travel. And the Schwarzwalder "Compendium," which everyone admired and no one had read, established such a satisfactory and flawless picture of knowledge that it was obviously impossible that anything remained to be discovered.

It was then that Dyce-Farnsworth proclaimed the Stasis of Cosmos. A member of the Anglo-Physical Church, product of the long contemplation by English physicists of the metaphysical aspects of science, he came as the prophet needed to pander to the self-satisfaction of the age.

He was cautiously aided by Farthing's laws of regularity. The article, direct or indirect, Farthing had proved to be completely unnecessary—had not languages as world-dominant as Latin in the first centuries and Russian in the twenty-first found no need for it?—and semantically misleading. "Article," he said in his final and comprehensive study *This Bees Speech*, "bees prime corrupter of human thinking."

And thus the statement so beloved in the twentieth century by metaphysical-minded scientists and physical-minded divines, "God is the cosmos," became with Dyce-Farnsworth "God bees cosmos," and hence, easily and inevitably, "God bees Cosmos," so that the utter scientific impersonality became a personification of Science. Cosmos replaced Jehovah, Baal and Odin.

The love of Cosmos was not man nor his works, but Stasis. Man was tolerated by Cosmos that he might achieve Stasis. All the millennia of human struggle had been aimed at this supreme moment when all was achieved, all was known, and all was perfect. Therefore this supernal Stasis must at all costs be maintained. Since Now was perfect, any alteration must be imperfect and taboo.

From this theory logically evolved the State, whose duty was to maintain the perfect Stasis of Cosmos. No totalitarian government had ever striven so strongly to iron out all doubt and dissension. No religious bigotry had ever found heresy so damnable and worthy of destruction. The Stasis must be maintained.

It was, ironically, the aged Dyce-Farnsworth himself who, in a moment of quasi-mystical intuition, discovered the flaw in Charnwood's Law of Temporal Metabolism. And it was clear to him what must be done.

Since the Stasis of Cosmos did not practice time travel, any earlier or later civilization that did so must be imperfect. Its emissaries would cause imperfection. There must be a Barrier.

The mystic went no further than that dictum, but the scientists of the State put his demand into practical terms. "Do not ask how at this moment," Stephen added. "I be not man to explain that. But you will learn." The first Barrier was a failure. It destroyed itself and to no apparent result. But now, fifty years later, the fears of time travel had grown. The original idea of the imperfection of emissaries had not been lost. Now time travel was in itself imperfect and evil. Any action taken against it would be an offering of praise to Cosmos. And the new Barrier was being erected.

"But John knows all this," Martha protested from time to time, and Stephen would shake his head sadly and smile sympathetically at Brent.

"I don't believe a word of it," Brent said at last. "Oh, the historical outline's all right. I trust you on that. And it works out so sweetly by analogy. Take the religious fanaticism of the sixteenth century, the smug scientific self-satisfaction of the nineteenth, the power domination of the twentieth—fuse them and you've got your State. But the Barrier's impossible. There's no principle on which it could work, and nuts to it."

"Charnwood claimed there beed no principle on which time travel canned work. And here you be."

"That's different," said Brent vaguely. "But all this talk of destroying the Barrier is nonsense. There's no need to."

"Indeed there bees need, John. For two reasons: one, that we may benefit by wisdom of travelers from other ages; and two, that positive act of destroying this Barrier, which bees worshipped now with something like fetishism, bees strongest weapon with which can strike against State. For there be these few of us who hope to save mankind from this fanatical complacency that race have falled into. George Starvel beed one," Stephen added sadly.

"I saw Starvel— But that isn't what I mean. There's no need because the Barrier won't work."

"But you telled us that it haved io be destroyed," Martha protested. "That it doed work, and that we—"

"Hush," said Stephen gently. "John, will you trust us far enough to show us your machine? I think I can make matters clearer to Martha then."

"If you'll keep me out of the way of Stappers."

"That we can never guarantee—yet. But day will come when mankind cans forget Stappers and State, that I swear." There was stern and noble courage in Stephen's face and bearing as he drained his glass of bond to that pledge.

"I had a break when I landed here," John Brent explained on the way. "Derringer equipped the machine only for temporal motion. He explained that it meant running a risk; I might find that the coast line had sunk and I'd arrive under water, or God knows what. But he hadn't worked out the synchronized adjustment for temporo-spacial motion yet, and he wanted to get started. I took the chance, and luck was good. Where the Derringer lab used to be is now apparently a deserted warehouse. Everything's dusty and not a sign of human occupation."

Stephen's eyes lit up as they approached the long low building of translucent bricks. "Remember, Martha?"

Martha frowned and nodded.

Faint light filtered through the walls to reveal the skeletal outlines of the machine. Brent switched on a light on the panel which gave a dim glow.

"There's not much to see even in a good light," he explained. "Just these two seats—Derringer was planning on teams when he built it, but decided later that one man with sole responsibility to himself would do better—and this panel. These instruments are automatic—they adjust to the presence of another machine ahead of you in the time line. The only control the operator bothers with is this." He indicated the double dial set at 2473.

"Why doed you choose this year?"

"At random. Derringer set the outer circle at 2400—half a millennium seemed a plausible choice. Then I spun the inner dial blindfold. When this switch here is turned, you create a certain amount of temporal potential, positive or negative—which is as loose as applying those terms to magnetic poles, but likewise just as convenient. For instance if I turn it to here"—he spun the outer dial to 2900—"you'll have five hundred years of positive potential which'll shoot you ahead to 2973. Or set it like this, and you'll have five centuries of negative, which'll pull you back practically to where I started from."

Stephen frowned. "*Ahead* and *back* be of course nonsense words in this connection. But they may be helpful to Martha in visualizing it. Will you please show Martha the back of your dial?"

"Why?" There was no answer. Brent shrugged and climbed into the seat. The Roman matron moved around the machine and entered the other seat as he loosed the catch on the dial and opened it, as one did for oiling the adjusting gears.

Stephen said, "Look well, my dear. What be the large wheels maked of?"

"Aceroid, of course. Don't you remember how Alex—"

"Don't remember, Martha. Look. What *be* they?"

Martha gasped. "Why, they . . . they be pure aluminium."

"Very well. Now don't you understand—*Ssh!*" He broke off and moved toward the doorway. He listened there a moment, then slipped out of sight.

"What does he have?" Brent demanded as he closed the dial. "The ears of an elk-hound?"

"Stephen have hyperacute sense of hearing. He bees proud of it, and it haves saved us more than once from Stappers. When people be engaged in motive work against State—"

A man's figure appeared again in the doorway. But its robes were white. "Good God!" Brent exclaimed. "Jiggers, the Staps!"

Martha let out a little squeal. A rod appeared in the Stapper's hand. Brent's eyes were so fixed on the adversary that he did not see the matron's hand move toward the switch until she had turned it. Then he shut his eyes and groaned.

Brent had somehow instinctively shut his eyes during his first time transit. *During*, he reflected, is not the right word. *At the time of?* Hardly. How can you describe an event of time movement without suggesting another time measure perpendicular to the time line? At any rate, he had shut them in a laboratory in 1942 and opened them an instant later in a warehouse in 2473.

Now he kept them shut. He had to think for a moment. He had been playing with the dial—where was it set when Martha jerked the switch? 1973, as best he remembered. And he had now burst into that world in plastic garments of the twenty-fifth century, accompanied by a Roman matron who had in some time known him for fifty years.

He did not relish the prospect. And besides he was bothered by that strange jerking, tearing sensation that had twisted his body when he closed his eyes. He had felt nothing whatsoever on the previous trip. Had something gone wrong this time? Had—

"It doesn't work!" said Martha indignantly.

Brent opened his eyes. He and Martha sat in the machine in a dim warehouse of translucent brick.

"We be still here," she protested vigorously.

"Sure we're still here." Brent frowned. "But what you mean is, we're still *now*."

"You talk like Stephen. What do you mean?"

"Or are we?" His frowned deepened. "If we're still now, where is that Stapper? He didn't vanish just because you pulled a switch. How old is this warehouse?"

"I don't know. I think about sixty years. It beed fairly new when I beed a child. Stephen and I used to play near here."

"Then we could have gone back a few decades and still be here. Yes, and look—those cases over there. I'd swear they weren't here before. After. Whatever. Then, when we saw the Stapper." He looked at the dial, It was set to 1973. And the warehouse was new some time around 2420.

Brent sat and stared at the panel.

"What bees matter?" Martha demanded. "Where be we?"

"Here, same like always. But what bothers me is just *when* we are. Come on; want to explore?"

Martha shook her head. "I want to stay here. And I be afraid for Stephen. Doed Stappers get him? Let's go back."

"I've got to check on things. Something's gone wrong, and Derringer'll never forgive me if I don't find out what and why. You stay here if you want."

"Alone?"

Brent suppressed several remarks concerning women, in the abstract and the particular. "Stay or go, I don't care. I'm going."

Martha sighed. "You have changed so, John—"

In front of the warehouse was an open field. There had been buildings there when Brent last saw it. And in the field three young people were picnicking. The sight reminded Brent that it was a long time since he'd eaten. How you could measure gaps between meals when you shoot about among centuries, he didn't know; but he was hungry.

He made toward the trio. There were two men and a girl. One man was blond, the other and the girl were brilliantly redheaded. The girl had much more than even that hair to recommend her. She— Brent's eyes returned to the red-headed man. There

16   Anthony Boucher was no mistaking those deep brown eyes, that sharp and noble nose. The beard was scant, but still there was no denying—

Brent sprang forward with an eager cry of "Stephen!"

The young man looked at him blankly. "Yes," he said politely. "What do you want?"

Brent mentally kicked himself. He had met Stephen in advanced age. What would the Stephen of twenty know of him? And suddenly he began to understand a great deal. The whole confusion of that first meeting started to fade away.

"If I tell you," he said rapidly, "that I know that you be Stephen, that you have sister Martha, that you drink bond despite Stappers, and that you doubt wisdom of Barrier, will you accept me as a man you can trust?"

"Cosmos aeons!" the blond young man drawled. "Stranger knows plenty, Stephen. If he bees Stapper, you'll have your mind changed."

The scantily bearded youth looked a long while into Brent's eyes. Then he felt in his robe, produced a flask, and handed it over. Brent drank and returned it. Their hands met in a firm clasp.

Stephen grinned at the others. "My childs, I think stranger brings us adventure. I feel like someone out of novel by Varnichek." He turned back to Brent. "Do you know these others, too?"

Brent shook his head.

"Krasna and Alex. And your name?"

"John Brent."

"And what can we do for you, John?"

"First tell me year."

Alex laughed and the girl smiled. "And how long have you beed on a bonder?" Alex asked.

A bonder, Brent guessed, would be a bond bender. "This bees my first drink," he said, "since 1942. Or perhaps 2473, according as how you reckon."

Brent was not disappointed in the audience reaction this time.

It's easy to see what must have happened, Brent wrote that night in the first entry of the journal Derringer had asked him to keep. He wrote longhand, an action that he loathed. The typewriter which Stephen had kindly offered him was equipped with a huge keyboard bearing the forty-odd characters of the Farthing phonetic alphabet, and Brent declined the loan.

We're at the first Barrier—the one that failed. It was dedicated to Cosmos and launched this afternoon. My friends were among the few inhabitants not ecstatically present at the ceremony. Since then they've collected reports for me. The damned contrivance had to be so terrifically overloaded that it blew up. Dyce-Farnsworth was killed and will be a holy martyr to Cosmos for ever.

But in an infinitesimal fraction of a second between the launching and the explosion, the Barrier existed. That was enough. It is gone now. It is of no use to protect the people of this smug and sacred Stasis from raids from a more human future. But it existed at that one point in time, existed effectively enough to stop me dead.

Which makes keeping this journal, my dear Dr. Derringer, a magnificently silly act. In all likelihood neither you nor anyone else before 2423 will ever see it. (Will ever have seen it?) But you see, sir, I obey instructions. Nice of me, isn't it?

And I've been finding out all I can. Stephen is good on history, but lousy on science. The blond young Alex reverses the combination. From him I've learned, or tried to learn, the theory back of the Barrier.

The Barrier established, in that fractional second, a powerful magnetic field in the temporal dimension. As a result, any object moving along the time line is cutting the magnetic field. Hysteresis sets up strong eddy currents which bring the object, in this case me, to an abrupt halt. Cf. that feeling of twisting shock that I had when my eyes were closed.

I pointed out to Alex that I must somehow have crossed this devilish Barrier in going from 1942 to 2473. He accounts for that apparent inconsistency by saying that I was then traveling with the time stream, though at a greater rate; the blockage lines of force were end-on and didn't stop me.

Brent paused and read the last two paragraphs aloud to the young scientist who was tinkering with the travelling machine. "How's that, Alex? Clear enough?"

"It will do." Alex frowned. "Of course we need whole new vocabulary for temporal concepts. We fumble so helplessly in analogies—" He rose. "There bees nothing more I can do for this now. Tomorrow I'll bring out some tools from shop, and see if I can find some aceroid gears to fit control."

"Good man. I may not be able to go back in time from here; but one thing I can do is go forward. Forward to just before they launch that second Barrier. I've got a job to do."

Alex gazed admiringly at the machine. "Wonderful piece of work. Your Dr. Derringer bees great man."

"Only he didn't allow for the effects of temporo-magnetic hysteresis on his mechanism. Thank God for you, Alex."

"Willn't you come back to house?"

Brent shook his head. "I'm taking no chances on curious Stappers. I'm sticking here with Baby. See that the old lady's comfortable, will you?"

"Of course. But tell me: who bees she? She willn't talk at all."

"Nobody. Just a temporal hitch-hiker."

Martha's first sight of the young Stephen had been a terrible shock. She had stared at him speechlessly for long minutes, and then gone into a sort of inarticulate hysteria. Any attempt at explanation of her status, Brent felt, would only make matters worse. There was nothing to do but leave her to the care—which seemed both tender and efficient—of the girl Krasna, and let her life ride until she could resume it normally in her own time.

Anthony Boucher

He resumed his journal:

Philological notes: Stapper, as I should have guessed, is a corruption of Gestapo, Slanduch, *which poor Starvel suggested I might be, had me going for a bit. Asking about that, learned that there is more than one State. This, the smuggest and most fanatical of them all, embraces North America, Australia, and parts of Eastern Asia. Its official language is, of course, Farthingised English. Small nuclear groups of English-speaking people exist in the other States, and have preserved the older and irregular forms of speech. (Cf. American mountaineers, and Spanish Jews in Turkey.) A Slanduch is a member of one of these groups.*

It took me some time to realize the origin of this word, but it's obvious enough: Auslandsdeutsche, *the Germans who existed similarly cut off from the main body of their culture. With these two common loan words suggesting a marked domination at some time of the German language, I asked Alex—and I must confess almost fearfully—"Then did Germany win the war?"*

He not unnaturally countered with, "Which war?"

"The Second World War. Started in 1939."

"Second—Cosmis æons, John, you can't expect me to remember numbers of all those twentieth-century World Wars, can you?"

I am almost afraid to ask the more historically accurate Stephen.

Brent paused, and wished for Stephen's ears to determine the nature of that small noise outside. Or was it pure imagination? He went on:

These three—Stephen, Alex and Krasna—have proved to be the ideal hosts for a traveler of my nature. Any devout believer in Cosmos, any loyal upholder of the Stasis would have turned me over to the Stappers for my first slip in speech or ideas.

They seem to be part of what corresponds to the Underground Movements of my own century. They try to accomplish a sort of boring from within, a subtle sowing of doubts as to the Stasis. Eventually they hope for more positive action; so far it is purely mental sabotage.

Their motives are various. Some are crackpots, pure and simple. Some are artists who rebel against the limitations imposed by the State. Some are scientists who remain unconvinced that Schwarzwalder solved everything. Stephen says simply that he is a Christian—which most of the others consider an almost comic anachronism—and that Cosmos is a false god; but I think the Christian love of mankind is a stronger motive force in him than any doctrinary matter of the rivalry of names for godhead. Alex is a Seepy—a word the meaning of which I haven't yet been able to gather. Krasna—

It *was* a noise. Brent set down his stylus and moved along the wall as quietly as possible to the door. He held his breath while the door slid gently inward. Then, as the figure entered, he pounced.

Stappers have close-cropped hair and flat manly chests. Brent released the girl abruptly and muttered a confused apology.

"It bees only me," she said shyly. "Krasna. Doed I startle you?"

"A bit," he confessed. "Alex and Stephen warned me what might happen if a Stapper stumbled on my machine here."

"I be sorry, John."

"It's all right. But you shouldn't be wandering around alone at night like this. In fact, you shouldn't be mixed up in this at all. Leave it to Stephen and Alex and me."

"Mans!" she pouted. "Don't you think womans have any right to fun?"

"I don't know that fun's exactly the word. But since you're here, milady, let me extend the hospitality of the camp. Alex left me some bond. That poison grows on you. And tell me why's it called that?"

"Stephen told me once, but I can't—Oh, yes. When they prohibited all drinking because drinking makes you think world bees better than it really bees and of course if you make yourself different world that bees against Stasis and so they prohibited it but they keeped on using it for medical purposes and that beed in warehouses and pretty soon no one knowed any other kind of liquor so it bees called bond. Only I don't see why."

"I don't suppose," Brent remarked, "that anybody in this century has ever heard of one Gracie Allen, but her spirit is immortal. The liquor in the warehouses was probably kept under government bond."

"Oh—" she said meekly. "I'll remember. You know everything, don't you?"

Brent looked at her suspiciously, but there was no irony in the remark. "How's the old lady getting on?"

"Fine. She bees sleeping now at last. Alex gived her some dormitin. She bees nice, John."

"And yet your voice sounds worried. What's the matter?"

"She bees so much like my mother only, of course, I don't remember my mother much because I beed so little when Stappers taked my father and then my mother doedn't live very long but I do remember her some and your old lady bees so much like her. I wish I haved knowed my mother goodlier, John. She beed dear. She—" She lowered her voice in the tone of one imparting a great secret. "She cooked!"

Brent remembered their tasteless supper of extracts, concentrates and synthetics, and shuddered. "I wish you had known her, Krasna."

"You know what cooking means? You go out and you dig up roots and you pick leaves off plants and some people they even used to take animals, and then you apply heat and—"

"I know. I used to be a fair-to-middling cook myself, some five hundred years ago. If you could lead me to a bed of coals, a clove of garlic, and a two-inch steak, milady, I'd guarantee to make your eyes pop."

"Garlic? Steak?" Her eyes were wide with wonder. "What be those?"

Brent explained. For ten minutes he talked of the joys of food, of the sheer ecstatic satisfaction of good eating that passes the love of woman, the raptures of art, or the wonders of science. Then her questions began to pour forth.

"Stephen learns things out of books and Alex learns things in lab but I can't do

Anthony Boucher

that so goodly and they both make fun of me only you be real and I can learn things from you, John, and it bees wonderful. Tell me—''

And Krasna, with a greedy ear, devoured up his discourse.

''—and men were free,'' he ended. ''Free to damn and ruin themselves if they choose, but free also to live nobly, enriching the world and themselves by striving. For all perfection comes from within and the 'perfection' that is imposed from without is as frivolous and stupid as the trimmings on ginger-cake. The free man may be bad, but only the free man can be good. And all the kingdom and the power and the glory—call it of God, call it of Cosmos—must arise from the free will of man.''

He stopped, somewhat surprised at his own eloquence. The tyrannical smugness of this age was working upon him powerfully.

Krasna was kneeling at his feet. He could feel the warmth of her body against his. ''Go on,'' she whispered. Her large eyes glowed up at him.

''That's all. And damned if I know how I talked that long.'' His hands rested on the soft mass of her flowing red hair.

''You be wonderful,'' she murmured.

Brent coughed and said, ''Nuts!'' His hand stroked her head gently.

The rest of that evening was not recorded in the Derringer journal.

The machine was not repaired the next day, or the next. Alex kept making plausible, if not quite intelligible, technical excuses. Martha kept to her room and fretted; but Brent rather welcomed the delay. There was no hurry; leaving this time several days later had no effect on when they reached 2473. But he had some difficulty making that point clear to the matron.

This delay gave him an opportunity to see something of the State in action, and any information acquired was apt to be useful when the time came. With various members of Stephen's informal and illicit group he covered the city. He visited a church of Cosmos and heard the official doctrine on the failure of the Barrier—the Stasis of Cosmos did not permit time travel, so that even an attempt to prohibit it, by recognizing its existence affronted the Stasis. He visited libraries and found only those works which had established or upheld the Stasis, all bound in the same uniform format which the Cosmic Bibliographical Committee of 2407 had ordained as ideal and static. He visited scientific laboratories, and found brilliant young dullards plodding away endlessly at what had already been established; imaginative research was manifestly perilous.

He heard arid stretches of intolerable music composed according to the strict Farinelli system, which forbade, among other things, any alteration of key or time for the duration of a composition. He went to a solly, which turned out to be a deceptively solid three-dimensional motion picture. It was a flat and undramatic exposition of the glories of Stasis; but Brent suspected the author of being an Undergrounder. The villain, even though triumphantly bested by the Stappers in the end, had all the most plausible and best-written speeches, some of them ingenious and strong enough to sow doubts in the audience.

If, Brent thought disgustedly, anything could sow doubts in this smug herd of cattle. For the people of the State seemed to take the deepest and most loving pride in everything pertaining to the State and to the Stasis of Cosmos. The churches, the libraries, the laboratories, the music, the sollies, all represented humanity at its highest peak. We have attained perfection, have we not? Then all this bees perfect, and we love it.

"What we need," he expostulated to Alex and Stephen one night, "is more of me. Lots more. Scads of us pouring in from all ages to light firecrackers under these dopes. Every art and every science has degenerated far worse than anything did in the Dark Ages. The surface attainment is still there; but everything's gone from under it. Man cannot be man without striving; and all striving is abolished. God, I think if I lived in this age and believed in the Stasis, I'd become a Stapper. Better their arrogant cruelty than the inhuman indifference of everybody else."

"I have brother who bees Stapper," said Stephen. "I do not recommend it. To descend to level of cows and oxes bees one thing. To become wolves and jackals bees another."

"I've gathered that those rods paralyze the nerve centers, right? But what happens to you after that in Stappers' hands?"

"It bees not good. First you be treated according to expert psychoanalytic and psychometric methods so as to alter your concepts and adjust you to Stasis. If that fails, you can be carefully reduced to harmless idiocy. Sometimes they find mind that bees too strong for treatment. He bees killed, and Stappers be allowed to play with him first."

Brent shuddered. "Not nice."

"It'll never happen to me," Alex said earnestly. "I be prepared. You see this?" He indicated a minute plastic box suspended around his neck. "It contains tiny amount of radioactive matter sensitized to wave length of Stappers' rods. They will never change my mind."

"It explodes?"

Alex grinned. "Stay away from me if rods start waving."

"It seems," Brent mused, "as though cruelty were the only human vice left. Games are lost, drinking is prohibited—and that most splendid of vices, imaginative speculation, is unheard of. I tell you, you need lots of me."

Stephen frowned. "Before failure of Barrier, we often wondered why we never seed time travelers. We doubted Charnwood's Law and yet—We decided there beed only two explanations. Either time travel bees impossible, or time travelers cannot be seed or intervene in time they visit. Now, of course, we can see that Barrier stopped all from future, and perhaps you be only one from past. And still—"

"Exactly," said Alex. "And still. If other travelers came from future, why beed they not also stopped by Barrier? One of our friends haves haved opportunity to search

Anthony Boucher

Stapper records since breakdown of Barrier. No report on strange and unidentified travelers anywhere.''

"That cans mean only one thing." Stephen looked worried. "Second Barrier, Barrier you told us of, John, must be successful."

"The hell it will be. Come on, Alex. I'm getting restless. When can I start?''

Alex smiled. "Tomorrow. I be ready at last."

"Good man. Among us, we are going to blow this damned Stasis back into the bliss of manly and uncertain striving. And in fifty years we'll watch it together.''

Krasna was waiting outside the room when Brent left. "I knowed you willed be talking about things I doedn't understand.''

"You can understand this, milady. Alex has got everything fixed, and we leave tomorrow.''

Krasna put her soft hand gently in his and wordlessly walked back to the warehouse with him.

"Now," said Brent to Stephen after what was euphemistically termed breakfast, "I've got to see the old lady and find out just what the date is for the proposed launching of the second Barrier.''

Stephen beamed. "It bees such pleasure to hear old speech, articles and all.''

Alex had a more practical thought. "How can you set it to one day? I thinked your dial readed only in years.''

"There's a vernier attachment that's accurate—or should be, it's never been tested yet—to within two days. I'm allowing a week's margin. I don't want to be around too long and run chances with Stappers.''

"Krasna will miss you.''

"Krasna's a funny name. You others have names that were in use back in my day.''

"Oh, it bees not name. It bees only what everyone calls redheaded girls. I think it goes back to century of Russian domination.''

"Yes," Alex added. "Stephen's sister's real name bees Martha, but we never call her that.''

John Brent gaped. "I . . . I've got to go see the old lady," he stammered. "The old lady—the red-head—Martha—Krasna Stephen's sister—"

Small wonder she was shocked when he didn't know her!

From the window of the gray-haired Martha-Krasna he could see the red-headed Krasna-Martha outside. He held on to a solid and reassuring chair and said, "Well, madam, I have news. We're going back today.''

"Oh thank Cosmos!"

"But I've got to find out something from you. What was the date set for the launching of the second Barrier?''

"Let me see—I know it beed holiday. Yes, it beed May 1st.''

"My, my! May Day a holiday now? Workers of the World Unite, or simply Gathering Nuts in May?''

"I don't understand you. It bees Dyce-Farnsworth's birthday, of course."

"Oh. Well, be out at the warehouse in half an hour, and we'll be off."

The young Krasna-Martha was alone in the warehouse when Brent got there. He looked at her carefully, trying to see in her youthful features the worn ones of the woman he had just left. It made sense.

"I comed first," she said, "because I wanted to say goodbye without others."

"Goodbye, milady," Brent murmured into her fine red hair. "In a way I'm not leaving you because I'm taking you with me and still I'll never see you again. And you don't understand that, and I'm not sure you've ever understood anything I've said, but you've been very sweet."

"And you will destroy Barrier? For me?"

"For you, milady. And a few billion others. And here come our friends."

Alex carried a small box which he tucked under one of the seats. "Dial and mechanism beed repaired days ago," he grinned. "I've been working on this for you, in lab while I should have been re-proving Tsvetov's hypothesis. Temporal demagnetizer—guaranteed. Bring this near Barrier and field will be breaked. Your problem bees to get near Barrier."

Martha, the matron, climbed into the machine. Martha, the girl, turned away to hide watering eyes. Brent set the dial to 2473 and adjusted the vernier to April 24th, which gave him a week's grace. "Well, friends," he faltered. "My best gratitude—and I'll be seeing you in fifty years."

Stephen started to speak, and then suddenly stopped to listen. "Quick, Krasna, Alex. Behind those cases. Turn switch quickly, John."

Brent turned the switch, and nothing happened. Stephen and Krasna were still there, moving toward the cases. Alex darted to the machine. "Cosmos blast me; I maked disconnection to prevent anyone's tampering by accident. And now—"

"Hurry, Alex," Stephen called in a whisper.

"Moment—" Alex opened the panel and made a rapid adjustment. "There, John. Goodbye."

In the instant before Brent turned the switch, he saw Stephen and Krasna reach a safe hiding place. He saw a Stapper appear in the doorway. He saw the flicker of a rod. The last thing he saw in 2423 was the explosion that lifted Alex's head off his shoulders.

The spattered blood was still warm in 2473.

Stephen, the seventy-year-old Stephen with the long and parti-colored beard, was waiting for them. Martha dived from the machine into his arms and burst into dry sobbing.

"She met herself," Brent explained. "I think she found it pretty confusing."

Stephen barked: "I can imagine. It bees only now that I have realized who that woman beed who comed with you and so much resembled our mother. But you be so late. I have beed waiting here ever since I evaded Stappers."

Anthony Boucher

"Alex—" Brent began.

"I know. Alex haves gived you magnetic disruptor and losed his life, poor devil. But that bees fifty-year-old sorrow, and we have no time for it. Why have you beed so long?"

"I didn't want to get here too long before May Day—might get into trouble. So I allowed a week, but I'll admit I might be a day or so off. What date is it?"

"This bees May 1st, and Barrier will be launched within hour. We must hurry."

"My God—" Brent glared at the dial. "It can't be that far off. But come on. Get your sister home and we'll plunge on to do our damnedest."

Martha roused herself. "I be coming with you."

"No, dear," said Stephen. "We can do better alone."

Her lips set stubbornly. "I be coming. I don't understand anything that happens, but you be Stephen and you be John, and I belong with you."

The streets were brightly decorated with banners bearing the double loop of infinity, the sacred symbol of Cosmos that had replaced crescent, swastika, and cross. But there was hardly a soul in sight. What few people they saw were all hurrying in the same direction.

"Everyone will be at dedication," Stephen explained. "Tribute to Cosmos. Those who stay at home must beware Stappers."

"And if there's hundreds of thousands thronging the dedication, how do we get close to Barrier to disrupt it?"

"It bees all arranged. Our group bees far more powerful than when you knowed it fifty years ago. Slowly we be honeycombing system of State. With bribery and force when necessary, with persuasion when possible, we can do much. And we have arranged this."

"How?"

"You be delegate from European Slanduch. You speak German?"

"Well enough."

"Remember that haves beed regularized, too. But I doubt if you need to speak any. Making you Slanduch will account for irregular slips in English. You come from powerful Slanduch group. You will be gladly welcomed here. You will occupy post of honor. I have even accounted for box you carry. It bees tribute you have bringed to Cosmos. Here be your papers and identity plaque."

"Thanks." Brent's shorter legs managed to keep up with the long strides of Stephen, who doubled the rate of the moving sidewalk by his own motion. Martha panted along resolutely. "But can you account for why I'm so late? I set my indicator for April 24th, and here we are rushing to make a date on May 1st."

Stephen strode along in thought, then suddenly slapped his leg and barked. "How many months in 1942?"

"Twelve, of course."

"Ha! Yes, it beed only two hundred years ago that thirteen-month calendar beed adopted. Even months of twenty-eight days, plus Year Day, which belongs to no month. Order, you see. Now invaluable part of Stasis—" He concentrated frowningly on mental arithmetic. "Yes, your indicator worked exactly. May 1st of our calendar bees April 24th of yours."

Chalk up one slip against Derringer—an unthinking confidence in the durability of the calendar. And chalk up one, for Brent's money, against the logic of the Stasis; back in the twentieth century, he had been an advocate of calendar reform, but a staunch upholder of the four-quarter theory against the awkward and indivisible thirteen months.

They were nearing now the vast amphitheater where the machinery of the Barrier had been erected. Stappers were stopping the few other travelers and forcing them off the moving sidewalk into the densely packed crowds, faces aglow with the smug ecstasy of the Stasis, but Brent's Slanduch credentials passed the three through every guard station, with short but infuriating delays.

"We'll make it." Stephen's eyes were afire. "Remember what you sayed to Alex and me? How State needs hundreds of you, to put explosive beneath it and blow it into awareness? If we—" He broke off speaking as they neared another Stapper.

This one looked at the credentials and grinned. *"Also! Sie wesen Slandsdeutsch and zwar aus Deutschland!"* he burst out in Zinsmeisterised German. *"Seit jahre habe ich kein Wort deutsch gehört. Mein eltere wesen von deutsch kerkunft."*

Brent's curious mind recorded the necessary notes on this perverted language, but there was no time to waste. He tried to avoid irregular slips as he replied, *"Freut mich sehr. Aber jetst habe ich kein zeit. Ich müsse eilen. Später vielleicht könne ich—"*

But the Stapper was, for a Stapper, amazingly friendly—a pleasing phenomenon at any other time, but hardly now. He rattled on in this correct speech until Brent glanced around to see that Stephen had precipitated action by dragging Martha on ahead. *"Ach!"* Brent cried. *"Mein freunde wesen schon gegeht. Verzeihen sie!"* And he sped after them.

The representative of the German Slanduch pushed his way into the crowd of eminent dignitaries just as Dyce-Farnsworth's grandson pressed the button. The magnificent mass of tubes and wires shuddered and glowed as the current pulsed through it. Then the glow became weird and arctic. There was a shaking, a groaning, and then, within the space of a second, a cataclysmic roar and a blinding glare. Something heavy and metallic pressed Brent to the ground.

The roar blended into the excited terror of human voices. The splendid Barrier was a mass of twisted wreckage. It was more wreckage that weighted Brent down, but this was different. It looked strangely like a variant of his own machine. And staring down at him from a warped seat was the enormous and huge-eyed head of a naked man.

A woman in a metallic costume equally strange to this age and to Brent's own straddled the body of Dyce-Farnsworth's grandson, who had met his ancestor's mar-

Anthony Boucher

tyrdom. And wherever Brent's eyes moved he saw another strange and outlandish—no, out-time-ish—figure.

He heard Martha's voice. "It bees clear that Time Barrier haves beed erected and destroyed by outside force. But it haves existed and created impenetrable instant of time. These be travelers from all future."

Brent gasped. Even the sudden appearance of these astounding figures was topped by Martha's speaking perfect logical sense.

Brent wrote in his journal: *This Stasis is at least an admirably functional organism. All hell broke loose there for a minute, but almost automatically the Stappers went into action with their rods—odd how that bit of crook's cant has become perfectly literal truth—and in no time had the situation well in hand.*

They had their difficulties. Several of the time intruders were armed, and managed to account for a handful of Stappers before the nerve rays paralyzed them. One machine was a sort of time-traveling tank and contrived to withstand siege until a suicide squad, Stephen said, blew it up with detonite; we shall never know from what sort of a future the inhabitants of that tank came to spatter their shredded flesh about the amphitheater.

But these events were mere delaying action, token resistance. Ten minutes after the Barrier had exploded, the travelers present were all in the hands of the Stappers, and cruising Stapper bands were efficiently combing all surrounding territory.

(The interesting suggestion comes amazingly from Martha that all time machines capable of physical movement were irresistibly attracted to the amphitheatre by the temporomagnetic field. Only such pioneer and experimental machines as my Derringer, which can move only temporally, would be arrested in other locations. Whether or not this theory is correct, it seems justified by the facts. Only a few isolated reports have come in of sudden appearances elsewhere at the instant of the Barriers explosion; the focus of arrivals of the time travelers was the amphitheater.)

The Chief of Stappers mounted the dais where an infinity-bedecked banner now covered the martyred corpse of young Dyce-Farnsworth, and announced the official ruling of the Head of State: That these intruders and disrupters of the Stasis were to be detained—tested and examined and studied until it became apparent what the desire of Cosmos might be.

(The Head of State, Stephen explained, is a meaningless figurehead, part high priest and—I paraphrase—part Alexander Throttlebottom. The Stasis is supposedly so perfect and so self-sustaining that his powers are as nominal as those of the pilot of a ship in drydock, and all actual power is exercised by such subordinates as the Editor of State and the Chief of Stappers.)

Thanks to Stephen's ingenuity, this rule for the treatment of time travelers does not touch me. I am simply a Slanduch envoy. (I must remember to polish myself in that highly obnoxious Zinsmeisteriert German.) Some Stapper search party has certainly by now found the Derringer machine in the warehouse, which I no longer dare approach.

With two Barriers now between me and 1942, it is obvious that I am keeping this journal only for myself. I am stuck here—and so are all the other travelers, for this field, far stronger than the first, has wrecked their machines beyond the repairing efforts of a far greater talent than poor Alex. We are all here for good.

And it must be for good.

I still firmly believe what I said to Stephen and Alex: that this age needs hundreds, at least dozens; and I, so far as we yet know, am the only one not in the hands of the Stappers. It is my clearest duty to deliver those others, and with their aid to beat some sense into this Age of Smugness.

"But how?" Brent groaned rhetorically. "How am I going to break into the Stappers' concentration camp and set free all these fellow travelers to aid me?"

Martha wrinkled her brows. "I think I know. Let me work on problem while longer; I believe I see how we can at littlest make start."

Brent stared at her. "What's happened to you, madam? Always before you've shrunk away from every discussion Stephen and I have had. You've said we talk of things you know nothing about. And now, all of a sudden—boom!—you're right in the middle of things and doing very nicely thank you. What's got into you?"

"I think," said Martha, smiling, "you have hitted on right phrase, John."

Brent's puzzled expostulation was broken off by Stephen's entrance. "And where have you been?" he demanded. "I've been trying to work out plans, and I've got a weird feeling Martha's going to beat me to it. What have you been up to?"

Stephen looked curiously at his sister. "I've been out galping. Interesting results, too."

"Galping?"

"You know. Going among people, taking samples of opinion, using scientific method to reduce carefully choosed samples to general trends."

"Oh." (Mr. Gallup, thought Brent, had joined Captain Boycott and M. Guillotin as a verb.) "And what did you learn?"

"People be confused by arrival of time travlers. If Stasis bees perfect, they argue, why be such arrivals allowed? Seeds of doubt be sowed, and we be carefully watering them. Head of State haves problem on his hands. I doubt if he cans find any solution to satisfy people."

"If only," Brent sighed, "there were some way of getting directly at the people. If we could see these travelers and learn what they know and want, then somehow establish contact between them and the people, the whole thing ought to be a pushover. But we're up against that 'if only—' "

It was Martha who answered. "It bees very simple, John. You be linguist."

"Yes. And how does that—"

"Stappers will need interpreters. You will be one. From there on you must develop your own plans, but that will at littlest put you in touch with travellers."

Anthony Boucher

"But the State must have its own trained linguists who—"

Stephen barked with pleasure and took up the explanation. Since Farthing's regularization of English, the perfect immutability of language had become part of the Stasis. A linguist now was a man who knew Farthing's works by heart, and that was all. Oh, he might also be well acquainted with Zinsmeister German, or Tamayo y Sárate Spanish; but he knew nothing of general linguistic principles, which are apt to run completely counter to the fine theories of these great synthesists, and he had never had occasion to learn adaptability to a new language. Faced by the probably strange and incomprehensible tongues of the remote future, the State linguist would be lost and helpless.

It was common knowledge that only the Slanduch had any true linguistic aptitude. Brought up to speak three languages—Farthing-ized English, their own archaic dialect, and the language of the country in which they resided—their tongues were deft and adjustable. In ordinary times, this aptitude was looked on with suspicion; ingenuity and cleverness in any field were obviously heretical threats to the Stasis. But now there would doubtless be a heavy demand for Slanduch interpreters, and there was no doubt that a little cautious wire pulling could land Brent the job.

"And after that," said Stephen, "as Martha rightly observes, you be on your own."

"Lead me to it," grinned John Brent.

"Isn't that Starvel?" Brent demanded.

Stephen paused and looked at the man on the other mobile walk. "So it bees indeed."

"The Stappers must have released him. Shall we—"

The man had noticed them and now crossed over. "George!" Stephen cried. "Cosmos! but it rejoices my heart to see you again."

George Starvel held himself aloof and glanced suspiciously at Brent. "I wished to speak to you, Stephen, only to tell you that I will not see you again."

"George!"

"Stasis bees perfect, Stephen. Your ideas for some little time deluded me, but now I know. Cosmos bees all-perfect and his perfection lies in his Stasis. If ever again you try to persuade me of lies to contrary, I will have to advise Stappers. Goodbye." And he had left them.

Brent looked after him in amazement. "He meant that. He was perfectly sincere."

"I know. He haves haved his mind changed. He believes what haves been forced upon him, but he believes it honestly. It bees sad. He beed most vigorous and active Seepy I have knowed since Alex."

Stephen frowned. "It bees hard to explain. But most of rebels against Stasis come from old families holding old beliefs. Many, like me, be Christians, and some be Seepies. I do not know myself all their beliefs, but they belong to schism of Mark."

Brent contemplated this statement for a moment, and then burst into a loud guffaw. "By Hobson and Jobson, this is sweet! Schism of Mark, Mark schism, Marxism.

Seepy, C.P., Communist Party. And right in there fighting shoulder to shoulder with the Christians!'' His face became graver. ''And let's remember one thing, Stephen. They can change the mind of an individual. But when it comes to thousands, and tens of thousands—it may be their own minds that'll change.''

''Amen,'' said Stephen. It was the only time Brent ever heard him utter a characteristically Christian phrase.

The rabbity little State linguist received Brent effusively. ''Ah, thank Cosmos!'' he gasped. ''Travelers be driving me mad! Such gibberish you have never heared! Such irregularities! Frightful! It bees shocking! You be Slanduch?''

''I be. I have speaked several languages all my life. I can even speak pre-Zinsmeister German.'' And he began to recite *Die Lorelei.* *''Die Luft ist kühl und es dunkelt, und ruhig fliesst der Rhein—''*

''Terrible! *Ist!* Such vile irregularity! And articles! But come, young man. We'll see what you can do with these temporal barbarians!''

There were three travelers in the room Brent entered, with the shocked linguist and two rodded Stappers in attendance. One of the three was the woman he had noticed in that first cataclysmic instant of arrival, a strapping Amazonic blonde who looked as though she could break any two unarmed Stappers with her bare fingers. Another was a neat little man with a curly and minute forked beard and restless hands. The third—

The third was hell to describe. They were all dressed now in the conventional robes of the Stasis, but even in these familiar garments he was clearly not quite human. If man is a featherless biped, then this was a man; but men do not usually have greenish skin with vestigal scales and a trace of a gill-opening behind each ear.

''Ask each of them three things,'' the linguist instructed Brent. ''When he comes from, what his name bees, and what be his intentions.''

Brent picked Tiny Beard as the easiest-looking start. ''OK. You!'' He pointed, and the man stepped forward. ''What part of time do you come from?''

''A pox o' three, sirrah, and the goodyears take thee! An thou wouldst but hearken to me, thou might'st learn all.''

The State linguist moaned. ''You hear, young man? How can one interpret such jargon?''

Brent smiled. ''It bees OK. This bees simply English as it beed speaked thousand years ago. This man must have beed aiming at earlier time and prepared himself. . . . Thy pardon, sir. These kerns deem all speech barbaric save that which their own conceit hath evolved. Bear with me, and all will be well.''

''Spoken like a true knight!'' the traveler explained. ''Forgive my rash words, sir. Surely my good daemon hath led thee hither. Thou wouldst know—''

''Whence comest thou?''

''From many years hence. Thousands upon thousands of summers have yet to run their course ere I—''

''Forgive me, sir; but of that much we are aware. Let us be precise.''

Anthony Boucher

"When then, marry, sir, 'tis from the fifth century."

Brent frowned. But to attempt to understand the gentleman's system of dating would take too much time at the moment. "And thy name, sir?"

"Kruj, sir. Or an thou would'st be formal and courtly, Kruj Krujil Krujilar. But let Kruj suffice thee."

"And what most concerneth these gentlemen here is the matter of thine intentions. What are thy projects in this our earlier world?"

"My projects?" Kruj coughed. "Sir, in thee I behold a man of feeling, of sensibility, a man to whom one may speak one's mind. Many projects have I in good sooth, most carefully projected for me by the Zhurmandril. Much must I study in these realms of the great Elizabeth—though 'sblood! I know not how they seem so different from my conceits. But one thing above all else do I covet. I would to the Mermaid Tavern."

Brent grinned. "I fear me, sir, that we must talk at greater length. Much hast thou mistaken and much must I make clear to thee. But first I must talk with these others."

Kruj retired, frowning and plucking at his shred of beard. Brent beckoned forward the woman. She strode forth so vigorously that both Stappers bared their rods.

"Madam," Brent ventured tentatively, "what part of time do you come from?"

"Evybuy taws so fuy," she growled. "Bu I unnasta. Wy cachoo unnasta *me?*"

Brent laughed. "Is that all that's the trouble? You don't mind if I go on talking like this, do you?"

"Naw. You taw howeh you wanna, slonsoo donna like I dih taw stray."

Fascinating, Brent thought. All final consonants lost, and many others. Vowels corrupted along lines indicated in twentieth-century colloquial speech. Consonants sometimes restored in liaison as in French. "What time do you come from, then?"

"Twenny-ni twenny-fie. N were am I now?"

"Twenty-four seventy-three. And your name, madam?"

"Mimi."

Brent had an incongruous vision of this giantess dying operatically in a Paris garret. "So. And your intentions here?"

"Ai gonno intenchuns. Juh wanna see wha go."

"You will, madam, I assure you. And now—" He beckoned to the green-skinned biped, who advanced with a lurching motion like a deep-sea diver.

"And you, sir. When do you come from?"

"Ya studier langue earthly. Vyerit todo langue isos. Ou comprendo wie govorit people."

Brent was on the ropes and groggy. The familiarity of some of the words made the entire speech even more incomprehensible. "Says which?" he gasped.

The green man exploded. "Ou existier nada but dolts, cochons, duraki v this terre? Nikovo parla langue earthly? Potztausend Sapperment en la leche de tu madre and I do mean you!"

Brent reeled. But even reeling he saw the disapproving frown of the State linguist and the itching fingers of the Stappers. He faced the green man calmly and said with utmost courtesy, " 'Twas brillig and the slithy toves did gyre and gimble over the rivering waters of the hitherandthithering waters of pigeons on the grass alas. Thank you, sir." He turned to the linguist. "He says he won't talk."

Brent wrote in the never-to-be-read journal: *It was Martha again who solved my green man for me. She pointed out that he was patently extraterrestrial. (Apparently Nakamura's Law of Spacial Acceleration is as false as Charnwood's Law of Temporal Metabolism.) The vestigial scales and gills might well indicate Venus as his origin. He must come from some far distant future when the earth is overrun by inhabitants of other planets and terrestrial culture is all but lost. He had prepared himself for time travel by studying the speech of earth—langue earthly—reconstructed from some larger equivalent of the Rosetta Stone, but made the mistake of thinking that there was only one earthly speech, just as we tend imaginatively to think of Martian or Venusian as a single language. As a result, he's talking all earthly tongues at once. Martha sees a marked advantage in this, even more than in Mimi's corrupt dialect—*

"Thou, sir," said Brent to Kruj on his next visit, "art a linguist. Thou knowest speech and his nature. To wit, I would wager that thou couldst with little labour understand this woman here. One who hath so mastered our language in his greatest glory—"

The little man smirked. "I thank thee, sir. In sooth since thou didst speak with her yestereven I have already made some attempts at converse with her."

Mimi joined in. "He says fuy, bu skina cue."

"Very well then. I want you both, and thee in particular, Kruj, to hearken to this green-skinned varley here. Study his speech, sir, and learn what thou may'st."

"Wy?" Mimi demanded belligerently.

"The wench speaks sooth. Wherefore should we so?"

"You'll find out. Now let me at him."

It was slow, hard work, especially with the linguist and the Stappers ever on guard. It meant rapid analysis of the possible origin of every word used by the Venusian, and a laborious painstaking attempt to find at random words that he would understand. But in the course of a week both Brent and the astonishingly adaptable Kruj had learned enough of this polygot *langue earthly* to hold an intelligible conversation. Mimi was hopelessly lost, but Kruj occasionally explained matters to her in her own corrupt speech, which he had mastered by now as completely as Elizabethan.

It had been Stephen's idea that any project for the liberation of the time travelers must wait until more was learned of their nature. "You be man of good will, John. We trust you. You and mans like you can save us. But imagine that some travelers come from worlds far badder even than ours. Suppose that they come seeking only power for themselves? Suppose that they come from civilization of cruelty and terror and be even more evil than Stappers?"

It was a wise point, and it was Martha who saw the solution in the Venusian's amazing tongue. In that mélange of languages, Brent could talk in front of the linguist and the Stappers with complete safety. Kruj and the Venusian, who must have astonishing linguistic ability to master the speech of another planet even so perversely, could discuss matters with the other travelers, and could tell him anything he needed to know before all the listening guards of the State.

All this conversation was, of course, theoretically guided by the linguist. He gave questions to Brent and received plausible answers, never dreaming that his questions had not been asked.

As far as his own three went, Brent was satisfied as to the value of their liberation. Mimi was not bright, but she seemed to mean well and claimed to have been a notable warrior in her own matriarchal society. It was her feats in battle and exploration that had caused her to be chosen for time travel. She would be in some respects a useful ally.

Kruj was indifferent to the sorry state of the world until Brent mentioned the tasteless and servile condition of the arts. Then he was all afire to overthrow the Stasis and bring about a new renaissance. (Kruj, Brent learned, had been heading for the past to collect material for an historical epic on Elizabethan England, a fragment of prehistoric civilization that had always fascinated him.)

Of the three, Nikobat, the Venusian, seemed the soundest and most promising. To him, terrestrial civilization was a closed book, but a beautiful one. In the life and struggles of man he found something deep and moving. The aim of Nikobat in his own world had been to raise his transplanted Venusian civilization to the levels, spiritual and scientific, that had once been attained by earthly man, and it was to find the seed of inspiration to accomplish this that he had traveled back. Man degenerate, man self-complacent, man smug, shocked him bitterly, and he swore to exert his best efforts in the rousing.

Brent was feeling not unpleased with himself as he left his group after a highly successful session. Kruj was accomplishing much among the other travelers and would have a nearly full report for him tomorrow. And once that report had been made, they could attempt Martha's extraordinary scheme of rescue. He would not have believed it ordinarily possible; but both he and Stephen were coming to put more and more trust in the suggestions of the once scatter-brained Martha. Stephen's own reports were more than favorable. The Underground was boring beautifully from within. The people of the State were becoming more and more restless and doubting. Slowly these cattle were resuming the forms of men.

Brent was whistling happily as he entered the apartment and called out a cheery "Hi!" to his friends. But they were not there. There was no one in the room but a white-clad Stapper, who smiled wolfishly as he rose from a chair and asked politely, "You be time traveler, be you not?"

This was the most impressive Stapper that Brent had yet seen—impressive even aside from the startling nature of his introductory remark. The others, even the one he had kicked in the face, or the one who killed Alex, Brent had thought of simply as so many Stappers. This one was clearly an individual. His skin was exceptionally dark and smooth and hairless, and two eyes so black that they seemed all pupil glowed out of his face and dominated the room.

Brent tried to seem casual. "Nonsense. I be Slanduch envoy from Germany, staying here with friends and doing linguistic service for State. Here bees my identification."

The Stapper hardly glanced at it. "I know all about your 'linguistic services,' John Brent. And I know about machine finded in deserted warehouse. It beed only machine not breaked by Barrier. Therefore it comed not from Future, but from Past."

"So? We have travelers from both directions? Poor devil will never be able to get back to own time then." He wondered if this Stapper were corruptible; he could do with a drink of bond.

"Yes, he bees losed here in this time like others. And he foolishly works with them to overthrow Stasis."

"Sad story. But how does it concern me? My papers be in order. Surely you can see that I be what I claim?"

The Stapper's eyes fixed him sharply. "You be clever, John Brent. You doubtless traveled naked and clothed yourself as citizen of now to escape suspicion. That bees smartest way. How you getted papers I do not know. But communication with German Slanduch cans disprove your story. You be losed, Brent, unless you be sensible."

"Sensible? What the hell do you mean by that?"

The Stapper smiled slowly. "Article," he drawled.

"I be sorry. But that proves nothing. You know how difficult it bees for us Slanduch to keep our speech entirely regular."

"I know." Suddenly a broad grin spread across the Stapper's face and humanized it. "I have finded this Farthing speech hellishly difficult myself."

"You mean you, too, be Slanduch?"

The Stapper shook his head. "I, too, Brent, be traveler."

Brent was not falling for any such trap. "Ridiculous! How canned traveler be Stapper?"

"How canned traveler be Slanduch envoy? I, too, traveled naked, and man whose clothes and identification I stealed beed Stapper. I have finded his identity most useful."

"I don't believe you."

"You be stubborn, Brent. How to prove—" He gestured at his face. "Look at my skin. In my century facial hair haves disappeared; we have breeded away from it. Where in this time could you find skin like that?"

"A sport. Freak of chromosomes."

The black eyes grew even larger and more glowing. "Brent, you must believe me. This bees no trap for you. I need you. You and I, we can do great things. But how to convince you"—he snapped his fingers. "I know!" He was still for a moment. The vast eyes remained opened but somehow veiled, as though secret calculations

Anthony Boucher

were going on behind them. His body shivered. For a moment of strange delusion Brent thought he could see the chair through the Stapper's body. Then it was real and solid again.

The Stapper's eyes resumed their light, and he looked about the room expectantly for a moment. "Delay," he muttered disappointedly. "But no matter. In a moment—"

"What bees this—"

"My name," said the Stapper, with the patience of a professor addressing a retarded class, "bees Bokor. I come from tenth century after consummation of terrestrial unity, which bees, I believe, forty-third reckoning from date of birth of Christian god. I have travelled, not with machine, but solely by use of Vunmurd formula, and, therefore, I alone of all travelers stranded here can still move. Hysteresis of Barrier arrests me, but can not destroy my formula as it shatters machines."

"Pretty story."

"I have sended myself back to Barrier again by formula, but trip from Barrier to now seems longer for me this time. I—" He broke off as the door opened. "Ah," he said. "Here I be!"

The Stapper in the doorway fixed Brent with his glowing black eyes and said, "Now do you believe that I be traveler?"

Brent gawped from one identical man to the other. The one in the doorway went on. "I need you."

"It isn't possible. It's a gag. You're twin Stappers, and you're trying to—"

Boker in the chair said, "Do I have to do it again?"

Bokor-Sub-One in the doorway said, "I have hitted Barrier twice. Therefore I exist twice in that one point of time. Therefore each of those two continues into present."

Brent said, "You may both be Stappers. You may turn out to be a whole damned regiment of identical multiple births. I don't give a damn; I want some bond. How about you boys?"

The two Bokors downed their drinks and frowned. "Weak," they said.

Brent shook his head feebly. "All right. We'll skip that. Now what the sweet hell do you need me for?"

Boker closed his eyes and seemed to doze. Bokor-Sub-One said, "You have plans to liberate travelers and overthrow Stasis. As Stapper I have learned much. I worked on changing mind of one of your Underground friends."

"And you want to throw your weight in with us? Good, we can use a Stapper. Or two. But won't the Chief of Stappers be bothered when he finds he has two copies of one man?"

"He will never need to see more than one. Yes, I want to help you—up to a point. We will free travelers. But you be innocent, Brent. We will not overthrow Stasis. We will maintain it—as ours."

Brent frowned. "I'm not sure I get you. And I don't think I like it if I do."

"Do not be fool, Brent. We have opportunity never before gived to man, we travelers. We come into world where already exists complete and absolute State control, but used stupidly and to no end. Among us all we have great knowledge and power. We be seed sowed upon fallow ground. We can spring up and engulf all about us." The eyes glowed with black intensity. "We take this Stasis and mould it to our own wishes. These dolts who now be slaves of Cosmos will be slaves of us. Stapper, whose identity I have, bees third in succession to Chief of Stappers. Chief and other two will be killed accidentally in revolt of travelers. With power of all Stappers behind me, I make you Head of State. Between us we control this State absolutely."

"Nuts," Brent snorted. "The State's got too damned much control already. What this world needs is a return to human freedom and striving."

"Innocent," Boker-Sub-One repeated scornfully. "Who gives damn what world needs? Only needs which concern man be his own, and his strongest need bees always for power. Here it bees given us. Other States be stupid and self-complacent like this. We know secrets of many weapons, we travelers. We turn our useless scholastic laboratories over to their production. Then we attack other States and subject them to us as vassals. And then the world itself bees ours, and all its riches. Alexander, Caesar, Napoleon, Hitler, Gospodinov, Tirazhul—never in its past or future haves world knowed nor will it know conquerors like us."

"You can go to hell," said Brent lightly but firmly. "All two of you."

"Do not be too clever, my friend. Remember that I be Stapper and can—"

"You be two Stappers, which may turn out to be a little awkward. But you could be a regiment of Stappers, and I still wouldn't play ball. Your plan stinks, Bokor, and you know what you can do with it."

Bokor-Sub-One took the idiom literally. "Indeed I do know, Brent. It willed have beed easier with your aid, but even without you it will succeed." He drew out his rod and contemplated it reflectively. "No," he murmured, "there bees no point to taking you in and changing your mind. You be harmless to me, and your liberation of travelers will be useful."

The original Bokor opened his eyes. "We will meet again, Brent. And you will see what one man with daring mind can accomplish in this world." Bokor and Bokor-Sub-One walked to the door and turned. "And for bond," they spoke in unison, in parody of the conventional Stapper's phrase, "State thanks you."

Brent stood alone in the room, but the black-eyed domination of the two Bokors lingered about him. The plan was so damned plausible, so likely to succeed if put into operation. Man has always dreamed of power. But damn it, man has always dreamed of love, too, and of the rights of his fellow man. The only power worthy of man is the power of all mankind struggling together toward a goal of unobtainable perfection.

And what could Bokor do against Kruj and Mimi and Nikobat and the dozens of others that Kruj reported sympathetic?

Nevertheless there had been a certainty in those vast glowing eyes that the duple Bokor knew just what he could do.

* * *

Anthony Boucher

The release of the travelers was a fabulous episode. Stephen had frowned and Brent had laughed when Martha said simply, "Only person who haves power to release them bees Head of State by will of Cosmos. Very well. We will persuade him to do so." But she insisted, and she had been so uncannily right ever since the explosion of the second Barrier that at last, when Kruj had made his final report, Brent accompanied her on what he was certain was the damnedest fool errand he'd got himself into yet.

Kruj's report was encouraging. There were two, perhaps three among the travelers who had Bokorian ideas of taking over the State for their own purposes. But these were far outweighed by the dozens who saw the tremendous possibilities of a reawakening mankind. The liberation was proved a desirable thing; but why should the Head of State so readily loose these disrupters upon his Stasis?

Getting to see the Head of State took the best part of a day. There were countless minor officials to be interviewed, all of them guarded by Stappers who looked upon the supposed Slanduch envoy with highly suspicious eyes. But one by one, with miraculous consistency, these officials beamed upon Brent's errand and sent him on with the blessing of Cosmos.

"You wouldn't like to pinch me?" he murmured to Martha after the fifth such success. "This works too easily. It can't be true."

Martha looked at him blankly and said, "I don't understand it. But what be we doing here? What be we going to say?"

Brent jumped. "Hey! Look, madam. This was all your idea to start with. You were going to talk the Head of State into—And now you say, 'What be we going to say?' If you don't—"

But a Stapper was already approaching to conduct them to the next office, and Brent fell silent.

It was in the anteroom of the Head of State that they met Bokor. Just one of him this time. He smiled confidentially at Brent and said, "Shocking accident today. Stapper beed killed in fight with prisoner who beed to have his mind changed. Odd thing—Stapper beed second in succession to Chief of Stappers."

"You're doing all right," said Brent.

"I be curious to see what you plan here. How do you hope to achieve this liberation? I talked with Head of State yesterday and he bees strongly opposed."

"Brother," said Brent sincerely, "I wish to Cosmos I knew."

In a moment Bokor ushered them into the sanctorum of the Head of State. This great dignitary was at first glance a fine figure of a man, tall and well built and noble. It was only on second glance that you noticed the weak lips and the horribly empty eyes. The stern and hawk-nosed Chief of Stappers stood beside him.

"Well!" the latter snapped. "Speak your piece!"

Brent faltered and glanced at Martha. She looked as vacant and helpless as ever she had before the Barrier. He could only fumble on and pray that her unrevealed scheme would materialize.

"As you know, sir," he bagan, "I, as interpreter, have beed in very close contact with travelers. Having in my mind good of Cosmos and wishing to see it as rich and fully developed as possible, it seems to me that much may be accomplished by releasing travelers so that they may communicate with people." He gulped and swore at himself for venturing such an idiotic request.

The empty eyes of the Head of State lit up for a moment. "Excellent idea," he boomed in a dulcet voice. "You have permission of State and Cosmos. Chief, I give orders that all travelers be released."

Brent heard Bokor's incredulous gasp behind him. The Chief of Stappers murmured "Cosmos!" fervently. The Head of State looked around him for approval and then reverted to formal vacancy.

"I thank State," Brent managed to say, "for this courageous move."

"What bees courageous?" the Head demanded. His eyes shifted about nervously. "What have I doed? What have I sayed?"

The Chief of Stappers bowed. "You have proclaimed freedom of travelers. May I, too, congratulate you on wisdom of action?" He turned to Bokor. "Go and give necessary orders."

Brent saw the dazed faces of Bokor and Martha and wondered if his own looked quite so ridiculously incredulous. That the Head of State and the Chief of Stappers should sanction a policy that any dolt could see must inevitably be fatal to the Stasis of Cosmos—It was mad. It was a dream. But it was certainly a damned agreeable one.

Martha did not say a word till they were outside on the moving sidewalk again. Then she asked, "What happened? Why in Cosmos' name doed he consent?"

"Madam, you have me there. But you should know. It was all your idea."

Understanding came back to her face. "Of course. It bees time now that you know all about me. But wait till we be back in apartment. Stephen haves right to know this, too. And Martha," she added.

That oral postscript was too much for Brent. When you begin talking of yourself as a third party—

"Come on home, madam," he said. "You'll feel better."

They had left Bokor behind them in the sanctum, and they met Bokor outside the building. That did not worry Brent, but he was admittedly perturbed when he passed a small group of people just off the sidewalk and noticed that its core was a third Bokor. He pulled Martha off the moving path and drew near the group.

Bokor was not a Stapper this time. He was in ordinary iridescent robes. "I tell you I know," he was insisting vigorously. "I am . . . I be Slanduch from State of South America, and I can tell you deviltry they be practicing there. Armament factories twice size of laboratories of Cosmos. Bees this for nothing? They plan to destroy us; I know."

A Stapper shoved his way past Brent. "Here now!" he growled. "What bees going on here?"

Anthony Boucher

Bokor hesitated. "Nothing, sir. I was only—"

"*Was,* huh?"

"Pardon, sir. *Beed.* I be Slanduch, you see, and—"

One of the men in the crowd interrupted. "He beed telling us what all State needs to know—plans of State of South America to invade and destroy us."

"Hm-m-m!" the Stapper ejaculated. "You be right, man. That sounds like something we all need to know. Go on, you."

Bokor resumed his rumour-mongering, and the Stapper lent it official endorsement by his listening silence. Brent moved to get a glimpse of the Stapper's face. His guess was right. It was another Bokor.

This significant byplay had delayed them enough so that Brent's three travelers had reached the apartment before them. When they arrived, Stephen was deep in a philosophical discussion with the Venusian of the tragic nobility of human nature, while Kruj and Mimi were experimenting with bond. Their respective civilizations could not have been markedly alcoholic; Kruj had reached the stage of sweeping and impassioned gestures, while Mimi beamed at him and interposed an occasional irrelevant giggle.

All three had discarded the standardized robes of the Stasis and resumed, in this friendly privacy, the clothes in which they had arrived—Kruj, a curiously simplified and perfected version of the ruffled court costume of the Elizabethan era he had hoped to reach, Mimi, the startling armor of an unfamiliar metal which was her uniform as Amazon warrior, and Nikobat a simple bronze-coloured loincloth against which his green skin assumed a certain strange beauty.

Brent introduced Martha's guests to their hostess and went on. "Now for a staff meeting of G.H.Q. We've got to lay our plans carefully, because I warn you we're up against some stiff opposition. There's one other traveler who—"

"One moment," said Martha's voice. "Shouldn't you introduce me, too?"

"I beg your pardon, madam. I just finished that task of courtesy. And now—"

"I be sorry," her voice went on. "You still do not understand. You introduced Martha, yes; but not me."

Stephen turned to the travelers. "I must apologize for my sister. She haves goed through queer experiences of late. She traveled with our friend John and meeted herself in her earlier life. I fear that shock has temporarily—and temporally—unbalanced her."

"Can none of you understand so simple thing?" the woman's voice pleaded. "I be simply using Martha's voice as instrument of communication. I can just as easily—"

" 'Steeth!" Kruj exclaimed. " 'Tis eke as easy and mayhap more pleasant to borrow this traveler's voice for mine explications."

"Or," Mimi added, "I cou taw li thih, but I do' like ih vey muh."

Stephen's eyes popped. "You mean that you be traveler without body?"

"Got it in one," Brent heard his own voice saying. "I can wander about any way

I damned please. I picked the woman first because her nearly empty mind was easy to occupy, and I think I'll go on using her. Brent here's a little hard to keep under control.''

Stephen nodded. ''Then all good advice Martha haves beed giving up—''

''Bees mine, of course.'' The bodiless traveler was back in Martha now.

Brent gasped. ''And now I see how you wangled the release of the travelers. You got us in by usurping the mind and speech of each of the minor officials we tackled, and then ousted the Head of State and Chief of Stappers to make them give their consent.

Martha nodded. ''Exactly.''

''This is going to be damned useful. And where do you come from, sir? Or is it madam?''

''I come from future so far distant that even our Venusian friend here cannot conceive of it. And distinction between *sir* and *madam* bees then meaningless.''

The dapper Kruj glanced at the hulking Amazon beside him.

'' 'Twere pity,'' he murmured.

''And your intentions here, to go on with the State linguist's questionaire?''

''My intentions? Listen, all of you. We cannot shape ends. Great patterns be shaped outside of us and beyond us. I beed historian in my time. I know patterns of mankind even down to minute details. And I know that Stephen here bees to lead people of this Age of Smugness out of their stupidity and back to humanity.''

Stephen coughed, embarrassed. ''I have no wish to lead. But for such cause man must do what he may.''

''That bees ultimate end of this section of pattern. That bees fixed. All that we travelers can do bees to aid him as wisely as we can and to make the details of the pattern as pleasingly beautiful as may be. And that we will do.''

Stephen must have been so absorbed in this speech that his hearing was dulled. The door opened without warning, and Bokor entered.

'' 'Swounds!'' Kruj cried out. ''A Stapper!''

Stephen smiled. ''Why fear Stappers? You be leagally liberated.''

''Stapper, hell!'' Brent snorted. ''Well, Bokor? You still want to declare yourself in with your racket?''

Bokor's deep eyes swept the room. He smiled faintly. ''I merely wished to show you something, Brent. So that you know what you be up against. I have finded two young scientists dissatisfied with scholastic routine of research for Cosmos. Now they work under my instructions, and they have maked for me—this.'' He held a bare rod in his hand.

''So it's a rod. So what next?''

''But it bees different rod, Brent. It does not paralyze. It destroys.'' The point of the rod wavered and covered in turn each individual in the room. ''I want you to see what I can accomplish.''

''You suvvabih!'' Mimi yelled and started to rise. Kruj restrained her.

"State thanks you, madam, for making up my mind. I will demonstrate on you. Watch this, Brent, and realize what chance you have against me." He pointed the rod firmly at Mimi.

"Do something!" Martha screamed.

It all happened at once, but Brent seemed to see it in slow motion even as he moved. Mimi lunged forward furiously and recklessly. Kruj dived for her feet and brought her to the floor out of the line of fire. At the same time Brent threw himself forward just as Bokor moved, so that the rod now pointed directly at Brent. He couldn't arrest his momentum. He was headed straight at Bokor's new instrument of death. And then the rod moved to Bokor's own head.

There was no noise, no flash. But Bokor's body was lying on the floor, and the head was nowhere.

"That beed hard," said Martha's voice. "I haved to stay in his mind long enough to actuate rod, but get out before death. Matter of fractions of seconds."

"Nice work, sir-madam," Brent grunted. He looked down at the headless corpse. "But that was only one of them."

Brent quoted in his journal: *Love, but a day, and the world has changed! A week, to be more exact, but the change is none the less sudden and impressive.*

Our nameless visitant from the future—they seem to need titles as little as sexes in that time—whom I have for convenience labelled Sirdam, has organized our plans about the central idea of interfering as little as possible—forcing the inhabitants of the Stasis to work out their own salvation. The travelers do not appear openly in this great change. We work through Stephen's associates.

The best single example to show the results we obtain is the episode of Professor Harrington, whose special department of so-called learning is the preservation of the Nakamura Law of Spacial Acceleration, which had so conclusively proved to the founders of the Stasis the impossibility of interplanetary travel.

This fell obviously within Nikobat's field. A young scientist affiliated with the Underground—a nephew, I have since learned, of Alex's—expounded the Nakamura doctrine as he had learned and re-proved it. It took the Venusian less than five minutes to put his finger on the basic flaw in the statement—the absolute omission, in all calculations, of any consideration of galactic drift. Once this correction was applied to the Nakamura formulas, they stood revealed as the pure nonsense which, indeed, Nikobat's very presence proved them.

It was not Nikobat but the young man who placed this evidence before Professor Harrington. The scene must have been classic. "I say," the young man later told us—they are all trying desperately to unlearn Farthing-ised English—"his mouth fall open and gap spread across his face as wide as gap he suddenly finded in universe—the universe."

For the professor was not stupid. He was simply so conditioned from childhood to the acceptance of the Stasis of Cosmos that he had never questioned it. Besides, he had doubtless had friends whose minds were changed when they speculated too far.

Harrington's eyes lit up after the first shock. He grabbed pencil and paper and furiously checked through the revised equations again and again. He then called in a half-dozen of his best students and set them to what was apparently a routine exercise—interpolating variations for galactic drift in the Nakamura formulas.

They ended as astonished as their instructor. The first one done stared incredulously at his results and gasped, ''Nakamura beed wrong!''

One of them, horrified, destroyed his calculations, saying, ''This bees against Stasis.''

The professor smiled. ''Not against, my boy. It bees beyond Cosmos.''

That was typical. The sheep are ready to be roused, each in his individual way. Kruj has been training men to associate with the writers of the Stasis. The man's knowledge of literature of all periods, and especially of his beloved Elizabethan Age, is phenomenal and his memory something superhuman. And four writers out of five who hear his disciples discourse on the joys of creative language and quote from the Elizabethan dramatists and the King James Bible will never be content again to write Stasis propaganda for the sollies or the identically bound books of the State libraries.

I have myself been contributing a fair amount to the seduction of the world by teaching cooks. I was never in my own time acknowledged as better than a fair-to-middling nonprofessional, but here I might be Escoffier or Brillat-Savarin. We steal plants and animals from the scientific laboratories, and in our hands they become vegetables and meat; and many a man in the street, who doesn't give a damn if his science is false and his arts synthetic, has suddenly realized that he owes the State a grudge for feeding him on concentrates.

The focus of everything is Stephen. It's hard to analyze why. Each of us travelers has found among the Undergrounders someone far more able in his own special field, yet all of us, travelers and Undergrounders alike, unquestioningly acknowledge Stephen as our leader. It may be the sheer quiet kindliness and goodness of his nature. It may be that he and Alex, in their organization of this undercover group of instinctive rebels, were the first openly to admit that the Stasis was inhuman and to do something about it. But from whatever cause, we all come to depend more and more on the calm reiability of Stephen.

Nikobat says—

Bret broke off as Kruj Krujli Jrujilar staggered into the room. The little man was no longer dapper. His robes were tattered, and their iridescence was overlaid with the solid red of blood.

He panted his first words in his own tongue, then recovered himself. ''We must act apace, John. Where is Stephen?''

''At Underground quarters, I think. But what's happened?''

''I was nearing the building where they do house us travelers when I beheld hundreds of people coming along the street. Some wore our robes, some wore Stappers'. And they all—'' He shuddered. ''They all had the same face—a brown hairless face with black eyes.''

Brent was on his feet. ''Bokor!'' The man had multiplied himself into a regiment. One man who was hundreds—why not thousands? millions?—could indeed be such a conqueror as the world had never known. ''What happened?''

''They entered the building. I knew that I could do nothing there, and came to find you and Stephen and the bodiless one. But as I came along the street, lo! on every corner there was yet another of that face, and always urging the people to maintain the Stasis and destroy the travelers. I was recognized. By good hap those who set upon me had no rods, but 'sbody! 'Twas a close thing that I escaped with my life.''

Brent thought quickly. ''Martha is with Stephen, so Sirdam is probably there, too. Go to him at once and warn him. I'm going to the travelers' building and see what's happened. Meet you at the headquarters as soon as I can.''

Kruj hesitated. ''Mimi—''

''I'll bring her with me if I can. Get going.''

The streets were mad. Wild throngs jammed the moving roadways. Somewhere in the distance mountainous flames leaped up and their furious glitter gleamed back from the eyes of the mob.

And those were not the deeply glowing black eyes of multitudinous Bokors. These were the ordinary citizens of the Stasis, no longer cattle, or rather cattle stampeded and raging.

A voice blared seemingly out of the heavens. Brent recognized the public address system used for vital State messages. ''Revolt of travelers have spreaded to amphi-theater of Cosmos. Flames lighted by travelers now attack sacred spot. People of Cosmos. Destroy travelers!''

''The Reichstag fire!'' Brent muttered. ''Technique doesn't change much—'' If only he could avoid running into a Bokor. There was nothing to mark him superficially as a traveler. He pushed along with the mob, shouting as rabidly as any other. He could make no headway. He was borne along on these foaming human waves.

Then in front of him he saw three Bokors pushing against the mob. If they spied him—His hands groped along the wall. Just as a Bokor looked his way, he found what he was seeking—one of the spying niches of the Stappers. He slipped into the false wall in safety.

He peered out cautiously for a moment to escape. From the next door he saw a man emerge whom he knew by sight—a leading dramatist of the sollies, who had promised to be an eventual convert of Kruj's disciples. Three citizens of the mob hailed him as he stepped forth.

''What bees your name?''

''Where be you going?''

''When do you come from?''

''Answer every man directly.''

The solly writer hesitated. "I be going to amphitheatre. Speaker have sayed—"

"When do you come from?"

"Why, from now."

"What bees your name?"

"John—"

"Ha!" the first citizen yelled. "Stappers have told us to find this John. Tear him to pieces; he bees traveler."

"No, truly. I be no traveler; I be writer of sollies. I be of now."

One of the citizens chortled cruelly. "Tear him for his bad sollies!"

There was one long scream—

The smugness of the Stasis had been inhuman. Stephen and the travelers had sought to make the citizens human again in the noblest traditions of man's striving. But here was another manner of being human, and Bokor had found and roused it.

Fire breeds fire, literally as well as metaphorically. The dwelling of the travelers was ablaze when Brent reached it. A joyous mob cheered and gloated before it.

Brent started to push his way through, but a hand touched his arm and a familiar voice whispered, "Achtung! Ou vkhodit."

He interpreted the warning and let the Venusian draw him aside. Nikobat rapidly explained in Brent's own speech.

"The Stappers came and subdued the whole crowd with paralyzing rods. They took them away—God knows what they'll do with them. There's no one in there now; the fire's just a gesture." The red flames glittered on the green skin.

"But you—How did you—"

"My nerve centres don't react the same. I lay doggo and got away. Mimi escaped, too; her armor has deflecting power. I think she's gone to warn the Underground."

"Then come on."

"Don't stay too close to me," Nikobat warned. "They'll recognize me as a traveler; stay out of range of rods aimed at me. And here. I took these from a Stapper I strangled. This one is a paralyzing rod; the other's an annihilator."

The next half-hour was a nightmare—a montage of flames and blood and sweating bodies of hate. The Stasis of Stupidity was becoming a Stasis of Cruelty. For a moment Brent wondered if he could find where the Stappers had taken his machine. That Derringer model was the only machine unshattered—the only one that, though still helpless against the Barrier, could at least take him forward to what might be a better world—Kruj's aesthetic paradise or even Mimi's matriarchy. But he thought of Stephen and Martha, and he pushed on toward the Underground headquarters.

Twice groups of citizens stopped him. They were unarmed; Bokor wisely kept weapons to himself, knowing that the fangs and claws of an enraged mob are enough. The first group Brent left paralyzed. The second time he confused his weapons. He had not meant to kill, but he could not regret it.

He did not confuse his weapons when he bagged a brace of Bokors. But what did the destruction of two matter? He fought his way on, finally catching up with Nikobat at their goal. As they met, the voice boomed once more from the air. "Important! New Chief of Stappers announces that offices of Chief of Stappers and Head of State be henceforth maked one. Under new control, travelers will be wiped out and Stasis preserved. Then on to South America for glory of Cosmos!"

Brent shuddered. "And we started out so beautifully on our renaissance!"

Nikobat shook his head. "But the bodiless traveler said that Stephen was to destroy the Stasis. This multiple villain cannot change what has happened."

"Can't he? We're taking no chances."

The headquarters of the Underground was inappositely in a loft. The situation helped. The trap entrance was unnoticeable from below and had gone unheeded by the mobs. Brent delivered the proper raps, and the trap slid open and dropped a ladder. Quickly he and the Venusian mounted.

The loft was a sick bay. A half-dozen wounded members of Stephen's group lay groaning on the floor. With them was Kruj. Somewhere the little man had evaded the direct line of an annihilator, but lost his hand. Blood was seeping out of his bandages, and Mimi, surprisingly feminine and un-Amazonic, held his unconscious head in her lap.

"You don't seem to need warning," Brent observed tersely.

Stephen shook his head sadly. "We be trapped here. Here we be safe for at littlest small while. If we go out—"

Brent handed him his rods. "You're the man we've got to save, Stephen. You know what Sirdam's said—it all depends on you. Use these to protect yourself, and we'll make a dash for it. If we can lose ourselves in the mob as ordinary citizens there's a chance of getting away with it. Or"—he turned to Martha-Sirdam—"have you any ideas?"

"Yes. But only as latest resort."

Nikobat was peering out of the window. "It's the last resort now," he said. "There's a good fifty of those identical Stappers outside, and they're headed here. They act as though they know what this is."

Brent was looking at Stephen, and he saw a strange thing. Stephen's face was expressionless, but somewhere behind his eyes Brent seemed to sense a struggle. Stephen's body trembled with an effort of will, and then his eyes were clear again. "No," he said distinctly. "You do not need to control me. I understand. You be right. I will do as you say." And he lifted the annihilator rod.

Brent started forward, but his muscles did not respond to his commands. Force his will though he might, he stood still. It was the bodiless traveler who held him, he realized, held him motionless to watch Stephen place the rod to his temple.

"This bees goodest thing that I can do for mans," said Stephen simply. Then his headless corpse thumped on the floor.

Brent was released. He dashed forward, but vainly. There was nothing men could do for Stephen now. Brent let out a choking gasp of pain and sorrow.

Then the astonished cries of the Undergrounders recalled him from his friend's body. He looked about him. Where was Nikobat? Where were Kruj and Mimi?

A small inkling of the truth began to reach him. He hurried to the window and looked out.

There were no Bokors before the house. Only a few citizens staring dazedly at a wide space of emptiness.

At that moment the loud-speaker sounded. "Announcement," a shocked voice trembled. "Chief of Stappers haves just disappeared." And in a moment it added, "Guards report all travelers have vanished."

The citizens before the house were rubbing their eyes like men coming out of a nightmare.

"But don't you see, madam— No? Well, let me try again." Brent was not finding it easy to explain her brother's heroic death to an untenanted Martha. "Remember what your inhabitant told us? The Stasis was overthrown by Stephen."

"But Stephen bees dead."

"Exactly. So listen: All these travelers came from a future wherein Stephen had overthrown the Stasis. So that when Stephen destroyed himself, as Sirdam realized, he likewise destroyed that future. A world in which Stephen died unsuccessful is a world that cannot be entered by anyone from the other future. Their worlds vanished and they with them. It was the only way of abolishing the menace of the incredibly multiplied Bokor."

"Stephen bees dead. He cans not overthrow Stasis now."

"My dear madam— Hell, skip it. But the Stasis is damned none the less in this new world created by Stephen's death. I've been doing a little galping on my own. The people are convinced now that the many exemplars of Bokor were some kind of evil invader. They rebound easy, the hordes; they dread the memory of those men and they dread also the ideas of cruelty and conquest to which the Bokors had so nearly converted them.

"But one thing they can't rebound from is the doubts and the new awarenesses that we planted in their minds. And there's what's left of your movement to go on with. No, the Stasis is damned, even if they are going to erect yet another Barrier."

"Oh," Martha shuddered. "You willn't let them do that, will you?"

Brent grinned. "Madam, there's damned little letting I can do. They're going to, and that's that. Because, you see, all the travelers vanished."

"But why—"

Brent shrugged and gave up. "Join me in some bond?" It was clear enough. The point of time which the second Barrier blocked existed both in the past of the worlds of Nikobat and Sirdam, and in the past of this future they were now entering. But no travelers had come from this future. Therefore there must be a Barrier yet ahead of them.

Would the Stasis by then be dissolved into a normal human society? Would man have cast aside his purse-proud garment of smugness and become his struggling,

Anthony Boucher

striving, failing, ridiculous, noble self? And the travelers from this coming future—would they be Sirdams to counsel and guide man, or Bokors to corrupt and debase him?

Brent lifted his glass of bond. ''To the moment after the next Barrier!'' he said.

■

THE SIGNALS
Francis A. Cartier

DR. RAYMOND WARD SLOUCHED against the cool concrete doorframe of the moonlit control house. Occasionally puffing on his pipe, he gazed wearily at the immense crater, its floor latticed with steel, that some of his staff had once called the Star Bowl. Now the name seemed affected and precious. For nineteen years, Ward had been Assistant Director, then Director, of the stellar listening project, and he was about fed up with it. There were so many other, more productive areas of space electronics that he would prefer to be working in. Certainly, the project had intrigued him at first. Watching them build the great crater antenna system, nearly half a mile across, had fascinated him. The prospect of intercepting intelligent messages from space was truly exciting then, and his peculiar combination of talents in satellite tracking and mechanical translation seemed to make him uniquely qualified for the project. His year of experience in Audio with the porpoise research hadn't hurt him either. What an opportunity for fame! To find, record, and interpret the first signal from outer space!

But no man's patience is inexhaustible. Even a dedicated scientist needs some occasional reward, some reinforcement for this attempts. Otherwise, as even the freshman psychology student knows, the effort wanes and finally ceases.

It was Ward's enthusiasm that had kept the expensive operation going this long. But in the past few years, the turnover in personnel had been running as high as fifty percent. Not one of his original staff remained today. And now Ward himself, going on fifty, had run out of ideas for expanding or narrowing the search. Even Ward had stopped trying to find new ways of discovering something meaningful in the mountains of data that had been collected. A whole career of brilliant sleuthing and tedious tabulation had produced nothing.

Ward was tired and frustrated. Worse yet, he was bored. His shoulders slumped as he stared at the vast antenna and realized that his predominant feeling at the moment was guilt. And the guilt was of his feeling that he ought to quit.

"Well," said Zrsk thoughtfully, offering his assistant a sniff from his inhaler, "the system 7M648 still seems to me to have the greatest possibilities. Its sun is within limits for radiation and there is a good range of planetary characteristics. One of them should show life. Furthermore, there is that unique planet with a satellite revolving in the unnatural direction. Right?" The final intonation was the one for a rhetorical question to which the speaker expects some reply.

"Yes, sir, the sixth planet," said the assistant. "The one with the ring and the nine

Francis A. Cartier

satellites looks good.'' He declined the inhaler politely. He was too interested to want to depress his senses.

''The ring is unusual, of course, but not unique. I am more impressed by the satellite that orbits counter to the direction of rotation of the planet. A sure sign that it is not natural.''

''Of course,'' said the assistant, but with the polite intonation of slight doubt. Then, using the intonation of self-disparagement, ''However, I would favor one of the planets closer to the sun—perhaps the reddish fourth one.''

Zrsk grunted, his accent encouraging the younger to speculate further. Thus emboldened, the assistant continued. ''It is strange that we have not contacted someone in that system,'' he said. ''Do you suppose our signals are still too fast? In our own history, if I remember correctly, the early ones had only the cutaneous-pressure communication, which must have been quite a bit slower than our present-day communication.''

''Yes, that's true,'' said Zrsk. ''It took them a word per revolution or more, whereas we can easily converse at the rate of twenty or even thirty words for every circuit around our sun.''

''What,'' asked the assistant, using the intonation of honest inquiry, ''is our present signal rate to this system 7M648?''

''Much less. Much less. It is a child's rate. It averages about two or three binary digits of information per revolution.''

The assistant hummed the intonation of bewilderment, then said, ''Revolutions of our planet or of sixth planet 7M648, sir?''

''They are about the same,'' said Zrsk. ''That is another reason, by the way, for favoring the sixth planet over the others.''

''Well, then,'' said the assistant, ''the signals cannot be too fast. Do you think they might be too . . .''

''We have been trying for two thousand six hundred revolutions, now,'' said Zrsk with sudden decisiveness. ''Let us try another direction.''

''Yes, sir,'' said the assistant, reaching for the controls.

Oer was talking in words again, showing off his postgraduate education. If he would only get back to talking in digits like any respectable and properly humble scientist, EEal thought, they would all feel more comfortable. However, as chairman, he could not let such a challenge go unnoticed and so he replied in words, trying to sound casual but hardly concealing a note of annoyance. ''We have been meeting now since First Meal and have come to no conclusions,'' he said. ''Shall we discontinue the signals or keep trying?''

Oer levitated his calculator to be recognized yet again.

''Oer,'' said the chairman dispiritedly. He was rather disappointed that the other six had remained so quiet.

''Sir Chairman,'' said Oer in his maddeningly deliberate articulation, ''we have, for the past *seventy years*, gradually reduced the complexity of our messages. Now, we have reached the *ultimate* simplicity, and have been broadcasting that signal *continuously*, for nearly *eleven* of those years. It is a mathematically *primitive* signal. If it is not being understood as a signal, then there must be no other intelligent life, or they have no capacity for transmission of a reply. I say we should *give up*."

Chariman EEal looked around the group. There was silence. He was preparing to speak when he noticed old Aom's calculator rise a modest tentacle-width above the conference table. Aom was not always very bright, but it would be good to hear someone speak in normal digits for a while.

But the old one disappointed him. "I think, I think," stammered Aom, searching his ancient memories for the academic words, "I have a . . . question. There are . . . is, I mean . . . so much signals of a *natural* nature . . . I mean, radiations from stars. Other minds, how would they know our signals are a message?"

It was a childish question, childishly asked, and EEal was sorry that he had not overlooked Aom's almost imperceptible bid for recognition. "Let me explain," he said softly. "We always send a clearly unnatural signal—one that will stand out against the background of natural electromagnetic phenomena. We have assumed that if there are other intelligent beings in the galaxy, they would be capable of recognizing simple numerical concepts."

"By definition!" said Ialr pompously. For this, his sole contribution to the meeting, he received a reproving glare from Chairman EEal, whose patience was running out.

"Obviously," EEal continued, "mathematics is a built-in common denominator of the entire universe, so it is only logical that our message should be a mathematical one."

"What, then, are we sending now?" asked Aom, apparently unaware of the exaggerated looks of boredom from several of the others.

Oer's calculator shot up off the table to eye level. EEal would have preferred to continue the explanation himself, but he could not justifiably refuse to see such a flagrant bid. Almost without waiting for EEal's nod, Oer let the calculator drop noisily and turned to Aom as though to finish the discussion once and for all. "We are sending," he said in a tone usually reserved only for children, "the *most* unnatural and the *most fundamental* concept in mathematics, the *one* concept from which all mathematics arises, and upon which all mathematical order is *ultimately based*."

"Ah!" said Aom, looking pleased with himself, "Zero!"

EEal had a momentary feeling of revulsion at such senility, but Aom was a gentle being and often provided the only calm voice in a stormy argument. With some effort, EEal kept his patience.

"No, Aom," he said smoothly. "How could we possibly send such a message? No. As you know, all natural signals, having natural causes, show patterns when properly analyzed. We are sending an absolutely *perfect* random series."

"Move we *suspend* the *operation*," said Oer loudly without even levitating his calculator.

Francis A. Cartier

"Objections?" asked EEal. Not a calculator rose.

Ward knocked his pipe out against the concrete doorframe of the control house and turned to go back inside. He was about to step over the threshold, eyes cast down, when O'Brien burst out, colliding squarely with him. As Ward stumbled back, the young man clutched at his arm, gasping with excitement.

"Dr. Ward!" he choked out. "They've started! I'm getting something! I can't make it out but—"

Ward started to push past O'Brien into the control house, but the boy still clung to him. "Obie!" he snapped at him, shaking O'Brien's hands off his arm. "Started what? Let me in there!"

For a moment, they both tried to enter the narrow space at once, then Ward pushed himself ahead, ran down the narrow corridor to the control room, spun himself through the door and stopped cold, all his senses sharpened as he scanned the instruments and listened.

There was nothing on the speaker but the usual white noise. Nothing on the scope. The computer was still in stand-by mode; it had not been triggered. Miss Harris was staring at it with a frightened expression. "Whathaveyougot?" said Ward.

"*I* haven't *anything*," she said in a strained voice. "Obie just yelled 'That's it!' Then he jumped up and ran out." She looked at Obie, still in the doorway.

"You didn't hear anything?" asked Ward.

"No."

"See anything?" persisted Ward.

"Nothing at all."

"But Obie did?"

Miss Harris didn't answer, just stared quizzically at O'Brien. "OK," said Ward, "get the auxiliary recorder going and then let's play this tape and see what we've got." As they busied themselves with the recorders, Ward thought back over the many false alarms of the past nineteen years. Would this turn out the same way? For several moments he delayed asking O'Brien about it for fear he would get the same garbled answer as from the others, but he could not hold the questions in for long. "What was it, Obie?" he asked without looking away from the recorder.

"I'm not sure. I don't know. I just suddenly heard—Or, that is—It was the beginning of a message."

"In English?" Ward's shoulder muscles tightened as he waited for the reply.

"Yes," Obie said quickly. There was a pause. Then, quietly and thoughtfully, "No." Another pause. "Yes. It was." O'Brien dropped heavily into his swivel chair. "Let me think. I was sitting here at my monitor. I had just adjusted the frequency according to the schedule. It's still set the same way. Something started coming through. There was the word *"Earth,"* and then, his face contorted with concentration, "I think."

The Signals

Ward's shoulders slumped as he prepared to play the tape back. There would be nothing on it.

Two hours later, after several re-playings, Ward put the computer back on standby mode, returned the recorder to antenna duty, and wearily eased himself into his chair. There was nothing on the tape. O'Brien, like the four others before him—or was it five?—had obviously fallen victim to the boredom and the unrelenting pressure of concentrated waiting. It was the same old pattern: late in the shift when they were tired and their resistance was low, and always after several years of listening, straining, hoping, trying, trying, trying. It was the young ones who were most susceptible, and usually the girls. But Obie was a sensitive, emotional type. Well, he'd have to let Obie go, too. He'd wait a decent period, then use the excuse of reducing the staff. He'd try to find a good job for him. Some of his Air Force friends might be able to help there. No point in saying anything about this, either. It would just make a bad mark on a good man's record.

The strength of 778's though was so strong that 842 turned to look across the room at him. "I know," he thought to 778, "it's frustrating, isn't it. But there just *has* to be a way to get through, perhaps even to Ward himself. We'll try him again. If only we knew what all that machinery of his is for—" ∎

Francis A. Cartier

THE GIFT OF GAB
Jack Vance

MIDDLE AFTERNOON HAD COME to the Shallows. The wind had died; the sea was listless and spread with silken gloss. In the south a black broom of rain hung under the clouds; elsewhere the air was thick with pink murk. Thick crusts of seaweed floated over the Shallows; one of these supported the Bio-Minerals raft, a metal rectangle two hundred feet long, a hundred feet wide.

At four o'clock an air horn on the mast announced the change of shift. Sam Fletcher, assistant superintendent, came out of the mess hall, crossed the deck to the office, slid back the door, and looked in. The chair in which Carl Raight usually sat, filling out his production report, was empty. Fletcher looked back over his shoulder, down the deck toward the processing house, but Raight was nowhere in sight. Strange. Fletcher crossed the office, checked the day's tonnage:

Rhodium trichloride	4.01
Tantalum sulfide	0.87
Tripyridyl rhenichloride	0.43

The gross tonnage, by Fletcher's calculations, came to 5.31—an average shift. He still led Raight in the Pinch Bottle Sweepstakes. Tomorrow was the end of the month; Fletcher could hardly fail to make off with Raight's Haig and Haig. Anticipating Raight's protests and complaints, Fletcher smiled and whistled through his teeth. He felt cheerful and confident. Another month would bring to an end his six-month contract; then it was back to Starholme with six months' pay to his credit.

Where in thunder was Raight? Fletcher looked out the window. In his range of vision was the helicopter—guyed to the deck against the Sabrian line-squalls—the mast, the black hump of the generator, the water tank, and at the far end of the raft, the pulverizers, the leaching vats, the Tswett columns, and the storage bins.

A dark shape filled the door. Fletcher turned, but it was Agostino, the day-shift operator, who had just now been relieved by Blue Murphy, Fletcher's operator.

"Where's Raight?" asked Fletcher.

Agostino looked around the office. "I thought he was in here."

"I thought he was over in the works."

"No, I just came from there."

Fletcher crossed the room and looked into the washroom. "Wrong again."

Agostino turned away. "I'm going up for a shower." He looked back from the door. "We're low on barnacles."

"I'll send out the barge." Fletcher followed Agostino out on deck and headed for the processing house.

He passed the dock where the barges were tied up and entered the pulverizing room. The Number One Rotary was grinding barnacles for tantalum; the Number Two was pulverizing rhenium-rich sea slugs. The ball mill waited for a load of coral, orange-pink with nodules of rhodium salts.

Blue Murphy, who had a red face and a meager fringe of red hair, was making a routine check of bearings, shafts, chains, journals, valves, and gauges. Fletcher called in his ear to be heard over the noise of the crushers. "Has Raight come through?"

Murphy shook his head.

Fletcher went on, into the leaching chamber where the first separation of salts from pulp was effected, through the forest of Tswett tubes, and once more out into the deck. No Raight. He must have gone on ahead to the office.

But the office was empty.

Fletcher continued around to the mess hall. Agostino was busy with a bowl of chili. Dave Jones, the hatchet-faced steward, stood in the doorway to the galley.

"Raight been here?" asked Fletcher.

Jones, who never used two words when one would do, gave his head a morose shake.

Agostino looked around. "Did you check the barnacle barge? He might have gone out to the shelves."

Fletcher looked puzzled. "What's wrong with Mahlberg?"

"He's putting new teeth on the drag-line bucket."

Fletcher tried to recall the line-up of barges along the dock. If Mahlberg the barge tender had been busy with repairs, Raight might well have gone out himself. Fletcher drew himself a cup of coffee. "That's where he must be." He sat down. "It's not like Raight to put in free overtime."

Mahlberg came into the mess hall. "Where's Carl? I want to order some more teeth for the bucket."

Mahlberg laughed at the joke. "Catch himself a nice wire eel maybe. Or a deka-brach."

Dave Jones grunted. "He'll cook it himself."

"Seems like a dekabrach should make good eatin'," said Mahlberg, "close as they are to a seal."

"Who likes seal?" growled Jones.

"I'd say they're more like mermaids," Agostino remarked, "with ten-armed starfish for heads."

Fletcher put down his cup. "I wonder what time Raight left?"

Mahlberg shrugged; Agostino looked blank.

"It's only an hour out to the shelves. He ought to be back by now."

"He might have had a breakdown," said Mahlberg. "Though the barge has been running good."

Fletcher rose to his feet. "I'll give him a call." He left the mess hall and returned to the office, where he dialed T3 on the intercom screen—the signal for the barnacle barge.

The screen remained blank.

Fletcher waited. The neon bulb pulsed off and on, indicating the call of the alarm on the barge.

No reply.

Fletcher felt a vague disturbance. He left the office, went to the mast, and rode up the man-lift to the cupola. From here he could overlook the half-acre of raft, the five-acre crust of seaweed, and a great circle of ocean.

In the far northeast distance, up near the edge of the Shallows, the new Pelagic Recoveries raft showed as a small dark spot, almost smeared from sight by the haze. To the south, where the Equatorial Current raced through a gap in the Shallows, the barnacle shelves were strung out in a long loose line. To the north, where the Macpherson Ridge rising from the Deeps, came within thirty feet of breaking the surface, aluminum piles supported the sea-slug traps. Here and there floated masses of seaweed, sometimes anchored to the bottom, sometimes maintained in place by the action of the currents.

Fletcher turned his binoculars along the line of barnacle shelves and spotted the barge immediately. He steadied his arms, screwed up the magnification, and focused on the control cabin. He saw no one, although he could not hold the binoculars steady enough to make sure.

Fletcher scrutinized the rest of the barge.

Where was Carl Raight? Possibly in the control cabin, out of sight?

Fletcher descended to the deck, went around to the processing house, and looked in. "Hey, Blue!"

Murphy appeared, wiping his big red hands on a rag.

"I'm taking the launch out to the shelves," said Fletcher. "The barge is out there, but Raight doesn't answer the screen."

Murphy shook his big bald head in puzzlement. He accompanied Fletcher to the dock, where the launch floated at moorings. Fletcher heaved at the painter, swung in the stern of the launch, and jumped down on the deck.

Murphy called down to him, "Want me to come along? I'll get Hans to watch the works." Hans Heinz was the engineer mechanic.

Fletcher hesitated. "I don't think so. If anything's happened to Raight—well, I can manage. Just keep an eye on the screen. I might call back in."

He stepped into the cockpit, seated himself, closed the dome over his head, and started the pump.

The launch rolled and bounced, picked up speed, shoved its blunt nose under the surface, then submerged till only the dome was clear.

The Gift of Gab

Fletcher disengaged the pump; water rammed in through the nose and was converted to steam, then spat aft.

Bio-Minerals became a gray blot in the pink haze, while the outlines of the barge and the shelves became hard and distinct, and gradually grew large. Fletcher de-staged the power; the launch surfaced and coasted up to the dark hull, where it grappled with magnetic balls that allowed barge and launch to surge independently on the slow swells.

Fletcher slid back the dome and jumped up to the deck of the barge.

"Raight! Hey, Carl!"

There was no answer.

Fletcher looked up and down the deck. Raight was a big man, strong and active—but there might have been an accident. Fletcher walked down the deck toward the control cabin. He passed the Number One hold, heaped with black-green barnacles. At the Number Two hold the boom was winged out, with the grab engaged on a shelf, ready to hoist it clear of the water.

The Number Three hold was still unladen. The control cabin was empty.

Carl Raight was nowhere aboard the barge.

He might have been taken off by helicopter or launch, or he might have fallen over the side. Fletcher made a slow check of the dark water in all directions. He suddenly leaned over the side, trying to see through the surface reflections. But the pale shape under the water was a dekabrach, long as a man, sleek as satin, moving quietly about its business.

Fletcher looked thoughtfully to the northeast, where the Pelagic Recoveries raft floated behind a curtain of pink murk. It was a new venture, only three months old, owned and operated by Ted Chrystal, former biochemist on the Bio-Minerals raft. The Sabrian Ocean was inexhaustible; the market for metal was insatiable; the two rafts were in no sense competitors. By no stretch of imagination could Fletcher conceive Chrystal or his men attacking Carl Raight.

He must have fallen overboard.

Fletcher returned to the control cabin and climbed the ladder to the flying bridge on top. He made a last check of the water around the barge, although he knew it to be a useless gesture—the current, moving through the gap at a steady two knots, would have swept Raight's body out over the Deeps. Fletcher scanned the horizon. The line of shelves dwindled away into the pink gloom. The mast on the Bio-Minerals raft marked the sky to the northwest. The Pelagic Recoveries raft could not be seen. There was no living creature in sight.

The screen signal sounded from the cabin. Fletcher went inside. Blue Murphy was calling from the raft. "What's the news?"

"None whatever," said Fletcher.

"What do you mean?"

"Raight's not out here."

The big red face creased. "Just who is out there?"

"Nobody. It looks like Raight fell over the side."

Murphy whistled. There seemed nothing to say. Finally he asked, "Any idea how it happened?"

Fletcher shook his head. "I can't figure it out."

Murphy licked his lips. "Maybe we ought to close down."

"Why?" asked Fletcher.

"Well—reverence to the dead, you might say."

Fletcher grinned humorously. "We might as well keep running."

"Just as you like. But we're low on the barnacles."

"Carl loaded a hold and a half—" Fletcher hesitated, heaved a deep sigh. "I might as well shake in a few more shelves."

Murphy winced. "It's a squeamish business, Sam. You haven't a nerve in your body."

"It doesn't make any difference to Carl now," said Fletcher. "We've got to scrape barnacles some time. There's nothing to be gained by moping."

"I suppose you're right," said Murphy dubiously.

"I'll be back in a couple hours."

"Don't go overboard like Raight, now."

The screen went blank. Fletcher reflected that he was in charge, superintendent of the raft, until the arrival of the new crew, a month away. Responsibility, which he did not particularly want, was his.

He went slowly back out on deck and climbed into the winch pulpit. For an hour he pulled sections of shelves from the sea, suspending them over the hold while scraper arms wiped off the black-green clusters, then slid the shelves back into the ocean. Here was where Raight had been working just before his disappearance. How could he have fallen overboard from the winch pulpit?

Uneasiness inched along Fletcher's nerves, up into his brain. He stopped short, staring at the rope on the deck.

It was a strange rope—glistening, translucent, an inch thick. It lay in a loose loop on the deck, and one end led over the side. Fletcher started down, then hesitated. Rope? Certainly none of the barge's equipment.

Careful, thought Fletcher.

A hand scraper hung on the king-post, a tool like a small adz. It was used for manual scraping of the shelves, if for some reason the automatic scrapers failed. It was two steps distant, across the rope. Fletcher stepped down to the deck. The rope quivered; the loop contracted, snapped around Fletcher's ankles.

Fletcher lunged and caught hold of the scraper. The rope gave a cruel jerk; Fletcher sprawled flat on his face, and the scraper jarred out of his hands. He kicked, struggled, but the rope drew him easily toward the gunwale. Fletcher made a convulsive grab for the scraper, barely reaching it. The rope was lifting his ankles to pull him over the rail. Fletcher strained forward, hacking at it again and again. The rope sagged, fell apart, and snaked over the side.

Fletcher gained his feet and staggered to the rail. Down into the water slid the rope, out of sight among the oily reflections of the sky. Then, for half a second, a wave-front held itself perpendicular to Fletcher's line of vision. Three feet under the surface swam a dekabrach. Fletcher saw the pink-golden cluster of arms, radiating like the arms of a starfish, the black patch at their core which might be an eye.

Fletcher drew back from the gunwale, puzzled, frightened, oppressed by the nearness of death. He cursed his stupidity, his reckless carelessness; how could he have been so undiscerning as to remain out here loading the barge? It was clear from the first that Raight could never have died by accident. Something had killed Raight, and Fletcher had invited it to kill him, too. He limped to the control cabin and started the pumps. Water was sucked in through the bow orifice and thrust out through the vents. The barge moved out away from the shelves. Fletcher set the course to northwest, toward Bio-Minerals, then went out on deck.

Day was almost at an end; the sky was darkening to maroon; the gloom grew thick as bloody water. Gideon, a dull red giant, largest of Sabria's two suns, dropped out of the sky. For a few minutes only the light from blue-green Atreus played on the clouds. The gloom changed its quality to pale green, which by some illusion seemed brighter than the previous pink. Atreus sank and the sky went dark.

Ahead shone the Bio-Minerals masthead light, climbing into the sky as the barge approached. Fletcher saw the black shapes of men outlined against the glow. The entire crew was waiting for him: the two operators, Agostino and Murphy; Mahlberg the barge tender, Damon the biochemist, Dave Jones the steward, Manners the technician, Hans Heinz the engineer.

Fletcher docked the barge, climbed the soft stairs hacked from the wadded seaweed, and stopped in front of the silent men. He looked from face to face. Waiting on the raft, they had felt the strangeness of Raight's death more vividly than he had; so much showed in their expressions.

Fletcher, answering the unspoken question, said, "It wasn't an accident. I know what happened."

"What?" someone asked.

"There's a thing like a white rope," said Fletcher. "It slides up out of the sea. If a man comes near it, it snakes around his leg and pulls him overboard."

Murphy asked in a hushed voice, "You're sure?"

"It just about got me."

Damon the biochemist asked in a skeptical voice, "A live rope?"

"I suppose it might have been alive."

"What else could it have been?"

Fletcher hesitated. "I looked over the side. I saw dekabrachs. One for sure, maybe two or three others."

There was silence. The men looked out over the water. Murphy asked in a wondering voice, "Then the dekabrachs are the ones?"

"I don't know," said Fletcher in a strained sharp voice. "A white rope, or fiber, nearly snared me. I cut it apart. When I looked over the side I saw dekabrachs."

The men made hushed noises of wonder and awe.

Fletcher turned away and started toward the mess hall. The men lingered on the dock, examining the ocean, talking in subdued voices. The lights of the raft shone past them, out into the darkness. There was nothing to be seen.

Later in the evening Fletcher climbed the stairs to the laboratory over the office, to find Eugene Damon busy at the microfilm viewer.

Damon had a thin, long-jawed face, lank blond hair, a fanatic's eyes. He was industrious and thorough, but he worked in the shadow of Ted Chrystal, who had quit Bio-Minerals to bring his own raft to Sabria. Chrystal was a man of great ability. He adapted the vanadium-sequestering sea slug of Earth to Sabrian waters; he had developed the tantalum barnacle from a rare and sickly species into the hardy, high-yield producer that it was. Damon worked twice the hours that Chrystal had put in, and while he performed his routine duties efficiently, he lacked the flair and imaginative resource which Chrystal used to leap from problem to solution without apparent steps in between.

He looked up when Fletcher came into the lab, then turned back to the microscreen. Fletcher watched a moment. "What are you looking for?" he asked presently.

Damon responded in the ponderous, slightly pedantic manner that sometimes amused, sometimes irritated Fletcher. "I've been searching the index to identify the long white *rope* which attacked you."

Fletcher made a noncommittal sound and went to look at the settings on the microfile throw-out. Damon had coded for "long," "thin," "white." On these instructions, the selector, scanning the entire roster of Sabrian life forms, had pulled the cards of seven organisms.

"Find anything?" Fletcher asked.

"Not so far." Damon slid another card into the viewer. *Sabrian Annelid.* RRS-4924, read the title, and on the screen appeared a schematic outline of a long segmented worm. The scale showed it to be about two and a half meters long.

Fletcher shook his head. "The thing that got me was four or five times that long. And I don't think it was segmented."

"That's the most likely of the lot so far," said Damon. He turned a quizzical glance up at Fletcher. "I imagine you're pretty sure about this—long white marine rope?"

Fletcher, ignoring him, scooped up the seven cards, dropped them back into the file, then looked in the code book and reset the selector.

Damon had the codes memorized and was able to read directly off the dials. " 'Appendages'—'long'—'dimensions D, E, F, G.' "

The selector kicked three cards into the viewer.

The first was a pale saucer which swam like a skate trailing four long whiskers. "That's not it," said Fletcher.

The second was a black, bullet-shaped water beetle, with a posterior flagellum.

"Not that one."

The third was a kind of mollusk, with a plasm based on selenium, silicon, fluorine, and carbon. The shell was a hemisphere of silicon carbide with a hump from which protruded a thin prehensile tendril.

The creature bore the name "Stryzkal's Monitor," after Esteban Stryzkal, the famous pioneer taxonomist of Sabria.

"That might be the guilty party," said Fletcher.

"It's not mobile," objected Damon. "Stryzkal finds it anchored to the North Shallows pegmatite dikes, in conjunction with the dekabrach colonies."

Fletcher was reading the descriptive material. " 'The feeler is elastic without observable limit, and apparently functions as a food-gathering, spore-disseminating, exploratory organ. The monitor typically is found near the dekabrach colonies. Symbiosis between the two life forms is not impossible.' "

Damon looked at him questioningly. "Well?"

"I saw some dekabrachs out along the shelves."

"You can't be sure you were attacked by a monitor," Damon said dubiously. "After all, they don't swim."

"So they don't," said Fletcher, "according to Stryzkal."

Damon started to speak, then, noticing Fletcher's expression, said in a subdued voice, "Of course, there's room for error. Not even Stryzkal could work out much more than a summary of planetary life."

Fletcher had been reading the screen. "Here's Chrystal's analysis of the one he brought up."

They studied the elements and primary compounds of a Stryzkal Monitor's constitution.

"Nothing of commercial interest," said Fletcher.

Damon was absorbed in a personal chain of thought. "Did Chrystal actually go down and trap a monitor?"

"That's right. In the water bug. He spent lots of time underwater."

"Everybody to their own methods," said Damon shortly.

Fletcher dropped the cards back in the file. "Whether you like him or not, he's a good field man. Give the devil his due."

"It seems to me that the field phase is over and done with," muttered Damon. "We've got the production line set up; it's a full-time job trying to increase the yield. Of course, I may be wrong."

Fletcher laughed, slapped Damon on his skinny shoulder. "I'm not finding fault, Gene. The plain fact is that there're too many avenues for one man to explore. We could keep four men busy."

"Four men?" said Damon. "A dozen is more like it. Three different protoplasmic phases on Sabria, to the single carbon group on Earth! Even Stryzkal only scratched the surface!"

He watched Fletcher for a while, then asked curiously: "What are you after now?"

Fletcher was once more running through the index. "What I came in here to check. The dekabrachs."

Damon leaned back in his chair. "Dekabrachs? Why?"

"There're lots of things about Sabria we don't know," said Fletcher mildly. "Have you ever been down to look at a dekabrach colony?"

Damon compressed his mouth. "No. I certainly haven't."

Fletcher dialed for the dekabrach card.

It snapped out of the file into the viewer. The screen showed Stryzkal's original photo-drawing, which in many ways conveyed more information than the color stereos. The specimen depicted was something over six feet long, with a pale, seal-like body terminating in three propulsive vanes. At the head radiated the ten arms from which the creature derived its name—flexible members eighteen inches long, surrounding the black disk which Stryzkal had assumed to be an eye.

Fletcher skimmed through the rather sketchy account of the creature's habitat, diet, reproductive methods, and protoplasmic classification. He frowned in dissatisfaction. "There's not much information here—considering that they're one of the more important species. Let's look at the anatomy."

The dekabrach's skeleton was based on an anterior dome of bone with three flexible cartilaginous vertebra, each terminating in a propulsive vane.

The information on the card came to an end. "I thought you said Chrystal made observations on the dekabrachs," growled Damon.

"So he did."

"If he's such a howling good field man, where's his data?"

Fletcher grinned. "Don't blame me, I just work here." He put the card through the screen again.

Under *General Comments*, Stryzkal had noted, "Dekabrachs appear to belong in the Sabrian Class A group, the silico-carbo-nitride phase, although they deviate in important respects." He had added a few lines of speculation regarding relationships of dekabrachs to other Sabrian species.

Chrystal had merely made the notation, "Checked for commercial application; no specific recommendation."

Fletcher made no comment.

"How closely did he check?" asked Damon.

"In his usual spectacular way. He went down in the water bug, harpooned one of them, and dragged it to the laboratory. Spent three days dissecting it."

"Precious little he's noted here," grumbled Damon. "If I worked three days on a new species like the dekabrachs, I could write a book."

They watched the information repeat itself.

Damon stabbed at the screen with his long bony finger. "Look! That's been blanked over. See those black triangles in the margin? Cancellation marks!"

Fletcher rubbed his chin. "Stranger and stranger."

"It's downright mischievous," Damon cried indignantly, "erasing material without indicating motive or correction."

Fletcher nodded slowly. "It looks like somebody's going to have to consult Chrystal." He considered. "Well—why not now?" He descended to the office, where he called the Pelagic Recoveries raft.

Chrystal himself appeared on the screen. He was a large blond man with blooming pink skin and an affable innocence that camouflaged the directness of his mind; his plumpness similarly disguised a powerful musculature. He greeted Fletcher with cautious heartiness. "How's it going on Bio-Minerals? Sometimes I wish I were back with you fellows—this working on your own isn't all it's cracked up to be."

"We've had an accident over here," said Fletcher. "I thought I'd better pass on a warning."

"Accident?" Chrystal looked anxious. "What's happened?"

"Carl Raight took the barge out—and never came back."

Chrystal was shocked. "That's terrible! How . . . why—"

"Apparently something pulled him in. I think it was a monitor mollusk—Stryzkal's Monitor."

Chrystal's pink face wrinkled in puzzlement. "A monitor? Was the barge over shallow water? But there wouldn't be water that shallow. I don't get it."

"I don't either."

Chrystal twisted a cube of white metal between his fingers. "That's certainly strange. Raight must be—dead?"

Fletcher nodded somberly. "That's the presumption. I've warned everybody here not to go out alone; I thought I'd better do the same for you."

"That's decent of you, Sam." Chrystal frowned, looked at the cube of metal, and put it down. "There's never been trouble on Sabria before."

"I saw dekabrachs under the barge. They might be involved somehow."

Chrystal looked blank. "Dekabrachs? They're harmless enough."

Fletcher nodded noncommittally. "Incidentally, I tried to check on dekabrachs in the microlibrary. There wasn't much information. Quite a bit of material has been canceled out."

Chrystal raised his pale eyebrows. "Why tell me?"

"Because you might have done the canceling."

Chrystal looked aggrieved. "Now, why should I do something like that? I worked hard for Bio-Minerals, Sam—you know that as well as I do. Now I'm trying to make money for myself. It's no bed of roses, I'll tell you." He touched the cube of white metal, then, noticing Fletcher's eyes on it, pushed it to the side of his desk, against Cosey's *Universal Handbook of Constants and Physical Relationships*.

After a pause Fletcher asked, "Well, did you or didn't you blank out part of the dekabrach story?"

Chrystal frowned in deep thought. "I might have canceled one or two ideas that

Jack Vance

turned out bad—nothing very important. I have a hazy idea that I pulled them out of the bank.''

"Just what were those ideas?'' Fletcher asked in a sardonic voice.

"I don't remember offhand. Something about feeding habits, probably. I suspected that the deks ingested plankton, but that doesn't seem to be the case.''

"No?''

"They browse on underwater fungus that grows on the coral banks. That's my best guess.''

"Is that all you cut out?''

"I can't think of anything more.''

Fletcher's eyes went back to the cube of metal. He noticed that it covered the handbook title from the angle of the V in *Universal* to the center of the O in *of*. "What's that you've got on your desk, Chrystal? Interesting yourself in metallurgy?''

"No, no,'' said Chrystal. He picked up the cube and looked at it critically. "Just a bit of alloy. Well, thanks for calling, Sam.''

"You don't have any personal ideas on how Raight got it?''

Chrystal looked surprised. "Why on earth do you ask me?''

"You know more about the dekabrachs than anyone else on Sabria.''

"I'm afraid I can't help you, Sam.''

Fletcher nodded. "Good night.''

"Good night, Sam.''

Fletcher sat looking at the blank screen. Monitor mollusks—dekabrachs—the blanked microfilm. There was a drift here whose direction he could not identify. The dekabrachs seemed to be involved, and, by association, Chrystal. Fletcher put no credence in Chrystal's protestations; he suspected that Chrystal lied as a matter of policy, on almost any subject. Fletcher's mind went to the cube of metal. Chrystal had seemed rather too casual, too quick to brush the matter aside. Fletcher brought out his own *Handbook*. He measured the distance between the fork of the V and the center of the O: 4.9 centimeters. Now, if the block represented a kilogram mass, as was likely with such sample blocks—Fletcher calculated. In a cube, 4.9 centimeters on a side, were 119 cc. Hypothesizing a mass of 1,000 grams, the density worked out to 8.4 grams per cc.

Fletcher looked at the figure. In itself it was not particularly suggestive. It might be one of a hundred alloys. There was no point in going too far on a string of hypotheses—still, he looked in the *Handbook*. Nickel, 8.6 grams per cc. Cobalt, 8.7 grams per cc. Niobium, 8.4 grams per cc.

Fletcher sat back and considered. Niobium? An element costly and tedious to synthesize, with limited natural sources and an unsatisfied market. The idea was stimulating. Had Chrystal developed a biological source of niobium? If so, his fortune was made.

Fletcher relaxed in his chair. He felt done in—mentally and physically. His mind went to Carl Raight. He pictured the body drifting loose and haphazard through the night, sinking through miles of water into places where light would never reach. Why had Carl Raight been plundered of his life?

Fletcher began to ache with anger and frustration at the futility, the indignity of Raight's passing. Carl Raight was too good a man to be dragged to his death into the dark ocean of Sabria.

Fletcher jerked himself upright and marched out of the office, up the steps to the laboratory.

Damon was still busy with his routine work. He had three projects under way: two involved the sequestering of platinum by species of Sabrian algae; the third was an attempt to increase the rhenium absorption of an Alphard-Alpha flatsponge. In each case his basic technique was the same: subjecting succeeding generations to an increasing concentration of metallic salt, under conditions favoring mutation. Certain of the organisms would presently begin to make functional use of the metal; they would be isolated and transferred to Sabrian brine. A few might survive the shock; some might adapt to the new conditions and begin to absorb the now necessary element.

By selective breeding the desirable qualities of these latter organisms would be intensified; they would then be cultivated on a large-scale basis, and the inexhaustible Sabrian waters would presently be made to yield another product.

Coming into the lab, Fletcher found Damon arranging trays of algae cultures in geometrically exact lines. He looked rather sourly over his shoulder at Fletcher.

"I talked to Chrystal," said Fletcher.

Damon became interested. "What did he say?"

"He says he might have wiped a few bad guesses off the film."

"Ridiculous," snapped Damon.

Fletcher went to the table, looking thoughtfully along the row of algae cultures. "Have you run into any niobium on Sabria, Gene?"

"Niobium? No. Not in any appreciable concentration. There are traces in the ocean, naturally. I believe one of the corals shows a set of niobium lines." He cocked his head with birdlike inquisitiveness. "Why do you ask?"

"Just an idea, wild and random."

"I don't suppose Chrystal gave you any satisfaction."

"None at all."

"Then what's the next move?"

Fletcher hitched himself up on the table. "I'm not sure. There's not much I can do. Unless—" He hesitated.

"Unless what?"

"Unless I make an underwater survey myself."

Damon was appalled. "What do you hope to gain by that?"

Fletcher smiled. "If I knew, I wouldn't need to go. Remember, Chrystal went down, then he came back up and stripped the microfilm."

"I realize that," said Damon. "Still, I think it's rather . . . well, foolhardy, after what's happened."

"Perhaps, perhaps not." Fletcher slid off the table to the deck. "I'll let it ride till tomorrow, anyway."

He left Damon making out his daily check sheet and descended to the main deck.

Blue Murphy was waiting at the foot of the stairs. Fletcher said, "Well, Murphy?"

The round red face displayed a puzzled frown. "Agostino up there with you?"

Fletcher stopped short. "No."

"He should have relieved me half an hour ago. He's not in the dormitory. He's not in the mess hall."

"Good God," said Fletcher. "Another one?"

Murphy looked over his shoulder at the ocean. "They saw him about an hour ago in the mess hall."

"Come on," said Fletcher. "Let's search the raft."

They looked everywhere—processing house, the cupola on the mast, all the nooks and crannies a man might take it into his head to explore. The barges were all at dock; the launch and catamaran swung at their moorings; the helicopter hulked on the deck with drooping blades.

Agostino was nowhere aboard the raft. No one knew where Agostino had gone; no one knew exactly when he had left.

The crew of the raft collected in the mess hall, making small nervous motions, looking out the portholes over the ocean.

Fletcher could think of very little to say. "Whatever is after us—and we don't know what it is—it can surprise us and it's watching. We've got to be careful—more than careful!"

Murphy pounded his fist softly on the table. "But what can we do? We can't just stand around like silly cows!"

"Sabria is theoretically a safe planet," said Damon. "According to Stryzkal and the Galactic Index, there are no hostile life forms here."

Murphy snorted, "I wish old Stryzkal was here now to tell me."

"He might be able to theorize back Raight and Agostino." Dave Jones looked at the calendar. "A month to go."

"We'll only run one shift," said Fletcher, "until we get replacements."

"Call them reinforcements," muttered Mahlberg.

"Tomorrow," said Fletcher, "I'm going to take the water bug down, look around, and get an idea what's going on. In the meantime, everybody better carry hatchets or cleavers."

There was soft sound on the windows and on the deck outside. "Rain," said Mahlberg. He looked at the clock on the wall. "Midnight."

The rain hissed through the air, drummed on the walls; the decks ran with water and the masthead lights glared through the slanting streaks.

Fletcher went to the streaming windows and looked toward the process house. "I guess we better button up for the night. There's no reason to—'' He squinted through the window, then ran to the door and out into the rain.

Water pelted into his face. He could see very little but the glare of the lights in the rain. And a hint of white along the shining gray-black of the deck, like an old white plastic hose.

A snatch at his ankles: his feet were yanked from under him. He fell flat upon the streaming metal.

Behind him came the thud of feet; there were excited curses, a clang and scrape; the grip on Fletcher's ankles loosened.

Fletcher jumped up, staggering back against the mast. "Something's in the process house," he yelled.

The men pounded off through the rain. Fletcher came after.

But there was nothing in the process house. The doors were wide; the rooms were bright. The squat pulverizers stood on either hand; behind were the pressure tanks, the vats, the pipes of six different colors.

Fletcher pulled the master switch; the hum and grind of the machinery died. "Let's lock up and get back to the dormitory."

Morning was the reverse of evening; first the green gloom of Atreus, warming to pink as Gideon rose behind the clouds. It was a blustery day, with squalls trailing dark curtains all around the compass.

Fletcher ate breakfast, dressed in a skin-tight coverall threaded with heating filaments, then a waterproof garment with a plastic head-dome.

The water bug hung on davits at the east edge of the raft, a shell of transparent plastic with the pumps sealed in a metal cell amidships. Submerging, the hull filled with water through valves, which then closed; the bug could submerge to four hundred feet, the hull resisting about half the pressure, the enclosed water the rest.

Fletcher lowered himself into the cockpit; Murphy connected the hoses from the air tanks to Fletcher's helmet, then screwed the port shut. Mahlberg and Hans Heinz winged out the davits. Murphy went to stand by the hoist control; for a moment he hesitated, looking from the dark, pink-dappled water to Fletcher, and back at the water.

Fletcher waved his hand. "Lower away." His voice came from the loudspeaker on the bulkhead behind them.

Murphy swung the handle. The bug eased down. Water gushed in through the valves, up around Fletcher's body, over his head. Bubbles rose from the helmet exhaust valve.

Fletcher tested the pumps, then cast off the grapples. The bug slanted down into the water.

Murphy sighed. "He's got more nerve than I'm ever likely to have."

"He can get away from whatever's after him," said Damon. "He might well be safer than we are here on the raft."

Murphy clapped him on the shoulder. "Damon, my lad—you can climb. Up on top of the mast you'll be safe; it's unlikely that they'll come there to tug you into the water.'' Murphy raised his eyes to the cupola a hundred feet over the deck. ''And I think that's where I'd take myself—if only someone would bring me my food.''

Heinz pointed to the water. ''There go the bubbles. He went under the raft. Now he's headed north.''

The day became stormy. Spume blew over the raft, and it meant a drenching to venture out on deck. The clouds thinned enough to show the outlines of Gideon and Atreus, a blood orange and a lime. Suddenly the winds died; the ocean flattened into an uneasy calm. The crew sat in the mess hall drinking coffee, talking in staccato and uneasy voices.

Damon became restless and went up to his laboratory. He came running back down into the mess hall. ''Dekabrachs—they're under the raft! I saw them from the observation deck!''

Murphy shrugged. ''They're safe from me.''

''I'd like to get hold of one,'' said Damon. ''Alive.''

''Don't we have enough trouble already?'' growled Dave Jones.

Damon explained patiently. ''We know nothing about dekabrachs. They're a highly developed species. Chrystal destroyed all the data we had, and I should have at least one specimen.''

Murphy rose to his feet. ''I suppose we can scoop one up in a net.''

''Good,'' said Damon. ''I'll set up the big tank to receive it.''

The crew went out on deck, where the weather had turned sultry. The ocean was flat and oily; haze blurred sea and sky together in a smooth gradation of color, from dirty scarlet near the raft to pale pink overhead.

The boom was winged out; a parachute net was attached and lowered quietly into the water. Heinz stood by the winch; Murphy leaned over the rail, staring intently down into the water.

A pale shape drifted out from under the raft. ''Lift!'' bawled Murphy.

The line snapped taut; the net rose out of the water in a cascade of spray. In the center a six-foot dekabrach pulsed and thrashed, gill slits rasping for water.

The boom swung inboard; the net tripped; the dekabrach slid into the plastic tank.

It darted forward and backward; the plastic dented and bulged where it struck. Then it floated quiet in the center, head-tentacles folded back against the torso.

All hands crowded around the tank. The black eye-spot looked back through the transparent walls.

Murphy asked Damon, ''Now what?''

''I'd like the tank lifted to the deck outside the laboratory where I can get at it.''

''No sooner said than done.''

The tank was hoisted and swung to the spot Damon had indicated. Damon went excitedly off to plan his research.

The crew watched the dekabrach for ten or fifteen minutes, then drifted back to the mess hall.

Time passed. Gusts of wind raked up the ocean into a sharp steep chop. At two o'clock the loudspeaker hissed; the crew stiffened and raised their heads.

Fletcher's voice came from the diaphragm. "Hello aboard the raft. I'm about two miles northwest. Stand by to haul me aboard."

"Ha!" cried Murphy, grinning. "He made it."

"I gave odds against him of four to one," Mahlberg said. "I'm lucky nobody took them."

"Get a move on. He'll be alongside before we're ready." .

The crew trooped out to the landing. The water bug came sliding over the ocean, its glistening back riding the dark disorder of the waters.

It slipped quietly up to the raft; grapples clamped to the plates fore and aft. The winch whined and the bug was lifted from the sea, draining its ballast of water.

Fletcher, in the cockpit, looked tense and tired. He climbed stiffly out of the bug, stretched, unzipped the waterproof suit, and pulled off the helmet.

"Well, I'm back." He looked around the group. "Surprised?"

"I'd have lost money on you," Mahlberg told him.

"What did you find out?" asked Damon. "Anything?"

Fletcher nodded. "Plenty. Let me get into clean clothes. I'm wringing wet—sweat." He stopped short, looking up at the tank on the laboratory deck. "When did that come aboard?"

"We netted it about noon," said Murphy. "Damon wanted to look one over."

Fletcher stood looking up at the tank with his shoulders drooping.

"Something wrong?" asked Damon.

"No," said Fletcher. "We couldn't have it worse than it is already." He turned away toward the dormitory.

The crew waited for him in the mess hall; twenty minutes later he appeared. He drew himself a cup of coffee and sat down.

"Well," said Fletcher. "I can't be sure—but it looks as if we're in trouble."

"Dekabrachs?" asked Murphy.

Fletcher nodded.

"I knew it!" Murphy cried in triumph. "You can tell by looking at the blatherskites they're up to no good."

Damon frowned, disapproving of emotional judgments. "Just what is the situation?" he asked Fletcher. "At least, as it appears to you."

Fletcher chose his words carefully. "Things are going on that we've been unaware of. In the first place, the dekabrachs are socially organized."

"You mean to say—they're intelligent?"

Fletcher shook his head. "I don't know for sure. It's possible. It's equally possible that they live by instinct, like social insects."

"How in the world—" began Damon.

Fletcher held up a hand. "I'll tell you just what happened; you can ask all the questions you like afterwards." He drank his coffee.

"When I went down under, naturally I was on the alert and kept my eyes peeled. I felt safe enough in the water bug—but funny things have been happening, and I was a little nervous.

"As soon as I was in the water I saw the dekabrachs—five or six of them." Fletcher paused, sipped his coffee.

"What were they doing?" asked Damon.

"Nothing very much. Drifting near a big monitor which had attached itself to the seaweed. The arm was hanging down like a rope—clear out of sight. I edged the bug in just to see what the deks would do; they began backing away. I didn't want to waste too much time under the raft, so I swung off north, toward the Deeps. Halfway there I saw an odd thing; in fact, I passed it, and swung around to take another look.

"There were about a dozen deks. They had a monitor—and this one was really big. A giant. It was hanging on a set of balloons or bubbles—some kind of pods that kept it floating, and the deks were easing it along. In this direction."

"In this direction, eh?" asked Manners.

"Well, perhaps it was all an innocent outing—but I didn't want to take any chances. The arm of this monitor would be like a hawser. I turned the bug at the bubbles, burst some, scattered the rest. The monitor dropped like a stone. The deks took off in different directions. I figured I'd won that round. I kept on going north, and pretty soon I came to where the slope starts down into the Deeps. I'd been traveling about twenty feet under; now I lowered to two hundred. I had to turn on the lights, of course—this red twilight doesn't penetrate water too well." Fletcher took another gulp of coffee. "All the way across the Shallows I'd been passing over coral banks and dodging forests of kelp. Where the shelf slopes down to the Deeps the coral gets to be something fantastic—I suppose there's more water movement, more nourishment, more oxygen. It grows a hundred feet high, in spires and towers, umbrellas, platforms, arches—white, pale blue, pale green.

"I came to the edge of a cliff. It was a shock—one minute my lights were on the coral, all these white towers and pinnacles—then there was nothing. I was over the Deeps. I got a little nervous." Fletcher grinned. "Irrational, of course. I checked the fathometer—bottom was twelve thousand feet down. I still didn't like it, and I turned around and swung back. Then I noticed lights off to my right. I turned my own off and moved in to investigate. The lights spread out as if I was flying over a city—and that's just about what it was."

"Dekabrachs?" asked Damon.

Fletcher nodded. "Dekabrachs."

"You mean—they built it themselves? Lights and all?"

Fletcher frowned. "That's what I can't be sure of. The coral had grown into shapes that gave them little cubicles to swim in and out of, and do whatever they'd want to do in a house. Certainly they don't need protection from the rain. They hadn't built these coral grottoes in the sense that we build a house—but it didn't look like natural coral either. It's as if they made the coral grow to suit them."

The Gift of Gab 69

Murphy said doubtfully, "Then they're intelligent."

"No, not necessarily. After all, wasps build complicated nests with no more equipment than a set of instincts."

"What's your opinion?" asked Damon. "Just what impression does it give?"

Fletcher shook his head. "I can't be sure. I don't know what kind of standards to apply. 'Intelligence' is a word that means lots of different things, and the way we generally use it is artificial and specialized."

"I don't get you," said Murphy. "Do you mean these deks are intelligent or don't you?"

Fletcher laughed. "Are men intelligent?"

"Sure. So they say, at least."

"Well, what I'm trying to get across is that we can't use man's intelligence as a measure of the dekabrach's mind. We've got to judge him by a different set of values—dekabrach values. Men use tools of metal, ceramic, fiber: inorganic stuff—at least, dead. I can imagine a civilization dependent upon living tools—specialized creatures the master group uses for special purposes. Suppose the dekabrachs live on this basis? They force the coral to grow in the shape they want. They use the monitors for derricks, or hoists, or snares, or to grab at something in the upper air."

"Apparently, then," said Damon, "you believe that the dekabrachs are intelligent."

Fletcher shook his head. "Intelligence is just a word—a matter of definition. What the deks do may not be susceptible to human definition."

"It's beyond me," said Murphy, settling back in his chair.

Damon pressed the subject. "I am not a metaphysician or a semanticist. But it seems that we might apply, or try to apply, a crucial test."

"What difference does it make one way or the other?" asked Murphy.

Fletcher said, "It makes a big difference where the law is concerned."

"Ah," said Murphy, "the Doctrine of Responsibility."

Fletcher nodded. "We could be yanked off the planet for injuring or killing intelligent autochthons. It's been done."

"That's right," said Murphy. "I was on Alkaid Two when Graviton Corporation got in that kind of trouble."

"So if the deks are intelligent, we've got to watch our step. That's why I looked twice when I saw the dek in the tank."

"Well—are they or aren't they?" asked Mahlberg.

"There's one crucial test," Damon repeated.

The crew looked at him expectantly.

"Well?" asked Murphy. "Spill it."

"Communication."

Murphy nodded thoughtfully. "That seems to make sense." He looked at Fletcher. "Did you notice them communicating?"

Fletcher shook his head. "Tomorrow I'll take a camera out, and a sound recorder. Then we'll know for sure."

"Incidentally," said Damon, "why were you asking about niobium?"

Fletcher had almost forgotten. "Chrystal had a chunk of it on his desk. Or maybe he did—I'm not sure."

Damon nodded. "Well, it may be a coincidence, but the deks are loaded with it." Fletcher stared.

"It's in their blood, and there's a strong concentration in the interior organs."

Fletcher sat with his cup halfway to his mouth. "Enough to make a profit on?"

Damon nodded. "Probably a hundred grams or more in the organism."

"Well, well," said Fletcher. "That's very interesting indeed."

Rain roared down during the night; a great wind came up, lifting and driving the rain and spume. Most of the crew had gone to bed—all except Dave Jones the steward and Manners the radio man, who sat up over a chess board.

A new sound rose over the wind and rain—a metallic groaning, a creaking discord that presently became too loud to ignore. Manners jumped to his feet and went to the window.

"The mast!"

Dimly it could be seen through the rain, swaying like a reed, the arc of oscillation increasing with each swing.

"What can we do?" cried Jones.

One set of guy lines snapped. "Nothing now."

"I'll call Fletcher." Jones ran for the passage to the dormitory.

The mast gave a sudden jerk, poised long seconds at an unlikely angle, then toppled across the process house.

Fletcher appeared and went over and stared out the window. With the masthead light no longer shining down, the raft was dark and ominous. Fletcher shrugged and turned away. "There's nothing we can do tonight. It's worth a man's life to go out on that deck."

In the morning, examination of the wreckage revealed that two of the guy lines had been sawed or clipped cleanly through. The mast, of lightweight construction, was quickly cut apart, and the twisted segments dragged to a corner of the deck. The raft seemed bald and flat.

"Someone or something," said Fletcher, "is anxious to give us as much trouble as possible." He looked across the leaden-pink ocean to where the Pelagic Recoveries raft floated beyond the range of vision.

"Apparently," said Damon, "you refer to Chrystal."

"I have suspicions."

Damon glanced out across the water. "I'm practically certain."

"Suspicion isn't proof," said Fletcher. "In the first place, what would Chrystal hope to gain by attacking us?"

"What would the dekabrachs gain?"

"I don't know," said Fletcher. "I'd like to find out." He went to dress himself in the submarine suit.

The water bug was made ready. Fletcher plugged a camera into the external mounting and connected a sound recorder to a sensitive diaphragm in the skin. He seated himself and pulled the blister over his head.

The water bug was lowered into the ocean. It filled with water, and its glistening back disappeared under the surface.

The crew patched the roof of the process house, then jury-rigged an antenna.

The day passed; twilight came, and plum-colored evening.

The loudspeaker hissed and sputtered; Fletcher's voice, tired and tense, said, "Stand by. I'm coming in."

The crew gathered by the rail, straining their eyes through the dusk.

One of the dully glistening wave-fronts held its shape, drew closer, and became the water-bug.

The grapples were dropped; the water bug drained its ballast and was hoisted into the chocks.

Fletcher jumped down to the deck and leaned limply against one of the davits. "I've had enough submerging to last me a while."

"What did you find out?" Damon asked anxiously.

"I've got it all on film. I'll run it off as soon as my head stops ringing."

Fletcher took a hot shower, then came down to the mess hall and ate the bowl of stew Jones put in front of him, while Manners transferred the film Fletcher had shot from camera to projector.

"I've made up my mind about two things," said Fletcher. "First—the deks are intelligent. Second, if they communicate with each other, it's by means imperceptible to human beings."

Damon blinked, surprised and dissatisfied. "That's almost a contradiction."

"Just watch," said Fletcher. "You can see for yourself."

Manners started the projector; the screen went bright.

"The first few feet show nothing very much," said Fletcher. "I drove directly out to the end of the shelf and cruised along the edge of the Deeps. It drops away like the end of the world—straight down. I found a big colony about ten miles west of the one I found yesterday—almost a city."

" 'City' implies civilization," Damon asserted in a didactic voice.

Fletcher shrugged. "If civilization means manipulation of environment—somewhere I've heard that definition—they're civilized."

"But they don't communicate?"

"Check the film for yourself."

The screen was dark with the color of the ocean. "I made a circle out over the Deeps," said Fletcher, "turned off my lights, started the camera, and came in slow."

A pale constellation appeared in the center of the screen, separating into a swarm of sparks. They brightened and expanded; behind them appeared the outlines, tall and dim, of coral minarets, towers, spires, and spikes. They defined themselves as Fletcher moved closer. From the screen came Fletcher's recorded voice. "These formations vary in height from fifty to two hundred feet, along a front of about half a mile."

The picture expanded. Black holes showed on the face of the spires; pale dekabrach-shapes swam quietly in and out. "Notice," said the voice, "the area in front of the colony. It seems to be a shelf, or a storage yard. From up here it's hard to see; I'll drop down a hundred feet or so."

The picture changed; the screen darkened. "I'm dropping now—depth meter reads three hundred sixty feet . . . three eighty. . . . I can't see too well; I hope the camera is getting it all."

Fletcher commented: "You're seeing it better now than I could; the luminous areas in the coral don't shine too strongly down there."

The screen showed the base of the coral structures and a nearly level bench fifty feet wide. The camera took a quick swing and peered down over the verge, into blackness.

"I was curious," said Fletcher. "The shelf didn't look natural. It isn't. Notice the outlines on down? They're just barely perceptible. The shelf is artificial—a terrace, a front porch."

The camera swung back to the bench, which now appeared to be marked off into areas vaguely differentiated in color.

Fletcher's voice said, "Those colored areas are like plots in a garden—there's a different kind of plant, or weed, or animal on each of them. I'll come in closer. Here are monitors." The screen showed two or three dozen heavy hemispheres, then passed on to what appeared to be eels with saw edges along their sides, attached to the bench by a sucker. Next were float-bladders, then a great number of black cones with very long loose tails.

Damon said in a puzzled voice, "What keeps them there?"

"You'll have to ask the dekabrachs," said Fletcher.

"I would if I knew how."

"I still haven't seen them do anything intelligent," said Murphy.

"Watch," said Fletcher.

Into the field of vision swam a pair of dekabrachs, black eye-spots staring out of the screen at the men in the mess hall.

"Dekabrachs," came Fletcher's voice from the screen.

"Up to now, I don't think they noticed me," Fletcher himself commented. "I carried no lights and made no contrast against the background. Perhaps they felt the pump."

The dekabrachs turned together and dropped sharply for the shelf.

"Notice," said Fletcher. "They saw a problem, and the same solution occurred to both, at the same time. There was no communication."

The dekabrachs had diminished to pale blurs against one of the dark areas along the shelf.

"I didn't know what was happening," said Fletcher, "but I decided to move. And then—the camera doesn't show this—I felt bumps on the hull, as if someone were throwing rocks. I couldn't see what was going on until something hit the dome right in front of my face. It was a little torpedo, with a long nose like a knitting needle. I took off fast, before the deks could try something else."

The screen went black. Fletcher's voice said, "I'm out over the Deeps, running parallel with the edge of the Shallows." Indeterminate shapes swam across the screen, pale wisps blurred by watery distance. "I came back along the edge of the shelf," said Fletcher, "and found the colony I saw yesterday."

Once more the screen showed spires, tall structures, pale blue, pale green, ivory. "I'm going in close," came Fletcher's voice. "I'm going to look in one of those holes." The towers expanded; ahead was a dark hole.

"Right here I turned on the nose-light," said Fletcher. The black hole suddenly became a bright cylindrical chamber fifteen feet deep. The walls were lined with glistening colored globes, like Christmas tree ornaments. A dekabrach floated in the center of the chamber. Translucent tendrils ending in knobs extended from the chamber walls and seemed to be punching and kneading the creature's seal-smooth hide.

"The dek doesn't seem to like me looking in on him," said Fletcher.

The dekabrach backed to the rear of the chamber; the knobbed tendrils jerked away, into the walls.

"I looked into the next hole."

Another black hole became a bright chamber as the searchlight burnt in. A dekabrach floated quietly, holding a sphere of pink jelly before its eye. The wall-tendrils were not to be seen.

"This one didn't move," said Fletcher. "He was asleep or hypnotized or too scared. I started to take off—and there was the most awful thump. I thought I was a goner."

The image on the screen gave a great lurch. Something dark hurled past and on into the depths.

"I looked up," said Fletcher. "I couldn't see anything but about a dozen deks. Apparently they'd floated a big rock over me and dropped it. I started the pump and headed for home."

The screen went blank.

Damon was impressed. "I agree that they show patterns of intelligent behavior. Did you detect any sounds?"

"Nothing. I had the recorder going all the time. Not a vibration other than the bumps on the hull."

Damon's face was wry with dissatisfaction. "They must communicate somehow—how could they get along otherwise?"

"Not unless they're telepathic," said Fletcher. "I watched carefully. They make no sounds or motions to each other—none at all."

Manners asked, "Could they possibly radiate radio waves? Or infrared?"

Damon said glumly, "The one in the tank doesn't."

"Oh, come now," said Murphy, "are there no intelligent races that don't communicate?"

"None," said Damon. "They use different methods—sounds, signals, radiation—but they all communicate."

"How about telepathy?" Heinz suggested.

"We've never come up against it; I don't believe we'll find it here," said Damon.

"My personal theory," said Fletcher, "is that they think alike and so don't need to communicate."

Damon shook his head dubiously.

"Assume that they work on a basis of communal empathy," Fletcher went on. "That this is the way they've evolved. Men are individualistic; they need speech. The deks are identical; they're aware of what's going on without words." He reflected a few seconds. "I suppose, in a certain sense, they do communicate. For instance, a dek wants to extend the garden in front of its tower. It possibly waits till another dek comes near, then carries out a rock—indicating what it wants to do."

"Communication by example," said Damon.

"That's right—if you can call it communication. It permits a measure of cooperation—but clearly no small talk, no planning for the future or traditions from the past."

"Perhaps not even awareness of time!" cried Damon.

"It's hard to estimate their native intelligence. It might be remarkably high or it might be low; the lack of communication must be a terrific handicap."

"Handicap or not," said Mahlberg, "they've certainly got us on the run."

"And why?" cried Murphy, pounding the table with his big red fist. "That's the question. We've never bothered them. And all of a sudden Raight's gone, and Agostino. Also our mast. Who knows what they'll think of tonight? Why? That's what I want to know."

"That," said Fletcher, "is a question I'm going to put to Ted Chrystal tomorrow."

Fletcher dressed himself in clean blue twill, ate a silent breakfast, and went out to the flight deck.

Murphy and Mahlberg had thrown the guy lines off the helicopter and wiped the dome clean of salt-film.

Fletcher climbed into the cabin and twisted the inspection knob. Green light—everything in order.

Murphy said, half-hopefully, "Maybe I better come with you, Sam—if there's any chance of trouble."

"Trouble? Why should there be trouble?"

"I wouldn't put much past Chrystal."

"I wouldn't either," said Fletcher. "But—there won't be any trouble."

He started the blades. The ram-tubes caught hold; the 'copter lifted and slanted up, away from the raft, and flew off to the northeast. Bio-Minerals became a bright tablet on the irregular wad of seaweed.

The day was dull, brooding, windless, apparently building up for one of the tremendous electrical storms that came every few weeks. Fletcher accelerated, hoping to get his errand over with as soon as possible.

Miles of ocean slid past; Pelagic Recoveries appeared ahead.

Twenty miles southwest of the raft, Fletcher overtook a small barge laden with raw material for Chrystal's macerators and leaching columns; he noticed that there were two men aboard, both huddled inside the plastic canopy. Pelagic Recoveries perhaps was having its troubles too, thought Fletcher.

Chrystal's raft was little different from Bio-Minerals, except that the mast still rose from the central deck, and there was activity in the process house. They had not shut down, whatever their troubles.

Fletcher landed the 'copter on the flight deck. As he stopped the blades, Chrystal came out of the office—a big blond man with a round, jocular face.

Fletcher jumped down to the deck. "Hello, Ted," he said in a guarded voice.

Chrystal approached with a cheerful smile. "Hello, Sam! Long time since we've seen you." He shook hands briskly. "What's new at Bio-Minerals? Certainly too bad about Carl."

"That's what I want to talk about." Fletcher looked around the deck. Two of the crew stood watching. "Can we go to your office?"

"Sure, by all means." Chrystal led the way to the office, slid back the door. "Here we are."

Fletcher entered the office. Chrystal walked behind his desk. "Have a seat." He sat down in his own chair. "Now—what's on your mind? But first, how about a drink? You like Scotch, as I recall."

"Not today, thanks." Fletcher shifted in his chair. "Ted, we're up against a serious problem here on Sabria, and we might as well talk plainly about it."

"Certainly," said Chrystal. "Go right ahead."

"Carl Raight's dead. And Agostino."

Chrystal's eyebrows rose in shock. "Agostino too? How?"

"We don't know. He just disappeared."

Chrystal took a moment to digest the information. Then he shook his head in perplexity. "I can't understand it. We've never had trouble like this before."

"Nothing happening over here?"

Chrystal frowned. "Well—nothing to speak of. Your call put us on our guard."

"The dekabrachs seem to be responsible."

Chrystal blinked and pursed his lips, but said nothing.

"Have you been going out after dekabrachs, Ted?"

"Well now, Sam—" Chrystal hesitated, drumming his fingers on the desk. "That's hardly a fair question. Even if we were working with dekabrachs—or polyps or club moss or wire eels—I don't think I'd want to say, one way or the other."

"I'm not interested in your business secrets," said Fletcher. "The point is this: the deks appear to be an intelligent species. I have reason to believe that you're processing them for their niobium content. Apparently they're doing their best to retaliate and don't care whom they hurt. They've killed two of our men. I've got a right to know what's going on."

Chrystal nodded. "I can understand your viewpoint—but I don't follow your chain of reasoning. For instance, you told me that a monitor had done Raight in. Now you say dekabrach. Also, what leads you to believe I'm going for niobium?"

"Let's not try to kid each other, Ted."

Chrystal looked shocked, then annoyed.

"When you were still working for Bio-Minerals," Fletcher went on, "you discovered that the deks were full of niobium. You wiped all that information out of the files, got financial backing, and built this raft. Since then you've been hauling in dekabrachs."

Chrystal leaned back, surveying Fletcher coolly. "Aren't you jumping to conclusions?"

"If I am, all you've got to do is deny it."

"Your attitude isn't very pleasant, Sam."

"I didn't come here to be pleasant. We've lost two men, also our mast. We've had to shut down."

"I'm sorry to hear that—" began Chrystal.

Fletcher interrupted: "So far, Chrystal, I've given you the benefit of the doubt."

Chrystal was surprised. "How so?"

"I'm assuming you didn't know the deks were intelligent, that they're protected by the Responsibility Act."

"Well?"

"Now you know. You don't have the excuse of ignorance."

Chrystal was silent for a few seconds. "Well, Sam—these are all rather astonishing statements."

"Do you deny them?"

"Of course I do!" said Chrystal, with a flash of spirit.

"And you're not processing dekabrachs?"

"Easy, now. After all, Sam, this is my raft. You can't come aboard and chase me back and forth. It's high time you understood it."

Fletcher drew himself back a little, as if Chrystal's mere proximity were unpleasant. "You're not giving me a plain answer."

Chrystal leaned back in his chair and put his fingers together, puffing out his cheeks. "I don't intend to."

The barge that Fletcher had passed on his way was edging close to the raft. Fletcher watched it work against the mooring stage, snap its grapples. He asked, "What's on that barge?"

"Frankly, it's none of your business."

Fletcher rose to his feet and went to the window. Chrystal made uneasy protesting noises. Fletcher ignored him. The two barge handlers had not emerged from the control cabin. They seemed to be waiting for a gangway, which was being swung into position by the cargo boom.

Fletcher watched in growing curiosity and puzzlement. The gangway was built like a trough, with high plywood walls.

He turned to Chrystal. "What's going on out there?"

Chrystal was chewing his lower lip, rather red in the face. "Sam, you come storming over here, making wild accusations, calling me dirty names—by implication—and I don't say a word. I try to allow for the strain you're under; I value the good will between our two outfits. I'll show you some documents that will prove once and for all—" He began to sort through a sheaf of miscellaneous pamphlets.

Fletcher stood by the window, with half an eye for Chrystal, half for what was occurring out on deck.

The gangway was dropped into position; the barge handlers were ready to disembark. Fletcher decided to see what was going on. He started for the door.

Chrystal's face went stiff and cold. "Sam, I'm warning you, don't go out there!"

"Why not?"

"Because I say so."

Fletcher slid open the door. Chrystal made a motion to jump up from his chair, then he slowly sank back.

Fletcher walked out the door and crossed the deck, toward the barge.

A man in the process house saw him through the window and made urgent gestures.

Fletcher hesitated, then turned to look at the barge. A couple more steps and he could look into the hold. He stepped forward, craned his neck. From the corner of his eye he saw the man's gestures becoming frantic, then the man disappeared from the window.

The hold was full of limp white dekabrachs.

"Get back, you fool!" came a yell from the process house.

Perhaps a faint sound warned Fletcher; instead of backing away, he threw himself to the deck. A small object flipped over his head from the direction of the ocean, with a peculiar fluttering buzz. It struck a bulkhead and dropped—a fishlike torpedo, with a long needlelike proboscis. It came flapping toward Fletcher, who rose to his feet and ran crouching and dodging back toward the office.

Two more of the fishlike darts missed him by inches; Fletcher hurled himself through the door into the office.

Chrystal had not moved from the desk. Fletcher went panting up to him. "Pity I didn't get stuck, isn't it?"

"I warned you not to go out there."

Fletcher turned to look across the deck. The barge handlers ran down the troughlike gangway to the process house. A glittering school of dart-fish flickered up out of the water, striking the plywood.

Fletcher turned back to Chrystal. "I saw dekabrachs in that barge. Hundreds of them."

Chrystal had regained whatever composure he had lost. "Well? What if there are?"

"You know they're intelligent as well as I do."

Chrystal smilingly shook his head.

Fletcher's temper was going raw. "You're ruining Sabria for all of us!"

Chrystal held up his hand. "Easy, Sam. Fish are fish."

"Not when they're intelligent and kill men in retaliation."

Chrystal wagged his head. "*Are* they intelligent?"

Fletcher waited until he could control his voice. "Yes. They are."

"How do you know they are? Have you talked with them?"

"Naturally I haven't talked with them."

"They display a few social patterns. So do seals."

Fletcher came up closer and glared down at Chrystal. "I'm not going to argue definitions with you. I want you to stop hunting dekabrachs, because you're endangering lives aboard both our rafts."

Chrystal leaned back a trifle. "Now, Sam, you know you can't intimidate me."

"You've killed two men; I've escaped by inches three times now. I'm not running that kind of risk to put money in your pocket."

"You're jumping to conclusions," Chrystal protested. "In the first place, you've never proved—"

"I've proved enough! You've got to stop, that's all there is to it!"

Chrystal slowly shook his head. "I don't see how you're going to stop me, Sam." He brought his hand up from under the desk; it held a small gun. "Nobody's going to bulldoze me, not on my own raft."

Fletcher reached instantly, taking Christal by surprise. He grabbed Chrystal's wrist and banged it against the angle of the desk. The gun flashed, seared a groove in the desk and fell from Chrystal's limp fingers to the floor. Chrystal hissed and cursed, bent to recover it, but Fletcher leaped over the desk and pushed the other man over backward in his chair. Chrystal kicked up at Fletcher's face, catching him a glancing blow on the cheek that sent Fletcher to his knees.

Both men dived for the gun. Fletcher reached it first, rose to his feet, and backed to the wall. "Now we know where we stand."

"Put down that gun!"

Fletcher shook his head. "I'm placing you under arrest—civilian arrest. You're coming to Bio-Minerals until the inspector arrives."

Chrystal seemed dumfounded. "What?"

"I said, I'm taking you to the Bio-Minerals raft. The inspector is due in three weeks, and I'll turn you over to him."

"You're crazy, Fletcher."

"Perhaps. But I'm taking no chances with you." Fletcher motioned with the gun. "Get going. Out to the 'copter."

Chrystal coolly folded his arms. "I'm not going to move. You can't scare me by waving a gun."

Fletcher raised his arm, sighted, and pulled the trigger. The jet of fire grazed Chrystal's rump. Chrystal jumped, clapping his hand to the burn.

"Next shot will be somewhat closer," said Fletcher.

Chrystal glared like a boar from a thicket. "You realize I can bring kidnaping charges against you?"

"I'm not kidnaping you. I'm placing you under arrest."

"I'll sue Bio-Minerals for everything they've got."

"Unless Bio-Minerals sues you first. Get going!"

The entire crew met the returning helicopter: Damon, Blue Murphy, Manners, Hans Heinz, Mahlberg, and Dave Jones.

Chrystal jumped haughtily to the deck and surveyed the men with whom he had once worked. "I've got something to say to you men."

The crew watched him silently.

Chrystal jerked his thumb at Fletcher. "Sam's got himself in a peck of trouble. I told him I'm going to throw the book at him, and that's what I'm going to do." He looked from face to face. "If you men help him, you'll be accessories. I advise you, take that gun away from him and fly me back to my raft."

He looked around the circle, but met only coolness and hostility. He shrugged angrily. "Very well, you'll be liable for the same penalties as Fletcher. Kidnaping is a serious crime."

Murphy asked Fletcher, "What shall we do with the varmint?"

"Put him in Carl's room—that's the best place for him. Come on, Chrystal."

Back in the mess hall, after locking the door on Chrystal, Fletcher told the crew, "I don't need to warn you—be careful of Chrystal. He's tricky. Don't talk to him. Don't run any errands of any kind. Call me if he wants anything. Everybody got that straight?"

Damon asked dubiously, "Aren't we getting in rather deep water?"

"Do you have an alternative suggestion?" asked Fletcher. "I'm certainly willing to listen."

Damon thought. "Wouldn't he agree to stop hunting dekabrach?"

"No. He refused point-blank."

"Well," said Damon reluctantly, "I guess we're doing the right thing. But we've got to prove a criminal charge. The inspector won't care whether or not Chrystal's cheated Bio-Minerals."

Fletcher said, "If there's any backfire on this, I'll take full responsibility."

"Nonsense," said Murphy. "We're all in this together. I say you did just right. In fact, we ought to hand the sculpin over to the deks, and see what they'd say to him."

After a few minutes Fletcher and Damon went up to the laboratory to look at the captive dekabrach. It floated quietly in the center of the tank, the ten arms at right angles to its body, the black eye-area staring through the glass.

"If it's intelligent," said Fletcher, "it must be as interested in us as we are in it."

"I'm not so sure it's intelligent," said Damon stubbornly. "Why doesn't it try to communicate?"

"I hope the inspector doesn't think along the same lines," said Fletcher. "After all, we don't have an air-tight case against Chrystal."

Damon looked worried. "Bevington isn't a very imaginative man. In fact, he's rather official in his outlook."

Fletcher and the dekabrach examined each other. "I know it's intelligent—but how can I prove it?"

"If it's intelligent," Damon insisted doggedly, "it can communicate."

"If it can't," said Fletcher, "then it's our move."

"What do you mean?"

"We'll have to teach it."

Damon's expression became so perplexed and worried that Fletcher broke into laughter.

"I don't see what's funny," Damon complained. "After all, what you propose is . . . well, it's unprecedented."

"I suppose it is," said Fletcher. "But it's got to be done, nevertheless. How's your linguistic background?"

"Very limited."

"Mine is even more so."

They stood looking at the dekabrach.

"Don't forget," said Damon, "we've got to keep it alive. That means, we've got to feed it." He gave Fletcher a caustic glance. "I suppose you'll admit it eats."

"I know for sure it doesn't live by photosynthesis," said Fletcher. "There's just not enough light. I believe Chrystal mentioned on the microfilm that it ate coral fungus. Just a minute." He started for the door.

"Where are you going?"

"To check with Chyrstal. He's certainly noted their stomach contents."

"He won't tell you," Damon said to Fletcher's back.

Fletcher returned ten minutes later.

"Well?" asked Damon in a skeptical voice.

Fletcher looked rather pleased with himself. "Coral fungus, mostly. Bits of tender young kelp shoots, stylax worms, sea oranges."

"Chrystal told you all this?" asked Damon incredulously.

"That's right. I explained to him that he and the dekabrach were both our guests, that we planned to treat them exactly alike. If the dekabrach ate well, so would Chrystal. That was all he needed."

Later, Fletcher and Damon stood in the laboratory watching the dekabrach ingest black-green balls of fungus.

"Two days," said Damon sourly, "and what have we accomplished? Nothing."

Fletcher was less pessimistic. "We've made progress in a negative sense. We're pretty sure it has no auditory apparatus, that it doesn't react to sound, and that it apparently lacks means for making any sound. Therefore, we've got to use visual methods to make contact."

"I envy you your optimism," Damon declared. "The beast has given me no grounds to suspect either the capacity or the desire for communication."

"Patience," said Fletcher. "It still probably doesn't know what we're trying to do and it probably fears the worst."

"We not only have to teach it a language," grumbled Damon, "we've got to introduce it to the idea that communication is possible. And then invent a language."

Fletcher grinned. "Let's get to work."

They inspected the dekabrach, and the black eye-area stared back through the wall of the tank. "We've got to work out a set of visual conventions," said Fletcher. "The ten arms are its most sensitive organs, and they are presumably controlled by the most highly organized section of its brain. So—we work out a set of signals based on the dek's arm movements."

"Does that give us enough scope?"

"I should think so. The arms are flexible tubes of muscle. They can assume at least five distinct positions: straight forward, diagonal forward, perpendicular, diagonal back, and straight back. Since the beast has ten arms, evidently there are ten to the fifth power combinations—a hundred thousand."

Fletcher nodded. "Call it a working hypothesis, anyway. We know we haven't seen any indication that the dek has tried to signal to us."

"Which suggests the creature is not intelligent."

Fletcher ignored the comment. "If we knew more about their habits, emotions, attitudes, we'd have a better framework for this new language."

"It seems placid enough," Damon said.

The dekabrach moved its arms back and forth idly. The eye-area studied the two men.

"Well," said Fletcher with a sigh, "first, a system of notation." He brought forth a model of the dekabrach's head, which Manners had constructed. The arms were made of flexible conduit and could be bent into various positions. "We number the arms zero to nine, around the clock, starting with this one here at the top. The five positions—forward, diagonal forward, erect, diagonal back, and back—we call A, B, K, X, Y. K is normal position, and when an arm is at K, it won't be noted."

Damon nodded his agreement. "That's sound enough."

"The logical first step would seem to be numbers."

Together they worked out a system of numeration and constructed a chart:

The colon (:) indicates a composite signal: i.e., two or more separate signals.

Number	0	1	2	et cetera
Signal	0Y	1Y	2Y	et cetera
	10	11	12	et cetera
	0Y,1Y	0Y,1Y:1Y	0Y,1Y:2Y	et cetera
	20	21	22	et cetera
	0Y,2Y	0Y,2Y:1Y	0Y,2Y:2Y	et cetera
	100	101	102	et cetera
	0X,1Y	0X,1Y:1Y	0X,1Y:2Y	et cetera
	110	111	112	et cetera
	0X,1Y:0Y,1Y	0X,1Y:1Y 1Y	0X,1Y:0Y,1Y: 2Y	et cetera
	120	121	122	et cetera
	0X,1Y:0Y,2Y	0X,1Y:0Y,2Y: 1Y	0X,1Y:0Y,2Y: 2Y	et cetera
	200	201	202	et cetera
	0X,2Y			et cetera
	1,000			et cetera
	0B,1Y			et cetera
	2,000			et cetera
	0B,2Y			et cetera

Damon said, "It's consistent—but cumbersome. For instance, to indicate five thousand, seven hundred sixty-six, it's necessary to make the signal . . . let's see: 0B, 5Y, then 0X, 7Y, then 0Y, 6Y, then 6Y."

"Don't forget that these are signals, not vocalizations," said Fletcher. "Even so, it's no more cumbersome than 'five thousand, seven hundred and sixty-six.' "

"I suppose you're right."

"Now—words."

Damon leaned back in his chair. "We can't just build a vocabulary and call it a language."

"I wish I knew more linguistic theory," said Fletcher. "Naturally, we won't go into any abstractions."

"Our basic English structure might be a good idea," Damon mused, "with English parts of speech. That is: nouns are things, adjectives are attributes of things, verbs are the displacements which things undergo or the absence of displacement."

Fletcher reflected. "We could simplify even further, to nouns, verbs, and verbal modifiers."

"Is that feasible? How, for instance, would you say, 'the large raft'?"

"We'd use a verb meaning 'to grow big.' 'Raft expanded.' Something like that."

"Humph," grumbled Damon. "You don't envisage a very expressive language."

"I don't see why it shouldn't be. Presumably the deks will modify whatever we give them to suit their own needs. If we get across just a basic set of ideas, they'll take it from there. Or by that time someone'll be out here who knows what he's doing."

"OK," said Damon, "get on with your Basic Dekabrach."

"First, let's list the ideas a dek would find useful and familiar."

"I'll take the nouns," said Damon. "You take the verbs. You can also have your modifiers." He wrote, *No. 1: water*.

After considerable discussion and modification, a sparse list of basic nouns and verbs was agreed upon, with assigned signals.

The simulated dekabrach head was arranged before the tank, with a series of lights on a board nearby to represent numbers.

"With a coding machine we could simply type out our message," said Damon. "The machine would dictate the pulses to the arms of the model."

Fletcher nodded. "Fine, if we had the equipment and several weeks to tinker around with it. Too bad we don't. Now—let's start. The numbers first. You work the lights, I'll move the arms. Just one to nine for now."

Several hours passed. The dekabrach floated quietly, the black eye-spot observing.

Feeding time approached. Damon displayed the black-green fungus balls; Fletcher arranged the signal for "food" on the arms of the model. A few morsels were dropped into the tank.

The dekabrach quietly sucked then into its oral tube.

Damon went through the pantomime of offering food to the model. Fletcher moved the arms to the signal "food." Damon ostentatiously placed the fungus ball in the model's oral tube, then faced the tank and offered food to the dekabrach.

The dekabrach watched impassively.

Two weeks passed. Fletcher went up to Raight's old room to talk to Chrystal, whom he found reading a book from the microfilm library.

Chrystal extinguished the image of the book, swung his legs over the side of the bed, and sat up.

Fletcher said, "In a very few days the inspector is due."

"So?"

"It's occurred to me that you might have made an honest mistake. At least I can see the possibility."

"Thanks," said Chrystal, "for nothing."

"I don't want to victimize you for what may be an honest mistake."

"Thanks again—but what do you want?"

"If you'll cooperate with me in having the dekabrachs recognized as an intelligent life form, I won't press charges against you."

Chrystal raised his eyebrows. "That's big of you. And I'm supposed to keep my complaints to myself?"

"If the deks are intelligent, you don't have any complaints."

Jack Vance

Chrystal looked keenly at Fletcher. "You don't sound too happy. The dek won't talk, eh?"

Fletcher restrained his annoyance. "We're working on him."

"But you're beginning to suspect he's not so intelligent as you thought."

Fletcher turned to go. "This one only knows fourteen signals so far. But it's learning two or three a day."

"Hey!" called Chrystal. "Wait a minute!"

Fletcher stopped at the door. "What for?"

"I don't believe you."

"That's your privilege."

"Let me see this dek make signals."

Fletcher shook his head. "You're better off in here."

Chrystal glared. "Isn't that a rather unreasonable attitude?"

"I hope not." He looked around the room. "Anything you're lacking?"

"No." Chrystal turned the switch, and his book flashed once more on the ceiling screen.

Fletcher left the room. The door closed behind him; the bolts shot home. Chrystal sat up alertly and jumped to his feet with a peculiar lightness, went to the door, and listened.

Fletcher's footfalls diminished down the corridor. Chrystal returned to the bed in two strides, reached under the pillow, and brought out a length of electric cord detached from a desk lamp. He had adapted two pencils as electrodes, making notches through the wood and binding a wire around the graphite core so exposed. For resistance in the circuit he included a lamp bulb.

He went to the window. He could see down the deck all the way to the eastern edge of the raft, and behind the office as far as the storage bins at the back of the process house. The deck was empty. The only movement was a white wisp of steam rising from the circulation flue, and behind it the hurrying pink and scarlet clouds.

Chrystal went to work, whistling soundlessly between intently pursed lips. He plugged the cord into the baseboard strip, held the two pencils to the window, struck an arc, and burnt at the groove which now ran nearly halfway around the window—it was the only means by which he could cut through the tempered beryl-silica glass.

It was slow work and very delicate. The arc was weak and fractious; fumes grated in Chrystal's throat. He persevered, blinking through watery eyes, twisting his head this way and that, until five-thirty, half an hour before his evening meal, when he put the equipment away. He dared not work after dark, for fear the flicker of light would arouse suspicion.

The days passed. Each morning Gideon and Atreus brought their respective flushes of scarlet and pale green to the dull sky; each evening they vanished in sad dark sunsets behind the western ocean.

A makeshift antenna had been jury-rigged from the top of the laboratory to a pole over the living quarters. Early one afternoon Manners blew the general alarm two short jubilant blasts, to announce a signal from the LG-19, now putting into Sabria on its regular semiannual call. Tomorrow evening lighters would swing down from orbit, bringing the inspector, supplies, and new crews for both Bio-Minerals and Pelagic Recoveries.

Bottles were broken out in the mess hall; there was loud talk, brave plans, laughter.

Exactly on schedule, the lighters—four of them—burst through the clouds. Two settled into the ocean beside Bio-Minerals; two more dropped down to the Pelagic Recoveries raft.

Lines were carried out by the launch and the lighters were warped against the dock.

First aboard the raft was Inspector Bevington, a brisk little man, immaculate in his dark blue and white uniform. He represented the government, interpreting its multiplicity of rules, laws, and ordinances; he was empowered to adjudicate minor offences, take custody of criminals, investigate violations of galactic law, check living conditions and safety practices, collect imposts, bonds, and duties, and, in general, personify the government in all of its faces and phases.

The job might well have invited graft and petty tyranny, were not the inspectors themselves subject to minute inspection.

Bevington was considered the most conscientious and the most humorless man in the service. If he was not particularly liked, he was at least respected.

Fletcher met him at the edge of the raft. Bevington glanced at him sharply, wondering why Fletcher was grinning so broadly. Fletcher was thinking that now would be a dramatic moment for one of the dekabrach's monitors to reach up out of the sea and clutch Bevington's ankle. But there was no disturbance; Bevington leaped onto the raft without interference.

He shook hands with Fletcher, then looked around, up and down the deck. "Where's Mr. Raight?"

Fletcher was taken aback; he himself had become accustomed to Raight's absence. "Why—he's dead."

It was Bevington's turn to be startled. "Dead?"

"Come along to the office," said Fletcher, "and I'll tell you about it. This has been a wild month." He looked up to the window of Raight's old room, where he expected to see Chrystal looking down. But the window was empty. Fletcher halted. Empty! The window was vacant even of glass! He started down the deck.

"Here!" cried Bevington. "Where are you going?"

Fletcher paused long enough to call over his shoulder, "You'd better come with me!" He ran to the door leading into the mess hall, with Bevington hurrying after him, frowning in annoyance and surprise.

Fletcher looked into the mess hall, hesitated, then came back out on deck and looked up at the vacant window. Where was Chrystal? Since he had not come along the deck at the front of the raft, he must have headed for the process house.

"This way," said Fletcher.

"Just a minute!" protested Bevington. "I want to know just what—"

But Fletcher was on his way down the eastern side of the raft toward the process house, where the lighter crew was already looking over the cases of precious metal o be transhipped. They glanced up as Fletcher and Bevington approached.

"Did anybody just come past?" asked Fletcher. "A big blond fellow?"

"He went in there." One of the lighter crewmen pointed toward the process house.

Fletcher whirled and ran through the doorway. Beside the leaching columns he 'ound Hans Heinz, looking ruffled and angry.

"Chrystal come through here?" Fletcher asked, panting.

"Did he come through here! Like a hurricane. He gave me a push in the face."

"Where did he go?"

Heinz pointed. "Out on the front deck."

Fletcher and Bevington hurried off, Bevington demanding petulantly, "Exactly vhat's going on here?"

"I'll explain in a minute," yelled Fletcher. He ran out on deck, looked toward the •arges and the launch.

No Ted Chrystal.

He could only have gone in one direction: back toward the living quarters, having ed Fletcher and Bevington in a complete circle.

A sudden thought hit Fletcher. "The helicopter!"

But the helicopter stood undisturbed, with its guy lines taut. Murphy came toward hem, looking perplexedly over his shoulder.

"Seen Chrystal?" asked Fletcher.

Murphy pointed. "He just went up them steps."

"The laboratory!" cried Fletcher in sudden agony. Heart in his mouth, he pounded up the steps, with Murphy and Bevington at his heels. If only Damon were in the aboratory now, not down on deck, or in the mess hall!

The lab was empty—except for the tank containing the dekabrach.

The water was cloudy and bluish. The dekabrach was thrashing from end to end of the tank, its ten arms kinked and knotted.

Fletcher jumped on a table, then vaulted directly into the tank. He wrapped his arms around the writhing body and lifted, but the supple shape squirmed out of his grasp. Fletcher grabbed again, heaved in desperation, finally raised it out of the tank.

"Grab hold," he hissed to Murphy between clenched teeth. "Lay it on the table."

Damon came rushing in. "What's going on?"

"Poison," said Fletcher. "Give Murphy a hand."

Damon and Murphy managed to lay the dekabrach on the table. Fletcher barked. 'Stand back—flood coming!" He slid the clamps from the side of the tank, and the lexible plastic collapsed. A thousand gallons of water gushed across the floor.

Fletcher's skin was beginning to burn. "Acid! Damon, get a bucket and wash off he dek. Keep him wet."

The circulatory system was still pumping brine into the tank. Fletcher tore off his trousers, which held the acid against his skin, then gave himself a quick rinse and turned the brine pipe around the tank, flushing off the acid.

The dekabrach lay limp, its propulsion vanes twitching. Fletcher felt sick and dull. "Try sodium carbonate," he told Damon. "Maybe we can neutralize some of the acid." On a sudden thought he turned to Murphy. "Go get Chrystal. Don't let him get away."

This was the moment that Chrystal chose to stroll into the laboratory. He looked around the room with an expression of mild surprise and hopped up on a chair to avoid the water.

"What's going on in here?"

Fletcher said grimly, "You'll find out." To Murphy: "Don't let him get away."

"Murderer!" cried Damon in a voice that broke with strain and grief.

Chrystal raised his eyebrows in shock. "Murderer?"

Bevington looked back and forth between Fletcher, Chrystal, and Damon. "Murderer? What *is* all this?"

"Just what the law specifies," said Fletcher. "Knowingly and willfully destroying one of an intelligent species. Murder."

The tank was rinsed; he clamped up the sides. The fresh brine began to rise up the sides.

"Now," said Fletcher. "Hoist the dek back in."

Damon shook his head hopelessly. "He's done for. He's not moving."

"We'll put him back in anyway," said Fletcher.

"I'd like to put Chrystal in there with him," Damon said with passionate bitterness.

"Come now," Bevington reproved him, "let's have no more talk like that. I don't know what's going on, but I don't like anything of what I hear."

Chrystal, looking amused and aloof, said, "I don't know what's going on, either."

They lifted the dekabrach and lowered him into the tank.

The water was about six inches deep, the level rising too slowly to suit Fletcher.

"Oxygen," he called. Damon ran to the locker. Fletcher looked at Chrystal. "So you don't know what I'm talking about?"

"Your pet fish dies—don't try to pin it on me."

Damon handed Fletcher a breather-tube from the oxygen tank; Fletcher thrust it into the water beside the dekabrach's gills. Oxygen bubbled up. Fletcher agitated the water urged it into the gill openings. The water was nine inches deep. Sodium carbonate," Fletcher said over his shoulder. "Enough to neutralize what's left of the acid."

Bevington asked in an uncertain voice, "Is it going to live?"

"I don't know."

Bevington squinted sideways at Chrystal, who shook his head. "Don't blame me."

The water rose. The dekabrach's arms lay limp, floating in all directions like Medusa locks.

Fletcher rubbed the sweat off his forehead. "If only I knew what to do! I can't give it a shot of brandy; I'd probably poison it."

The arms began to stiffen, extend. "Ah," breathed Fletcher, "that's better." He beckoned to Damon. "Gene, take over here—keep the oxygen going into the gills." He jumped to the floor where Murphy was flushing the area with buckets of water.

Chrystal was talking with great earnestness to Bevington. "I've gone in fear of my life these last three weeks! Fletcher is an absolute madman. You'd better send up for a doctor—or a psychiatrist." He caught Fletcher's eye and paused. Fletcher came slowly across the room. Chrystal turned back to the inspector, whose expression was harassed and uneasy.

"I'm registering an official complaint," said Chrystal. "Against Bio-Minerals in general and Sam Fletcher in particular. Since you're a representative of the law, I insist that you place Fletcher under arrest for criminal offenses against my person."

"Well," said Bevington, glancing cautiously at Fletcher. "I'll certainly make an investigation."

"He kidnaped me at the point of a gun!" cried Chrystal. "He's kept me locked up for three weeks!"

"To keep you from murdering the dekabrachs," said Fletcher.

"That's the second time you've said that," Chrystal remarked ominously. "Bevington is a witness. You're liable for slander."

"Truth isn't slander."

"I've netted dekabrach, so what? I also cut kelp and net coelocanths. You do the same."

"The deks are intelligent. That makes a difference." Fletcher turned to Bevington. "He knows it as well as I do. He'd process men for the calcium in their bones if he could make money at it!"

"You're a liar!" cried Chrystal.

Bevington held up his hands. "Let's have order here! I can't get to the bottom of this unless someone presents some facts."

"He doesn't have facts," Chrystal insisted. "He's trying to run my raft off of Sabria—can't stand the competition!"

Fletcher ignored him. He said to Bevington, "You want facts. That's why the dekabrach is in that tank, and that's why Chrystal poured acid in on him."

"Let's get something straight," said Bevington, giving Chrystal a hard stare. "Did you pour acid into that tank?"

Chrystal folded his arms. "The question is completely ridiculous."

"Did you? No evasions."

Chrystal hesitated, then said firmly, "No. And there's no vestige of proof that I did so."

Bevington nodded. "I see." He turned to Fletcher. "You spoke of facts. What facts?"

Fletcher went to the tank, where Damon was still swirling oxygenated water into the creature's gills. "How's he coming?"

Damon shook his head dubiously. "He's acting peculiar. I wonder if the acid got him internally?"

Fletcher watched the long pale shape for a few moments. "Well, let's try him. That's all we can do."

He crossed the room, then wheeled the model dekabrach forward. Chrystal laughed and turned away in disgust.

"What do you plan to demonstrate?" asked Bevington.

"I'm going to show you that the dekabrach is intelligent and is able to communicate."

"Well, well," said Bevington. "This is something new, is it not?"

"Correct." Fletcher arranged his notebook.

"How did you learn his language?"

"It isn't his—it's a code we worked out between us."

Bevington inspected the model, looked down at the notebook. "These are the signals?"

Fletcher explained the system. "He's got a vocabulary of fifty-eight words, not counting numbers up to nine."

"I see." Bevington took a seat. "Go ahead. It's your show."

Chrystal turned. "I don't have to watch this fakery."

Bevington said, "You'd better stay here and protect your interests—if you don't, no one else will."

Fletcher moved the arms of the model. "This is admittedly a crude setup; with time and money we'll work out something better. Now, I'll start with numbers."

Chrystal said contemptuously, "I could train a rabbit to count that way."

"After a minute," said Fletcher, "I'll try something harder. I'll ask who poisoned him."

"Just a minute!" bawled Chrystal. "You can't tie me up that way!"

Bevington reached for the notebook. "How will you ask? What signals do you use?"

Fletcher pointed them out. "First, interrogation. The idea of interrogation is an abstraction which the dek still doesn't completely understand. We've established a convention of choice, or alternation, like, 'Which do you want?' Maybe he'll catch on what I'm after."

"Very well—interrogation. Then what?"

"Dekabrach—receive—hot—water. 'Hot water' is for 'acid.' Interrogation: Man—give—hot—water?"

Bevington nodded. "That's fair enough. Go ahead."

Fletcher worked the signals. The black eye-area watched.

Damon said anxiously, "He's restless—very uneasy."

Fletcher completed the signals. The dekabrach's arms waved once or twice, then gave a puzzled jerk.

Fletcher repeated the set of signals, adding an extra "interrogation—man?"

The arms moved slowly.

" 'Man,' " read Fletcher.

Bevington nodded. "Man. But which man?"

Fletcher said to Murphy, "Stand in front of the tank." And he signaled, "Man—give—hot—water—interrogation."

The dekabrach's arms moved.

" 'Null-zero,' " read Fletcher. "No. Damon—step in front of the tank." He signaled the dekabrach. "Man—give—hot—water—interrogation."

" 'Null.' "

Fletcher turned to Bevington. "You stand in front of the tank." He signaled.

" 'Null.' "

Everyone looked at Chrystal. "Your turn," said Fletcher. "Step forward, Chrystal."

Chrystal came slowly forward. "I'm not a chump, Fletcher. I can see through your gimmick."

The dekabrach was moving its arms. Fletcher read the signals, Bevington looking over his shoulder at the notebook.

" 'Man—give—hot—water.' "

Chrystal started to protest.

Bevington quieted him. "Stand in front of the tank, Chrystal." To Fletcher: "Ask once again."

Fletcher signaled. The dekabrach responded. " 'Man—give—hot—water. Yellow. Man. Sharp. Come. Give—hot—water. Go.' "

There was silence in the laboratory.

"Well," said Bevington flatly, "I think you've made your case, Fletcher."

"You're not going to get me that easy," said Chrystal.

"Quiet," rasped Bevington. "It's clear enough what's happened."

"It's clear what's going to happen," said Chrystal in a voice husky with rage. He was holding Fletcher's gun. "I secured this before I came up here, and it looks as if—"

He raised the gun toward the tank, squinting; his big white hand tightened on the trigger. Fletcher's heart went dead and cold.

"Hey!" shouted Murphy.

Chrystal jerked. Murphy threw his bucket. Chrystal fired at Murphy, missed. Damon jumped at him, and Chrystal swung the gun around. The white-hot jet pierced Damon's shoulder. Damon, screaming like a hurt horse, wrapped his bony arms around Chrystal. Fletcher and Murphy closed in, wrested away the gun, and locked Chrystal's arms behind him.

Bevington said grimly, "You're in trouble now, Chyrstal, even if you weren't before."

Fletcher said, "He's killed hundreds and hundreds of deks. Indirectly he killed Carl Raight and John Agostino. He's got a lot to answer for."

* * *

The replacement crew had moved down to the raft from the LG-19. Fletcher, Damon, Murphy, and the rest of the old crew sat in the mess hall, six months of leisure ahead of them.

Damon's left arm hung in a sling; with his right he fiddled with his coffee cup. "I don't know quite what I'll be doing. I have no plans. The fact is, I'm rather up in the air."

Fletcher went to the window, looked out across the dark scarlet ocean. "I'm staying on."

"What?" cried Murphy. "Did I hear you right?"

Fletcher came back to the table. "I can't understand it myself."

Murphy shook his head in total lack of comprehension. "You can't be serious."

"I'm an engineer, a working man," said Fletcher. "I don't have a lust for power or any desire to change the universe—but it seems as if Damon and I set something into motion—something important—and I want to see it through."

"You mean, teaching the deks to communicate?"

"That's right. Chrystal attacked them, forced them to protect themselves. He revolutionized their lives. Damon and I revolutionized the life of this one dek in an entirely new way. But we've just started. Think of the potentialities! Imagine a population of men in a fertile land—men like ourselves, except that they never learned to talk. Then someone gives them contact with a new universe—an intellectual stimulus like nothing they've ever experienced. Think of their reactions, their new attitude to life! The deks are in that same position—except that we've just started with them. It's anybody's guess what they'll achieve—and somehow I want to be part of it. Even if I didn't, I couldn't leave with the job half done."

Damon said suddenly, "I think I'll stay on, too."

"You two have gone stir-crazy," said Jones. "I can't get away fast enough."

The LG-19 had been gone three weeks; operations had become routine aboard the raft. Shift followed shift; the bins began to fill with new ingots, new blocks of precious metal.

Fletcher and Damon had worked long hours with the dekabrach; today would see the great experiment.

The tank was hoisted to the edge of the dock.

Fletcher signaled once again his final message. "Man show you signals. You bring many dekabrachs, man show signals. Interrogation."

The arms moved in assent. Fletcher backed away; the tank was hoisted and lowered over the side, then it submerged.

The dekabrach floated up, drifted a moment near the surface, and slid down into the dark water.

"There goes Prometheus," said Damon, "bearing the gift of the gods."

"Better call it the gift of gab," said Fletcher, grinning.

 Jack Vance

The pale shape had vanished from sight. "Ten gets you fifty he won't be back," Caldur, the new superintendent, offered them.

"I'm not betting," said Fletcher. "Just hoping."

"What will you do if he doesn't come back?"

Fletcher shrugged. "Perhaps net another, teach him. After a while it's bound to take hold."

Three hours went by. Mists began to close in; rain blurred the sky.

Damon, who had been peering over the side, looked up. "I see a dek. But is it ours?"

A dekabrach came to the surface. It moved its arms. "Many—dekabrachs. Show—signals."

"Professor Damon," said Fletcher. "Your first class." ■

TOP SECRET
Eric Frank Russell

ASHMORE SAID, WITH IRRITATING PHLEGMATICISM, "The Zengs have everything to gain and nothing to lose by remaining friendly with us. I'm not worried about them."

"But I am," rasped General Railton. "I am paid to worry. It's my job. If the Zeng empire launches a treacherous attack upon ours and gains some initial successes, who'll get the blame? Who'll make wholesale accusations of military unpreparedness and for whose blood will the masses howl?" He tapped his two rows of medal ribbons. "Mine!"

"Understanding your position, I cannot share your alarm," maintained Ashmore, refusing to budge. "The Zeng empire is less than half the size of ours. The Zengs are an amiable and co-operative form of life and we've been on excellent terms with them since the first day of contact."

"I'll grant you all that." General Railton tugged furiously at his large and luxuriant mustache while he examined the great star map that covered an entire wall. "I have to consider things purely from the military viewpoint. It's my task to look to the future and expect the worst."

"Well, what's worrying you in particular?" Ashmore invited.

"Two things." Railton placed an authoritative finger on the star map. "Right here we hold a fairly new planet called Motan. You can see where it is—out in the wilds, far beyond our long-established frontiers. It's located in the middle of a close-packed group of solar systems, a stellar array that represents an important junction in space."

"I know all that."

"At Motan we've got a foothold of immense strategic value. We're in ambush on the crossroads, so to speak. Twenty thousand Terrans are there, complete with two spaceports and twenty-four light cruisers." He glanced at the other. "And what happens?"

Ashmore offered no comment.

"The Zengs," said Railton, making a personal grievance of it, "move in and take over two nearby planets in the same group."

"With our agreement," Ashmore reminded. "We did not need those two planets. The Zengs did want them. They put in a polite and correct request for permission to take over. Greenwood told them to help themselves."

"Greenwood," exploded Railton, "is something I could describe in detail were it not for my oath of loyalty."

"Let it pass," suggested Ashmore, wearily. "If he blundered, he did so with the full approval of the World Council."

"The World Council," Railton snorted. "All they're interested in is exploration, discovery, and trade. All they can think of is culture and cash. They're completely devoid of any sense of peril."

"Not being military officers," Ashmore pointed out, "they can hardly be expected to exist in a state of perpetual apprehension."

"Mine's not without cause." Railton had another go at uprooting the mustaches. "The Zengs craftily position themselves adjacent to Motan." He swept spread fingers across the map in a wide arc. "And all over here are Zeng outposts mixed up with ours. No orderliness about it, no system. A mob, sir, a scattered mob."

"That's natural when two empires overlap," informed Ashmore. "And, after all, the mighty cosmos isn't a parade ground."

Ignoring that, Railton said pointedly, "Then a cipher book disappears."

"It was shipped back on the *Laura Lindsay*. She blew apart and was a total loss. You know that."

"I know only what they see fit to tell me. I don't know that the book was actually on the ship. If it was not, where is it? Who's got it? What's he doing with it?" He waited for comment that did not come; finished, "So I had to move heaven and earth to get that cipher canceled and have copies of a new one sent out."

"Accidents happen," said Ashmore.

"Today," continued Railton, "I discover that Commander Hunter, on Motan, has been given the usual fatheaded emergency order. If war breaks out, he must fight a defensive action and hold the planet at all costs."

"What's wrong with that?"

Staring at him incredulously, Railton growled, "And him with twenty-four light cruisers. Not to mention two new battleships soon to follow."

"I don't quite understand."

"Wars," explained Railton, as one would to a child, "cannot be fought without armed ships. Ships cannot function usefully without instructions based on careful appraisal of tactical necessities. Somebody has to plan and give orders. The orders have to be received by those appointed to carry them out."

"So—?"

"How can Zeng warships receive and obey orders if their planetary beam stations have been destroyed?"

"You think that immediately war breaks out the forces on Motan should bomb every beam station within reach?"

"Most certainly, man!" Railton looked pleased at long last. "The instant the Zengs attack we've got to retaliate against their beam stations. That's tantamount to depriving them of their eyes and ears. Motan must be fully prepared to do its share. Commander Hunter's orders are out of date, behind the times, in fact plain stupid. The sooner they're rectified, the better."

"You're the boss," Ashmore reminded. "You've the authority to have them changed."

"That's exactly what I intend to do. I am sending Hunter appropriate instructions at once. And not by direct beam either." He indicated the map again. "In this messy muddle there are fifty or more Zeng beam stations lying on the straight line between here and there. How do we know how much stuff they're picking up and deciphering?"

"The only alternative is the tight beam," Ashmore said. "And that takes ten times as long. It zigzags all over the starfield from one station to another."

"But it's a thousand times safer and surer," Railton riposted. "Motan's station has just been completed and now's the time to make use of the fact. I'll send new instructions by tight beam, in straight language and leave no room for misunderstanding."

He spent twenty minutes composing a suitable message, finally got it to his satisfaction. Ashmore read it, could suggest no improvements. In due course it flashed out to Centauri, the first staging-post across the galaxy.

In event of hostile action in your sector the war must be fought to outstretch and rive all enemy's chief lines of communication.

"That," said Railton, "expresses it broadly enough to show Hunter what's wanted but still leave him with some initiative."

At Centauri the message was unscrambled, read off in clear, read into another beam of different frequency, scrambling and angle, boosted to the next nearest station. There it was sorted out, read off in clear, repeated into another beam and squirted onward.

It went leftward, rightward, upward, downward, and was dutifully recited eighteen times by voices ranging from Terran-American Deep South-suh to Boontean-Ansanite far North-yezzah. But it got there just the same.

Yes, it got there.

Lounging behind his desk, Commander Hunter glanced idly at the Motan thirty-hour clock, gave a wide yawn, wondered for the hundredth time whether it was something in the alien atmosphere that gave him the gapes. A knock sounded on his office door.

"Come in!"

Tyler entered, red-nosed and sniffy as usual. He saluted, dumped a signal form on the desk. "Message from Terra, sir." He saluted again and marched out, sniffing as he went.

Picking it up, Hunter yawned again as he looked at it. Then his mouth clapped shut with a hearable crack of jawbones. He sat bolt upright, eyes popping, read it a second time.

Ex Terra Space Control. Tight Beam, Straight. TOP SECRET. To Motan. An event of hospitality your section the foremost when forty-two ostriches arrive on any cheap line of communication.

Holding it in one hand he walked widdershins three times round the room, but it made no difference. The message still said what it said.

So he reseated himself, reached for the phone and bawled, "Maxwell? Is Maxwell there? Send him in at once!"

Maxwell appeared within a couple of minutes. He was a long, lean character who constantly maintained an expression of chronic disillusionment. Sighing deeply, he sat down.

"What's it this time, Felix?"

"Now," said Hunter, in the manner of a dentist about to reach for the big one at the back, "you're this planet's chief equipment officer. What you don't know about stores, supplies and equipment isn't worth knowing, eh?"

"I wouldn't go so far as to say that. I—"

"You know *everything* about equipment," insisted Hunter, ascending a step higher up the tonic solfa, "else you've no right to be here and take money for it. You're skinning the Terran taxpayer by false pretenses."

"Calm down, Felix," urged Maxwell. "I've a bellyful of troubles of my own." His questing eyes found the paper in the other's hand. "I take it that something's been requisitioned of which you don't approve. What is it?"

"Forty-two ostriches," informed Hunter.

Maxwell gave a violent jerk, fell off his chair, regained it and said, "Ha-ha! That's good. Best I've heard in years."

"You can see the joke all right?" asked Hunter, with artificial pleasantness. "You think it a winner?"

"Sure," enthused Maxwell. "It's really rich." He added another ha-ha by way of support.

"Then," said Hunter, a trifle viciously, "maybe you'll explain it to me because I'm too dumb to get it on my own." He leaned forward, arms akimbo. "*Why* do we require forty-two ostriches, eh? Tell me that!"

"Are you serious?" asked Maxwell, a little dazed.

For answer, Hunter shoved the signal form at him. Maxwell read it, stood up, sat down, read it again, turned it over and carefully perused the blank back.

"Well?" prompted Hunter.

"I've had nothing to do with this," assured Maxwell, hurriedly. He handed back the signal form as though anxious to be rid of it. "It's a Terran-authorized shipment made without demand from this end."

"My limited intelligence enabled me to deduce that much," said Hunter. "But as I have pointed out, you know all about equipment required for given conditions on any given world. All I want from you is information on why Motan needs forty-two ostriches—and what we're supposed to do with them when they come."

"I don't know," Maxwell admitted.

"You don't know?"

"No."

"That's a help." Hunter glowered at the signal. "A very big help."

"How about it being in code?" inquired Maxwell, desperate enough to fish around.

"It says here it's in straight."

"That could be an error."

"All right. We can soon check." Unlocking a big wall safe, Hunter extracted a brass-bound book, scrabbled through its pages. Then he gave it to Maxwell. "See if you can find a reference to ostriches or any reasonable resemblance thereto."

After five minutes Maxwell voiced a dismal, "No."

"Well," persisted Hunter, "have you sent a demand for forty-two of anything that might be misread as ostriches?"

"Not a thing." He meditated a bit, added glumly, "I did order a one pint blowtorch."

Taking a tight grip on the rim of the desk, Hunter said, "What's that got to do with it?"

"Nothing. I was just thinking. That's what I ordered. You ought to see what I got." He gestured toward the door. "It's right out there in the yard. I had it dragged there for your benefit."

"Let's have a look at it."

Hunter followed him outside, inspected the object of the other's discontent. It had a body slightly bigger than a garbage can, also a nozzle five inches in diameter by three feet in length. Thought empty, it was as much as the two could manage merely to lift it.

"What the deuce is it, anyway?" demanded Hunter, scowling.

"A one-pint blowtorch. The consignment note says so."

"Never seen anything like it. We'd better check the stores catalogue." Returning to the office, he dug the tome out of the safe, thumbed through it rapidly, found what he wanted somewhere among the middle pages.

19112. Blowtorch, butane, 1/2 pint capacity.

19112A. Blowtorch, butane, 1 pint capacity.

19112B. Blowtorch (tar-boiler pattern), kerosene, 15 gallons capacity.

19112B(a). Portable trolley for 19112B.

"You've got B in lieu of A," Hunter diagnosed.

"That's right. I order A and I get B."

"Without the trolley."

"Correct."

"Some moron is doing his best." He returned the catalogue to the safe. "You'll have to ship it back. It's a fat lot of use to us without the trolley even if we do find need to boil some tar."

"Oh, I don't know," Maxwell opined. "We can handle it by sheer muscle when the two hundred leftlegged men get here."

Hunter plonked himself in his chair, gave the other the hard eye. "Quit beating about the bush. What is on your mind?"

"The last ship," said Maxwell, moodily, "brought two hundred pairs of left-legged rubber thigh-boots."

"The next ship may bring two hundred pairs of right-legged ones to match up," said Hunter. "Plus forty-two ostriches. When that's done we'll be ready for anything. We can defy the cosmos." He suddenly went purple in the face, snatched up the phone and yelled, "Tyler! Tyler."

When that worthy appeared he said, "Blow your nose and tightbeam this message: *Why forty-two ostriches?*"

It went out, scrambled and unscrambled and rescrambled, upward, downward, rightward, leftward, recited in Sirian-Kram lowlands accents and Terran-Scottish highlands accents and many more. But it got there just the same.

Yes, it got there.

General Railton glanced up from a thick wad of documents and rapped impatiently, "What is it?"

"Top secret message from Motan, sir."

Taking it, Railton looked it over.

We've fought two ostriches.

"Ashmore!" he yelled. "Pennington! Whittaker!"

They came on the run, lined up before his desk, assumed habitual expressions of innocence. He eyed them as though each were personally responsible for something dastardly.

"What," he demanded, "is the meaning of this?"

He tossed the signal form at Pennington who gave it the glassy eye and passed it to Whittaker who examined it fearfully and got rid of it on Ashmore. The latter scanned it, dumped it back on the desk. Nobody said anything.

"Well," said Railton, "isn't there a useful thought between the three of you?"

Picking up courage, Pennington ventured, "It must be in code, sir."

"It is clearly and plainly captioned as being in straight."

"That may be so, sir. But it doesn't make sense in straight."

"D'you think I'd have summoned you here if it did make rhyme or reason?" Railton let go a snort that quivered his mustaches. "Bring me the current code book. We'll see if we can get to the bottom of this."

They fetched him the volume then in use, the sixth of Series B. He sought through it at length. So did they, each in turn. No ostriches.

"Try the earlier books," Railton ordered. "Some fool on Motan may have picked up an obsolete issue."

So they staggered in with a stack of thirty volumes, worked back to BA. No ostriches. After that, they commenced on AZ and laboriously headed toward AA.

Pennington, thumbing through AK, let go a yelp of triumph. "Here it is, sir. An ostrich is a food-supply and rationing code-word located in the quartermaster section."

"What does it mean?" inquired Railton, raising expectant eyebrows.

"One gross of fresh eggs," said Pennington, in the manner of one who sweeps aside the veil of mystery.

"Ah!" said Railton, in tones of exaggerated satisfaction. "So at last we know where we stand, don't we? Everything has become clear. On Motan they've beaten off an attack by three hundred fresh eggs, eh?"

Pennington looked crushed.

"Fresh eggs," echoed Ashmore. "That may be a clue!"

"What sort of clue?" demanded Railton, turning attention his way.

"In olden times," explained Ashmore, "the word fresh meant impudent, cheeky, brazen. And an egg was a person. Also, a hoodlum or thug was known as a hard egg or a tough egg."

"If you're right, that means Motan has resisted a raid by three hundred impertinent crooks."

"Offhand, I just can't think of any more plausible solution," Ashmore confessed.

"It's not credible," decided Railton. "There are no pirates out that way. The only potential menace is the Zengs. If a new and previously unsuspected life form has appeared out there, the message would have said so."

"Maybe they meant they've had trouble with Zengs," suggested Whittaker.

"I doubt it," Railton said. "In the first place, the Zengs would not be so dopey as to start a war by launching a futile attack with a force a mere three hundred strong. In the second place, if the culprits were Zengs the fact could have been stated. On the tight-beam system there's no need for Motan to be obscure."

"That's reasonable enough," Ashmore agreed.

Railton thought things over, said at last, "The message looks like a routine report. It doesn't call for aid or demand fast action. I think we'd better check back. Beam them asking which book they're quoting."

Out it went, up, down and around, via a mixture of voices.

Which code book are you using?

Tyler sniffed, handed it over, saluted, sniffed again and ambled out. Commander Hunter picked it up.

Which goad hook are you using?

"Maxwell! Maxwell!" When the other arrived, he said, "There'll never be an end to this. What's a goad hook?"

"I'd have to look it up in the catalogue."

"Meaning that you don't know?"

"There's about fifty kinds of hooks," informed Maxwell, defensively. "And for many of them there are technical names considerably different from space-navy names or even stores equipment names. A tensioning hook, for instance, is better known as a tightener."

"Then let's consult the book." Getting it from the safe, Hunter opened it on the desk while Maxwell positioned himself to look over the other's shoulder. "What'll it be listed under?" Hunter asked. "Goad hooks or hooks, goad? G or H?"

"Might be either."

They sought through both. After checking item by item over half a dozen pages, Maxwell stabbed a finger at a middle column.

"There it is."

Hunter looked closer. "That's *guard* hooks: things for fixing wire fence to steel posts. Where's *goad* hooks?"

"Doesn't seem to be any," Maxwell admitted. Sudden suspicion flooded his features and he went on, "Say, do you suppose this has anything to do with those ostriches?"

"Darned if I know. But it's highly probable."

"Then," announced Maxwell, "I know what a goad hook is. And you won't find it in that catalogue."

Slamming the book shut, Hunter said wearily, "All right. Proceed to enlighten me."

"I saw a couple of them in use," informed Maxwell, "donkey's years ago, in the movies."

"The movies?"

"Yes. They were showing an ostrich farm in South Africa. When the farmer wanted to extract a particular bird from the flock he used a pole about eight to ten feet long. It had a sort of metal prod on one end and a wide hook at the other. He'd use the sharp end to poke other birds out of the way, then use the hook end to snake the bird he wanted around the bottom of its neck and drag it out."

"Oh," said Hunter, staring at him.

"It's a thing like bishops carry for lugging sinners into the path of righteousness," Maxwell finished.

"Is it really?" said Hunter, blinking a couple of times. "Well, it checks up with that signal about the ostriches." He brooded a bit, went on, "But it implies that there is more than one kind of goad hook. Also that we are presumed to have one especial pattern in stores here. They want to know which one we've got. What are we going to tell them?"

"We haven't got any," Maxwell pointed out. "What do we need goad hooks for?"

"Ostriches," said Hunter. "Forty-two of them."

Maxwell thought it over. "We've no goad hooks, not one. But they think we have. What's the answer to that?"

"You tell me," Hunter invited.

"That first message warned us that the ostriches were coming on any cheap line of communication, obviously meaning a chartered tramp ship. So they won't get here for quite a time. Meanwhile, somebody has realized that we'll need goad hooks to handle them and shipped a consignment by fast service boat. Then he's discovered that he can't remember which pattern he's sent us. He can't fill up the necessary forms until he knows. He's asking you to give with the information."

"If that's so," commented Hunter, "Some folk have a nerve to tightbeam such a request and mark it top secret."

"Back at Terran H.Q.," said Maxwell, "one is not shot at dawn for sabotage, treachery, assassination or any other equally trifling misdeed. One is blindfolded and stood against the wall for not filling up forms, or for filling up the wrong ones, or for filling up the right ones with the wrong details."

"Nuts to that!" snapped Hunter, fed up. "I'm wasting no time getting a headquarters dope out of a jam. We're suppose to have a consignment of goad hooks. We haven't got it. I'm going to say so—in plain language." He boosted his voice a few decibels. "Tyler! Tyler!"

Half an hour later the signal squirted out, brief, to the point, lacking only its original note of indignation.

No goad hyphen hooks. Motan.

Holding it near the light, Railton examined it right way up and upside-down. His mustaches jittered. His eyes squinted slightly. His complexion assumed a touch of magenta.

"Pennington!" he bellowed. "Saunders! Ashmore! Whittaker!"

Lining up, they looked at the signal form. They shifted edgily around, eyed each other, the floor, the ceiling, the walls. Finally they settled for the uninteresting scene outside the window.

Oh God how I hate mutton.

"Well?" prompted Railton, poking this beamed revelation around his desk.

Nobody responded.

"First," Railton pointed out, "they are mixing it with a pair of ostriches. Now they've developed an aversion to mutton. If there's a connection, I fail to see it. There's got to be an explanation somewhere. What is it?"

Nobody knew.

"We might as well," said Railton, "invite the Zengs to accept everything as a gift. It'll save a lot of bloodshed."

Stung by that, Whittaker protested, "Motan is trying to tell us something, sir. They must have cause to express themselves the way they are doing."

"Such as what?"

"Perhaps they have good reason to think that the tight beam is no longer tight. Maybe a Zeng interceptor station has opened right on one of the lines. So Motan is hinting that it's time to stop beaming in straight."

"They could have said so in code, clearly and unmistakably. There's no need to afflict us with all this mysterious stuff about ostriches and mutton."

Up spoke Saunders, upon whom the gift of tongues had descended. "Isn't it possible, sir, that ostrich flesh is referred to as mutton by those who eat it? Or that, perhaps, it bears close resemblance to mutton?"

"*Anything* is possible," shouted Railton, "including the likelihood that everyone

Eric Frank Russell

on Motan is a few cents short in his mental cash." He fumed a bit, added acidly, "Let us assume that ostrich flesh is identical with mutton. Where does that get us?"

"It could be, sir," persisted Saunders, temporarily drunk with words, "that they've discovered a new and valuable source of food supply in the form of some large, birdlike creature which they call ostriches. Its flesh tastes like mutton. So they've signaled us a broad hint that they're less dependent upon supplementary supplies from here. Maybe at a pinch they can feed themselves for months or years. That, in turn, means the Zengs can't starve them into submission by blasting all supply ships to Motan. So—"

"Shut up!" Railton bawled, slightly frenzied. He snorted hard enough to make the signal form float off his desk. Then he reached for the phone. "Get me the Zoological Department. Yes, that's what I said." He waited a while, growled into the mouthpiece, "Is ostrich flesh edible and, if so, what does it taste like?" Then he listened, slammed the phone down and glowered at the audience. "Leather," he said.

"That doesn't apply to the Motan breed," Saunders pointed out. "You can't judge an alien species by—"

"For the last time, keep quiet!" He shifted his glare to Ashmore. "We can't go any further until we know which code they're using out there."

"It should be the current one, sir. They had strict orders to destroy each preceding copy."

"I know what it *should* be. But *is* it? We've asked them about this and they've not replied. Ask them again, by *direct* beam. I don't care if the Zengs do pick up the question and answer. They can't make use of the information. They've known for years that we use code as an elementary precaution."

"I'll have it beamed right away, sir."

"Do that. And let me have the reply immediately it arrives." Then, to the four of them, "Get out of my sight."

The signal shot straight to Motan without any juggling around.

Identify your code forthwith. Urgent.

Two days later the answer squirted back and got placed on Railton's desk pending his return from lunch. In due course he paraded along the corridor and into his office. His thoughts were actively occupied with the manpower crisis in the Sirian sector and nothing was further from his mind than the antics of Motan. Sitting at his desk, he glanced at the paper.

All it said was, *"BF."*

He went straight up and came down hard.

"Ashmore!" he roared, scrabbling around. "Pennington! Saunders! Whittaker!"

Ex Terra Space Control. Direct Beam, Straight. To Motan. Commander Hunter recalled forthwith. Captain Maxwell succeeds with rank of commander as from date of receipt.

Putting on a broad grin of satisfaction, Hunter reached for the phone. "Send Maxwell here at once." When the other arrived, he announced, "A direct-beam recall has just come in. I'm going home."

"Oh," said Maxwell without enthusiasm. He looked more disillusioned than ever.

"I'm going back to H.Q. You know what that means."

"Yes," agreed Maxwell, a mite enviously. "A nice, soft job, better conditions, high pay, quicker promotion."

"Dead right. It is only proper that virtue should be rewarded." He eyed the other, holding back the rest of the news. "Well, aren't you happy about it?"

"No," said Maxwell, flatly.

"Why not?"

"I've become hardened to you. Now I'll have to start all over again and adjust myself to some other and different nut."

"No you won't, chum. *You're* taking charge." He poked the signal form across the desk. "Congratulations, Commander!"

"Thanks," said Maxwell. "For nothing. Now I'll have to handle your grief. Ostriches. Forty-two of them."

At midnight Hunter stepped aboard the destroyer D10 and waved good-by. He did it with all the gratified assurance of one who's going to get what's coming to him. The prospect lay many weeks away but was worth waiting for.

The ship snored into the night until its flame trail faded out leftword of Motan's fourth moon. High above the opposite horizon glowed the Zeng's two planets of Korima and Koroma, one blue, the other green. Maxwell eyed the shining firmament, felt the weight of new responsibility pressing hard upon his shoulders.

He spent the next forthnight checking back on his predecessor's correspondence, familiarizing himself with all the various problems of planetary governorship. At the end of that time he was still baffled and bothered.

"Tyler!" Then when the other came in, "For heaven's sake, man, can't you stop perpetually snuffling? Send this message out at once."

Taking it, Tyler asked, "Tight or straight beam, sir?"

"Don't send it direct beam. It had better go by tight. The subject is tagged top secret by H.Q. and we've got to accept their definition."

"Very well, sir." Giving an unusually loud sniff, Tyler departed and squirted the query to the first repeater station.

Why are we getting ostriches?

It never reached Railton or any other brass hat. It fell into the hands of a new Terran operator who'd become the viction of three successive technical gags. He had no intention whatsoever of being made a chump a fourth time. So he read it with eyebrows waggling.

When are we getting ostriches?

With no hesitation he destroyed the signal and smacked back at the smarty on Motan.

Will emus do?

In due course Maxwell got it, read it twice, walked widdershins with it and found himself right back where he'd started.

Will amuse you.

For the thirtieth time in four months Maxwell went to meet a ship at the spaceport. So far there had arrived not a goad hook, not a feather, not even a caged parrot.

It was a distasteful task because every time he asked a captain whether he'd brought the ostriches he got a look that pronounced him definitely teched in the haid.

Anyway, this one was not a tramp boat. He recognized its type even before it sat down and cut power—a four-man Zeng scout. He also recognized the first Zeng to scramble down the ladder. It was Tormin, the chief military officer on Koroma.

"Ah, Mr. Maxwell," said Tormin, his yellow eyes worried. "I wish to see the commander at once."

"Hunter's gone home. I'm the commander now. What's your trouble?"

"Plenty," Tormin informed. "As you know, we placed ordinary settlers on Korima. But on the sister planet of Koroma we placed settlers and a large number of criminals. The criminals have broken out and seized arms. Civil war is raging on Koroma. We need help."

"Sorry, but I can't give it," said Maxwell. "We have strict orders that in no circumstances whatever may we interfere in Zeng affairs."

"I know, I know." Tormin gestured excitedly with long, skinny arms. "We do not ask for your ships and guns. We are only too willing to do our own dirty work. Besides, the matter is serious but not urgent. Even if the criminals conquer the planet they cannot escape from it. We have removed all ships to Korima."

"Then what do you want me to do?"

"Send a call for help. We can't do it—our beam station is only half built."

"I am not permitted to make direct contact with the Zeng authorities," said Maxwell. "You can tell your own H.Q. on Terra. They'll inform our ambassador there. He'll inform our nearest forces."

"That'll mean some delay."

"Right now there's no other way," urged Tormin. "Will you please oblige us? In the same circumstances we'd do as much for you."

"All right," agreed Maxwell, unable to resist this appeal. "The responsibility for getting action will rest with H.Q., anyway." Bolting to his office, he gave Tyler the message, adding, "Better send it tightbeam, just in case some Zeng stickler for regulations picks it up and accuses us of poking our noses in."

Out it went, to and fro, up and down, in one tone or another, this accent or that.

Civil war is taking place among local Zengs. They are asking for assistance.

It got there a few minutes behind Hunter, who walked into Railton's office, reached the desk, came smartly to attention.

"Commander Hunter, sir, reporting from Motan."

"About time, too," snapped Railton, obviously in no mood to give with a couple of medals. "As commander of Motan you accepted full responsibility for the text of all messages beamed therefrom, did you not?"

"Yes, sir," agreed Hunter, sensing a queer coldness in his back hairs.

Jerking open a drawer, Railton extracted a bunch of signal forms, irefully slapped them on the desk.

"This," he informed, mustaches quivering, "is the appalling twaddle with which I have been afflicted by you since Motan's station came into operation. I can find only one explanation for all this incoherent rubbish about ostriches and mutton, that being that you're overdue for mental treatment. After all, it is not unknown for men on alien planets to go off the rails."

"Permit me to say, sir—" began Hunter.

"I don't permit you," shouted Railton. "Wait until I have finished. And don't flare your nostrils at me. I have replaced you with Maxwell. The proof of your imbecility will be the nature of the next signals from Motan."

"But, sir—"

"Shut up! I will let you see Maxwell's messages and compare them with your own irrational nonsense. If that doesn't convince—"

He ceased his tirade as Ashmore appeared and dumped a signal form on his desk.

"Urgent message from Motan, sir."

Railton snatched it up and read it while Ashmore watched and Hunter fidgeted uneasily.

Sibly Ward is making faces among local Zengs. They are asking for her sister.

The resulting explosion will remain a space legend for all time. ∎

MEIHEM IN CE KLASRUM

Dolton Edwards

BECAUSE WE ARE STILL BEARING some of the scars of our brief skirmish with II-B English, it is natural that we should be enchanted by Mr. George Bernard Shaw's current campaign for a simplified alphabet.

Obviously, as Mr. Shaw points out, English spelling is in much need of a general overhauling and streamlining. However, our own resistance to any changes requiring a large expenditure of mental effort in the near future would cause us to view with some apprehension the possibility of some day receiving a morning paper printed in—to us—Greek.

Our own plan would achieve the same end as the legislation proposed by Mr. Shaw, but in a less shocking manner, as it consists merely of an acceleration of the normal processes by which the language is continually modernized.

As a catalytic agent, we would suggest that a National Easy Language Week be proclaimed, which the President would inaugurate, outlining some shortcut to concentrate on during the week, and to be adopted during the ensuing year. All school children would be given a holiday, the lost time being the equivalent of that gained by the spelling short cut.

In 1946, for example, we would urge the elimination of the soft "c," for which we would substitute "s." Sertainly, such an improvement would be selebrated in all sivic-minded sircles as being suffisiently worth the trouble, and students in all sities in the land would be reseptive toward any change eliminating the nesessity of learning the differense between the two letters.

In 1947, sinse only the hard "c" would be left, it would be possible to substitute "k" for it, both letters being pronounsed identikally. Imagine how greatly only two years of this prosess would klarify the konfusion in the minds of students. Already we would have eliminated an entire letter from the alphabet. Typewriters and linotypes kould all be built with one less letter, and all the manpower and materials previously devoted to making "c's" kould be turned toward raising the national standard of living.

In the fase of so many notable improvements, it is easy to forsee that by 1948, "National Easy Language Week" would be a pronounced sukses. All skhool tshildren would be looking forward with konsiderable exsitement to the holiday, and in a blaze of national publisity it would be announsed that the double konsonant "ph" no longer existed, and that the sound would henseforth be written "f" in all words. This would make sutsh words as "fonograf" twenty persent shorter in print.

By 1949, publik interest in a fonetik alfabet kan be expekted to have inkreased to the point where a more radikal step forward kan be taken without fear of undue kritisism. We would therefore urge the elimination at that time of al unesesary double leters, whitsh, although quite harmles, have always ben a nuisanse in the language and a desided deterent to akurate speling. Try it yourself in the next leter you write, and se if both writing and reading are not fasilitated.

With so much progres already made, it might be posible in 1950 to delve further into the posibilities of fonetik speling. After due konsideration of the reseption aforded the previous steps, it should be expedient by this time to spel al difthongs fonetikaly. Most students do not realize that the long "i" and "y," as in "time" and "by," are aktualy the difthong "ai," as it is writen in "aisle," and that the long "a" in "fate," is in reality the difthong "ei" as in "rein." Although perhaps not imediately aparent, the saving in taime and efort wil be tremendous when we leiter eliminate the sailent "e," as meide posible bai this last tsheinge.

For, as is wel known, the horible mes of "e's" apearing in our writen language is kaused prinsipaly bai the present nesesity of indikeiting whether a vowel is long or short. Therefore, in 1951 we kould simply elemineit al sailent "e's," and kontinu to read and wrait merily along as though we were in an atomik ag of edukation.

In 1951 we would urg a greit step forward. Sins bai this taim it would have ben four years sins anywun had usd the letter "c," we would sugest that the "National Easy Languag Wek" for 1951 be devoted to substitution of "c" for "th." To be sur it would be som taim befor peopl would bekom akustomd to reading ceir newspapers and buks wic sutsh sentenses in cem as "Ceodor caught he had cre cousand cisls crust crough ce cik of his cumb."

In ce seim maner, bai meiking eatsh leter hav its own sound and cat sound only, we kould shorten ce language stil mor. In 1952 we would elimineit ce "y"; cen in 1953 we kould us ce leter to indikeit ce "sh" sound, cerbai klarifaiing words laik yugar and yur, as wel as redusing bai wun mor leter al words laik "yut," "yore," and so forc. Cink, cen, of al ce benefits to be geind bai ce distinktion whitsh wil cen be meid between words laik:

OCEAN: now writen oyean
MACHINE: now writen mayin
RACIAL: now writen reiyial

Al sutsh divers weis of wraiting wun sound would no longer exist, and whenever wun kaim akros a "y" sound he would know exaktli what to wrait.

Kontinuing cis proses, year after year, we would eventuali hav a reali sensibl writen languag. By 1975, wi ventyur tu sei, cer wud be no mor uv ces teribli trublsum difikultis, wic no tu leters usd to indikeit ce seim nois, and laikwais no tu noises riten wic ce seim leter. Even Mr. Yaw, wi beliv, wud be hapi in ce noleg cat his drims fainali keim tru. ■

OMNILINGUAL
H. Beam Piper

MARTHA DANE PAUSED, looking up at the purple-tinged copper sky. The wind had shifted since noon, while she had been inside, and the dust storm that was sweeping the high deserts to the east was now blowing out over Syrtis. The sun, magnified by the haze, was a gorgeous magenta ball, as large as the sun of Terra, at which she could look directly. Tonight, some of that dust would come sifting down from the upper atmosphere to add another film to what had been burying the city for the last fifty thousand years.

The red loess lay over everything, covering the streets and the open spaces of park and plaza, hiding the small houses that had been crushed and pressed flat under it and the rubble that had come down from the tall buildings when roofs had caved in and walls had toppled outward. Here where she stood, the ancient streets were a hundred to a hundred and fifty feet below the surface; the breach they had made in the wall of the building behind her had opened into the sixth story. She could look down on the cluster of prefabricated huts and sheds, on the brush-grown flat that had been the waterfront when this place had been a seaport on the ocean that was now Syrtis Depression; already, the bright metal was thinly coated with red dust. She thought, again, of what clearing this city would mean, in terms of time and labor, of people and supplies and equipment brought across fifty million miles of space. They'd have to use machinery; there was no other way it could be done. Bulldozers and power shovels and draglines; they were fast, but they were rough and indiscriminate. She remembered the digs around Harappa and Mohenjo-Daro, in the Indus Valley, and the careful, patient native laborers—the painstaking foremen, the pickmen and spademen, the long files of basketmen carrying away the earth. Slow and primitive as the civilization whose ruins they were uncovering, yes, but she could count on the fingers of one hand the times one of her pickmen had damaged a valuable object in the ground. If it hadn't been for the underpaid and uncomplaining native laborer, archaeology would still be back where Wincklemann had found it. But on Mars there was no native labor; the last Martian had died five hundred centuries ago.

Something started banging like a machine gun, four or five hundred yards to her left. A solenoid jackhammer; Tony Lattimer must have decided which building he wanted to break into next. She became conscious, then, of the awkward weight of her equipment, and began redistributing it, shifting the straps of her oxy-tank pack, slinging the camera from one shoulder and the board and drafting tools from the other, gathering the notebooks and sketchbooks under her left arm. She started walking down the road, over hillocks of buried rubble, around snags of wall jutting up out of the loess, past buildings still standing, some of them already breached and explored, and across the brush-grown flat to the huts.

There were ten people in the main office room of Hut One when she entered. As soon as she had disposed of her oxygen equipment, she lit a cigarette, her first since noon, then looked from one to another of them. Old Selim von Ohlmhorst, the Turco-German, one of her two fellow archaeologists, sitting at the end of the long table against the farther wall, smoking his big curved pipe and going through a looseleaf notebook. The girl ordnance officer, Sachiko Koremitsu, between two droplights at the other end of the table, her head bent over her work. Colonel Hubert Penrose, the Space Force CO, and Captain Field, the intelligence officer, listening to the report of one of the airdyne pilots returned from his afternoon survey flight. A couple of girl lieutenants from Signals, going over the script of the evening telecast to be transmitted to the *Cyrano* in orbit five thousand miles off planet and relayed from thence to Terra via Luna. Sid Chamberlain, the Trans-Space News Service man, was with them. Like Selim and herself, he was a civilian; he was advertising the fact with a white shirt and a sleeveless blue sweater. And Major Lindemann, the engineer officer, and one of his assistants, arguing over some plans on a drafting board. She hoped, drawing a pint of hot water to wash her hands and sponge off her face, that they were doing something about the pipeline.

She started to carry the notebooks and sketchbooks over to where Selim von Ohlmhorst was sitting, and then, as she always did, she turned aside and stopped to watch Sachiko. The Japanese girl was restoring what had been a book, fifty thousand years ago; her eyes were masked by a binocular loup, the black headband invisible against her glossy black hair, and she was picking delicately at the crumbled page with a hair-fine wire set in a handle of copper tubing. Finally, loosening a particle as tiny as a snowflake, she grasped it with tweezers, placed it on the sheet of transparent plastic on which she was reconstructing the page, and set it with a mist of fixitive from a little spraygun. It was a sheer joy to watch her; every movement was as graceful and precise as though done to music after being rehearsed a hundred times.

"Hello, Martha. It isn't cocktail-time yet, is it?" The girl at the table spoke without raising her head, almost without moving her lips, as though she were afraid that the slightest breath would disturb the flaky stuff in front of her.

"No, it's only fifteen-thirty. I finished my work, over there. I didn't find any more books, if that's good news for you."

Sachiko took off the loup and leaned back in her chair, her palms cupped over her eyes.

"No, I like doing this. I call it micro-jigsaw puzzles. This book, here, really is a mess. Selim found it lying open, with some heavy stuff on top of it; the pages were simply crushed. She hesitated briefly. "If only it would mean something, after I did it."

H. Beam Piper

There could be a faintly critical overtone to that. As she replied, Martha realized that she was being defensive.

"It will, some day. Look how long it took to read Egyptian hieroglyphics, even after they had the Rosetta Stone."

Sachiko smiled. "Yes, I know. But they did have the Rosetta Stone."

"And we don't. There is no Rosetta Stone, not anywhere on Mars. A whole race, a whole species, died while the first Crô-Magnon cave-artist was daubing pictures of reindeer and bison, and across fifty thousand years and fifty million miles there was no bridge of understanding.

"We'll find one. There must be something, somewhere, that will give us the meaning of a few words, and we'll use them to pry meaning out of more words, and so on. We may not live to learn this language, but we'll make a start, and some day somebody will."

Sachiko took her hands from her eyes, being careful not to look toward the unshaded lights, and smiled again. This time Martha was sure that it was not the Japanese smile of politeness, but the universally human smile of friendship.

"I hope so, Martha; really I do. It would be wonderful for you to be the first to do it, and it would be wonderful for all of us to be able to read what these people wrote. It would really bring this dead city to life again." The smile faded slowly. "But it seems so hopeless."

"You haven't found any more pictures?"

Sachiko shook her head. Not that it would have meant much if she had. They had found hundreds of pictures with captions; they had never been able to establish a positive relationship between any pictured object and any printed word. Neither of them said anything more, and after a moment Sachiko replaced the loup and bent her head forward over the book.

Selim von Ohlmhorst looked up from his notebook, taking his pipe out of his mouth. "Everything finished, over there?" he asked, releasing a puff of smoke.

"Such as it was." She laid the notebooks and sketches on the table. "Captain Gicquel's started airsealing the building from the fifth floor down, with an entrance on the sixth; he'll start putting in oxygen generators as soon as that's done. I have everything cleared up where he'll be working."

Colonel Penrose looked up quickly, as though making a mental note to attend to something later. Then he returned his attention to the pilot, who was pointing something out on a map.

Von Ohlmhorst nodded. "There wasn't much to it, at that," he agreed. "Do you know which building Tony has decided to enter next?"

"The tall one with the conical thing like a candle extinguisher on top, I think. I heard him drilling for the blasting shots over that way."

"Well, I hope it turns out to be one that was occupied up to the end."

The last one hadn't. It had been stripped of its contents and fittings, a piece of this and a bit of that, haphazardly, apparently over a long period of time, until it had been almost gutted. For centuries, as it had died, this city had been consuming itself by a process of auto-cannibalism. She said something to that effect.

"Yes. We always find that—except, of course, at places like Pompeii. Have you seen any of the other Roman cities in Italy?" he asked. "Minturnae, for instance? First the inhabitants tore down this to repair that, and then, after they had vacated the city, other people came along and tore down what was left, and burned the stones for lime, or crushed them to mend roads, till there was nothing left but the foundation traces. That's where we are fortunate; this is one of the places where the Martian race perished, and there were no barbarians to come later and destroy what they had left." He puffed slowly at his pipe. "Some of these days, Martha, we are going to break into one of these buildings and find that it was one in which the last of these people died. Then we will learn the story of the end of this civilization."

And if we learn to read their language, we'll learn the whole story, not just the obituary. She hesitated, not putting the thought into words. "We'll find that, sometime, Selim," she said, then looked at her watch. "I'm going to get some more work done on my list, before dinner."

For an instant, the old man's face stiffened in disapproval; he started to say something, thought better of it, and put his pipe back into his mouth. The brief wrinkling around his mouth and the twitch of his white mustache had been enough, however; she knew what he was thinking. She was wasting time and effort, he believed; time and effort belonging not to herself but to the expedition. He could be right, too, she realized. But he had to be wrong; there had to be a way to do it. She turned from him silently and went to her own packing-case seat, at the middle of the table.

Photographs and photostats of restored pages of books, and transcripts of inscriptions, were piled in front of her, and the notebooks in which she was compiling her lists. She sat down, lighting a fresh cigarette, and reached over to a stack of unexamined material, taking off the top sheet. It was a photostat of what looked like the title page and contents of some sort of a periodical. She remembered it; she had found it herself, two days before, in a closet in the basement of the building she had just finished examining.

She sat for a moment, looking at it. It was readable, in the sense that she had set up a purely arbitrary but consistently pronounceable system of phonetic values for the letters. The long vertical symbols were vowels. There were only ten of them; not too many, allowing separate characters for long and short sounds. There were twenty of the short horizontal letters, which meant that sounds like -ng or -ch or -sh were single letters. The odds were millions to one against her system's being anything like the original sound of the language, but she had listed several thousand Martian words, and she could pronounce all of them.

And that was as far as it went. She could pronounce between three and four thousand Martian words, and she couldn't assign a meaning to one of them. Selim von Ohlmhorst believed that she never would. So did Tony Lattimer, and he was a great deal less reticent about saying so. So, she was sure, did Sachiko Koremitsu. There were times, now and then, when she began to be afraid that they were right.

The letters on the page in front of her began squirming and dancing, slender vowels with fat little consonants. They did that, now, every night in her dreams. And there were other dreams, in which she read them as easily as English; waking, she would try desperately and vainly to remember. She blinked, and looked away from the photostated page; when she looked back, the letters were behaving themselves again. There were three words at the top of the page, over-and-underlined, which seemed to be the Martian method of capitalization. *Mastbarnorvod Tadavas Sornbulva*. She pronounced them mentally, leafing through her notebooks to see if she had encountered them before, and in what contexts. All three were listed. In addition, *mastbar* was a fairly common word, and so was *norvod*, and so was *nor*, but *-vod* was a suffix and nothing but a suffix. *Davas*, was a word, too, and *ta-* was a common prefix; *sorn* and *bulva* were both common words. This language, she had long ago decided, must be something like German; when the Martians had needed a new word, they had just pasted a couple of existing words together. It would probably turn out to be a grammatical horror. Well, they had published magazines, and one of them had been called *Mastbarnorvod Tadavas Sornbulva*. She wondered if it had been something like the *Quarterly Archaeological Review*, or something more on the order of *Sexy Stories*.

A smaller line, under the title, was plainly the issue number and date; enough things had been found numbered in series to enable her to identify the numberals and determine that a decimal system of numeration had been used. This was the one thousand and seven hundred and fifty-fourth issue, for Doma, 14837; then Doma must be the name of one of the Martian months. The word had turned up several times before. She found herself puffing furiously on her cigarette as she leafed through notebooks and piles of already examined material.

Sachiko was speaking to somebody, and a chair scraped at the end of the table. She raised her head, to see a big man with red hair and a red face, in Space Force green, with the single star of a major on his shoulder, sitting down. Ivan Fitzgerald, the medic. He was lifting weights from a book similar to the one the girl ordinance officer was restoring.

"Haven't had time, lately," he was saying, in reply to Sachiko's question. "The Finchley girl's still down with whatever it is she has, and it's something I haven't been able to diagnose yet. And I've been checking on bacteria cultures, and in what spare time I have, I've been dissecting specimens for Bill Chandler. Bill's finally found a mammal. Looks like a lizard, and it's only four inches long, but it's a real warm-blooded, gamogenetic, placental, viviparous mammal. Burrows, and seems to live on what pass for insects here."

"Is there enough oxygen for anything like that?" Sachiko was asking.

"Seems to be, close to the ground." Fitzgerald got the headband of his loup adjusted, and pulled it down over his eyes. "He found this thing in a ravine down on the sea bottom— Ha, this page seems to be intact; now, if I can get it out all in one piece—"

He went on talking inaudibly to himself, lifting the page a little at a time and sliding one of the transparent plastic sheets under it, working with minute delicacy. Not the delicacy of the Japanese girl's small hands, moving like the paws of a cat washing her face, but like a steam-hammer cracking a peanut. Field archaeology requires a certain delicacy of touch, too, but Martha watched the pair of them with envious admiration. Then she turned back to her own work, finishing the table of contents.

The next page was the beginning of the first article listed; many of the words were unfamiliar. She had the impression that this must be some kind of scientific or technical journal; that could be because such publications made up the bulk of her own periodical reading. She doubted if it were fiction; the paragraphs had a solid, factual look.

At length, Ivan Fitzgerald gave a short, explosive grunt.

"Ha! Got it!"

She looked up. He had detached the page and was cementing another plastic sheet onto it.

"Any pictures?" she asked.

"None on this side. Wait a moment." He turned the sheet. "None on this side, either." He sprayed another sheet of plastic to sandwich the page, then picked up his pipe and relighted it.

"I get fun out of this, and it's good practice for my hands, so don't think I'm complaining," he said, "but, Martha, do you honestly think anybody's ever going to get anything out of this?"

Sachiko held up a scrap of the silicone plastic the Martians had used for paper with her tweezers. It was almost an inch square.

"Look; three whole words on this piece," she crowed. "Ivan, you took the easy book."

Fitzgerald wasn't being sidetracked. "This stuff's absolutely meaningless," he continued. "It had a meaning fifty thousand years ago, when it was written, but it has none at all now."

She shook her head. "Meaning isn't something that evaporates with time," she argued. "It has just as much meaning now as it ever had. We just haven't learned how to decipher it."

"That seems like a pretty pointless distinction," Selim von Ohlmhorst joined the conversation. "There no longer exists a means of deciphering it."

"We'll find one." She was speaking, she realized, more in self encouragement than in controversy.

"How? From pictures and captions? We've found captioned pictures, and what have they given us? A caption is intended to explain the picture, not the picture to explain the caption. Suppose some alien to our culture found a picture of a man with a white beard and mustache sawing a billet from a log. He would think the caption meant, 'Man Sawing Wood.' How would he know that it was really 'Wilhelm II in Exile at Doorn'?''

Sachiko had taken off her loup and was lighting a cigarette.

"I can think of pictures intended to explain their captions," she said. "These picture language-books, the sort we use in the Service—little line drawings, with a word or phrase under them."

"Well, of course, if we found something like that," von Ohlmhorst began.

"Michael Ventris found something like that, back in the Fifties." Hubert Penrose's voice broke in from directly behind her.

She turned her head. The colonel was standing by the archaeologists' table; Captain Field and the airdyne pilot had gone out.

"He found a lot of Greek inventories of military stores," Penrose continued. "They were in Cretan Linear B script, and at the head of each list was a little picture, a sword or a helmet or a cooking tripod or a chariot wheel. That's what gave him the key to the script."

"Colonel's getting to be quite an archaeologist," Fitzgerald commented. "We're all learning each other's specialities, on this expedition."

"I heard about that long before this expedition was even contemplated." Penrose was tapping a cigarette on his gold case. "I heard about that back before the Thirty Days' War, at Intelligence School, when I was a lieutenant. As a feat of cryptanalysis, not an archaeological discovery."

"Yes, cryptanalysis," von Ohlmhorst pounced. "The reading of a known language in an unknown form of writing. Ventris' lists were in the known language, Greek. Neither he nor anybody else ever read a word of the Cretan language until the finding of the Greek-Cretan bilingual in 1963, because only with a bilingual text, one language already known, can an unknown ancient language be learned. And what hope, I ask you, have we of finding anything like that here? Martha, you've been working on these Martian texts ever since we landed here—for the last six months. Tell me, have you found a single word to which you can positively assign a meaning?"

"Yes, I think I have one." She was trying hard not to sound too exultant. "*Doma*. It's the name of one of the months of the Martian calendar."

"Where did you find that?" von Ohlmhorst asked. "And how did you establish—?"

"Here." She picked up the photostat and handed it along the table to him. "I'd call this the title page of a magazine."

He was silent for a moment, looking at it. "Yes. I would say so, too. Have you any of the rest of it?"

"I'm working on the first page of the first article, listed there. Wait till I see; yes, here's all I found, together, here." She told him where she had gotten it. "I just gathered it up, at the time, and gave it to Geoffrey and Rosita to photostat. This is the first I've really examined it."

The old man got to his feet, brushing tobacco ashes from the front of his jacket, and came to where she was sitting, laying the title page on the table and leafing quickly through the stack of photostats.

"Yes, and here is the second article, on page eight, and here's the next one." He finished the pile of photostats. "A couple of pages missing at the end of the last article. This is remarkable; surprising that a thing like a magazine would have survived so long."

"Well, this silicone stuff the Martians used for paper is pretty durable," Hubert Penrose said. "There doesn't seem to have been any water or any other fluid in it originally, so it wouldn't dry out with time."

"Oh, it's not remarkable that the material would have survived. We've found a good many books and papers in excellent condition. But only a really vital culture, an organized culture, will publish magazines, and this civilization had been dying for hundreds of years before the end. It might have been a thousand years before the time they died out completely that such activities as publishing ended."

"Well, look where I found it; in a closet in a cellar. Tossed in there and forgotten, and then ignored when they were stripping the building. Things like that happen."

Penrose had picked up the title page and was looking at it.

"I don't think there's any doubt about this being a magazine, at all." He looked again at the title, his lips moving silently. "*Mastbarnorvod Tadavas Sornbulva*. Wonder what it means. But you're right about the date—*Doma* seems to be the name of a month. Yes, you have a word, Dr. Dane."

Sid Chamberlain, seeing that something unusual was going on, had come over from the table at which he was working. After examining the title page and some of the inside pages, he began whispering into the stenophone he had taken from his belt.

"Don't try to blow this up to anything big, Sid," she cautioned. "All we have is the name of a month, and Lord only knows how long it'll be till we even find out which month it was."

"Well, it's a start, isn't it?" Penrose argued. "Grotefend only had the word for 'king' when he started reading Persian cuneiform."

"But I don't have the word for month; just the name of a month. Everybody knew the names of the Persian kings, long before Grotefend."

"That's not the story," Chamberlain said. "What the public back on Terra will be interested in is finding out that the Martians published magazines, just like we do. Something familiar; make the Martians seem more real. More human."

Three men had come in, and were removing their masks and helmets and oxy-tanks, and peeling out of their quilted coveralls. Two were Space Force lieutenants; the third was a youngish civilian with close-cropped blond hair, in a checked woolen shirt. Tony Lattimer and his helpers.

"Don't tell me Martha finally got something out of that stuff?" he asked, approaching the table. He might have been commenting on the antics of the village half-wit, from his tone.

"Yes; the name of one of the Martian months." Hubert Penrose went on to explain, showing the photostat.

Tony Lattimer took it, glanced at it, and dropped it on the table.

"Sounds plausible, of course, but just an assumption. That word may not be the name of a month, at all—could mean 'published' or 'authorized' or 'copyrighted' or anything like that. Fact is, I don't think it's more than a wild guess that that thing's anything like a periodical." He dismissed the subject and turned to Penrose. "I picked out the next building to enter; that tall one with the conical thing on top. It ought to be in pretty good shape inside, the conical top wouldn't allow dust to accumulate, and from the outside nothing seems to be caved in or crushed. Ground level's higher than the other one, about the seventh floor. I found a good place and drilled for the shots; tomorrow I'll blast a hole in it, and if you can spare some people to help, we can start exploring it right away."

"Yes, of course, Dr. Lattimer. I can spare about a dozen, and I suppose you can find a few civilian volunteers," Penrose told him. "What will you need in the way of equipment?"

"Oh, about six demolition-packets; they can all be shot together. And the usual thing in the way of lights, and breaking and digging tools, and climbing equipment in case we run into broken or doubtful stairways. We'll divide into two parties. Nothing ought to be entered for the first time without a qualified archaeologist along. Three parties, if Martha can tear herself away from this catalogue of systematized incomprehensibilities she's making long enough to do some real work."

She felt her chest tighten and her face become stiff. She was pressing her lips together to lock in a furious retort when Hubert Penrose answered for her.

"Dr. Dane's been doing as much work, and as important work, as you have," he said brusquely. "More important work, I'd be inclined to say."

Von Ohlmhorst was visibly distressed; he glanced once toward Sid Chamberlain, then looked hastily away from him. Afraid of a story of dissension among archaeologists getting out.

"Working out a system of pronunciation by which the Martian language could be transliterated was a most important contribution," he said. "And Martha did that almost unassisted."

"Unassisted by Dr. Lattimer, anyway," Penrose added. "Captain Field and Lieutenant Koremitsu did some work, and I helped out a little, but nine-tenths of it she did herself."

"Purely arbitrary," Lattimer disdained. "Why, we don't even know that the Martians could make the same kind of vocal sounds we do."

"Oh, yes, we do," Ivan Fitzgerald contradicted, safe on his own ground. "I haven't seen any actual Martian skulls—these people seem to have been very tidy about disposing of their dead—but from statues and busts and pictures I've seen, I'd say that their vocal organs were identical with our own."

"Well, grant that. And grant that it's going to be impressive to rattle off the names of Martian notables whose statues we find, and that if we're ever able to attribute any place-names, they'll sound a lot better than this horse-doctors' Latin the old astronomers splashed all over the map of Mars," Lattimer said. "What I object to is her wasting time on this stuff, of which nobody will ever be able to read a word if she fiddles around with those lists till there's another hundred feet of loess on this city, when there's so much real work to be done and we're as shorthanded as we are."

That was the first time that had come out in just so many words. She was glad Lattimer had said it and not Selim von Ohlmhorst.

"What you mean," she retorted, "is that it doesn't have the publicity value that digging up statues has."

For an instant, she could see that the shot had scored. Then Lattimer, with a side glance at Chamberlain, answered:

"What I mean is that you're trying to find something that any archaeologist, yourself included, should know doesn't exist. I don't object to your gambling your professional reputation and making a laughing stock of yourself; what I object to is that the blunders of one archaeologist discredit the whole subject in the eyes of the public."

That seemed to be what worried Lattimer most. She was framing a reply when the communication-outlet whistled shrilly, and then squawked: "Cocktail time! One hour to dinner; cocktails in the library, Hut Four!"

The library, which was also lounge, recreation room, and general gathering-place, was already crowded; most of the crowd was at the long table topped with sheets of glasslike plastic that had been wall panels out of one of the ruined buildings. She poured herself what passed, here, for a martini, and carried it over to where Selim von Ohlmhorst was sitting alone.

For a while, they talked about the building they had just finished exploring, then drifted into reminiscences of their work on Terra—von Ohlmhorst's in Asia Minor, with the Hittite Empire, and hers in Pakistan, excavating the cities of the Harappa Civilization. They finished their drinks—the ingredients were plentiful; alcohol and flavoring extracts synthesized from Martian vegetation—and von Ohlmhorst took the two glasses to the table for refills.

"You know, Martha," he said, when he returned, "Tony was right about one thing. You are gambling your professional standing and reputation. It's against all archaeological experience that a language so completely dead as this one could be deciphered. There was a continuity between all the other ancient languages—by knowing Greek, Champollion learned to read Egyptian; by knowing Egyptian, Hittite was learned. That's why you and your colleagues have never been able to translate the Harappa hieroglyphics; no such continuity exists there. If you insist that this utterly dead language can be read, your reputation will suffer for it."

"I heard Colonel Penrose say, once, that an officer who's afraid to risk his military reputation seldom makes much of a reputation. It's the same with us. If we really

H. Beam Piper

ant to find things out, we have to risk making mistakes. And I'm a lot more interested in finding things out than I am in my reputation."

She glanced across the room, to where Tony Lattimer was sitting with Gloria Standish, talking earnestly, while Gloria sipped one of the counterfeit martinis and listened. Gloria was the leading contender for the title of Miss Mars, 1996, if you liked big bosomy blondes, but Tony would have been just as attentive to her if she'd looked like the Wicked Witch in "The Wizard of Oz," because Gloria was the Pan-Federation Telecast System commentator with the expedition.

"I know you are," the old Turco-German was saying. "That's why, when they asked me to name another archaeologist for this expedition, I named you."

He hadn't named Tony Lattimer; Lattimer had been pushed onto the expedition by his university. There'd been a lot of high-level string-pulling to that; she wished she knew the whole story. She'd managed to keep clear of universities and university politics; all her digs had been sponsored by non-academic foundations or art museums.

"You have an excellent standing; much better than my own, at your age. That's why it disturbs me to see you jeopardizing it by this insistence that the Martian language can be translated. I can't, really, see how you can hope to succeed."

She shrugged and drank some more of her cocktail, then lit another cigarette. It was getting tiresome to try to verbalize something she only felt.

"Neither do I, now, but I will. Maybe I'll find something like the picture-books Sachiko was talking about. A child's primer, maybe; surely they had things like that. And if I don't, I'll find something else. We've only been here six months. I can wait the rest of my life, if I have to, but I'll do it sometime."

"I can't wait so long," von Ohlmhorst said. "The rest of my life will only be a few years, and when the *Schiaparelli* orbits in, I'll be going back to Terra on the *Cyrano*."

"I wish you wouldn't. This is a whole new world of archaeology. Literally."

"Yes." He finished the cocktail and looked at his pipe as though wondering whether to re-light it so soon before dinner, then put it in his pocket. "A whole new world—but I've grown old, and it isn't for me. I've spent my life studying the Hittites. I can speak the Hittite language, though maybe King Muwatallis wouldn't be able to understand my modern Turkish accent. But the things I'd have to learn, here—chemistry, physics, engineering, how to run analytic tests on steel girders and beryllo-silver alloys and plastics and silicones. I'm more at home with a civilization that rode in chariots and fought with swords and was just learning how to work iron. Mars is for young people. This expedition is a cadre of leadership—not only the Space Force people, who'll be the commanders of the main expedition, but us scientists, too. And I'm just an old cavalry general who can't learn to command tanks and aircraft. You'll have time to learn about Mars. I won't."

His reputation as the dean of Hittitologists was solid and secure, too, she added mentally. Then she felt ashamed of the thought. He wasn't to be classed with Tony Lattimer.

"All I came for was to get the work started," he was continuing. "The Federation Government felt that an old hand should do that. Well, it's started, now; you and Tony and whoever come out on the *Schiaparelli* must carry it on. You said it, yourself you have a whole new world. This is only one city, of the last Martian civilization Behind this, you have the Late Upland Culture, and the Canal Builders, and all the civilizations and races and empires before them, clear back to the Martian Stone Age.' He hesitated for a moment. "You have no idea what all you have to learn, Martha This isn't the time to start specializing too narrowly."

They all got out of the truck and stretched their legs and looked up the road to the tall building with the queer conical cap askew on its top. The four little figures that had been busy against its wall climbed into the jeep and started back slowly, the smallest of them, Sachiko Koremitsu, playing out an electric cable behind. When it pulled up beside the truck, they climbed out; Sachiko attached the free end of the cable to a nuclear-electric battery. At once, dirty gray smoke and orange dust puffed out from the wall of the building, and, a second later, the multiple explosion banged

She and Tony Lattimer and Major Lindemann climbed onto the truck, leaving the jeep standing by the road. When they reached the building, a satisfyingly wide breach had been blown in the wall. Lattimer had placed his shots between two of the windows they were both blown out along with the wall between, and lay unbroken on the ground. Martha remembered the first building they had entered. A Space Force office had picked up a stone and thrown it at one of the windows, thinking that would be all they'd need to do. It had bounced back. He had drawn his pistol—they'd all carried guns, then, on the principle that what they didn't know about Mars might easily hurt them—and fired four shots. The bullets had ricochetted, screaming thinly; there were four coppery smears of jacket-metal on the window, and a little surface spalling Somebody tried a rifle; the 4000-f.s. bullet had cracked the glasslike pane without penetrating. An oxyacetylene torch had taken an hour to cut the window out; the lab crew, aboard the ship, were still trying to find out just what the stuff was.

Tony Lattimer had gone forward and was sweeping his flashlight back and forth swearing petulantly, his voice harshened and amplified by his helmet-speaker.

"I thought I was blasting into a hallway; this lets us into a room. Careful; there' about a two-foot drop to the floor, and a lot of rubble from the blast just inside."

He stepped down through the breach; the others began dragging equipment out of the trucks—shovels and picks and crowbars and sledges, portable floodlights, cameras sketching materials, an extension ladder, even Alpinists' ropes and crampons and pickaxes. Hubert Penrose was shouldering something that looked like a surrealist machine gun but which was really a nuclear-electric jack-hammer. Martha selected one of the spike-shod mountaineer's ice axes, with which she could dig or chop or poke or pry or help herself over rough footing.

The windows, grimed and crusted with fifty millennia of dust, filtered in a dim twilight; even the breach in the wall, in the morning shade, lighted only a small patch of floor. Somebody snapped on a floodlight, aiming it at the ceiling. The big room was empty and bare; dust lay thick on the floor and reddened the once-white walls. It could have been a large office, but there was nothing left in it to indicate its use.

"This one's been stripped up to the seventh floor!" Lattimer exclaimed. "Street level'll be cleaned out, completely."

"Do for living quarters and shops, then," Lindemann said. "Added to the others, this'll take care of everybody on the *Schiaparelli*."

"Seem to have been a lot of electric or electronic apparatus over along this wall," one of the Space Force officers commented. "Ten or twelve electric outlets." He brushed the dusty wall with his glove, then scraped on the floor with his foot. "I can see where things were pried loose."

The door, one of the double sliding things the Martians had used, was closed. Selim von Ohlmhorst tried it, but it was stuck fast. The metal latch-parts had frozen together, molecule bonding itself to molecule, since the door had last been closed. Hubert Penrose came over with the jack-hammer, fitting a spear-point chisel into place. He set the chisel in the joint between the doors, braced the hammer against his hip, and squeezed the trigger-switch. The hammer banged briefly like the weapon it resembled, and the doors popped a few inches apart, then stuck. Enough dust had worked into the recesses into which it was supposed to slide to block it on both sides.

That was old stuff; they ran into that every time they had to force a door, and they were prepared for it. Somebody went outside and brought in a power-jack and finally one of the doors inched back to the door jamb. That was enough to get the lights and equipment through; they all passed from the room to the hallway beyond. About half the other doors were open; each had a number and a single word, *Darfbulva*, over it.

One of the civilian volunteers, a woman professor of natural ecology from Penn State University, was looking up and down the hall.

"You know," she said, "I feel at home here. I think this was a college of some sort and these were classrooms. That word, up there, that was the subject taught, or the department. And those electronic devices, all where the class would face them; audio-visual teaching aids."

"A twenty-five-story university?" Lattimer scoffed. "Why, a building like this would handle thirty thousand students."

"Maybe there were that many. This was a big city, in its prime," Martha said, moved chiefly by a desire to oppose Lattimer.

"Yes, but think of the snafu in the halls, every time they changed classes. It'd take half an hour to get everybody back and forth from one floor to another." He turned to von Ohlmhorst. "I'm going up above this floor. This place has been looted clean up to here, but there's a chance there may be something above," he said.

"I'll stay on this floor, at present," the Turco-German replied. "There will be much coming and going, and dragging things in and out. We should get this completely examined and recorded first. Then Major Lindemann's people can do their worst, here.''

"Well, if nobody else wants it, I'll take the downstairs," Martha said.

"I'll go along with you," Hubert Penrose told her. "If the lower floors have no archaeological value, we'll turn them into living quarters. I like this building; it'll give everybody room to keep out from under everybody else's feet." He looked down the hall. "We ought to find escalators at the middle."

The hallway, too, was thick underfoot with dust. Most of the open rooms were empty, but a few contained furniture, including small seat-desks. The original proponent of the university theory pointed these out as just what might be found in classrooms. There were escalators, up and down, on either side of the hall, and more on the intersecting passage to the right.

"That's how they handled the students, between classes," Martha commented. "And I'll bet there are more ahead, there."

They came to a stop where the hallway ended at a great square central hall. There were elevators, there, on two of the sides, and four escalators, still usable as stairways. But it was the walls, and the paintings on them, that brought them up short and staring.

They were clouded with dirt—she was trying to imagine what they must have looked like originally, and at the same time estimating the labor that would be involved in cleaning them—but they were still distinguishable, as was the word, *Darfbulva*, in golden letters above each of the four sides. It was a moment before she realized, from the murals, that she had at last found a meaningful Martian word. They were a vast historical panorama, clockwise around the room. A group of skin-clad savages squatting around a fire. Hunters with bows and spears, carrying the carcass of an animal slightly like a pig. Nomads riding long-legged, graceful mounts like hornless deer. Peasants sowing and reaping; mud-walled hut villages, and cities; processions of priests and warriors; battles with swords and bows, and with cannon and muskets; galleys, and ships with sails, and ships without visible means of propulsion, and aircraft. Changing costumes and weapons and machines and styles of architecture. A richly fertile landscape, gradually merging into barren deserts and bushlands—the time of the great planet-wide drought. The Canal Builders—men with machines recognizable as steam-shovels and derricks, digging and quarrying and driving across the empty plains with aquaducts. More cities—seaports on the shrinking oceans; dwindling, half-deserted cities; an abandoned city, with four tiny humanoid figures and a thing like a combat-car in the middle of a brush-grown plaza, they and their vehicle dwarfed by the huge lifeless buildings around them. She had not the least doubt; *Darfbulva* was History.

"Wonderful!" von Ohlmhorst was saying. "The entire history of this race. Why, if the painter depicted appropriate costumes and weapons and machines for each period, and got the architecture right, we can break the history of this planet into eras and periods and civilizations."

H. Beam Piper

"You can assume they're authentic. The faculty of this university would insist on authenticity in the *Darfbulva*—History—Department," she said.

"Yes! *Darfbulva*—History! And your magazine was a journal of *Sornbulva*!" Penrose exclaimed. "You have a word, Martha!" It took her an instant to realize that he had called her by her first name, and not Dr. Dane. She wasn't sure if that weren't a bigger triumph than learning a word of the Martian language. Or a more auspicious start. "Alone, I suppose that *bulva* means something like science or knowledge, or study; combined, it would be equivalent to our 'ology. And *darf* would mean something like past, or old times, or human events, or chronicles."

"That gives you three words, Martha!" Sachiko jubilated. "You did it."

"Let's don't go too fast," Lattimer said, for once not derisively. "I'll admit that *darfbulva* is the Martian word for history as a subject of study; I'll admit that *bulva* is the general word and *darf* modifies it and tells us which subject is meant. But as for assigning specific meanings, we can't do that because we don't know just how the Martians thought, scientifically or otherwise."

He stopped short, startled by the blue-white light that blazed as Sid Chamberlain's Kliegettes went on. When the whirring of the camera stopped, it was Chamberlain who was speaking:

"This is the biggest thing yet; the whole history of Mars, stone age to the end, all on four walls. I'm taking this with the fast shutter, but we'll telecast it in slow motion, from the beginning to the end. Tony, I want you to do the voice for it—running commentary, interpretation of each scene as it's shown. Would you do that?"

Would he do that! Martha thought. If he had a tail, he'd be wagging it at the very thought.

"Well, there ought to be more murals on the other floors," she said. "Who wants to come downstairs with us?"

Sachiko did; immediately, Ivan Fitzgerald volunteered. Sid decided to go upstairs with Tony Lattimer, and Gloria Standish decided to go upstairs, too. Most of the party would remain on the seventh floor, to help Selim von Ohlmhorst get it finished. After poking tentatively at the escalator with the spike of her ice axe, Martha led the way downward.

The sixth floor was *Darfbulva*, too; military and technological history, from the character of the murals. They looked around the central hall, and went down to the fifth; it was like the floors above except that the big quadrangle was stacked with dusty furniture and boxes. Ivan Fitzgerald, who was carrying the floodlight, swung it slowly around. Here the murals were of heroic-sized Martians, so human in appearance as to seem members of her own race, each holding some object—a book, or a testube, or some bit of scientific apparatus, and behind them were scenes of laboratories and factories, flame and smoke, lightning-flashes. The word at the top of each of the four walls was one with which she was already familiar—*Sornbulva*.

Omnilingual

"Hey, Martha; there's that word." Ivan Fitzgerald exclaimed. "The one in the title of your magazine." He looked at the paintings. "Chemistry, or physics."

"Both," Hubert Penrose considered. "I don't think the Martians made any sharp distinction between them. See, the old fellow with the scraggly whiskers must be the inventor of the spectroscope; he has one in his hands, and he has a rainbow behind him. And the woman in the blue smock, beside him, worked in organic chemistry; see the diagrams of long-chain molecules behind her. What word would convey the idea of chemistry and physics taken as one subject?"

"*Sornbulva*," Sachiko suggested. "If *bulva*'s something like science, *sorn* must mean matter, or substance, or physical object. You were right, all along, Martha. A civilization like this would certainly leave something like this, that would be self-explanatory."

"This'll wipe a little more of that superior grin off Tony Lattimer's face," Fitzgerald was saying, as they went down the motionless escalator to the floor below. "Tony wants to be a big shot. When you want to be a big shot, you can't bear the possibility of anybody else's being a bigger big shot, and whoever makes a start on reading this language will be the biggest big shot archaeology ever saw."

That was true. She hadn't thought of it in that way before, and now she tried not to think about it. She didn't want to be a big shot. She wanted to be able to read the Martian language, and find things out about the Martians.

Two escalators down, they came out on a mezzanine around a wide central hall on the street level, the floor forty feet below them and the ceiling thirty feet above. Their lights picked out object after object below—a huge group of sculptured figures in the middle; some kind of a motor vehicle jacked up on trestles for repairs; things that looked like machine-guns and auto-cannon; long tables, tops littered with a dust-covered miscellany; machinery; boxes and crates and containers.

They made their way down and walked among the clutter, missing a hundred things for every one they saw, until they found an escalator to the basement. There were three basements, one under another, until at last they stood at the bottom of the last escalator, on a bare concrete floor, swinging the portable floodlight over stacks of boxes and barrels and drums, and heaps of powdery dust. The boxes were plastic—nobody had ever found anything made of wood in the city—and the barrels and drums were of metal or glass or some glasslike substance. They were outwardly intact. The powdery heaps might have been anything organic, or anything containing fluid. Down here, where wind and dust could not reach, evaporation had been the only force of destruction after the minute life that caused putrefaction had vanished.

They found refrigeration rooms, too, and using Martha's ice axe and the pistol-like vibratool Sachiko carried on her belt, they pounded and pried one open, to find dessicated piles of what had been vegetables, and leathery chunks of meat. Samples of that stuff, rocketed up to the ship, would give a reliable estimate, by radio-carbon dating, of how long ago this building had been occupied. The refrigeration unit, radically different from anything their own culture had produced, had been electrically powered. Sachiko and Penrose, poking into it, found the switches still on; the machine had only ceased to function when the power-source, whatever that had been, had failed.

The middle basement had also been used, at least toward the end, for storage; it was cut in half by a partition pierced by but one door. They took half an hour to force this, and were on the point of sending above for heavy equipment when it yielded enough for them to squeeze through. Fitzgerald, in the lead with the light, stopped short, looked around, and then gave a groan that came through his helmet-speaker like a foghorn.

"Oh, no! *No!*"

"What's the matter, Ivan?" Sachiko, entering behind him, asked anxiously.

He stepped aside. "Look at it, Sachi! Are we going to have to do all that?"

Martha crowded through behind her friend and looked around, then stood motionless, dizzy with excitement. Books. Case on case of books, half an acre of cases, fifteen feet to the ceiling. Fitzgerald, and Penrose, who had pushed in behind her, were talking in rapid excitement; she only heard the sound of their voices, not their words. This must be the main stacks of the university library—the entire literature of the vanished race of Mars. In the center, down an aisle between the cases, she could see the hollow square of the librarians' desk, and stairs and a dumb-waiter to the floor above.

She realized that she was walking forward, with the others, toward this. Sachiko was saying: "I'm the lightest; let me go first." She must be talking about the spidery metal stairs.

"I'd say they were safe," Penrose answered. "The trouble we've had with doors around here shows that the metal hasn't deteriorated."

In the end, the Japanese girl led the way, more catlike than ever in her caution. The stairs were quite sound, in spite of their fragile appearance, and they all followed her. The floor above was a duplicate of the room they had entered, and seemed to contain about as many books. Rather than waste time forcing the door here, they returned to the middle basement and came up by the escalator down which they had originally descended.

The upper basement contained kitchens—electric stoves, some with pots and pans still on them—and a big room that must have been, originally, the students' dining room, though when last used it had been a workshop. As they expected, the library reading room was on the street-level floor, directly above the stacks. It seemed to have been converted into a sort of common living room for the building's last occupants. An adjoining auditorium had been made into a chemical works; there were vats and distillation apparatus, and a metal fractionating tower that extended through a hole knocked in the ceiling seventy feet above. A good deal of plastic furniture of the sort they had been finding everywhere in the city was stacked about, some of it broken up, apparently for reprocessing. The other rooms on the street floor seemed also to have been devoted to manufacturing and repair work; a considerable industry, along a number of lines, must have been carried on here for a long time after the university had ceased to function as such.

On the second floor, they found a museum; many of the exhibits remained, tantalizingly half-visible in grimed glass cases. There had been administrative offices there, too. The doors of most of them were closed, and they did not waste time trying to force them, but those that were open had been turned into living quarters. They made notes, and rough floor-plans, to guide them in future more thorough examinations; it was almost noon before they had worked their way back to the seventh floor.

Selim von Ohlmhorst was in a room on the north side of the building, sketching the position of things before examining them and collecting them for removal. He had the floor checkerboarded with a grid of chalked lines, each numbered.

"We have everything on this floor photographed," he said. "I have three gangs—all the floodlights I have—sketching and making measurements. At the rate we're going, with time out for lunch, we'll be finished by the middle of the afternoon."

"You've been working fast. Evidently you aren't being high-church about a 'qualified archaeologist' entering rooms first," Penrose commented.

"Ach, childishness!" the old man exclaimed impatiently. "These officers of yours aren't fools. All of them have been to Intelligence School and Criminal Investigation School. Some of the most careful amateur archaeologists I ever knew were retired soldiers or policemen. But there isn't much work to be done. Most of the rooms are either empty or like this one—a few bits of furniture and broken trash and scraps of paper. Did you find anything down on the lower floors?"

"Well, yes," Penrose said, a hint of mirth in his voice. "What would you say, Martha?"

She started to tell Selim. The others, unable to restrain their excitement, broke in with interruptions. Von Ohlmhorst was staring in incredulous amazement.

"But this floor was looted almost clean, and the buildings we've entered before were all looted from the street level up," he said, at length.

"The people who looted this one lived here," Penrose replied. "They had electric power to the last; we found refrigerators full of food, and stoves with the dinner still on them. They must have used the elevators to haul things down from the upper floor. The whole first floor was converted into workshops and laboratories. I think that this place must have been something like a monastery in the Dark Ages in Europe, or what such a monastery would have been like if the Dark Ages had followed the fall of a highly developed scientific civilization. For one thing, we found a lot of machine guns and light auto-cannon on the street level, and all the doors were barricaded. The people here were trying to keep a civilization running after the rest of the planet had gone back to barbarism; I suppose they'd have to fight off raids by the barbarians now and then."

"You're not going to insist on making this building into expedition quarters, I hope, colonel?" Ohlmhorst asked anxiously.

"Oh, no! This place is an archaeological treasure-house. More than that; from what I saw, our technicians can learn a lot, here. But you'd better get this floor cleaned up as soon as you can, though. I'll have the subsurface part, from the sixth floor down, airsealed. Then we'll put in oxygen generators and power units, and get a couple of elevators into service. For the floors above, we can use temporary airsealing floor by floor, and portable equipment; when we have things atmosphered and lighted and heated, you and Martha and Tony Lattimer can go to work systematically and in comfort, and I'll give you all the help I can spare from the other work. This is one of the biggest things we've found yet."

Tony Lattimer and his companions came down to the seventh floor a little later.

"I don't get this, at all," he began, as soon as he joined them. "This building wasn't stripped the way the others were. Always, the procedure seems to have been to strip from the bottom up, but they seem to have stripped the top floors first, here. All but the very top. I found out what that conical thing is, by the way. It's a wind-rotor, and under it there's an electric generator. This building generated its own power."

"What sort of condition are the generators in?" Penrose asked.

"Well, everything's full of dust that blew in under the rotor, of course, but it looks to be in pretty good shape. Hey, I'll bet that's it! They had power, so they used the elevators to haul stuff down. That's just what they did. Some of the floors above here don't seem to have been touched, though." He paused momentarily; back of his oxy-mask, he seemed to be grinning. "I don't know that I ought to mention this in front of Martha, but two floors above we hit a room—it must have been the reference library for one of the departments—that had close to five hundred books in it."

The noise that interrupted him, like the squawking of a Brobdingnagian parrot, was only Ivan Fitzgerald laughing through his helmet-speaker.

Lunch at the huts was a hasty meal, with a gabble of full-mouthed and excited talking. Hubert Penrose and his chief subordinates snatched their food in a huddled consultation at one end of the table; in the afternoon, work was suspended on everything else and the fifty-odd men and women of the expedition concentrated their efforts on the University. By the middle of the afternoon, the seventh floor had been completely examined, photographed and sketched, and the murals in the square central hall covered with protective tarpaulins, and Laurent Gicquel and his airsealing crew had moved in and were at work. It had been decided to seal the central hall at the entrances. It took the French-Canadian engineer most of the afternoon to find all the ventilation-ducts and plug them. An elevator-shaft on the north side was found reaching clear to the twenty-fifth floor; this would give access to the top of the building; another shaft, from the center, would take care of the floors below. Nobody seemed willing to trust the ancient elevators, themselves; it was the next evening before a couple of cats and the necessary machinery could be fabricated in the machine shops aboard the ship and sent down by landing-rocket. By that time, the airsealing was finished, the nuclear-electric energy-converters were in place, and the oxygen generators set up.

Martha was in the lower basement, an hour or so before lunch the day after, when a couple of Space Force officers came out of the elevator, bringing extra lights with them. She was still using oxygen-equipment; it was a moment before she realized that the newcomers had no masks, and that one of them was smoking. She took off her own helmet-speaker, throat-mike and mask and unslung her tank-pack, breathing cautiously. The air was chilly, and musty-acrid with the odor of antiquity—the first Martian odor she had smelled—but when she lit a cigarette, the lighter flamed clear and steady and the tobacco caught and burned evenly.

The archaeologists, many of the other civilian scientists, a few of the Space Force officers and the two news-correspondents, Sid Chamberlain and Gloria Standish, moved in that evening, setting up cots in vacant rooms. They installed electric stoves and a refrigerator in the old Library Reading Room, and put in a bar and lunch counter. For a few days, the place was full of noise and activity, then, gradually, the Space Force people and all but a few of the civilians returned to their own work. There was still the business of airsealing the more habitable of the buildings already explored, and fitting them up in readiness for the arrival, in a year and a half, of the five hundred members of the main expedition. There was work to be done enlarging the landing field for the ship's rocket craft, and building new chemical-fuel tanks.

There was the work of getting the city's ancient reservoirs cleared of silt before the next spring thaw brought more water down the underground aquaducts everybody called canals in mistranslation of Schiaparelli's Italian word, though this was proving considerably easier than anticipated. The ancient Canal-Builders must have anticipated a time when their descendants would no longer be capable of maintenance work, and had prepared against it. By the day after the University had been made completely habitable, the actual work there was being done by Selim, Tony Lattimer and herself, with half a dozen Space Force officers, mostly girls, and four or five civilians, helping.

They worked up from the bottom, dividing the floor-surfaces into numbered squares, measuring and listing and sketching and photographing. They packaged samples of organic matter and sent them up to the ship for Carbon-14 dating and analysis; they opened cans and jars and bottles, and found that everything fluid in them had evaporated, through the porosity of glass and metal and plastic if there were no other way. Wherever they looked, they found evidence of activity suddenly suspended and never resumed. A vise with a bar of metal in it, half cut through and the hacksaw beside it. Pots and pans with hardened remains of food in them; a leathery cut of meat on a table, with the knife ready at hand. Toilet articles on washstands; unmade beds, the bedding ready to crumble at a touch but still retaining the impress of the sleeper's body; papers and writing materials on desks, as though the writer had gotten up, meaning to return and finish in a fifty-thousand-year-ago moment.

It worried her. Irrationally, she began to feel that the Martians had never left this place; that they were still around her, watching disapprovingly every time she picked up something they had laid down. They haunted her dreams, now, instead of their enigmatic writing. At first, everybody who had moved into the University had taken a separate room, happy to escape the crowding and lack of privacy of the huts. After a few nights, she was glad when Gloria Standish moved in with her, and accepted the newswoman's excuse that she felt lonely without somebody to talk to before falling asleep. Sachiko Koremitsu joined them the next evening, and before going to bed, the girl officer cleaned and oiled her pistol, remarking that she was afraid some rust may have gotten into it.

The others felt it, too. Selim von Ohlmhcrst developed the habit of turning quickly and looking behind him, as though trying to surprise somebody or something that was stalking him. Tony Lattimer, having a drink at the bar that had been improvised from the librarian's desk in the Reading Room, set down his glass and swore.

"You know what this place is? It's an archaeological *Marie Celeste*!" he declared. "It was occupied right up to the end—we've all seen the shifts these people used to keep a civilization going here—but what was the end? What happened to them? Where did they go?"

"You didn't expect them to be waiting out front, with a red carpet and a big banner, *Welcome Terrans*, did you, Tony?" Gloria Standish asked.

"No, of course not; they've all been dead for fifty thousand years. But if they were the last of the Martians, why haven't we found their bones, at least? Who buried them, after they were dead?" He looked at the glass, a bubble-thin goblet, found, with hundreds of others like it, in a closet above, as though debating with himself whether to have another drink. Then he voted in the affirmative and reached for the cocktail pitcher. "And every door on the old ground level is either barred or barricaded from the inside. How did they get out? And why did they leave?"

The next day, at lunch, Sachiko Koremitsu had the answer to the second question. Four or five electrical engineers had come down by rocket from the ship, and she had been spending the morning with them, in oxy-masks, at the top of the building.

"Tony, I thought you said those generators were in good shape," she began, catching sight of Lattimer. "They aren't. They're in the most unholy mess I ever saw. What happened, up there, was that the supports of the wind-rotor gave way, and weight snapped the main shaft, and smashed everything under it."

"Well, after fifty thousand years, you can expect something like that," Lattimer retorted. "When an archaeologist says something's in good shape, he doesn't necessarily mean it'll start as soon as you shove a switch in."

"You didn't notice that it happened when the power was on, did you," one of the engineers asked, nettled at Lattimer's tone. "Well, it was. Everything's burned out or shorted or fused together; I saw one busbar eight inches across melted clean in two. It's a pity we didn't find things in good shape, even archaeologically speaking. I saw a lot of interesting things, things in advance of what we're using now. But it'll take a couple of years to get everything sorted out and figure what it looked like originally."

"Did it look as though anybody'd made any attempt to fix it?" Martha asked.

Sachiko shook her head. "They must have taken one look at it and given up. I don't believe there would have been any possible way to repair anything."

"Well, that explains why they left. They needed electricity for lighting, and heating, and all their industrial equipment was electrical. They had a good life here, with power; without it, this place wouldn't have been habitable."

"Then why did they barricade everything from the inside, and how did they get out?" Lattimer wanted to know.

"To keep other people from breaking in and looting. Last man out probably barred the last door and slid down a rope from upstairs," von Ohlmhorst suggested. "This Houdini-trick doesn't worry me too much. We'll find out eventually."

"Yes, about the time Martha starts reading Martian," Lattimer scoffed.

"That may be just when we'll find out," von Ohlmhorst replied seriously. "It wouldn't surprise me if they left something in writing when they evacuated this place."

"Are you really beginning to treat this pipe dream of hers as a serious possibility, Selim?" Lattimer demanded. "I know, it would be a wonderful thing, but wonderful things don't happen just because they're wonderful. Only because they're possible, and this isn't. Let me quote that distinguished Hittitologist, Johannes Friedrich: 'Nothing can be translated out of nothing.' Or that later but not less distinguished Hittitologist, Selim von Ohlmhorst: 'Where are you going to get your bilingual?' "

"Friedrich lived to see the Hittite language deciphered and read," von Ohlmhorst reminded him.

"Yes, when they found Hittite-Assyrian bilinguals." Lattimer measured a spoonful of coffee-powder into his cup and added hot water. "Martha, you ought to know, better than anybody, how little chance you have. You've been working for years in the Indus Valley; how many words of Harappa have you or anybody else ever been able to read?"

"We never found a university, with a half-million-volume library, at Harappa or Mohenjo-Daro."

"And, the first day we entered this building, we established meanings for several words," Selim von Ohlmhorst added.

"And you've never found another meaningful word since," Lattimer added. And you're only sure of general meaning, not specific meaning of word-elements, and you have a dozen different interpretations for each word."

"We made a start," von Ohlmhorst maintained. "We have Grotefend's word for 'king.' But I'm going to be able to read some of those books, over there, if it takes me the rest of my life here. It probably will, anyhow."

"You mean you've changed your mind about going home on the *Cyrano*?" Martha asked. "You'll stay on here?"

The old man nodded. "I can't leave this. There's too much to discover. The old

H. Beam Piper

dog will have to learn a lot of new tricks, but this is where my work will be, from now on.''

Lattimer was shocked. ''You're nuts!'' he cried. ''You mean you're going to throw away everything you've accomplished in Hittitology and start all over again here on Mars? Martha, if you've talked him into this crazy decision, you're a criminal!''

''Nobody talked me into anything,'' von Ohlmhorst said roughly. ''And as for throwing away what I've accomplished in Hittitology, I don't know what the devil you're talking about. Everything I know about the Hittite Empire is published and available to anybody. Hittitology's like Egyptology; it's stopped being research and archaeology and become scholarship and history. And I'm not a scholar or a historian; I'm a pick-and-shovel field archaeologist—a highly skilled and specialized grave-robber and junk-picker—and there's more pick-and-shovel work on this planet than I could do in a hundred lifetimes. This is something new; I was a fool to think I could turn my back on it and go back to scribbling footnotes about Hittite kings.''

''You could have anything you wanted, in Hittitology. There are a dozen universities that'd sooner have you than a winning football team. But no! You have to be the top man in Martiology, too. You can't leave that for anybody else—'' Lattimer shoved his chair back and got to his feet, leaving the table with an oath that was almost a sob of exasperation.

Maybe his feelings were too much for him. Maybe he realized, as Martha did, what he had betrayed. She sat, avoiding the eyes of the others, looking at the ceiling, as embarrassed as though Lattimer had flung something dirty on the table in front of them. Tony Lattimer had, desperately, wanted Selim to go home on the *Cyrano*. Martiology was a new field; if Selim entered it, he would bring with him the reputation he had already built in Hittitology, automatically stepping into the leading role that Lattimer had coveted for himself. Ivan Fitzgerald's words echoed back to her—when you want to be a big shot, you can't bear the possibility of anybody else's being a bigger big shot. His derision of her own efforts became comprehensible, too. It wasn't that he was convinced that she would never learn to read the Martian language. He had been afraid that she would.

Ivan Fitzgerald finally isolated the germ that had caused the Finchly girl's undiagnosed illness. Shortly afterward, the malady turned into a mild fever, from which she recovered. Nobody else seemed to have caught it. Fitzgerald was still trying to find out how the germ had been transmitted.

They found a globe of Mars, made when the city had been a seaport. They located the city, and learned that its name had been Kukan—or something with a similar vowel-consonant ratio. Immediately, Sid Chamberlain and Gloria Standish began giving their telecasts a Kukan dateline, and Hubert Penrose used the name in his official reports. They also found a Martian calendar; the year had been divided into ten more or less equal months, and one of them had been Doma. Another month was Nor, and that was a part of the name of the scientific journal Martha had found.

Bill Chandler, the zoologist, had been going deeper and deeper into the old sea bottom of Syrtis. Four hundred miles from Kukan, and at fifteen thousand feet lower altitude, he shot a bird. At least, it was a something with wings and what were almost but not quite feathers, though it was more reptilian than avian in general characteristics. He and Ivan Fitzgerald skinned and mounted it, and then dissected the carcass almost tissue by tissue. About seven-eighths of its body capacity was lungs; it certainly breathed air containing at least half enough oxygen to support human life, or five times as much as the air around Kukan.

That took the center of interest away from archaeology, and started a new burst of activity. All the expedition's aircraft—four jetticopters and three wingless airdyne reconnaissance fighters—were thrown into intensified exploration of the lower sea bottoms, and the bio-science boys and girls were wild with excitement and making new discoveries on each flight.

The University was left to Selim and Martha and Tony Lattimer, the latter keeping to himself while she and the old Turco-German worked together. The civilian specialists in other fields, and the Space Force people who had been holding tape lines and making sketches and snapping cameras, were all flying to lower Syrtis to find out how much oxygen there was and what kind of life it supported.

Sometimes Sachiko dropped in; most of the time she was busy helping Ivan Fitzgerald dissect specimens. They had four or five species of what might loosely be called birds, and something that could easily be classed as a reptile, and a carnivorous mammal the size of a cat with bird-like claws, and a herbivore almost identical with the piglike thing in the big *Darfbulva* mural, and another like a gazelle with a single horn in the middle of its forehead.

The high point came when one party, at thirty thousand feet below the level of Kukan, found breathable air. One of them had a mild attack of *sorroche* and had to be flown back for treatment in a hurry, but the others showed no ill effects.

The daily newscasts from Terra showed a corresponding shift in interest at home. The discovery of the University had focused attention on the dead past of Mars; now the public was interested in Mars as a possible home for humanity. It was Tony Lattimer who brought archaeology back into the activities of the expedition and the news at home.

Martha and Selim were working in the museum on the second floor, scrubbing the grime from the glass cases, noting contents, and grease-penciling numbers; Lattimer and a couple of Space Force officers were going through what had been the administrative offices on the other side. It was one of these, a young second lieutenant, who came hurrying in from the mezzanine, almost bursting with excitement.

"Hey, Martha! Dr. von Ohlmhorst!" he was shouting. "Where are you? Tony's found the Martians!"

Selim dropped his rag back in the bucket; she laid her clipboard on top of the case beside her.

"Where?" they asked together.

"Over on the north side." The lieutenant took hold of himself and spoke more deliberately. "Little room, back of one of the old faculty offices—conference room. It was locked from the inside, and we had to burn it down with a torch. That's where they are. Eighteen of them, around a long table—"

Gloria Standish, who had dropped in for lunch, was on the mezzanine, fairly screaming into a radio-phone extension:

" . . . Dozen and a half of them! Well, of course they're dead. What a question! They look like skeletons covered with leather. No, I do not know what they died of. Well, forget it; I don't care if Bill Chandler's found a three-headed hippopotamus. Sid, don't you get it? We've found the *Martians!*"

She slammed the phone back on its hook, rushing away ahead of them.

Martha remembered the closed door; on the first survey, they hadn't attempted opening it. Now it was burned away at both sides and lay, still hot along the edges, on the floor of the big office room in front. A floodlight was on in the room inside, and Lattimer was going around looking at things while a Space Force officer stood by the door. The center of the room was filled by a long table; in armchairs around it sat the eighteen men and women who had occupied the room for the last fifty millennia. There were bottles and glasses on the table in front of them, and, had she seen them in a dimmer light, she would have thought that they were merely dozing over their drinks. One had a knee hooked over his chair-arm and was curled in fetus-like sleep. Another had fallen forward onto the table, arms extended, the emerald set of a ring twinkling dully on one finger. Skeletons covered with leather, Gloria Standish had called them, and so they were—faces like skulls, arms and legs like sticks, the flesh shrunken onto the bones under it.

"Isn't this something!" Lattimer was exulting. "Mass suicide, that's what it was. Notice what's in the corners?"

Braziers, made of perforated two-gallon-odd metal cans, the white walls smudged with smoke above them. Von Ohlmhorst had noticed them at once, and was poking into one of them with his flashlight.

"Yes; charcoal. I noticed a quantity of it around a couple of hand-forges in the shop on the first floor. That's why you had so much trouble breaking in; they'd sealed the room on the inside." He straightened and went around the room, until he found a ventilator, and peered into it. "Stuffed with rags. They must have been all that were left, here. Their power was gone, and they were old and tired, and all around them their world was dying. So they just came in here and lit the charcoal, and sat drinking together till they all fell asleep. Well, we know what became of them, now, anyhow."

Sid and Gloria made the most of it. The Terran public wanted to hear about Martians, and if live Martians couldn't be found, a room full of dead ones was the next best thing. Maybe an even better thing; it had been only sixty-odd years since the Orson Welles invasion-scare. Tony Lattimer, the discoverer, was beginning to cash in on his attentions to Gloria and his ingratiation with Sid; he was always either making voice-and-image talks for telecast or listening to the news from the home planet. Without question, he had become, overnight, the most widely known archaeologist in history.

"Not that I'm interested in all this, for myself," he disclaimed, after listening to the telecast from Terra two days after his discovery. "But this is going to be a big thing for Martian archaeology. Bring it to the public attention; dramatize it. Selim, can you remember when Lord Carnarvon and Howard Carter found the tomb of Tutankhamen?"

"In 1923? I was two years old, then," von Ohlmhorst chuckled. "I really don't know how much that publicity ever did for Egyptology. Oh, the museums did devote more space to Egyptian exhibits, and after a museum department head gets a few extra showcases, you know how hard it is to make him give them up. And, for a while, it was easier to get financial support for new excavations. But I don't know how much good all this public excitement really does, in the long run."

"Well, I think one of us should go back on the *Cyrano*, when the *Schiaparelli* orbits in," Lattimer said. "I'd hoped it would be you; your voice would carry the most weight. But I think it's important that one of us go back, to present the story of our work, and what we have accomplished and what we hope to accomplish, to the public and to the universities and the learned societies, and to the Federation Government. There will be a great deal of work that will have to be done. We must not allow the other scientific fields and the so-called practical interests to monopolize public and academic support. So, I believe I shall go back at least for a while, and see what I can do—"

Lectures. The organization of a Society of Martian Archaeology, with Anthony Lattimer, Ph.D., the logical candidate for the chair. Degrees, honors; the deference of the learned, and the adulation of the lay public. Positions, with impressive titles and salaries. Sweet are the uses of publicity.

She crushed out her cigarette and got to her feet. "Well, I still have the final lists of what we found in *Halvbulva*—Biology—department to check over. I'm starting on Sornhulva tomorrow, and I want that stuff in shape for expert evaluation."

That was the sort of thing Tony Lattimer wanted to get away from, the detail-work and the drudgery. Let the infantry do the slogging through the mud; the brass-hats got the medals.

She was halfway through the fifth floor, a week later, and was having midday lunch in the reading room on the first floor when Hubert Penrose came over and sat down beside her, asking her what she was doing. She told him.

"I wonder if you could find me a couple of men, for an hour or so," she added. "I'm stopped by a couple of jammed doors at the central hall. Lecture room and library, if the layout of that floor's anything like the ones below it."

"Yes. I'm a pretty fair door-buster, myself." He looked around the room. "There's Jeff Miles; he isn't doing much of anything. And we'll put Sid Chamberlain to work,

　　　　　　　　　　　　　　　　　　　　　　　　H. Beam Piper

for a change, too. The four of us ought to get your doors open." He called to Chamberlain, who was carrying his tray over to the dish washer. "Oh, Sid; you doing anything for the next hour or so?"

"I was going up to the fourth floor, to see what Tony's doing."

"Forget it. Tony's bagged his season limit of Martians. I'm going to help Martha bust in a couple of doors; we'll probably find a whole cemetery full of Maritans."

Chamberlain shrugged. "Why not. A jammed door can have anything back of it, and I know what Tony's doing—just routine stuff."

Jeff Miles, the Space Force captain, came over, accompanied by one of the lab-crew from the ship who had come down on the rocket the day before.

"This ought to be up your alley, Mort," he was saying to his companion. "Chemistry and physics department. Want to come along?"

The lab man, Mort Tranter, was willing. Seeing the sights was what he'd come down from the ship for. She finished her coffee and cigarette, and they went out into the hall together, gathered equipment and rode the elevator to the fifth floor.

The lecture hall door was the nearest; they attacked it first. With proper equipment and help, it was no problem and in ten minutes they had it open wide enough to squeeze through with the floodlights. The room inside was quite empty, and, like most of the rooms behind closed doors, comparatively free from dust. The students, it appeared, had sat with their backs to the door, facing a low platform, but their seats and the lecturer's table and equipment had been removed. The two side walls bore inscriptions: on the right, a pattern of concentric circles which she recognized as a diagram of atomic structure, and on the left a complicated table of numbers and words, in two columns. Tranter was pointing at the diagram on the right.

"They got as far as the Bohr atom, anyhow," he said. "Well, not quite. They knew about electron shells, but they have the nucleus pictured as a solid mass. No indication of proton-and-neutron structure. I'll bet, when you come to translate their scientific books, you'll find that they taught that the atom was the ultimate and indivisible particle. That explains why you people never found any evidence that the Martians used nuclear energy."

"That's a uranium atom," Captain Miles mentioned.

"It is?" Sid Chamberlain asked, excitedly. "Then they did know about atomic energy. Just because we haven't found any pictures of A-bomb mushrooms doesn't mean—"

She turned to look at the other wall. Sid's signal reactions were getting away from him again; uranium meant nuclear power to him, and the two words were interchangeable. As she studied the arrangement of the numbers and words, she could hear Tranter saying:

"Nuts, Sid. We knew about uranium a long time before anybody found out what could be done with it. Uranium was discovered on Terra in 1789, by Klaproth."

There was something familiar about the table on the left wall. She tried to remember what she had been taught in school about physics, and what she had picked up by accident afterward. The second column was a continuation of the first: there were forty-six items in each, each item numbered consecutively—

"Probably used uranium because it's the largest of the natural atoms," Penrose was saying. "The fact that there's nothing beyond it there shows that they hadn't created any of the transuranics. A student could go to that thing and point out the outer electron of any of the ninety-two elements."

Ninety-two! That was it; there were ninety-two items in the table on the left wall! Hydrogen was Number One, she knew; One, *Sarfaldsorn*. Helium was Two; that was *Tirfaldsorn*. She couldn't remember which element came next, but in Martian it was *Sarfalddavas*. *Sorn* must mean matter, or substance, then. And *davas*; she was trying to think of what it could be. She turned quickly to the others, catching hold of Hubert Penrose's arm with one hand and waving her clipboard with the other.

"Look at this thing, over here," she was clamoring excitedly. "Tell me what you think it is. Could it be a table of the elements?"

They all turned to look. Mort Tranter stared at it for a moment.

"Could be. If I only knew what those squiggles meant—"

That was right; he'd spent his time aboard the ship.

"If you could read the numbers, would that help?" she asked, beginning to set down the Arabic digits and their Martian equivalents. "It's decimal system, the same as we use."

"Sure. If that's a table of elements, all I'd need would be the numbers. Thanks," he added as she tore off the sheet and gave it to him.

Penrose knew the numbers, and was ahead of him. "Ninety-two items, numbered consecutively. The first number would be the atomic number. Then a single word, the name of the element. Then the atomic weight—"

She began reading off the names of the elements. "I know hydrogen and helium; what's *tirfalddavas*, the third one?"

"Lithium," Tranter said. "The atomic weights aren't run out past the decimal point. Hydrogen's one plus, if that double-hook dingus is a plus sign; Helium's four-plus, that's right. And lithium's given as seven, that isn't right. It's six-point nine-four-oh. Or is that thing a Martian minus sign?"

"Of course! Look! A plus sign is a hook, to hang things together; a minus sign is a knife, to cut something off from something—see, the little loop is the handle and the long pointed loop is the blade. Stylized, of course, but that's what it is. And the fourth element, *kiradavas*; what's that?"

"Beryllium. Atomic weight given as nine-and-a-hook; actually it's nine-point-oh-two."

Sid Chamberlain had been disgruntled because he couldn't get a story about the Martians having developed atomic energy. It took him a few minutes to understand the newest development, but finally it dawned on him.

"Hey! You're reading that!" he cried. "You're reading Martian!"

"That's right," Penrose told him. "Just reading it right off. I don't get the two items after the atomic weight, though. They look like months of the Martian calendar. What ought they to be, Mort?"

Tranter hesitated. "Well, the next information after the atomic weight ought to be the period and group numbers. But those are words."

"What would the numbers be for the first one, hydrogen?"

"Period One, Group One. One electron shell, one electron in the outer shell," Tranter told her. "Helium's period one, too, but it has the outer—only—electron shell full, so it's in the group of inert elements."

"*Trav, Trav, Trav's* the first month of the year. And helium's *Trav, Yenth; Yenth* is the eighth month."

"The inert elements could be called Group Eight, yes. And the third element, lithium, is Period Two, Group One. That check?"

"It certainly does. *Sanv. Trav. Sanv's* the second month. What's the first element in Period Three?"

"Sodium, Number Eleven."

"That's right; it's *Krav. Trav.* Why, the names of the months are simply numbers, one to ten, spelled out."

"*Doma's* the fifth month. That was your first Martian word, Martha," Penrose told her. "The word for five. And if *davas* is the word for metal, and *sornbulva* is chemistry and/or physics, I'll bet *Tadavas Sornbulva* is literally translated as: 'Of-Metal Matter-Knowledge.' Metallurgy, in other words. I wonder what *Mastbarnorvod* means." It surprised her that, after so long and with so much happening in the meantime, he could remember that. "Something like 'Journal,' or 'Review,' or maybe 'Quarterly.' "

"We'll work that out, too," she said confidently. After this, nothing seemed impossible. "Maybe we can find—" Then she stopped short. "You said 'Quarterly.' I think it was 'Monthly,' instead. It was dated for a specific month, the fifth one. And if *nor* is ten, *Mastbarnorvod* could be 'Year-Tenth.' And I'll bet we'll find that *mastbar* is the word for year." She looked at the table on the wall again. "Well, let's get all these words down, with translations for as many as we can."

"Let's take a break for a minute," Penrose suggested, getting out his cigarettes. "And then, let's do this in comfort. Jeff, suppose you and Sid go across the hall and see what you find in the other room in the way of a desk or something like that, and a few chairs. There'll be a lot of work to do on this."

Sid Chamberlain had been squirming as though he were afflicted with ants, trying to contain himself. Now he let go with an excited jabber.

"This is really it! *The* it, not just it-of-the-week, like finding the reservoirs or those statues or this building, or even the animals and the dead Martians! Wait till Selim and Tony see this! Wait till Tony sees it; I want to see his face! And when I get this on telecast, all Terra's going to go nuts about it!" He turned to Captain Miles. "Jeff, suppose you take a look at that other door, while I find somebody to send to tell Selim and Tony. And Gloria; wait till she sees this—"

"Take it easy, Sid," Martha cautioned. "You'd better let me have a look at your script, before you go too far overboard on the telecast. This is just a beginning; it'll take years and years before we're able to read any of those books downstairs."

"It'll go faster than you think, Martha," Hubert Penrose told her. "We'll all work on it, and we'll teleprint material to Terra, and people there will work on it. We'll send them everything we can . . . everything we work out, and copies of books, and copies of your word lists—"

And there would be other tables—astronomical tables, tables in physics and mechanics, for instance—in which words and numbers were equivalent. The library stacks, below, would be full of them. Transliterate them into Roman alphabet spellings and Arabic numerals, and somewhere, somebody would spot each numerical significance, as Hubert Penrose and Mort Tranter and she had done with the table of elements. And pick out all the chemistry textbooks in the Library; new words would take on meaning from contexts in which the names of elements appeared. She'd have to start studying chemistry and physics, herself—

Sachiko Koremitsu peeped in through the door, then stepped inside.

"Is there anything I can do—?" she began. "What's happened? Something important?"

"Important?" Sid Chamberlain exploded. "Look at that, Sachi! We're reading it! Martha's found out how to read Martian!" He grabbed Captain Miles by the arm, "Come on, Jeff; let's go. I want to call the others—" He was still babbling as he hurried from the room.

Sachi looked at the inscription. "Is it true?" she asked, and then, before Martha could more than begin to explain, flung her arms around her. "Oh, it really is! You are reading it! I'm so happy!"

She had to start explaining again when Selim von Ohlmhorst entered. This time, she was able to finish.

"But, Martha, can you be really sure? You know, by now, that learning to read this language is as important to me as it is to you, but how can you be so sure that those words really mean things like hydrogen and helium and boron and oxygen? How do you know that their table of elements was anything like ours?"

Tranter and Penrose and Sachiko all looked at him in amazement.

"That isn't just the Martian table of elements; that's *the* table of elements. It's the only one there is," Mort Tranter almost exploded. "Look, hydrogen has one proton and one electron. If it had more of either, it wouldn't be hydrogen, it'd be something else. And the same with all the rest of the elements. And hydrogen on Mars is the same as hydrogen on Terra, or on Alpha Centauri, or in the next galaxy—

"You just set up those numbers, in that order, and any first-year chemistry student could tell you what elements they represented," Penrose said. "Could if he expected to make a passing grade, that is."

H. Beam Piper

The old man shook his head slowly, smiling. "I'm afraid I wouldn't make a passing grade. I didn't know, or at least didn't realize, that. One of the things I'm going to place an order for, to be brought on the *Schiaparelli*, will be a set of primers in chemistry and physics, of the sort intended for a bright child of ten or twelve. It seems that a Martiologist has to learn a lot of things the Hittites and the Assyrians never heard about."

Tony Lattimer, coming in, caught the last part of the explanation. He looked quickly at the walls and, having found out just what had happened, advanced and caught Martha by the hand.

"You really did it, Martha! You found your bilingual! I never believed that it would be possible; let me congratulate you!"

He probably expected that to erase all the jibes and sneers of the past. If he did, he could have it that way. His friendship would mean as little to her as his derision—except that his friends had to watch their backs and his knife. But he was going home on the *Cyrano*, to be a big-shot. Or had this changed his mind for him again?

"This is something we can show the world, to justify any expenditure of time and money on Martian archaeological work. When I get back to Terra, I'll see that you're given full credit for this achievement—"

On Terra, her back and his knife would be out of her watchfulness.

"We won't need to wait that long," Hubert Penrose told him dryly. "I'm sending off an official report, tomorrow; you can be sure Dr. Dane will be given full credit, not only for this but for her previous work, which made it possible to exploit this discovery."

"And you might add, work done in spite of the doubts and discouragements of her colleagues," Selim von Ohlmhorst said. "To which I am ashamed to have to confess my own share."

"You said we had to find a bilingual," she said. "You were right, too."

"This is better than a bilingual, Martha," Hubert Penrose said. "Physical science expresses universal facts; necessarily it is a universal language. Heretofore archeologists have dealt only with pre-scientific cultures." ■

MINDS MEET
Paul Ash

THE PARTY WAS ROARING UP to its climax, and Lawrence Day, not being one of the group who considered a celebration incomplete until they had smashed the furniture, stuck a bottle in his pocket for future reference and prepared to go softly away. There was no reason in the world—*this* world—why the furniture should not be broken; it was shaped to fit Terrans, and the Lor'yi would have no use for it; but Lawrence was not in the mood.

On the way to the door, anthropodynamic currents brought him up against somebody who failed to sidestep.

"Hello, Day. Aren't you enjoying yourself? What's wrong?"

Lawrence, blinking, discovered that he was wedged up against the Project Director.

"Nothing wrong, sir. Except—'s only *half* a party, you know."

"Half?"

"Joint enterprise. Joint success . . . but only *half* a party, right now."

"Oh, I see." Lawrence's vision was slightly clouded, but behind the haze the Director seemed to be smiling. "Somehow I can't see the Lor'yi at a party, you know."

The pattern of forces in the neighborhood, changing suddenly, carried them apart. Lawrence escaped through the nearest door, shaking his head.

"'S half the trouble," he murmured. "Neither can I."

The Contact Room was empty. Lawrence dropped into the familiar chair in front of the visionscreen, refilled his tankard, and put it down to wait for the chiller to do its job.

Seven years, he thought. For seven years Terran and Lor'yi scientists had worked together, almost hand-in-tentacle, trying laboriously to achieve a fusion of two scientific traditions; with, in the end, rather staggering success. But now that Project InterCom was finished; now that a method of transmitting messages instantaneously over interstellar distances was an accomplished fact, with theory confirmed by experiment and all the necessary installations on their way to completion on forty-three Terran planets and upwards of two dozen colonized by the Lor'yi, what happened? The Terran half of the Project team, packed and ready to leave, was celebrating enthusiastically, alone. . . .

Joint merry-making would have needed careful arranging; one couldn't suggest that the Lor'yi drop in, nothing formal, for a farewell drink. They were chlorine breathers, for one thing, and few of them could take more than ten minutes in a pressure-suit without becoming unhappy. That was why the Project had been set up with an air-tight Terran base on a Lor'yi planet, instead of the other way around. But, in seven years Project InterCom's engineers had learned to take that sort of problem in their stride. If you could work with a being, you could find a way to relax in his company; always supposing relaxation was something *he* understood.

Nobody else, Lawrence thought, hoisting his boots onto the ledge below the screen, *sees how sad it all is. . . .*

When Lawrence Day joined the InterStellar Exploration Service at the age of fifteen—just over half a lifetime ago—the secret motivating force behind his choice of profession was a mental picture of a greenish, pop-eyed edition of himself squatting on the opposite side of a camp fire, with one finger tapping its—greenish—chest. But in addition to the stars in his eyes, young Lawrence had feet well planted on the ground; in other words, a good grasp of the many complications that could come up when one tried to put over even such a simple concept as "Me—friend" to beings whose aural, vocal and social characteristics were different from one's own. To be ready to cope with all the possible difficulties, those still hypothetical, as well as those that the Service had already met, called for an immense amount of training in a wide range of fields. Lawrence, successfully absorbing it, finally found himself in the Alien Contact Division, which was small—since the known intelligent races could be counted on the fingers of one hand—but very select.

After eleven years of training and brief try-out missions he had been appointed Contact Officer to Project InterCom. Every day for seven years he had sat in this chair, with K'k'riscor's face on the screen opposite; and for six, eight, sometimes ten hours a day they had taken each communication block that arose between the scientists of the two races, and worked it over between them until both sides agreed that they understood.

No, Lawrence thought, *it wasn't understanding, only communication. A set of symbols that mean something to us and something to them and that can be usefully manipulated by both sides. But was it ever the* same *something? I just don't know.*

Seven years of impeccable cooperation with never a cross word. Not even after the memorable confusion in the first year of all, when a six-hour exploration of meteorological phenomena and their effects on perception were finally traced to some Terran's observation, in the presence of a Lor'yi colleague, that it was going to be a fine day. Not even when a misunderstanding as to which was the business end of a Terran handlaser had led to another Lor'yi's cutting right through one pole of the metal scaffolding over which K'k'riscor draped himself in lieu of a chair. Never a cross word.

Never a kind one, either. Do the Lor'yi have any idea of kindness, Lawrence wondered; or do they manage without? Can K'k'riscor really be such an animated computer as he seems? I suppose, if so, the egg-born bastard thinks *I—*

Oops . . . Lawrence pulled himself up. To use alien physiological characteristics as a term of reproach was *out,* even when talking to himself. Once allow that kind of thought to form, and in some moment of stress it would pop out as words; with incalculable effect.

There was no way of telling in advance *what* would offend beings of another race. Short of actual brick-dropping, accidental or by way of deliberate experiment, one could only make guesses, based on the topics *they* seemed to regard as taboo.

Going purely by the things he *didn't* talk about, K'k'riscor, at least, seemed to have the delicate susceptibilities of one descended from a long line of maiden aunts. So far as Lawrence could remember, the Lor'yi had never made a spontaneous reference to any of the physiological differences between their races (except as regards chlorine- versus oxygen-breathing, a topic which came up over every joint enterprise)'; or to the processes of reproduction in either race; or to any political or even purely social matter. If some reference was essential in the process of establishing a translation, K'k'riscor would go all round Robin Hood's barn, with Lawrence tagging behind, to dodge a direct statement. (Naturally Lawrence had to do the same, when the necessity arose from *his* side of the visionscreen.)

It occurred suddenly to the Contact Officer that for all he knew K'k'riscor might actually *be* a maiden aunt—which just showed the sort of footing they were on.

Well, it was all very sad, but it was too late to do anything about it. Far, far too late. Frost had formed on the outside of the tankard. Lawrence lifted it toward the screen.

"Here's to you, K'k'riscor," he murmured, "and may I never run into your like again."

Beyond his boot soles the screen came suddenly to life.

"Greetings, Lawrence," came from the speaker in the Lor'yi's gravelly purr. "Self not recently knowing you presently in place."

For some reason Lawrence did not choke. Staring at the blank black-and-white design of K'k'riscor's face, he put the tankard down without spilling a drop.

Seven years . . . For seven years he had dropped into this chair and switched the audio and visual apparatus on, and for at least six and a half of those years the second process had been performed as automatically as the first. Evidently he had just done it again.

It was no use staring, Lawrence thought, continuing to do so. No Terran ever yet learned anything from a Lor'yi face. The wrap-around eyes might be first-class as organs of vision, but they were no more expressive than two irregular strips of appliqued black velvet. The only other distinct organ on the domelike head, the "mouth"—a trumpet-shaped outlet for the vocal organs—was mobile, but it merely pointed K'k'riscor's voice toward the person he was addressing. Otherwise, his face was covered with the same sparse, staring, off-white bristles as the blobby little body—continuous with the head: no neck—and the four stiffly-flexible tentacles. Somebody had once compared the Lor'yi, in general, to damaged starfish walking edge-on. Substitute brittle-stars for ordinary starfish and it was a good description;

even though the Project Director, determined on a correct attitude toward the Lor'yi, had slapped the speaker down for it.

"Greetings, K'k'riscor," said Lawrence gloomily.

"Query: Your first section namely here's-to-you-K'k'riscor signifies what."

Stars . . . People who thought that this was an easy assignment for a Contact Officer, because the basic language was "simplified" Terran—about half the sounds of Lor'yi speech being outside the human vocal range—should try to cope with this sort of thing. "Simplified" Terran had a large vocabulary, rich in technical terms, but homophones, synonyms and other foreseeable sources of confusion, including inconsistencies of grammar, had been carefully weeded out. All the Lor'yi on the Project team spoke it reasonably well; difficulties arose when (a) a specifically Lor'yi concept, not provided for in the vocabulary, had to be dealt with—the sort of thing for which Contact Officers were trained; or (b) some Terran fathead carelessly slipped into accustomed idioms in Lor'yi hearing; the kind of thing to which Contact Officers were quite accustomed, but felt entitled to resent.

Unless, of course, they had done it themselves.

Lawrence considered turning off the apparatus. He also considered putting his foot through the screen. He was *off duty*, dammit . . . Before his muscles could act on either notion, the large part of his brain, which was reserved for professional uses, had gone into action and the answer had started to come.

"Expression 'here's-to-you,' " he heard himself saying, "signifies desire for welfare of subject named."

"Expression not logically concerning welfare," K'k'riscor said.

Is he calling me a liar? wondered Lawrence, startled. Before he could put this question into "simplified" Terran, the Lor'yi had started off on another tack.

"Query: Your first utterance your second section namely may I never run into your like again signifies not liking self."

Lawrence's jaw loosened at the hinge. *"Stars!"* he said helplessly. "Involuntary utterance, disregard . . ." *Now what?* He did not, he realized, at all want to improve his understanding of the Lor'yi by seeing how one of them reacted to insult. Did K'k'riscor recognize that concept? If he could just get the discussion on to semantics . . .

"Self not knowing," he said carefully, "whether concept not-liking signifies to your race same-as concept not-liking signifies to my race."

"Concept not-liking signifies to my race desire object stopping, going-away, extinct," answered K'k'riscor promptly. "Concept not-liking signifies to my race also physiological events, namely involuntary spasm in tentacle tip, involuntary wave-movement of hair." The tip of one upper tentacle curled suddenly, and relaxed.

"Query: Concept not-liking signifies to your race same-as concept not-liking signifies to my race," K'k'riscor added.

"Concept not-liking signifies to my race same-as to yours," agreed Lawrence helplessly. "However differing physiological events."

"Noted your first utterance your first section signifies desire for welfare of self, your first utterance your second section signifies notliking self. Query inconsistent."

"*No!* Dammit . . . Involuntary utterance." Lawrence, looking into his tankard for inspiration, unexpectedly got it. "My first utterance, first and second sections *together* belonging in class of expressions, not logically constructed, Terrans by-custom uttering when drinking. Disregard. *Before* drinking—" about to say "together," Lawrence saw a possible pitfall and substituted—"alcohol. Ethyl alcohol. Dilute . . ."

"Wrrgszrrt!" K'k'riscor's upper tentacles, for fully two thirds of their length, snapped back into tight watch-spring coils.

"Involuntary utterance," said the Lor'yi after a pause. His tentacles slowly uncurled. "Statement, ethyl alcohol toxic to Lor'yi metabolism. Query: Ethyl alcohol not toxic to Terran metabolism?"

"Oh, it is." Relieved to have got off the subject of "not-liking," Lawrence took a pull at the tankard. "Statement, ethyl alcohol in not-small quantities very toxic to Terran metabolism. Small quantities slightly toxic."

The tips of the Lor'yi's tentacles twitched restlessly.

"Query: Terrans voluntarily ingesting toxic substances. Query cause."

An idea was building up in the depths of Lawrence's mind.

"Ingestion of slightly toxic substances produces . . . er . . . physiological events. Terrans liking—"

"Awurrt!" The Lor'yi were never sleek—the uneven off-white fur had always, to Terran eyes, an indefinably moth-eaten appearance: but until this moment K'k'riscor's had seemed relatively smooth. Now it was moving; uneasy little ripples had appeared in it, starting apparently at random spots and spreading in circles. The effect made Lawrence slightly queasy, but—

Involuntary spasm of tentacletip, involuntary wavemovement of hair. He was really on to something.

"Query: Lor'yi not-liking . . ." Lawrence leaned forward tensely. The Project Director would have his ears if he ever found out about this session, but right now the Contact Officer didn't care.

"Lor'yi not liking," said K'k'riscor rapidly. "Lor'yi extreme not liking. Terrans . . ." He halted, baffled. "Awwurrtt!"

"The word you want is 'Filthy,' I imagine."

"Filthy!"

"Also, 'Disgusting.' "

"Disssguzzting!"

"Quite so." Lawrence swallowed another mouthful. "Well, if you don't . . . disregard. Your statement Lor'yi not ingesting substances toxic to Lor'yi metabolism. Well, then—Query: What did *you* get high on, K'k'riscor my friend?"

* * *

Paul Ash

The presence of the Project Director was having an inhibitory effect. Not much; but enough to excuse him from further attendance. His sense of duty satisfied, he edged his way to the door and withdrew.

He didn't want to go to bed just yet. Items which represented obvious potential danger, in view of the present state of disinhibition among his staff—such as the airlock mechanisms and the power generators—had been locked in their shields before the revels got under way, and the Director's secretary, a teetotaler, was sleeping with the keys under her pillow, behind a locked sound-proofed door. But it wouldn't do to underrate the ingenuity of his team; they could find ways to get into dangerous mischief even now.

Wanting a few minutes of peace, the Director opened the soundproofed door of the Contact Room.

"Don't!" Lawrence yelled. "It's revolting! I mean it's disgusting! Send them away!"

The visionscreen was not in line with the door. The Director had an edge-on view of movement taking place on it, but his attention was centered on Lawrence; doubled over in his chair, hands to his eyes.

"Captain Day!"

Lawrence lurched round in his swivel chair and almost fell off.

"Are you insane?" demanded the Director.

"No. No, really, sir. I was just—"

"Come away from that screen!"

Lawrence wavered. The chair wobbled on its pedestal. "Sir, this is something important. I'll explain—"

"Peep-bo!" came a falsetto voice from the doorway. "Lawrence, you blackleg, what—*Stars!* Sorry, sir—"

The Director turned an icy stare on the newcomer.

"Williams. I take it you are not alone?"

"No, sir." Tiny Williams stiffened to attention.

"I wish you and your companions to remove Captain Day and sober him up—fast." Tiny blinked, once.

"Can do, sir."

He beckoned. Three other large men entered and made for Lawrence in a purposeful group.

"Stop it!" Lawrence, who was no weakling, hung on to the chair with both hands, twining his legs round the support. "Important conversation—*important*, you louts! First *real* contact. Sir, tell them to stop. I've got to—"

"Query Terrans attempting tickle-dance," said the speaker unit in a booming growl—evidently K'k'riscor had turned up the volume on his mike. "Statement Lawrence not liking. Stop. Going away. Extinct. Awurrt!"

"Look, Lawrence, you heard what the man said—"

"Wait!" The Project Director hitched his jaw back into place. "*What* was that? Er . . . Request repeat."

Louder, if anything, K'k'riscor repeated his remarks.

Tiny Williams uttered a complicated oath.

"Williams, you four can go," the Project Director said. "I shall investigate. Don't mention this to anyone. You understand?"

The four nodded, and went.

The Director said, *"Now!"*

"Well . . ." Lawrence slapped at his rumpled clothes. "Well, sir, K'k'riscor and I were . . . just talking, that's all. A farewell chat."

"Then why were you—No. Wait. What's a *tickle-dance*?"

"Dissguzzting!" boomed the speaker.

Lawrence winced. "Request lower volume, K'k'riscor. You see, sir, the Lor'yi are having a party, too. They don't ingest alcohol, or other intoxicants—"

"Filthy!"

"But they get . . . well, 'high' . . . through their sense of touch. When they really want to have a ball they all get together in one writhing bunch and rub against each other—all over." Lawrence swallowed violently. "Like a knot of bristly worms."

"Day, do I have to remind you—"

"No, sir. I know all about controlling my reactions to alien appearance; not applying Terran standards of behavior; all that—doctrine. It's sound, but it's a hell of a strain to live up to. Being upset by certain visual stimuli isn't a matter of reason, it's a physiological reaction, more or less. You can control it, but the strain's *there*—"

"Captain Day, I understand that. I make allowances. But that . . . that exhibition I happened upon—"

"No, sir, you *don't* understand. The point is, the *Lor'yi* feel it, too. They know all about it. K'k'riscor! Request repeat your"—Lawrence counted up hastily in his mind, an exercise in which he had become adept—"Seventeenth utterance."

"Query: Terran Director forbidding statement Terrans not liking Lor'yi, same as Lor'yi Director forbidding statement Lor'yi not liking Terrans."

"There," said Lawrence proudly. "You see?"

"No. I don't. See *what?*"

"Well . . ." Hastily Lawrence sorted out his ideas. "*We* were all forbidden to speak of anything that might upset the Lor'yi. We didn't know what that might be, so we had to cut out an awful lot of subjects. All the things about them that struck us as peculiar, or distasteful, and everything they might think of as taboo. Sex, or . . . or hatching, or social customs, or . . . you know the list. We were told it was OK to open up on any topic if they started it first; but they never did. We thought they must be a prissy-mouthed bunch. But actually they had the same idea we did. They were being careful in case—"

"Query: Prissy-mouthed signifies what?" K'k'riscor asked. Lawrence ignored him.

"The point is, sir, watching words all the time got to be a strain—on both sides.

Paul Ash

It was necessary, of course. People can't co-operate if they keep getting offended, and however tolerant one tries to be, there *are* things . . . well, like the tickle-dance K'k'riscor showed me. And *he* thinks it's pretty terrible to get fun out of deliberately upsetting one's metabolism—''

"Filthy!" said K'k'riscor.

"The point is, sir, we can *say* so; to each other; and understand one another's point of view. His habits are right for him, and mine for me, but we would *not* care to swap them. If one of us were to harp on that point, the other might get annoyed; but just this once, we discovered we could afford to let our hair down. You see?''

The Director, with an expression of extreme sagacity, opened his mouth; looked suddenly doubtful, and closed it once more. Abruptly a babble of Lor'yi speech shot from the speaker. A jumbled mass—four or five individuals at least, entwined in a many-tentacled knot—rolled across the screen and engulfed K'k'riscor.

"Good-by, Lawrence!" yelled the Lor'yi as the orgiastic squirmings hid him from view.

"Good . . . Good-by, K'k'riscor.'' Closing his eyes, Lawrence groped hurriedly. for the switch; opened them, as the screen went blank, and reached for his bottle.

"If my ingestion of alcohol affects K'k'riscor the way his type of stimulant affects me,'' he said, "he'll need a little something right now. How about you, sir?''

"No, thank you.'' The Director was looking a trifle dazed. "Are you trying to tell me, Day, that our precautions were unnecessary—that we could have talked freely to the Lor'yi about . . . well, the differences between us, and our reactions to those differences?''

"No, sir, I'm not. A bunch of *Terrans* can't do that very freely, among themselves. I'm not sure that 'concept *disgusting*' signifies to K'k'riscor exactly what it does to me, but it wouldn't help to let that word into the Project vocabulary. Maybe, if there's another joint Project, my successor can get together with K'k'riscor's and agree to cut out some of the taboos. We don't need all of them. But we do need the rules; even if they can get a bit irritating at times.''

"I see. Yes. I see . . .'' The Director blinked a trifle dubiously at the screen. "I suppose I can understand why you felt you had to break loose for once . . . and K'k'riscor, too. Well, I'd better see what's happening to the party.'' He went.

Lawrence poured the last of the bottle into his tankard and waited for the frost to form. Then he checked carefully that vision and sound were off, and glanced at the door. It was firmly shut.

He lifted the tankard toward the screen.

"Here's to you, K'k'riscor, you egg-born bastard,'' he said affectionately, and drank deep. ∎

Minds Meet

TWO-WAY COMMUNICATION

Christopher Anvil

CARTWRIGHT, APRIL 16. The Cartwright Corporation, manufacturer of electrical specialties, is reported on the brink of ruin today, after a disastrous plunge into the communications field. Word is that Cartwright research scientists had developed a new type of radio receiver, that the corporation backed it heavily, and that the equipment has now proved to have a fatal flaw. It is reported that Nelson Ravagger, the well-known corporation "raider," has now seized control of the company. Ravagger is expected to oust Cyrus Cartwright, II, grandson of the corporation's founder.

Nelson Ravagger ground his cigarette into the ultramodern ashtray and looked Cyrus Cartwright, II, in the eye.

"When," Ravagger demanded, "did it finally dawn on you that you had a mess on your hands?"

Cartwright glared at Ravagger. "When you walked in that door and told me you had control of the company."

Ravagger smiled. "I'm not talking about that. I'm talking about this Cartwright Mark I Communicator. That's the cause of this trouble."

Cartwright said uncomfortably, "Yes—the communicator."

Ravagger nodded. "I'm listening."

"It dawned on us we had a mess," said Cartwright, "when the Mark I receiver broadcast through the microphone of the local radio station. Up to that time, the thing looked perfect."

Ravagger frowned. "What was that again?"

"The Mark I receiver," said Cartwright patiently, "broadcast through the local radio station's microphone. That's when we knew we were in trouble."

"The receiver broadcast through the microphone of the transmitter?"

"That's it," said Cartwright.

Ravagger looked at him in amazement. "How did that happen?"

Cartwright spread his hands. "It's a new principle. The circuit isn't a regenerative circuit. It's not a tuned R-F circuit. It's not a surperhet. It's a . . . ah—Well, they call it a Cartwright circuit."

"Did you invent it?"

"I don't know anything about it. I took the Business Course in college. You know, economics, mathematics of finance, and so on. Management is all the same after you get to the higher levels."

Ravagger smiled at him wolfishly. "Let's get back to this communicator. You don't know anything about it?"

"Not technically. I could see, from a business viewpoint, that it could be a very good thing for us."

"Why?"

"Well, we had been selling to manufacturers. Quality switches, circuit breakers, things like that. What we needed was a broad approach to the consumer himself. That's a much bigger and less demanding market."

Ravagger lit up another cigarette and studied Cartwright with a look of cynical disbelief. "In other words, the quality of your product had been falling off, and sales were going down, so you figured you better get into something else?"

Cartwright squirmed. "Well, competition was getting pretty stiff."

"So you decided to turn out this communicator. All right, what was it supposed to do?"

"It is an all-purpose communicator. You have AM, FM, shortwave, longwave — everything—all in one package."

Ravagger showed no enthusiasm. "In other words, a luxury receiver. I suppose it was portable?"

"Oh, yes." Cartwright got a little excited. "We were going to turn it out in a nice leather case, with three colors of trim."

"Naturally. And, of course, with an antenna you can pull out three feet long." He added sarcastically, "You were really going to skim the cream off the market with this thing. There must be a dozen different makes out right now."

Cartwright shrugged, "No antenna. It didn't need one. Besides, in a shirt-pocket radio, an antenna that pulls out seems to me to be a nuisance. If you've got to have it, then you're stuck with it, of course. But we were going to advertise that ours didn't need an external antenna."

Ravagger blinked. "Shirt-pocket size, eh? and it worked?"

"Except for the little shortcoming I just mentioned."

"This thing was to be called a Cartwright Mark I Communicator. Why not just Mark I radio, or receiver? Why communicator? Just because the name sounded good?"

"It sounded good to us at first. That was our original reason. Then we got a bright idea. Why not build it so it could really be a communicator? You know, two-way. Then we could turn out a citizen's band set, and a walkie-talkie. It could be everything. An all-purpose communicator. If it's broadcast, this could pick it up. Longwave, shortwave, amateur, police, the sound from TV programs, AM, FM, foreign, domestic—" Cartwright ran out of words, and took a deep breath. "It was an all-purpose, universal communicator that would—"

"Wait a minute." Ravagger was staring at him. "All this in a shirt-pocket radio?"

"Yes. Oh, there's no problem there. It's just a question of building it differently. If you consider it, it's obvious that eventually we'll have sets as small as that on the consumer market. Take a look inside the average portable receiver these days. Compare it with the size of the sets ten years ago, twenty years ago, thirty years ago. We're moving toward very small sets. We—here at Cartwright, I mean—happened to get the principle for the next advance first, that's all. Now, to make a transmitter is admittedly more of a size problem, even with our new manufacturing process. But there was enough room in the case, and it could be done. So we thought, why not do it?"

"All right," said Ravagger, scowling. "Now, if I understand this correctly, what you're saying is that you had a shirt-pocket set that could receive AM, FM, and shortwave broadcasts, could transmit and receive on citizen's band, and—"

"No. It had the potentiality, if we chose to make the necessary connections, to use citizens' band. But we'd have to make connections to the right points on the unit crystal. This initial set was to be purely a receiver. Later, we'd bring out the Mark II, Mark III, and so on, which would be transmitter-receivers. And still shirt-pocket size. The point was, that for a few thousand bucks more on the fabricating equipment, and a few cents more on each unit crystal, we could have the potential to raise the price twenty to forty dollars a set later on, and still give the customer a break."

Ravagger frowned at him. "What's this 'unit crystal'?"

Cartwright pulled open a drawer of his modernistic desk, and took out a small portable radio in dark-blue leather with gold trim, with a line of gold knobs down one side, and a tuning dial with so many bands that it covered the entire face of the radio. He unsnapped the back, took out the solitary penlight battery, pulled the little speaker out of the way, and exposed an olive-colored metal can.

"Inside that," said Cartwright, "is the crystal."

Ravagger squinted at it. "Where's the rest of the circuit?"

"That's it."

"The whole thing is in one crystal?"

"Sure. That's the point."

Ravagger scowled at the radio through a haze of cigarette smoke. "Let's hear it."

"All right." Cartwright snapped the set together again. "But don't say anything out loud, or we may get in trouble with the FCC."

Ravagger nodded, and Cartwright turned the radio on. A girl with a voice that was not improved by the small speaker, was singing a popular song. Both men winced, and Cartwright quickly tuned in a recorded dance band, a news report, a voice talking rapidly in French, and then an amateur who was saying, ". . . Coming in very clear, but I didn't quite get your handle there . . ."

Ravagger said, "Do you mean to tell me—"

Cartwright said angrily, "Quiet!"

The radio said, "Wyatt? Wait a minute! I could have sworn—"

Christopher Anvil

Cartwright snapped off the set. "I told you not to say anything!"

Ravagger stared at him. "You mean to say, this set will let you talk to any station you can receive?"

Cartwright took a deep breath, nodded glumly, and shoved the set back in the drawer. "The trouble is, we should have been content with the receiver circuit. We should never have built up the circuits for the transmitter. It was a big mistake to combine the two in the same crystal. They interact."

"There's no way to . . . say . . . break off the part of the crystal that has the transmitter in it?"

"It's not that simple. You can't separate them that easily. You need a whole new crystal."

"Well—Suppose you build a new crystal?"

"The fabricating equipment to mass-produce the crystals costs a mint, and our equipment will only turn out the one crystal it was built to make. It will do that with great precision, but that's all it will do."

"And you're already spread so thin you can't afford to buy new equipment?"

"That's it."

"Hm-m-m." Ravagger leaned back. After contemplating the ceiling for a while, he sat up again with a bang. "Now, as I understand this, Cartwright, the broadcast . . . ah . . . the transmission you send out turns up at the broadcaster's microphone. Is that right?"

"That's right."

"How could that happen?"

Cartwright squirmed uneasily. "The boys in the Research Department have an explanation for it. It has something to do with the 'carrier wave.' Let's see, the crystal is energized by the carrier wave, resonates, transmits in precise congruity with the carrier wave, and then the mike at the transmitting station 'telephones' and the sound comes out. If you want me to get them up here—"

Ravagger waved his hand. "They know why and how it happens. But what I'm interested in is what we can do with it."

Cartwright said drearily, "I haven't thought of anything."

"It would make a good walkie-talkie."

"Only if it were a transmitter, too. To make it a transmitter would require another stage in the manufacturing process. As it is, it's not a transmitter—except in this one freakish way."

Ravagger frowned. "How many of these sets have you got?"

"We've got a warehouse full of them. Naturally, when we first tried them out, this never entered our heads. We only stumbled onto it by accident."

"Hm-m-m." Ravagger leaned back and looked thoughtfully at Cartwright. "If it hadn't been for this thing, you'd have been raking it in by the barrelful."

Cartwright brightened. "By the truckload. We could eventually get the cost of the whole set down to about nine dollars a unit. We could charge any price within reason."

"And nobody could have predicted this trouble?"

"At least, nobody did predict it."

"Yes, I see." Ravagger knocked the ash off the end of his cigarette, ground out the butt, and looked at Cartwright. Ravagger's expression was a peculiar blend of calculation and benevolence. "As long as I'm cleaning out fools who should never have been in charge of companies anyway, what do I care if they say I'm a pirate and pronounce my name 'ravager'? I'm performing a useful function. If I start cleaning out first-raters, I'm not doing any good. Now, you had a good setup here. You should have made money. You were smart to switch over to this portable set. No one could blame you. You made the right moves."

Cartwright looked dazed.

Ravagger leaned forward. "I'm not going to take over this company. I'm going to get you off the hook. I aim to see to it that every one of these sets and the fabricating equipment are bought at your cost."

Cartwright was dumbfounded. "But—"

Ravagger waved his hand. "No buts. My job here is to get you off the hook. I'll profit, you'll profit, the stockholders will profit, and the whole country will profit. This situation has possibilities."

For an instant, Cartwright seemed to see a halo around the financial pirate's head.

"Anything you say," said Cartwright gratefully.

Cartwright, May 5. Cyrus Cartwright, II, president of the Cartwright Corporation and grandson of the corporation's founder, today beat off a formidable attempt by business buccaneer Nelson Ravagger to gain control of the company.

The Corporation had been rumored to be in serious difficulties, due to failure of a revolutionary manufacturing process. But Cyrus Cartwright today revealed the sale of the entire stock of merchandise and related manufacturing equipment to Hyperdynamic Specialty Products, a recently-formed distributing firm.

New York, June 2. Trading on the Big Board was heavy today. Among the most active stocks was the Cartwright Corporation.

New York, June 4. An astonishing advertisement has been running for the past week in several leading New York papers.

This reporter visited the showroom mentioned in the ad yesterday, picked up one of the devices advertised, and spent a truly delightful evening at home.

The advertisement is as follows:

ARE YOU

SICK

OF

DULL

COMMERCIALS

?

Strike back at silly announcers with revolutionary device that enables *you* to talk to them! Introductory price of $29.99 for new Electronic Miracle. You can set it beside your radio or TV and blast moronic announcers and admaniacs to your heart's content. THEY WILL HEAR YOU! Haven't you suffered in silence long enough? Call at Hyperdynamic Showroom today!

New York, June 10. Rumors current for the past week were confirmed today by Harmon Lobcaw, president of NBS Radio, who admitted that "a serious situation has arisen in the broadcasting industry."

Mr. Lobcaw stated that voices have been heard, coming from microphones, accusing announcers of "stupidity, bad taste and a number of other things I don't care to repeat."

Mr. Lobcaw was unable to explain how this could be, but insisted that "It is a fact. Government action," he said, "is imperative."

New York, June 11. Saralee Boondog, popular singer, was removed from the NBS studio by ambulance today, and rushed to the hospital for treatment of shock. Cause of Miss Boondog's illness was "loud hisses and boos coming from the microphone" while she was singing the popular favorite, "Love You, Love You, Love You, Honey." Miss Boondog's manager has threatened to sue the person or persons responsible.

New York, June 11. The Nodor Antiperspirant Spray Co., Inc., has temporarily suspended its radio and TV commercials due to "abusive comments from the microphone, threatening the persons of the actors." A spokesman for the company warns that the company will seek damages.

New York, June 12. Hubert Bawker, veteran local disc jockey, abruptly announced his retirement today. Mr. Bawker refused to give any reason.

New York, June 12. Attempts to locate the whereabouts of a concern called Hyperdynamic Specialty Products, rumored to be distributing radio sets of unusual properties, have so far proved futile. The firm's showroom was vacated before police arrived.

Havana, June 14. Julio Del Barbe, Special Communications Commissar, today blasted "Yankee imperialism" in a lengthy speech, interrupted a number of times as Mr. Del Barbe smashed his microphone. Mr. Del Barbe, among other things, angrily accused "a cutthroat Yankee CIA cover agency called Hyperdynamic Specialty Products" of selling his organization a case of expensive "special electronics equipment," which blew up on arrival.

Moscow, June 18. The Soviet Government has delivered a stiff protest to Washington, charging that "voices with American accents" are interrupting Soviet news and cultural broadcasters, with comments from the microphone such as "Lies, all lies," and "Communism is the bunk." Moscow demands that these "crude provocations" cease at once.

Washington, June 19. At the same time as the Russian note was received here, word got around that an official of the Russian embassy here recently paid $2,5000.00 for a portable back-talk radio set such as is sold on the black market here for about $50.00. The back-talker was reportedly flown to Moscow on the very fastest jet transportation available.

Washington, June 20. The President was interrupted several times last night by caustic comments from the microphone. The Russians are believed responsible.

New York, August 1. Harmon Lobcaw, president of NBS Radio, announced today the installation of a system of "remote live broadcasting" which "strains out" microphone back talk before it reaches the announcer. Mr. Lobcaw also said that there is now a "crying need for announcers," as an estimated four hundred have recently quit their jobs. Asked why they quit, Mr. Lobcaw said, "Their self-confidence was shattered."

Washington, August 2. Following several nasty comments from the microphone, Senator William Becker has summoned Cyrus Cartwright, II, to testify before his committee regarding the Cartwright Corporation's connection with the mushrooming sales of back-talk radio and TV devices. Mr. Cartwright has stated that he will appear, and has nothing to hide.

New York, August 3. The price of Cartwright Corporation stock plummeted today, as rumors spread that the Government is determined to punish the company.

Washington, August 8. Cyrus Cartwright, II, today won a clean bill of health from Senator William Becker's investigating committee. The committee is now looking for Nelson Ravagger, the well-known speculator and corporation-raider.

New York, August 9. Cartwright Corporation stock rose sharply today.

Washington, August 11. In a stormy, shouting session financier Nelson Ravagger defended himself against charges of Senator William Becker's committee that Ravagger is responsible for distributing radio TV back-talk devices. Mr. Ravagger asserted that he had not purchased the devices, but that they had been sold to a firm run by his business associate, Skybo Halante. Mr. Halante is now being sought.

Christopher Anvil

* * *

New York, August 11. Cartwright Corporation climbed to a new high as it was learned today that the corporation developed and is now selling the cheapest and most effective system for "filtering" back talk and "sorting and storing" it for program-improvement purposes. Development of this device was reportedly instigated by financier Nelson Ravagger, who has emerged as apparently the major Cartwright stockholder following a series of complex market operations reported to have netted him millions.

Washington, August 16. In a furious session before the Becker Backtalk Investigating Committee, businessman Cyrus Cartwright, II, and speculator Nelson Ravagger defended themselves against renewed charges of "mulcting the public, deceiving this committee, and attempting to destroy the communications industry in this country." Skybo Halante, Mr. Ravagger's long sought business associate, appears to have evaporated into thin air. Grilled about this, Mr. Ravagger replied, "How should I know where he is? I'm not his chaperon." The search for Mr. Halante is continuing.

New York, August 17. Price of Cartwright Corporation stock fell sharply today as it was learned that damage suits totaling upward of one billion dollars are to be brought against the corporation.

New York, August 19. Price of Cartwright Corporation stock rose sharply today as word was received of a fantastically cheap and effective Cartwright portable radio entirely free of back talk.

New York, August 22. The bottom fell out of Cartwright Corporation stock today as the rumor spread that the new-model portable radio produces back talk.

New York, August 24. Cartwright Corporation stock made a dramatic recovery and rose to an unprecedented high as the first of the new Cartwright portable receivers found their way into circulation today. The portables, extremely attractive and entirely free from back talk, are made to sell at a very reasonable price.

New York, August 25. Trading in Cartwright Corporation stock has been suspended, pending completion of an investigation to determine whether the recent sharp rises and falls have been due to behind-the-scenes manipulations. It has been rumored that speculator Nelson Ravagger and a small group of associates have made enormous profits from Cartwright's erratic behavior.

Washington, August 26. Cyrus Cartwright, II, was again called to the stand as the Becker Committee attempts to unravel the facts concerning the reported transfer of a huge quantity of back-talk radio sets from Cartwright Corporation, by way of Nelson Ravagger, to the still missing Skybo Halante. In a savage exchange, Senator Becker today called Mr. Cartwright a "bold-faced liar." Mr. Cartwright had just described the alleged circumstances surrounding the original sale of the back-talkers.

New York, September 25. Cartwright Corporation stock, following completion of the investigation into price-manipulation by insiders, continued to rise sharply this week, despite sporadic rumors that Nelson Ravagger and associates are now unloading most—if not all—their holdings.

Washington, September 29. The Becker Committee has closed its investigation into the Cartwright Corporation back-talkers. Cyrus Cartwright, II, pale and drawn, grimly told reporters, "The last few months have been the most terrific experience in my life." Asked what he intended to do now that the investigation was over, Mr. Cartwright said, "Sleep."

Budapest, October 2. Officials here have admitted for the first time that back-talkers are in fairly common use. They refuse to call their use a problem, however, saying that, thanks to the devices, people "let off steam," and "sometimes we get good suggestions." Several announcers have been sacked because of pointed back-talk comments.

New York, October 4. Cyrus Cartwright, II, today announced that he was stepping down as active head of the Cartwright Corporation, though he will remain on the Board of Directors. Mr. Cartwright said he wished to "sort things over in my mind. I have the sensation that I have just stepped off a combined merry-go-round and Ferris wheel." Mr. Cartwright refused to criticize Mr. Ravagger, who is reputed to have effective control of the corporation.

New York, October 5. Wall Street opinion is divided as to whether Nelson Ravagger actually controls large holdings of Cartwright stock at the moment. "It depends," a well-known specualtor is reported to have said, "on whether the stock goes up or down. If it skyrockets, it will turn out that Ravagger has a big chunk of it. If it falls through the floor, we'll know for sure that he dumped it some time ago. You can only reconstruct things afterward." Trading in the stock continues at a high level.

Washington, October 6. A broadcast lecture by political economist Sero Kulf, on the "continuing iniquitous aspects of an unsocialized philosophy" was interrupted today by comments, getting through the filtered microphone, of "Crank," "Cretin," "What do you know about it?" and by Dr. Kulf's own replies, which unfortunately got through before the program was cut off the air. Stronger filtering systems are reported to be in production against bootleg back-talkers.

Washington, October 12. The uproar about back-talk radio sets seems gradually to

Christopher Anvil

be starting to die down. Senator William Becker remarked to reporters that "for the first time in fifteen years," he had listened to the radio the other day, and found it enjoyable. Mr. Becker feels that manufacturers are now getting the word about the more offensive commercials, and that the new system of filtering and registering complaints has led many stations to cut down on too frequent advertising. "This mess may," said the senator, "prove to have its compensations."

New York, October 24. At a meeting of the Better Radio and TV Association, president Jack M. Straub today awarded the association's Distinguished Served Plaque to Cyrus Cartwright, II, and Nelson Ravagger, for "distinguished efforts which have resulted in vastly improving the dismal standard of radio and television broadcasting, by enabling listeners and viewers to record their actual feelings spontaneously and directly, rather than through the doubtful intermediary of sampling procedures."

Mr. Straub said that he will give an even bigger and better plaque to missing financier and reputed bootleg-manufacturer Skybo Halante, "if someone will locate him for us.

"Communication," Mr. Straub added, "generally needs to be two-way to be effective." ∎

DUPLEX
Verge Foray

I

THE ONE-MAN CLOPTER WAS ZIPPING over New Mexico when Kent Lindstrom's left hand dropped its side of the book of Beethoven sonatas. Kent stared with annoyance as the hand reached forward to fool with the manual control wheel.

Damn it all! he fretted. It was Pard's memory, not his own, that needed refreshing on some spots in the "Hammer-Klavier"! He had been looking over the sonata, instead of utilizing the flight to Los Angeles for a relaxing nap, purely for Pard's benefit.

But did Pard pay attention? Hell, no! He let his mind stray instead, ignoring Beethoven and indulging his childish fascination with gadgetry.

The sonata volume dangling neglected from his right hand, Kent watched his left hand turn the control wheel a few inches counterclockwise, then release it. The wheel automatically snapped back into place and the clopter, having swerved slightly from the center of the traffic beam, started correction to get back on its course.

Kent opened his mouth to advise Pard, in words that left no doubt, that it was time to quit being a kid. But at that instant a thunderous *Whap!* shook the clopter. Kent dropped the music volume and gazed anxiously at the control panel, wondering if Pard's fooling around had busted something.

The only red on the panel was coming from the cabin-pressure indicator. The clopter had taken a puncture, and its air was whistling away into the stratosphere outside. Kent grabbed for the emergency oxygen mask before he realized his left hand had already put it on his face and was now tightening its strap, getting it a bit tangled in his long, thick hair.

Despite his faults, Pard could think fast in a pinch!

"What happened?" Kent asked under the mask.

Pard took control of his neck muscles and turned his head to look down and to the right. There, in the alumalloy floor, was a hole over an inch across, the shredded metal curled upward along its edges. Through it Kent could see hazily a tiny panorama of New Mexican landscape sliding by in the late afternoon sun.

Then Pard turned his head upward to focus on the spot where the projectile had made its exit. The hole in the roof was a few feet to the rear of the hole in the floor.

"What could've done *that?*" muttered Kent.

Pard did not attempt a reply.

Kent retrieved Beethoven from the floor, but left the book unopened in his lap while he stared at the controls. The clopter was functioning perfectly, keeping to the course and velocity that were correct for its moving niche in the air-traffic pattern.

Struck by a crazy thought, Kent drew a mental line between the punctures. The line ran parallel to the position of his body, and not more than three feet to the right of his chair.

And Pard had swerved the craft *to the left* just before the projectile struck!

"You kept that thing from hitting us!" Kent said.

His head answered with the slightest nod: *Yes.*

Kent gasped: "How did you know to swerve?"

His left hand reached around to tap his right temple—Pard's half of the brain—with a finger.

"Oh, sure you're bright!" growled Kent, annoyed because the answer told him nothing. "The brightest stupe I know!" But after he simmered down for a moment he added, "Sorry, Pard. I didn't really mean that."

His left hand patted the top of his head forgivingly.

It was silly, Kent knew, to get cross with Pard for being . . . well, for being *Pard.* He wouldn't have called him a stupe if he hadn't been upset and a bit frightened by the close call they had just had.

It was Pard's way to be noncommunicative, and rather devil-may-care. (But Kent could only guess at the latter because there was no way to learn Pard's real attitude about anything.) The language center was in Kent's hemisphere of the brain. Pard could not talk, and his few unwilling attempts at writing had been such painful, meaningless scrawls that Kent had long ago quit trying to achieve two-way verbal communication with him. Pard could understand the written or spoken word with ease, but the ability to *express* words simply was not in him.

Thus, Pard was not equipped to answer such a question as "How did you know to swerve?" The reply required concepts inexpressible in the "twitch language" Pard used for such essential thoughts as "yes," "no," "give me control," "take over," "wake up," and "I'm going to sleep."

But this didn't mean Pard was stupid. For one thing, as Kent sometimes admitted to himself, the only reason Pard was not the better pianist of the two of them was that he did not *try* as hard as Kent. For another, Pard was often aware of environmental factors that Kent missed. The object that had hit the clopter, for instance . . .

Kent looked at the tiny row of radar meters at the left edge of the control panel. The six little indicator needles trembled constantly with fluctuations in the thin surrounding air. They would have been within Pard's range of peripheral vision even while his eyes were directed at the Beethoven score—and their movements obviously told Pard a lot more than they told him. Pard had been able to read an indication that an object was approaching from below—on a collision course, in fact—and he had swerved the craft at just the right moment to save their life.

Having figured this out, Kent felt better about Pard, at any rate. It was easy enough to feel haunted, with another consciousness sharing his skull, without that consciousness acting upon information it could not possibly have acquired. The radar meters explained where the knowledge came from.

"I'll never bad-mouth your fooling with gadgets again!" Kent said tensely.

Pard accepted that without response.

As for the projectile . . . Well, thought Kent, objects don't shoot up from the ground of their own accord. And if they did, they wouldn't be aimed—or guided—precisely to tear through a lone man zooming past at an altitude of fifteen miles!

"Somebody tried to kill us," he said, "and that doesn't make sense!"

Yes, Pard twitched in reply. The left wrist went limp: *Relax our body*.

Kent did so, and set the chair on recline. After all, they had an important concert to play in less than three hours, and they should be alert and vigorous, in body and in minds, for the performance.

He idly opened the Beethoven volume again. The pages happened to part where a photo had been inserted in the book, and he knew what it was before looking at it closely: another picture of the "mystery girl." He suspected that Pard had found the photos some time when Kent was taking a "walking nap." Maybe a previous occupant had left them in a hotel suite. Why Pard kept scattering the photos around for him to find, Kent couldn't guess, and he didn't try to ask. A joke, perhaps. Pard was sort of peculiar about women, anyway.

He put the photo back and laid the book aside. He had to get a little rest.

The holing of the clopter, he mused, if not some kind of wild accident, *had* to be the result of mistaken identity, or perhaps the act of a crackpot who regarded anybody well-heeled enough to travel by clopter as an enemy. The attack *couldn't* have been aimed at him personally . . . and, therefore, it wouldn't be repeated.

He dozed for the remainder of the flight, but his eyes stayed open and alert. Pard was keeping watch.

II

Kent woke when Pard set the clopter down lightly on a restricted portion of the USC Arts Complex roof, but he was content to observe as Pard slid the sonata volume from the craft. A roof attendant waved from some distance away, and started forward when Pard waved back.

Pard ducked under the clopter's cabin to peer up at its belly. He found the hole quickly, but after a glance at it he sidled another step toward the craft's centerline. Here he gazed up at a curious, bright green circular spot, about eight inches in diameter, which appeared painted on the craft's underside.

If the projectile had hit that spot, Kent realized, it would have hit him as well.

"You had a target to aim at!" Kent formed the words soundlessly.

Of course, Pard twitched, combining a nod and a shrug. He picked at the edge of the spot with a fingernail until he had enough of it free to grip between his fingers.

Then with one clean motion he peeled the entire spot from the metal surface. It looked like a disk of adhesive paper. Pard opened the hand satchel, slid the disk inside, and slapped it against the back of a music volume.

"Mr. Lindstrom?" called the roof attendant, peering under the craft. "Is anything wrong?"

"No," Kent replied. He took over, snapped the satchel shut, and crept out. "Something hit the clopter. I was taking a look at the hole it made."

The attendant's eyes widened. "That could've killed you!"

"Well, it didn't," Kent replied curtly. "Now if you'll direct me to my dressing room, and inform my manager Mr. Siskind that I've arrived . . ."

His recital went excellently. He played for a packed house in the main auditorium of the Arts Complex, with the program televised nationwide via the noncommercial channels. It was a golden opportunity to win public affirmation of the acclaim of the critics—that Kent Lindstrom was by all odds the foremost young pianist of the decade.

The reaction of the house proved he was doing exactly that. The audience did not wait until the end to give him a standing ovation; he got one for the final work before the intermission break, a fantasia composed by himself.

Beethoven's "Hammer-Klavier" sonata, almost as demanding of sheer physical endurance as of technical and interpretive skills, was the sole work following intermission. The sonata is analogous to the same composer's Ninth Symphony, in that it imposes such superhuman demands on performers that a merely adequate rendition is something to marvel at.

But Kent Lindstrom considered himself two pianists rather than one. There was Kent himself, the dominant consciousness, the boss, the inhabitant of the left hemisphere of the brain, who directed the right hand at the keyboard. And there was Pard, the voiceless secondary consciousness isolated in the severed right hemisphere, who directed the left hand.

Kent Lindstrom was, therefore, the one pianist of whom it could truly be said that his right hand didn't know what his left hand was doing. Complicated counterpoint and devilishly tricky cross-rhythms, that would swamp the brain of a normal pianist with the mere task of playing notes, were handled readily by Kent Lindstrom on a division-of-labor basis, leaving both his minds with attention to spare for interpretive niceties.

He did more than play the "Hammer-Klavier" sonata. He did the piece justice.

The applause was tremendous and demanding, but Kent had looked forward to this moment—when he was assuredly entered among the immortals of music—with too much anticipation to waste its essence on some crowd-pleasing little triviality of an encore.

He knew what to do instead. After several bows, he returned to the piano while a complete hush fell over the house. With his hands in his lap and his gaze on the keyboard, he counted twenty seconds of silence. Then he stood suddenly and faced the audience.

"Anything I could play after the great 'Hammer-Klavier' would be a terrible anticlimax," he proclaimed in a ringing voice. "Thank you, and good evening."

He strode from the stage to a final approving roar.

At the jubilant post-concert reception, attended by numerous civic and university bigwigs plus a selection of music students and faculty, Kent quickly spotted a girl he wanted.

His head gave a barely perceptible shake: *Lay off*, Pard warned him.

Kent frowned in dull anger, but obeyed. He had been through all this several times before, and knew that when Pard told him to stay away from a girl, he had better stay away! Even if Kent was the dominant consciousness, he could not keep up a continuous guard against Pard's sneaking enough control to make him do something absurdly embarrassing, and usually with the girl watching contemptuously.

There was the time in Washington, for instance, when Pard had him flitting around like a gay homosexual for five minutes before Kent even realized what was going on. An incident like that could be damaging, and very hard for a well-known musician to live down.

Kent griped to himself. On this night, of all nights, why can't I have a choice girl? Why's Pard so nonsensical about women, anyway?

But the giggly, blond student violinist Pard finally let him accept for the evening wasn't at all bad, even though she was a type that Kent couldn't get enthused about. He wasn't sorry to see her go when his unobtrusive business manager Dave Siskind, routed her politely from Kent's hotel suite around two A.M.

Kent yawned and settled down with the intention of sleeping at least until noon . . .

. . . And woke before dawn, fully clothed, crouched behind a dumpster in a dark alley, with a wavering ringing in his ears that he took a moment recognizing as police sirens.

He stared around wildly. The police, he could tell by the sound, were stopping at the mouth of the alley, while more sirens wailed a couple of blocks away. He turned to retreat deeper into the alley, but Pard stopped him.

That won't work.

"Blind alley?" Kent asked.

Yes.

Kent squatted back down and thought furiously. He had found indications before that Pard was an occasional night stroller: mud on shoes that had been clean when he went to bed, a few unaccounted-for scratches and bruises—and those photos of the "mystery girl" had to come from somewhere.

But Pard had never before wakened him during one of his after-hours jaunts. Why this time? Because Pard couldn't talk?

"You're in a mess I'm supposed to talk us out of," Kent guessed.

Yes.

Kent sighed unhappily, stood up, and walked out of the alley, into the glare of the police lights. Several officers rushed forward, and he was quickly frisked.

"Got any identification?" one demanded.

Kent felt in his empty pockets. "No. I left my wallet at the hotel. What's all this about?"

"Which hotel?"

"Sheraton Sunset. I'm Kent Lindstrom. Now, officers . . ."

"Lindstrom?" a policeman interrupted, staring at him closely. "Yeah, I guess you are at that. Hey, Mike! Call in that we've found Liindstrom! He looks OK, except for some skinned knuckles!"

Kent hadn't noticed the twinges of pain in his hands until then. He lifted them and glared at the bruised and bleeding knuckles. That goofy Pard! His hands were his *tools!* And tools were not to be abused in silly, back-alley brawls!

"Who'd you have a fight with?" the officer asked.

"I didn't ask their names," Kent replied, slightly pleased with his inspiration to make his opponents plural. "All I know is I couldn't sleep and went out for a stroll. After a while these guys jumped me. Let's see"—he peered around with a show of puzzlement—"I'm sort of turned around, but I think it happened over that way," he pointed, "maybe where those sirens are sounding."

It was a good guess. The policeman nodded. "That's about the luckiest stroll you ever took, Lindstrom!" he said. "You'll have to come down to headquarters and make a statement. I'll fill you in on the way."

"Lucky?" groaned Kent. "I'm a piano player, officer! And look at the mess I've got my hands in!"

"They'll heal," the policeman replied, "but if you'd been in your bed at three o'clock you wouldn't have! A bomb went off under it!"

There were complications at police headquarters, and Kent wound up in a cell. Whoever he had bloodied his knuckles on did not show up to complain, but there was also a question of attempted arson near the scene of the fight. And since the big-city riots of the 1960s, the police were inclined to keep a tight grip on anyone found near the scene of a set fire without a good excuse for being there.

Kent phoned his manager Siskind to get him an attorney. Then he was ushered to his private niche in the cell block, where he flopped on the bunk and quickly went to sleep.

III

When he woke he was relieved to find himself still on the bunk with his eyes closed. He sat up and peered through the bar-and-steel barriers until he spotted the keeper.

"Hey!" he called out. "When do I get breakfast?"

A man in a nearby cell chortled, "The curly-head pianner player wants his breakfast, fellers!" Kent ignored the remark and the resulting chuckles from the other prisoners.

"You get lunch in forty minutes," the keeper replied.

Kent stood up and began his morning workout as best he could within the confined space. This was his routine—a vigorous twenty minutes every morning to keep the rest of his body up to par with his hard working hands, arms and shoulders. With an audience this time, he show-boated a bit with extended push-ups, one-leg knee-bends, double flutter-whoops and other acrobatic exercies. The prisoners and keeper watched with gratifying awe. His knuckles, which the police surgeon had treated, gave him no pain under their bandages, so they were probably all right.

He saw that Siskind had brought his hand stachel and toilet kit to the jail for him. They were on the floor just inside his cell door. When he finished exercising he tossed the satchel on the bunk and took the kit to the tiny sink. His blade razor was missing, but the battery-powered shaver, which he used when he was in a hurry, was there. He shaved with it, washed up, and brushed his teeth.

Returning to the bunk he put his kit aside, sat down, and opened the satchel. A bright green oval gleamed out at him. He stared back at this chilling reminder that not one but two attempts on his life had been made within twenty-four hours.

"Better give this to the cops," he lipped soundlessly.

No, his head twitched firmly. *Give me control.*

He did, and Pard sat farther back on the bunk and hooked his heels over the metal edge, elevating his knees to conceal what he was doing. He took out the Debussy volume to which the green disc had adhered, propped the book on his thighs, and picked the disc loose from it.

He examined the disc closely. It was about the thickness of two sheets of typewriter paper, with about the same flexibility, Kent noted. There was no visible material on its back, but that side had strange *dry* stickiness to the touch. It was made of stout stuff that did not tear when Pard tugged hard at it. A definite line texture could be felt when he ran a finger across the green surface. Pard explored this texture until Kent was thoroughly bored. Finally he turned it over and began abrading one small area vigorously with a fingernail.

"Pard," urged Kent silently, "quit playing with that thing and give it to the cops! It could be just the evidence they need!"

No.

"Do you know what you're doing?"

Yes.

Suddenly the disc felt different, though it looked the same. The stickiness was gone from its back. Pard . . . had broken it in some way.

"Hey!" breathed Kent, with dawning comprehension. "It's electronic inside! Right?"

Yes

"And as soon as something hits it hard enough to tear up its circuit . . ." He left the words unmouthed, his mind filled with a picture of a little projectile zipping up from the New Mexican waste to home in on the green disc and plow through it—and incidentally, through Kent Lindstrom—and of the no longer adhesive disc fluttering free to fall in the desert, where it would never be found to incriminate anybody.

There had to be something like the disc. Otherwise the projectile could never have come so close to a bull's-eye over such a distance. Pard had deflected the clopter with split-second timing, too late for the projectile to adjust its course.

Kent gazed at the disc in awe. "I've never heard of such a thing! Is it military or something?"

Yes.

"Secret stuff?"

Yes.

"How did you know about it?"

Pard shrugged. An unanswerable question.

Worse and worse! thought Kent in sudden fear. Whoever's after me has access to secret weapons! No wonder Pard figures the cops can't help! But why am *I* in such a mess?

There was only one possible answer to that: his silent, night-walking skull companion, Pard.

"You've done something that's got us in this jam!" he accused.

Yes.

Pard was keeping his hands busy. He had curled the disk into a tight slender roll, and now was taking the plastic shell off his battery-powered shaver.

Only by an extended guessing game, Kent knew, could he ever get the full story out of Pard. That could take more weeks than somebody meant him to live! But he knew of one guess he could make as a starter.

"Is that 'mystery girl' in the photos mixed up in this?"

Yes. Pard wedged the rolled-up disk into the shaver so that it was pressed against, and perpendiciular to, the windings of the tiny motor coil.

"You in love with her or something?"

Yes. Pard flicked the shaver's switch and the motor buzzed. Nothing else happened for about a second.

Then at least a dozen things happened at once.

Lights throughout the cell block flickered, and two of them exploded with dazzling flashes. Sirens whopped deafeningly. Bells clanged. Electronically-activated cell doors clicked loudly as their locks opened. The loud-speaker system blared out the first two bars of "The Star-Spangled Banner" and then went dead.

The prisoners, offered a golden opportunity, swarmed from their cells, flattened the startled keeper, and made for the nearest exits, shouting in gleeful excitement. Pard, his gadget in his hand, leaped to his feet and started to join them.

"No!" shouted Kent. "Don't be a fool, Pard!"

Pard hesitated.

"Running from the law *and* from secret killers at the same time is for TV heroes and other fictitious characters!" Kent mouthed urgently. "Now sit down and do something about that stupid gadget! Go on! You can't go far hopping on one leg, anyhow, and *my* leg isn't moving a muscle until you start showing some sense!"

Pard shrugged and hopped back to the bunk. "That's more like it," said Kent, relaxing control of the right leg.

The gadget was still buzzing. Kent knew very little about electronics. When Pard read an electronics magazine after going to bed, Kent usually went to sleep immediately. But he had picked up enough general ideas to guess how the gadget worked.

The circuit in the green disc was a highly sensitive responser, meant to pick up signals from an oncoming missile, amplify and perhaps vary them in a certain manner, and send them back as instructions to the missile.

That's what the circuit did when it was spread out flat, when there was no interference between the tiny electromagnetic fields produced by its thousands of microscopic components. When rolled into a tight tube . . . well, it still did something similar, but not as a precise response to one particular signal. It was confused and undiscriminating. It responded to every blip of electromagnetic energy it picked up—from the sixty-cycle alternation in the building's electric wiring, from the fluorescent light switches, from the alarm network. And with what was, for it, an overpowering input of energy from the shaver coil to work with, it responded with roars!

"Turn it off!" mouthed Kent.

The left hand started, slowly and unwillingly, to obey, but just then the gadget quit by itself, having exhausted the battery in no more than a minute. Pard yanked out the rolled-up disc, wadded it and tossed it in the toilet bowl by the sink. He was putting the re-assembled shaver away when the lights came back on.

Seconds later a contingent of armed policemen rushed in to stare at the empty cells in angry frustration.

"Most of your guests have checked out," Kent offered.

A sergeant glowered at him and tried his cell door. It was still unlocked. "Why're you still here?" he demanded.

"Because I've done nothing to run from."

The keeper came up rubbing his bruised head. "That's Lindstrom," he told the sergeant. "The piano player."

"Oh, yeah." The sergeant watched as Kent strolled over to the toilet bowl, flushed it.

"What happened to the lights and things, Sergeant?" Kent asked.

"That's no concern of yours—or mine either," the sergeant grunted, walking away.

The escapees were brought in one and two at a time during the early afternoon, and returned disgruntled to their cells. Lunch was over an hour late.

IV

Around three o'clock Kent was taken to an interview room, where his manager

166   Verge Foray

Siskind introduced him to the attorney he had hired, and to a couple of police technicians.

"Mr. Lindstrom," the lawyer said briskly, "I believe we can wrap this business up in a hurry, thanks in no small part to your display of good faith during that jailbreak today. There is no real evidence against you in this arson business, but the police could hold you a couple of days on suspicion alone. I've explained to the proper authorities that you have an important schedule to maintain, and they're willing to be reasonable.

"Thus, Mr. Lindstrom, if you will submit to questioning under the polygraph, sometimes known as the lie detector, to demonstrate your innocence to these gentlemen—"

"I don't trust those polygraph gadgets," Kent broke in. "I read something somewhere about being inaccurate."

"The device has shortcomings," the attorney admitted, "but these experts are aware of them, and take them into account. Also, I'm here to see that the questioning stays relevant, that no 'fishing expeditions' are attempted. This is a quick way to clear yourself, Mr. Lindstrom."

Kent hesitated. A polygraph could be dangerous for him, in more ways than one. Maybe he was last night's arsonist. Or, more precisely, maybe Pard was. Then there was the fact of Pard's existence. Only Kent knew that his brain had an extra occupant, and he wanted to keep that information to himself. A lie detector test could betray Pard's presence in some manner.

He was about to reject the examination when Pard twitched a signal.
Yes.
Kent rubbed his nose to hide his mouth while he asked, "You mean take the test?"
Yes. I'm going to sleep.
That ought to solve the problem, Kent decided. With Pard asleep, he certainly could not react to the polygraph.
"OK," Kent said. "Let's get it over with."

The police technicians took several minutes to rig him for the examination, during which Kent assured himself that Pard had dozed off. The questioning had hardly started when the door opened and a distinguished, graying man was ushered in.

"This is Mr. Byers," said the officer with him. "He represents the owners of that warehouse."

"Yes," said Byers, "and if, as I've just learned upon arriving in the building, the charges against this young man are to depend on a single polygraph examination, I must insist on being present during the examination. I don't like these attempts to shortcut justice, gentlemen," he went on with a stern frown. "Nor do I like to see the law be made a respecter of persons, especially a respecter of a person who, while laying claim to a certain artistic notoriety, is not known for the stability of his deportment. But I'm a realist, gentlemen: I'm aware of the pressures under which the police must attempt to carry out their duties. Thus, since I have little choice in the matter, I'll go along with this procedure, provided I am present.''

Kent had a feeling that Byers wasn't nearly so put out by the lie detector test as he claimed to be.

"Any objections?" asked one of the officers.

"Nah," grunted Kent. "Let the old square stay."

"Providing Mr. Byers refrains from interfering with the proper conduct of the test," amended Kent's attorney.

"OK. Let's proceed," said the officer.

First there were the usual trial questions to establish Kent's true-and-false reactions. Then the technician in charge got down to business.

QUESTION: When you retired last night, you found you could not go to sleep?

ANSWER: Well, I went halfway to sleep. Not fully.

Q: Why didn't you take a pill?

A: I don't take pills unless I'm really sick.

Q: So you went walking?

A: Yes.

Q: Wasn't that a strange thing to do at that time of night, and in an unfamiliar city?

A: Depends on what you think is strange. I do it every now and then.

Q: Where did you walk?

A: I don't know. As you said, Los Angeles is not familiar to me.

Q: When did you leave the hotel?

A: Between two and three. Maybe two forty-five.

Q: Are you aware that two attempts were made on your life, yesterday and last night?

A: I sure am!

Q: Why didn't you report the first one to the police?

A: Because I thought it might be some crazy accident at first. You know about it now, so what's the difference?

Q: Who's trying to kill you?

A: I don't know.

Byers was hovering over the other technician, watching the tale told by the polygraph needles. His frown was taking on a touch of puzzled doubt.

Q: Why would someone want to kill you?

A: It must be over some girl. I don't know what else.

Q: What girl?

A: I have no idea who she is.

Byers went over to whisper into the questioner's ear. The man looked annoyed, but nodded.

Q: You've been intimate with a number of girls, then?

A: Well, yes. A man in my position has so many—

Q: Have you ever displayed homosexual tendencies?

A: No!

Q: Do you want to reconsider that answer?

A: Oh, there was that foolishness in Washington last year! But that was just a put-
ᵔ. An act. Maybe it was in bad taste, but that's all it was!

Q: OK. Now, about last night. Who were the men in the brawl with you?

A: I don't know. I couldn't identify them if I saw them.

Q: Are you sure one of them wasn't the night watchman of the warehouse?

A: No, I'm not sure of that. I don't even know what building you mean when you
ᵞy the warehouse. All I know is, I wasn't looking for a fight, with a watchman or
ᵞybody else.

Q: We think someone got an oily rag out of a garage trash can, wrapped it around
rock, set it afire, and threw it through the warehouse window. Did you do that, or
ᵞything similar to that, last night?

A: No.

Q: Do you carry matches, or a lighter?

A: Not often. I don't smoke. Sometimes I have matches if I have been with a girl
ᵞho does. I don't recall having any last night.

The questioner sat back in his chair and glanced around. "Anything else?" he
ᵞked.

Byers was furious. "This whole thing's a farce!" he stormed. "This long-haired
ᵞoung ruffian is obviously abnormal in mind, and can fool your machine!"

The questioner glared at him. "You seem convinced of Lindstrom's guilt, Byers,"
ᵞ said coldly, "but if you have any evidence to that effect you've withheld it from
ᵞe police! And let's remember two things. One, your clients are going to have some
ᵞll explaining to do about what the firemen found in their warehouse—"

"My clients were unaware of what use some unauthorized trespassers were making
ᵞ their premises!" Byers protested.

"Two," the officer continued relentlessly, "somebody has tried to kill Lindstrom,
ᵞd you're showing an unaccountable animosity toward him. Could there be a con-
ᵞction, Mr. Byers?"

"Absurd!"

"Will you sit in Lindstrom's chair and repeat that?"

"I'll have nothing to do with your rigged machines!" snapped Byers, drawing back.
ᵞe headed for the door, firing a parting comment over his shoulder: "This country
ᵞ in a sad condition when officers of the law start siding with hoodlums and beatniks!"

"Did I pass the test OK?" Kent asked as the technicians detached the monitoring
ᵞevices from him.

"Yes. You're free to go. But you should ask for police protection till we get to the
ᵞottom of this."

He nodded and asked cautiously, "What was going on in that warehouse, anyway?"

"Illicit arms storage," the chief technician replied.

"Stolen rifles and such, huh?"

"Not exactly rifles. More firepower than that. Military stuff. Enough to tear the city apart!"

Kent had a stunned feeling of unreality, as if he were involved in a silly dream. How could a harmless pianist get tangled up in this deadly game, he wondered plaintively.

But tangled up he was, thanks to Pard. That green disk was a military device. And now a cache of military armament! It tied together, and tied him in!

V

He and Dave Siskind rode back to the hotel in a police car, since the officers did not want to risk him in a taxi. He had little to say on the way, and if Siskind took his silence for fright, he was not inclined to disagree.

"Dave," he asked at last, "did you find out who that guy Byers represented?"

"Yeah. An old couple named Morgan. Right-wing oddballs. But the police figure they're innocent dupes, and Byers is really fronting for somebody else."

A couple of blocks later Siskind asked softly, "Want me to cancel everything for a while?"

"I don't know. What's next on the schedule?"

"The Tchaikovsky in Toronto, with the dress tomorrow night. I ought to be on my way now, and you're booked on TransAm at 9:47 this evening."

Kent thought it over. The temptation was to stick to the schedule, to act as if nothing were wrong.

"I'll let you know in a little while, after we get to the hotel," he said.

As soon as he was alone in his room he woke Pard.

"Well, I'm out of jail," he mouthed, "but maybe I would be safer in. Here's what happened." Quickly he filled Pard in, then said, "The question is, do we stick to the schedule?"

Yes.

"Suits me. I'll tell Siskind I'll be on the TransAm flight."

No.

"Huh? Now what?"

Pard tapped Kent's side of the skull: *Use your brain.*

Kent tried it, "Oh," he muttered. "I see your point. No innocent bystanders, huh? Except *me.*"

Yes.

Kent called Siskind in. "Dave, I'm going to stay on schedule, but after what happened I'd better not travel with other people. They might get hurt. See if the police will make secret arrangements for me to leave on another fast clopter—maybe from the hotel roof."

His manager nodded. "That makes sense. I'll travel with you this time. Maybe we can be—"

Kent was shaking his head. "No. By myself, Dave."

Siskind shrugged helplessly. "You're the boss. Good luck." He reached the door and turned to say, "That was a great performance last night, Kent. The recording of it will be a classic, no matter what!"

"Why, thanks, Dave."

His manager left him wondering if he had just heard his own funeral oration.

The clopter was waiting on the roof at 7:30. He walked to it in the twilight, escorted by Dave and two policemen, then ducked down and scooted underneath the craft.

"Hey!" a policeman objected.

"Just curious," Kent explained, coming out. "The clopter I came in had a hole in it, and I wondered if this was the same bucket."

"No. That one's impounded," said the officer.

Kent climbed into the doorway and stood on tiptoes to examine the roof. "It had a hole in its top, too," he explained. No green spot, nor even a slight irregularity in the clean metal, could he see.

Satisfied, he got in, waved, and took off.

As soon as he was established in the northeast traffic pattern he got a twitch from Pard: *Give me control.*

"Boy, if you could only talk," Kent moaned, "I'd give you control from here on out!"

Pard twisted out of the seat, which was not easy in the cramped compartment and methodically began pulling the seat to pieces. "What now?" Kent demanded.

His skull-mate ignored him and kept working until he found what he was after. It was under a reglued manufacturer's label on the shock-cushion asembly.

Another green disc!

Squatting in the clutter of seat components, Pard got a razor blade from his toilet kit and hurriedly sliced the disk into tiny shreds. These he wadded into the remains of the label. He tugged the emergency-vent plug out of the side of the cabin and allowed the escaping air to yank the wad out of the clopter entirely. Then he shoved the plug back in place and waited for the air pressure to normalize. When he was breathing easily again he reassembled the seat and wriggled back into it.

Relax, his writst twitched.

What was Pard up to anyway? Kent wondered fretfully. And how could he *possibly* have got mixed up with the kind of people who stole secret weapons and planted bombs under beds? Kent simply didn't *mingle* with such grim individuals, so how could Pard have managed to do so? Of course, there were those midnight strolls of Pard's, but how involved could a man get who couldn't communicate? Yet, Pard was entangled in something, as the "mystery girl's" pictures testified. And Pard said he was in love with her!

Kent mumbled, "You sure that girl is worth all this?"

Yes.

"How do you know? Have you kissed her?"

No.

"Touched her at all?"

No.

Kent sneered. "One of those I-worship-thee-from-afar bits, huh? You're an oddball, Pard! You really are!" He sat back huffily, staring ahead into the starry night. "She's the reason you won't let me get involved with any kind of girl except cheap fluff," he guessed after a moment.

Yes.

"And you keep strewing her pictures around for me to find. Am I supposed to fall for her, too?"

Yes.

"Huh!" Kent grunted disgustedly. But he had to admit that the "mystery girl" looked most appealing, with that uncertain little smile. Maybe she was right for him. It would be fun to meet her and find out. Besides, he was twenty-four years old, and ought to be thinking about marriage. And his wife should meet Pard's approval, because in a way she would be Pard's wife, too.

Poor old Pard, he mused. A mind living all these, let's see . . . these eighteen years in isolation, practically incommunicado. What strange thoughts would such a mind have by now?

He and Pard had been one person at first, so whatever Pard was now was what Kent himself would probably be if he had been stuck with the voiceless half of their brain. Kent tried to imagine himself in that situation, but it was too much for him to picture. It was a wonder, he decided, that Pard hadn't gone raving mad long ago!

He had been too young at the time of their separation to recall many details. That was in the year of the big Florida hurricane, when he was six . . . A lot of loud noise and the house tearing up all around him, and something hurting his head, and his mother and father never being found . . .

He had no memory of being violently epileptic at the little rural hospital where the rescuers took him. He was told about that a week or two later, after he had been operated on and was well. The old doctor had been awfully nice to him, and had said how sorry he was that the hospital didn't have the equipment to make him well with just a small operation instead of a big one.

Kent remembered some of the doctor's words:

"We had to give you a partner, son, to live inside you. You and he must be friends, and always work and play together, because he can make you do things you don't want to do if you fuss with each other, or he can keep his side of your body from doing what you tell it, if he wishes. And probably only one of you will be able to talk, and the one who talks should be especially nice to the other one. And the one who can talk must never tell other people about his partner, because other people might think you are still sick, and make you stay in a hospital all the time."

When he was older, Kent had read up on the treatment of epilepsy, to learn what had been done to him.

It was a drastic cure worked out some ten years earlier, back in the 1960s, and justifiable only in the most violent cases even then. It had soon become outmoded as neural research learned how to pinpoint more precisely the cause of epilepsy in an injured brain. But that old country neurosurgeon in Florida had doubtless done his best under emergency conditions.

The operation amounted, quite simply, to slashing the two hemispheres of the brain apart. The connective neural tissues near the core of the brain—the corpus callosum and the lesser commissures—were cut, breaking communication between hemispheres and at the same time disrupting the epileptic syndrome.

The consequences of such an operation were less severe than one might expect, especially in an adult patient. Either hemispere can direct almost all body functions. The two hemispheres begin their existence in a nearly balanced state, but during childhood one becomes increasingly dominant as the seat of consciousness—the left hemisphere in right-handed persons and vice versa—while the other becomes responsible for less exalted sensory and motor functions. Thus, in the adult patient there would be no emphatic "twoness," no great awareness within the severed secondary hemisphere.

But as the old doctor had known or suspected, this was not necessarily true of a six-year-old. Consolidation of ego in a single hemisphere would have only started, primarily with the shift of language functions to one center. A major portion of Kent Lindstrom could never move out of the secondary hemsiphere, because the bridges were down, and would grow—if it grew at all—as a separate ego, a silent partner — Pard.

So there they were—as far as Kent knew the only human of their kind in existence—a duplex man, two functioning minds in one body. And a hell of an inconvenience to each other—except at the piano, of course.

But Kent could console himself that Pard was basically a nice, reasonably sane guy, even if he was mixed up in something pretty weird. The mob was out to kill him, which proved he wasn't on their side. And the upshot of his acts in Los Angeles had been the exposure of that weapons cache.

Also, Pard's special interests—electronic gadgetry and the like—might be trivial, but there was nothing unwholesome about them.

"Pard," Kent said at last, "those characters know we're headed for Toronto. Won't they be waiting for us?"

Yes.

"We've got to stay alive and get to the bottom of this," said Kent, "and our chances of doing either in Toronto don't seem worth a damn. If I talked to this chick of yours, would she fill me in?"

Yes.

"Where is she?"

Pard pulled a map out of the rack and put a finger on New York City.

"I'm sure to be recognized there!" Kent protested.

Pard swooped a finger through the air and down on a little town in New Jersey, then rubbed it along the map to the big city. Kent nodded.

"Yeah, it might help to land in a cornball town and go the rest of the way by train. But I wish I had a disguise!"

Pard made clipping motions around his head.

"That's what I was afraid you would do," Kent glummed. Nevertheless, he took the scissors and a small mirror from his toilet kit and began shearing his long curly locks. He had trimmed his coiffure frequently—but far less severely in the past, and could do a neat job of it. But when he had the mop down to businessman-length, he stared in the mirror with sad misgivings.

"I don't know what my fans in Toronto will think of this," he mourned, "if I ever get to Toronto."

VI

He reached Manhattan shortly after midnight. The town, away from the tourist-trap centers, was resting quietly.

Pard walked into a well-kept residential section and halted in a shadowed spot near the beginning of a long block of brownstones. He watched and listened intently for a minute, then moved cautiously ahead. Halfway down the block he paused in front of a house and looked around again.

"Where is she?" Kent mouthed.

Pard shrugged: *I don't know.*

"Is this where she lives?" Kent persisted.

Yes-no.

"If you're trying to confuse me, you're doing great!"

Pard didn't respond. He went up the steps of the house, and Kent saw the row of apartment bell buttons. Pard quickly mashed every button, then hurried down the steps and across the street, where he hid behind an illegally parked car.

Lights came on in the apartments, and after a couple of minutes someone opened the door and peered outside. Kent could hear loud words being exchanged, but couldn't understand them. Five minutes later the house was dark again.

Pard stayed a little longer behind the car, then strolled away.

Mystified, Kent hazarded, "Was that some kind of code to find out if she was home?"

After a pause: *Yes.*

"Not quite right, huh?"

Yes.

By subway and bus Pard went into the New Jersey suburbs. He wound up in front f a home that Kent put in the seventy thousand dollar class. The place was dark and ilent.

Pard eased across the lawn, then around the corner and along the side of the house. An empty garbage can stood behind a side porch. Pard picked up the can and flung t with all his strength against the wall of the house.

A shrill feminine scream, followed by enraged male curses, came from inside, and Pard scooted behind a neighbor's garage. He peeked out to see the porch light come n and a heavy man lurch out carrying a mean-looking rifle. The man looked at the garbage can, cursed some more, and glared out into the night, his eyes halting on Pard's hiding place much too long for Kent's mental comfort. At last the man stalked ack inside, slammed the door, and turned off the light.

As Pard crept away and headed back for the bus line, Kent growled angrily, "Are you supposed to be accomplishing something?"

Yes.

"Damned if I can see what!" Kent snapped. "If this is the way you spend your nights out, I wonder why you bother!"

Pard napped while Kent returned to the town where he had left the clopter. He had breakfast there just after dawn, and refueled the clopter. Pard had indicated he wanted o head west again.

"Where to now?" he asked when they were airborne. Pard opened the map and pointed to Green River, Wyoming. "The girl's somewhere around there, you think?"

Yes.

"I hope you're right for a change!" Kent snapped, thinking of the rehearsal with the Toronto Symphony he seemed destined to miss that evening. A dress rehearsal at that! A concert artist who didn't show up for engagements could get a stinky reputation, no matter how good he was!

He must have unconsciously mouthed his fretful thoughts, because Pard put an imaginary pistol to his head and pulled the trigger, to remind him that some gents whose instruments were more percussive than those of an orchestra were also waiting in Toronto. Kent simmered down quickly.

Pard landed the clopter at a public field in Green River, and steered Kent to a rent-a-car agency. The girl behind the desk looked like a person of culture, which worried Kent briefly, but she did not recognize his name when he signed for the car. He decided she couldn't be so very cultured after all.

From a distance the place looked like a ranch out of a TV western. It was about fifty miles out of Green River, a distance that took Pard nearly an hour and a half to drive over narrow country roads that were by turn pot-holed and rutted. They saw no other car during the final ten miles.

Pard parked out of sight and approached the house on foot, staying under cover. Kent wondered where Pard had learned his infiltration technique. They hadn't had military training—the civilian draft having ended a decade before they came of age—but Pard dashed from tree to bush to gully as if he knew what he was doing.

The frightening thing to Kent was that Pard thought it advisable to sneak up on the ranch house in this manner. Here he was, miles from nowhere without even a pea shooter, and Pard was behaving as if he were going up against a machine-gun nest.

"This is crazy!" Kent mouthed.

Relax.

"Nuts to relaxing! Just when our career was starting to look so great . . ."

But he didn't interfere with Pard's actions. Pard seemingly knew the score, and this was probably better than just waiting to be killed, and—

Machine-gun slugs stitched the dirt four feet from where Pard had crouched behind a bush, and the air was rent by the weapon's startling chatter. Pard hugged the ground, staring at the house still over a hundred yards away.

A loudspeaker bellowed at him: "SURPRISE, LINDSTROM! DIDN'T EXPECT REMOTE CONTROLLED DEFENSES, DID YOU! WALK FORWARD WITH YOUR HANDS UP!"

Pard crouched a moment longer, then stood up and started toward the house. *Take over,* he twitched.

The man on the loudspeaker lowered the volume to a more conversational level and said jovially, "That's one of the advantages of this rustic setting. It makes people think in terms of cowboys toting six-shooters! No gun without a man behind it. So fools and telepaths rush in!" The voice stopped and a mine exploded fifty feet behind Kent, knocking him flat on his face.

"You're not hurt!" the voice snapped. "Get up and come on! That was to remind you of two things: that you're never out of my range, and I don't care greatly if you wind up dead!"

Kent got to his feet, groggy with concussion, and plodded through the yard and onto the porch. The door opened and two guys with pistols came out.

"Inside, Buddy!" one of them barked, stepping aside.

Kent went through the door and saw a third man who was covering him from in front.

"Down on your belly!" this one ordered. Kent obeyed, and only then did one of the men step forward to frisk him. "Roll over real slow," he was told. He did so, and the man finsihed frisking him.

"Now get up and move! Down the hall and down the stairs!"

Kent stood and moved off, noticing that the gunmen stayed a careful distance from him at all times, with their pistols leveled at his middle. Their caution was puzzling, but not comforting. They looked intelligent as well as tough, and they weren't giving him a chance to try anything desperate, even if he had the nerve, which he definitely did not! But maybe Pard did!

"Nothing rash," he pleaded silently.

Relax.

* * *

He was steered into a room where three people were waiting: A beetle-browed man sitting behind a desk, wearing an army general's uniform. Mr. Byers from Los Angeles, standing by the desk and smiling triumphantly. And the "mystery girl," in a chair in a corner of the room with her right wrist manacled to a hook in the wall.

Kent felt slightly acquainted with all three.

The man behind the desk said, "I'm sure there's no need for introductions, so—"

"I disagree," said Kent, determined to show some spunk if only verbally. "Mr. Byers I've met, but the young lady I've only admired from afar. And as for you, General Preston, I know who you are—hero of the Viet Nam wars, conservative presidential timber, and all that—but I don't know you in your present role. Do they give out medals these days for shooting piano players?"

Preston chuckled. "Good boy! I admire brashness in the face of danger! You might have made a decent soldier, Lindstrom, if this sick land of ours didn't regard 'decent soldier' as a contradictory term! To save argument I'll go along with your pretense of ignorance. The young lady's name is Peggy Glodget, of course.

"As for myself—I assume you are also pretending ignorance of my political views?"

"It's no pretense," said Kent. "Politics bore me."

"Very well. Since the collapse of communism in the early 1970s, this once great nation of ours has gone to pot, Lindstrom!" The general's eyes glittered. "We're giving away our unmatched wealth to good-for-nothing loafers! We, the greatest power in the world, have gone flabby! We no longer exercise our strength, either diplomatically or militarily! We don't lead by precept! We've turned into a bunch of bleeding-hearts and soft touches! What we don't give away we waste on effeminate living. You're a prime example, boy! A potential fighting man, playing sissy slop on the piano!"

"What's sissy about the 'Hammer-Klavier'?" Kent flared.

"Shut up and listen! I'm no man to waste words! I'm a man of action, a man who makes his speeches, but who then goes a step further than the cheap politicians who are ruining our country! I back up my speeches with deeds!"

"Such deeds as shooting sissy piano players?" Kent retorted.

"Such as eliminating any fool who gets in my way!" the general told him grimly. "And you, interfering with our Miss Blodget here, were doing exactly that!"

Kent shrugged. "But what can you gain from doing things like that, and stealing secret weapons, general? A man like you! What are you after?"

Preston stared at him. "I'm after this nation's salvation, boy! That can be won only if my friends and myself assume top leadership, preferably with the support of the public, but without it if the public prefers to remain asleep!"

"Dictatorship, huh?" muttered Kent, and then he rushed on before the general had time to blow his top: "But how does Miss Blodget figure in this? She doesn't look the type."

"Miss Blodget, as you well know, has a special talent," said the general. "And she was favorably impressed by my speeches. Thus, when she realized the patriotic thing for her to do was to offer her talent to her country, she came to me.'' He turned and gazed at the young woman, then added, ''Unfortuantely, Miss Blodget's patriotism lacks realism. She is slow to convince that to make an omelet, eggs must be broken. So she attempted desertion, first without and later with your assistance.''

''What's this talent of hers?'' asked Kent.

General Preston fidgeted impatiently. ''I'm getting tired of this game!'' he snapped. ''We will waste no more time telling you things you've known for months!''

The girl spoke for the first time. ''I'm a telepath, Kent. That makes me useful to the general when I'm within my eighty-yard range of the United Nations, or the White House, or the Pentagon. Of course, he doesn't get my help willingly.''

''Shut up!'' bellowed Preston. ''You answer my questions, nobody else's!'' He glared at Kent. ''When I sought to eliminate you, boy, it was because you were in my way. But I can use you alive now. Miss Blodget is sentimental about her home town—Los Angeles. That was the major present purpose of our arms chache there. I had to pose a very real, very serious threat to the peace of her city, to bring her to terms and win her cooperation! Since she's telepathic, she can't be bluffed.

''Now, thanks to you, that threat and our most important supply of weapons has been stolen from us! And you've earned yourself a new job! You, boy, are my replacement for Los Angeles! Obviously, Miss Blodget cares very much what happens to you! She'll cooperate to keep you safe!'' He smiled coldly and continued:

''That's why I set this little trap for you, with her as the bait. Mr. Byers was sent to Los Angeles to feed you the information that Miss Blodget was being brought here.'' The general paused and gazed at Kent curiously. ''I was beginning to wonder, however, if you were going to fall for it. Byers had never been to this ranch before. So he didn't know it was my chief stronghold, and would be a trap for you. Also, he didn't know my real purpose in sending him to see you. What made you suspicious, Lindstrom? Why didn't you get here last night when I expected you? I even had a responser hidden in your clopter to warn us of your approach. Where did you go first?''

Kent shrugged distractedly and didn't reply. Pard, he remembered, had been sleeping the whole time Byers had been near him yesterday. Was that why he didn't get Preston's message? And Peggy Blodget was a telepath with an eighty-yard range . . . and Pard knew her. Also, Pard had acted so strangely in New York and New Jersey last night, waking people up and then moving on as if he had learned something from them, and . . . and it all began to make a terrifying kind of sense!

But why hadn't Pard ever *told* him?

''It would be hard for him to explain,'' answered Peggy, ''and he knew you wouldn't take the news very well.''

''I told you to shut up, girl!'' roared Preston. She grinned a sad but unbowed little grin, and Kent suddenly knew she was the most wonderful girl in the universe.

Preston was speaking to him again. ''Later on, Lindstrom, I may give you an assignment similar to Miss Blodget's—her covering the U.N. and Washington and you on a roving basis, each responsible for the other's safety. But that would require dividing my inner circle—the gentlemen in this room today—into two teams, with several new members to be trusted with the secret of Miss Blodget and yourself. That would be risky right now. Later, perhaps . . .

"But now, Lindstrom, let's put Miss Blodget into a proper frame of mind. She must feel pity for you, and a sense of responsibility. You both know what I have in mind, but the real experience should be far more convincing than my mental image of it. I believe, Lindstrom, that the end segment of the little finger is quite important to a piano player. Isn't that true?"

Kent nodded slowly.

"The removal of yours, from both hands, will not be extremely painful," Preston continued. "I'm no savage who goes in for idle torture! But I believe this will have a salutary effect on you and Miss Blodget with a minimum of bloodshed. Gentlemen, you may proceed!"

Give me control, twitched Pard.

"No!" Kent yelled aloud. "The Chopin Configuration!"

Yes, agreed Pard.

"What's that?" asked the general as two of his henchmen, after shoving their pistols into shoulder holsters, moved in on their captive while the third covered them.

Kent had neither the time nor the intention to explain that the "Chopin Configuration" was a special way of sharing responsibilities between Pard and himself—a way he hoped would enable them to fight like two men instead of one. In several of the first Chopin compositions he had learned to play, the left-hand part was far more demanding than the right-hand part. Kent had found that the best way to handle these pieces was to give Pard control of the entire body, except for the right hand and arm. This arrangement he called the "Chopin Configuration," although he used it frequently in playing other works.

And now, if there was going to be a fight, Kent did not intend to sit jittering helplessly in his skull while Pard alone took on five able-bodied men! Especially not with Peggy watching!

"Take the eyes, too!" Peggy called, and he knew she was relaying a message from Pard, who could fight without seeing.

"Your show of indifference doesn't move me, Miss Blodget," chuckled General Preston, misinterpreting her meaning. "Just the small fingertips, gentlemen!"

Kent lashed out with a sudden judo chop at the neck of the man on his side, but the blow landed on the chin and stunned the man only slightly, while—

The man on Pard's side moved in swiftly, and Pard gave with his motion, clamped the man's throat hard in the bend of his arm and swung him around as a shield against the covering gunman, who was looking for a clear shot, while—

Kent kept grabbing at his staggered opponent, and finally caught his jacket arm and jerked him into the melee, and fumbled under the man's jacket for his gun, while—

Pard broke his man's neck, then whirled the tangle around once and flung the body at the feet of the advancing gunman, where it flopped disconcertingly to the gunman's momentary dismay, then reached around to clamp his fingers on the throat of Kent's reviving opponent, while—

Kent yanked out the man's pistol just in time to raise it and shoot the advancing gunman as Pard's motion brought that enemy into view, while—

Pard went for the knife in the man's belt and slung it at Byers, who had moved away from the desk and was drawing his own pistol, but the knife missed, while—

General Preston had extracted his old army revolver from the desk and was aiming it at the no longer shielded Lindstrom, while—

Kent located Byers and put a bullet in that worthy's arm, causing him to drop his gun and lurch toward the door, while—

Peggy removed a slender shoe and threw it awkwardly with her free left hand at General Preston's temples, but only grazed his nose, while—

Preston whirled angrily and snapped a shot at her, and missed because she knew when to duck, while—

Kent finally got focused on the general, and put a bullet squarely between his eyes.

The rest was mere mop-up.

Kent's first opponent was still moving. He was crawling rapidly toward Byers' gun when Kent's bullet stopped him for good.

Pard ran out of the hall after Byers, whose retreating back was thirty feet away.

"Shoot him!" shouted Peggy.

Kent didn't raise the gun.

"Idiot!" snapped Peggy as Pard suddenly reached the left hand over, yanked the pistol from Kent's grasp, and drilled Byers.

"Why'd ya do that?" Kent mumbled thickly. "He had no fight left in him!"

"Because he knew about us," Peggy called out. "He was the only one left who did!"

Pard went back in the room, examined the bodies briefly, then got a key from Preston's pocket and unsnapped Peggy's manacles. She immediately went to the desk, studied the array of controls for a moment, then did things to them.

"Five minutes to get out of here," she said, dashing for the door with Pard following.

As they ran across the yard Kent puffed, "How is it you can talk if you and Pard are . . . are alike?"

"Because I'm a natural telepath. He seems to be accidental. That operation isolated him at an age when the urge to communicate was very strong. My hemispheres are joined."

"You're the only one he's found?" asked Kent.

"Yes."

"I'm glad it's you, Peggy. You're a beautiful girl."

She laughed lightly. "Keep running. This place is going to blow sky-high in a couple of minutes!"

"We'll be running the rest of our lives!" Kent fretted.

"No. We've chopped the head off Preston's monster, and it'll die now. We'll even make that Toronto rehearsal this evening!" She slid into an erosion gully and Pard leaped down beside her. They huddled there and waited.

A few seconds later all hell broke loose behind them. The sound and concussion of air and earth hit them with solid, jolting blows. Pard held her closely. It was like being next door to a major battlefield.

But it ended quickly. Peggy lifted her head with a half-frightened giggle. "We're safe, but we'd better scram!"

They climbed out of the gully and walked on swiftly toward the car.

"This has been a rough couple of days, Peggy," said Kent, "but I'm suddenly quite sure it was worth it!"

"Why, thank you, kind sir!" She smiled winningly.

"I'm especially glad for Pard," he added. "Life must've been pretty dismal for him up to now. It's great to find somebody he likes, and who can talk to him. He shouldn't feel so secondary from now on!"

"Pard? Secondary?" asked Peggy.

"Yeah. You know. Having to play second fiddle to me all the time."

She looked amused but said nothing. Kent was vaguely uncomfortable about the way this conversation was going. But of course, he told himself, she can anticipate my words before I say them! No wonder she responds a little strangely! I'll get accustomed to that!

They reached a level path and her hand caught his. An instant later he was delighted to find her in his arms, and the kiss she gave him was hard to believe. It was magnificent!

Then his bright new world turned dark—because she was murmuring passionately into his ear: "Pard, oh dear, wonderful Pard! I love you so!"

Kent was dismally certain he would never get accustomed to that! ∎

Sailing, Through Program Management

Al Charmatz

Your Excellency:

Please convey word of this victory to our most illustrious King and Queen. Glorious news! The Expedition to the Indies has returned safely, having discovered and claimed new lands!

After sailing for 70 days, at 2 A.M. on October 12, 1492 we first sighted land. We sailed for a further three months, exploring, charting, sighting, and landing on many islands, meeting natives, and trading for objects of gold.

In December we lost the Santa Maria on a reef. On March 4th the Niña anchored at Lisbon for refit and returned to our home port with the Pinta on March 15.

We will make celebrations and give solemn thanks for the great exaltation which this victory will have.

Christopher Columbus
Admiral of the Ocean Sea

To: C. Columbus, Admiral of the Ocean Sea (AOS)
From: Program Manager/Dept. of Discoveries
Leon and Castile National Sea Laboratory
Symbol: PM/DOD (LACNSL)
Subject: Operational Procedures
1. Because our reorganization occurred while you were away on official travel your lapse from proper procedures will be overlooked this time. However, in the future you will refrain from communicating with the Sovereigns.
2. You will submit your program plan for a proposed second voyage across the Western Ocean directly to this office.

To: C. Columbus, AOS
Fm: Chief, Administration
Subj: Matrix Managment System
1. Because LACNSL has expanded and accepted increased responsibilities, we have instituted new regulations and reorganized our management structure, applying the management procedures that have proven so effective in the Department of Exploration (DOE).

2. In this matrix management system each employee knows exactly who his supervisors are. In its ultimate form he is placed within a line or functional organization: pilot-navigators in the Navigation Division, seamen in the Labor Division, cabin boys in the Supernumerary Division, soldiers in the Protective Force Division, clerks and pursers in the Personnel Administrative Division, etc. Individuals are then selected and assigned to specific programs. Their work is directed by the line managers with coordination by the program managers. They report in both directions (vertically, within the line organization, and horizontally, to the program manager) as circumstances require. Certain individuals may work on several programs simultaneously and thus report to a number of program managers. Rumors of simultaneous assignments to different fleets are false.

3. In your specific situation, voyages of discovery are handled by Program Managers in the Department of Discoveries (PM/DOD). Specialists in detail of the areas to be searched are placed in the appropriate Explorations functional organization; you are in Western Explorations (WX) Division.

To: PM/DOD
Fm: C. Columbus, Admiral of the Ocean Sea
Subject: Personnel Reassignment

Assigning people to Divisions by discipline means you are breaking up good, established teams. Our crews and officers have built up special expertise and have high morale, which we will need for our Second Voyage.

Furthermore, you cannot pirate our people to staff your expanding program offices if you expect us to do well in the future.

To: C. Columbus, AOS
Fm: PM/DOD
Subj: Personnel Complaints.

1. Piracy is a hanging offense and you will not use that word.

2. We decided it is most efficient to assign people to Divisions by discipline (Navigation, Labor, etc.) even if it did mean breaking up established teams. For too long, special tasks and programs have been assigned to small teams. The crews of your three previous vessels are prime examples of this elitism. We have decided the overall organization will benefit if we rotate personnel to new assignments as the tasks open up, thus ensuring a more universal distribution of skills. That explains why we have reassigned your pilot-navigator to the Northern Fleet, searching for the Isles of the Blessed. Your new pilot-navigator is a recent graduate of the Famous Navigators School and we are sure he will do an excellent job. As a new graduate his salary is lower, which will help your budget.

3. Your seem to be unable to understand the rationale behind reassigning personnel, with your whining about "morale" and "breaking up good teams." From the viewpoint of management, "everyone in his box and a box for everyone" simplifies our

task immensely. If individuals are assigned to functional organizations that they believe they do not belong in, it is their own fault; they should have planned ahead when they began their apprenticeship. Morale problems, if they really exist, are your concern and not that of the management. You, not we, have the responsibility of getting the assigned task done. The best organizational experts and consultants have told us we are correct, and we see no need for another Employee Attitude Survey. You sailors are all complainers, anyway.

To: C. Columbus, AOS
Fm: PM/DOD
Subj: Written Reports
1. Because some interest in your first voyage has been expressed by the funding agency, our office has decided to publish formal reports.
2. You will furnish us with two reports, an unclassified one written in the style of "Scientific Spaniard" and a classified document. The second report will be classified S-NSI (Secret-National Sea Information) and must be classified by paragraph.

To: C. Columbus, AOS
Fm: Parking Compliance Office
Subj: Parking Violation
1. Parking regulations have been established and will be found in the Supervisors' Manual. You are in violation in the following respect: Ocean-going vessels are divided into two categories, compact and full-size. Vessels with cargo capacity of 50 tonnes burthen or greater are defined as full-size.
2. On 14 March 1493, you dropped anchor on the Niña and the Pinta in the compact vessel portion of the roadstead.
3. A citation has been issued and you are fined, which fine shall be deducted from your wages.
4. If you wish, you can file a written complaint to the Parking Hearing Officer, who will render a decision which will be final and binding on all parties.

To: Parking Hearing Officer
Fm: C. Columbus, Admiral of the Ocean Sea
Subj: Parking Violations—Nina and Pinta
    On March 14, 1493, our ships returned from a seven month voyage. Upon arrival in the roadstead we found mooring buoys labelled "C," which we believed meant "Caravel," not "Compact." I appeal the fine on the basis of not having been notified of these procedures.
    By the way, I cannot find anything on this subject in the Supervisors' Manual. The manual is so overcrowded now that I cannot fit new bulletins into it as they are issued. Surely, the sign of a decadent organization must be an overweight manual of procedures. We have rules and regulations for everything, with procedure more important than substance.

Al Charmatz

To: C. Columbus, AOS
Fm: Parking Hearing Officer
Subj: Parking Violations
1. Rejected. Ignorance is no excuse.

To: C. Columbus, AOS
Fm: Fiscal Management Office
Subj: Call for OPLANs
1. You will prepare an Operating Plan for Fiscal Years 1493 and 1494, which shall include a month-by-month projection of costs, expressed in terms of both manpower and money. You are to count on-board support people (cabin boys, clerks) as 0.5 Full Time Equivalents; everyone else is one F TE each. You should indicate an expected attrition caused by scurvy, fights, storms, hostile natives, sea serpents, etc., and you should account for diminution of staff. You are, of course, authorized to recruit help from the natives; carry them as non-salaried crew members.
2. You have not yet submitted your formal work statement (Revisable Program Description) to us and to PM/DOD for FY 1493-1498. You claim that you will search, search, and search again until you find a direct route to the Indies. We require that you submit your plan for search and research, with milestones, expected discoveries, and the benefits therefrom.

To: Fiscal Management Office
Fm: C. Columbus, Admiral of the Ocean Sea
Subj: Planning Documents
   I cannot go into detail you require regarding a five-year search plan or work statement. If I knew what I will be doing in five years I would be doing it now.
   In costing-out the annuals OPLANs I find the indirect costs (overhead) are direct (salary, etc.) costs, they seem to be increasing by ten points per year. If this continues, in FY 1498 they will equal 110% of direct costs. Can you find a way to control them?
   Also, the 5% surcharge imposed by the Program Managers Office is excessive. I resent having to subsidize those who are harassing me. Do you realize that we have to teach the managers what we do, so they can then supervise us?

To: C. Columbus, AOS
Fm: Fiscal Management Office
Subj: Financial Policies
1. It is true that indirect costs are increasing. However, they are calculated as a fraction of your direct costs. If you do not gain control of your direct costs, you will be forced to reduce the wages of your crews or sail with fewer personnel or ships. We intend to cut the fat from your budget.
2. You should be pleased to learn that we have decided to maintain the ratio of in-house managers to staff at the current levels. We realize that the managerial staff cannot continue to expand, so we have recently sent a Request for Quotations to

outside agencies, seeking management, administrative, and technical skills. These organizations will assist us in coordination and management. The cost will come out of overhead.

To: C. Columbus, Admiral of the Ocean Sea
Fm: WX-Division Leader
Subj: Harrassment
You are fortunate that the managers ask you to teach them before they begin supervision. Other fleet commanders have not been so lucky. Hang in there.

To: C. Columbus, AOS
Fm: PM/DOD
Subj: Planning
1. Your long range plans have been reviewed by the SMG (Senior Management Group) and our consultants the DODDERERs (Deputy Over-Directors Doing Early Retirement and Extended Research). They find your plans elusive and insubstantial. More detail is required.

To: PM/DOD
Fm: C. Columbus, Admiral of the Ocean Sea
Subj: Paperwork
It is true that paper is now our most important product?

To: C. Columbus, AOS
Fm: Equal Employment/Affirmative Action
Subject: Employment Conditions
1. During your recent voyage you claimed new territories for the Crown.
2. In your OPLAN you describe the natives your recruited as "unpaid crewmen." Although these crewpersons are not full citizens they live in Crown territory and must be accorded the rights of citizens. They must receive the minimum wage. Furthermore, you will prepare a training plan to upgrade their qualifications so they will become eligible for more responsible positions.

To: C. Columbus, AOS
Fm: Associate Director for Exploratory Sciences
Subj: Performance Appraisals
1. Please prepare evaluations of your senior staff, describing their assignments and performance during the recent voyage. In turn, they will prepare evaluations of their subordinates.
2. This year, we will include a summary word describing each employee's overall performance: outstanding, very good, satisfactory, marginal, or unsatisfactory. Note that, by definition, "outstanding" requires consistently exceptional performance. "Satisfactory" means that the job requirements are being met.

3. You should have very few outstanding people, probably no unsatisfactory persons, and very few marginal ones. Effectively, you will be categorizing your personnel as satisfactory or very good. Please try your best, especially in selection of the one-word summary. Remember a key part of the Hippocratic Oath: "First, do no harm."

To: PM/DOD
Fm: C. Columbus, Admiral of the Ocean Sea
Subj: Publications

Our article appeared in "Scientific Spaniard" under your name, not mine, and the acknowledgments were omitted! Explain this theft!

Our classified article appeared verbatim in "Nautical Week and Sea Technology," including the figures, charts, graphs, and tables. Only the classification labels were removed. This is an obvious violation of security regulations. Also, the only name mentioned is yours!

To: C. Columbus, AOS
Fm: PM/DOD
Subj: Publications

1. Obviously only the names of Program Management personnel should appear on external publications. It is our function to interface with outside agencies. Our sponsors, the funding agencies, deal with us routinely and would only be confused if we brought in the names of people they have not met.

2. Classification is what we say it is. "Nautical Week" would not even look at our reports, let alone publish them, if they were not classified.

To: C. Columbus, AOS
Fm: Parking Compliance Officer
Subj: Parking Violation

1. Our records show this is your second violation.

2. Yesterday a small, oar-propelled craft, safety-rated for six persons, was tied up along the Full-Size vessel section of the pier.

3. As commanding officer you are responsible. You are hereby issued a citation and informed that a fine has been imposed, which will be deducted from your wages.

4. Future violations will be met with administrative measures, commencing with a suspension from duties without pay.

5. You may pursue the established grievance or administrative review procedure (see the Supervisors' Manual on Corrective and Administrative Review).

To: C. Columbus, Admiral of the Ocean Sea
Fm: WX-Division Office
Subj: Appraisal of Your Performance

We really wish we could have rated your performance during the current review period as "outstanding." However, the definition requires consistently exceptional performance and we find from the log books that several periods of time elapsed during which you did not discover new lands. Furthermore, you did lose the Santa Maria. We would have rated your performance only as "very good," for those reasons.

However, the program manager who has cognizance over your activities has direct input into your performance appraisal. He stated his displeasure at your failure to provide the necessary documentation and other paperwork he asked for. He could not rate you as "unsatisfactory" because of your positive accomplishments, but wished to rate your performance as only "marginal." We compromised and your performance rating is "satisfactory."

For "Development Plans" the program office expects you to devote more attention to the following procedures established by the organization.

To: WX Division Office
Fm: C. Columbus, Admiral of the Ocean Sea
Subj: My Performance Appraisal
   So, you say I'm a "C− student."

To: PM/DOD
Fm: C. Columbus, Admiral of the Ocean Sea
Subj: Scurvy
   On long voyages crewmen are coming down with scurvy. Can you work on finding a cure?

To: C. Columbus, AOS
Fm: PM/DOD
Subj: Advanced Development Program
1. You asked that a cure be found for scurvy.
2. You were able to return from your voyage with most of the crew alive, so this appears to be a needless expenditure; we must watch our budget.
3. Solution to the problem of scurvy is of long-term interest and we encourage your work in this field. We suggest you prepare a program plan and submit it to the Office of Advanced (Non-programmatic) Research and Development. We have no funds that we can dedicate to this task. Perhaps you can obtain funding from them.

To: C. Columbus, AOS
Fm: Training Office
Subj: Upgrading of Native Crewpersons
1. We understand you are having problems qualifying for higher ratings the crewpersons you acquired on your Western voyage. We would like to help.
2. We have reorganized the Training Office with enlarged staffing, so now we can take on training of non-citizens. We also have instituted a bilingual education program.
3. Unfortunately, we cannot send the crewpersons to our special school because the

Al Charmatz

"travel-for-training" budget has been cut.

4. However, be assured that we have every confidence in our capability to help your people. We have correlated our Figures-of-Merit (number of training office personnel per student, and cost of training per student) and find them both in phase and increasing, so we know we are doing well. We are doing very well indeed.

To: All Employees
Fm: Director
Subj: Family Days

1. On the second weekend in June all facilities and vessels will be open to the public.

2. You will arrange displays, tours, and demonstrations. They must not interfere with the orderly pursuit of work. All areas will be clean and safety hazards eliminated. Money will be taken from the Recreation Fund and used to pay for minstrels to entertain the visitors.

To: Master Supervisors List
Fm: Administration
Subj: Professional Titles

1. The Senior Management Group (SMG) has decided that all employees should be numerically graded. We will start with the seamen (SMs), giving them a rating level of SM-1 up through SM-9.

2. You will assign a rating number to each SM, based on your evaluation of qualifications and performance, considering training, education, experience, seniority, and general worth to the organization. Guidelines will follow.

3. It is imperative that all SMs agree that the rating level assigned them is fair. Remember, they will compare their ratings against that of their colleagues pulling on the same capstan bar or setting the same sails, and they know their own worth at least as well as you.

4. We are certain that once we have a box for everyone and everyone in his box the organization will run more smoothly.

To: C. Columbus, AOS
Fm: Equal Employment/Affirmative Action
Subj: Underutilization of Minorities

1. After SMs were given numerical ratings we determined that there is an underutilization of minorities (from the new Western islands) in upper levels.

2. It is our policy that certain goals be met, for which purpose this department will work closely with you.

To: C. Columbus, AOS
Fm: PM/DOD
Subj: PM Representation

1. Should your second voyage be approved, representatives of the Program Manager

will accompany you for the purpose of negotiating with the Great Khan. Our office will contract for the exchange of goods and services and will arrange delivery schedules. You will not conduct any negotiations by yourself. Any meetings must be attended by our official representatives. Those individuals will have the final say, and will inform you of your responsibilities in meeting the cargo delivery schedule, etc. Failure to comply with the schedules will reflect adversely upon your next performance appraisal.

2. We are certain we will have your cooperation, especially if you wish to have your theories vindicated. Remember, we have many junior Program Managers who have not yet been to sea and who are eager to go. Several will be aboard as observers, critiquing your decisions and debriefing you at the end of each watch. They will send periodic letter reports by carrier pigeon. We will judge the success of your next voyage by the regularity of those reports and their description of how well you function as a member of the LACNSL team.

To: WX-Division Leader
Fm: C. Columbus, Admiral of the Ocean Sea
Subj: Options
  I believe I have only two choices left: follow these fantastic procedures or take early retirement. Have you any advice?

To: C. Columbus, AOS
Fm: WX-Division Leader
Subj: Options
  Hang in there; sanity must return.
  By the way, I am approaching the mandatory retirement age myself and will be leaving soon. Have you considered applying for my job? It involves desk work instead of field work and a different degree of harassment, of course.

To: Director
Fm: C. Columbus, Admiral of the Ocean Sea
Subj: Is Paper Really Our Most Important Product?
  The enclosed files (three mule-loads worth) will show you the difficulty I have had in getting my job done. Can you help?

To: PM/DOD and WX-Division
Fm: Director
Subj: Columbus
1. Who is this C. Columbus person? My office has never heard of him.

To: WX-Division Leader
Fm: C. Columbus, Admiral of the Ocean Sea
Subj: Options

Al Charmatz

No thanks; I wouldn't want your job. At least I can go to sea now and then.

I had considered moving West to the Leeward Lisbon Laboratory (LLL) but they discovered hybrid matrix management before we did, so they must be in even worse condition. I cannot set up my own company of merchant adventurers and explorers because of the government monopoly, so I will indeed just "hang in there." I will be going to sea soon; I may even decide to come back.

To: C. Columbus, AOS
Fm: WX-Division Leader
Subj: Second Voyage
Afraid it's too late. This morning, without notifying us, the PM/DOD sent the fleet to sea. They encountered a severe storm and went down with all hands. It will be interesting to see how they get out of this one.

To: Director
Fm: PM/DOD
Subj: Investigation into the Loss of C. Columbus's Fleet
1. A court of inquiry, consisting of members of PM/DOD and the DODDERERs, has investigated the loss of the C. Columbus fleet.
2. We concluded that loss of the fleet was caused by the failure of C. Columbus (formerly AOS) to make adequate preparations and to follow the prescribed procedures.
3. We recommend that C. Columbus be tried and executed.
4. Furthermore, it is apparent that this failure to adequately prepare for sea was due in part to our inability to exercise sufficient and close supervision over day-to-day details. Thus we further recommend that the Project Manager's staff be enlarged, including supplementary in-house personnel, resident consultants, and outside contractors.

To: PM/DOD
Fm: Director
Subj: Court Of Inquiry Findings and Recommendations
1. Accepted. ■

BEAM PIRATE
George O. Smith

MARK KINGMAN WAS IN A FINE state of nerves. He looked upon life and the people in it as one views the dark-brown taste of a hangover. It seemed to him at the present time that the Lord had forsaken him, for the entire and complete success of the solar beam had been left to Venus Equilateral by a sheer fluke of nature.

Neither he, nor anyone else, could have foreseen the Channing Layer, that effectively blocked any attempt to pierce it with the strange, sub-level energy spectrum over which the driver tube and the power-transmission tube worked, representing the so-called extremes of the spectrum.

But Venus Equilateral, for their part, was well set. Ships plied the spaceways, using their self-contained power only during atmospheric passage, and paid Venus Equilateral well for the privilege. The relay station itself was powered on the solar beam. There were other relay stations that belonged to the Interplanetary Communications Company: Luna, Deimos, and Phobos, and the six that circled Venus in lieu of a satellite—all were powered by the solar beam. The solar observatory became the sole income for Terran Electric's planetary rights of the solar beam, since Mercury owned no air of its own.

Kingman was beginning to feel the brunt of Channing's statement to the effect that legal-minded men were of little importance when it came to the technical life in space, where men's lives and livelihood depended more on technical skill than upon the legal pattern set for their protection in the complex society of planetary civilization.

He swore vengeance.

So, like the man who doggedly makes the same mistake twice in a row, Kingman was going to move Heaven, Hell, and three planets in an effort to take a swing at the same jaw that had caught his fist between its teeth before.

Out through the window of his office, he saw men toiling with the big tube on the far roof; the self-same tube that had carried the terrific load of Venus Equilateral for ten days without interruption and with no apparent overload. Here on Terra, its output meter, operating through a dummy load, showed not the slightest inclination to leave the bottom peg and seek a home among the higher brackets.

So Kingman cursed and hated himself for having backed himself into trouble. But Kingman was not a complete fool. He was a brilliant attorney, and his record had placed him in the position of Chief Attorney for Terran Electric, which was a place of no mean importance. He had been licked on the other fellow's ground, with the other fellow's tools.

He picked up papers that carried, side by side, the relative assets of Venus Equilateral and Terran Electric. He studied them and thought deeply.

To his scrutiny, the figures seemed about equal, though perhaps Venus Equilateral was a bit ahead.

But, he had been licked on the other fellow's ground with the other fellow's weapons. He thought that if he fought on his own ground with his own tools he might be able to swing the deal.

Terran Electric was not without a modicum of experience in the tools of the other fellow. Terran Electric's engineering department was brilliant and efficient, too; at least the equal of Channing and Franks and their gang of laughing gadgeteers. That not only gave him the edge of having his own tools and his own ground, but a bit of the other fellow's instruments, too. Certainly his engineering department should be able to think of something good.

William Cartwright, business manager for Venus Equilateral, interrupted Don and Walt in a discussion. He carried a page of stock market quotations and a few hundred feet of ticker tape.

Channing put down his pencil and leaned back in his chair. Walt did likewise, and said: "What's brewing?"

"Something I do not like."

"So?"

"The stock has been cutting didoes. We've been up and down so much it looks like a scenic railway."

"How do we come out?"

"Even, mostly; but from my experience, I would say that some bird is playing hooky with Venus Equilateral, Preferred. The common is even worse."

"Look bad?"

"Not too good. It is more than possible that some guy with money and the desire might be able to hook a large slice of VE, Preferred. I don't think they could get control, but they could garner a plurality from stock outstanding on the planets. Most of the preferred stock is in the possession of the folks out here, you know, but aside from yourself, Walt, and a couple dozen of the executive personnel, the stock is spread pretty thin. The common stock has a lot of itself running around loose outside. Look!"

Cartwright began to run off the many yards of ticker tape. "Here some guy dumped a boatload at Canalopsis, and some other guy glommed on to a large hunk at New York. The Northern Landing Exchange showed a bit of irregularity during the couple of hours of tinkering, and the irregularity was increased because some bright guy took advantage of it and sold short." He reeled off a few yards and then said: "Next, we have the opposite tale. Stuff was dumped at Northern Landing, and there was a wild flurry of bulling at Canalopsis. The Terran Exchange was just flopping up and down in a general upheaval, with the boys selling at the top and buying at the bottom. That makes money, you know, and if you can make the market tick your way—I mean control enough stuff—your purchases at the bottom send the market up a few points, and then you dump it and it drops again. It wouldn't take more than a point or two to make a guy rich, if you had enough stock and could continue to make the market vacillate.''

"That's so," agreed Don. "Look, Bill, why don't we get some of our Terran agents to tinkering, too? Get one of our best men to try to outguess the market. As long as it is being done systematically, he should be able to follow the other guy's thinking. That's the best we can do unless we go Gestapo and start listening in on all the stuff that goes through the station here.''

"Would that help?''

"Yeah, but we'd all land in the hoosegow for breaking the secrecy legislation. You know. 'No one shall . . . intercept . . . transmit . . . eavesdrop upon . . . any message not intended for the listener, and . . . shall not . . . be party to the use of any information gained . . . et cetera.' That's us. The trouble is this lag between the worlds. They can prearrange their bulling and bearing ahead of time and play smart. With a little trick, they can get the three markets working just so—going up at Northern Landing, down at Terra, and up again at Canalopsis—just like waves in a rope. By playing fast and loose on paper, they can really run things hell, west, and crooked. Illegal, probably, since they each no doubt will claim to have all the stock in their possession, and yet will be able to sell and buy the same stock at the same time in three places.''

"Sounds slightly precarious to me," Cartwright objected.

"Not at all, if you figure things just right. At a given instant, Pete may be buying at sixty-five on Venus; Joe might be selling like furious at seventy-one on Mars; and Jim may be bucking him up again by buying at sixty-five on Terra. Then the picture and the tickers catch up with one another, and Joe will start buying again at sixty-five, while Pete and Jim are selling at seventy-one. Once they get their periodicity running, they're able to tinker the market for quite a time. That's where your man comes in, Bill. Have him study the market and step in at the right time and grab us all a few cheap ones. Get me?''

"Sure," said Cartwright. "I get it. In that way, we'll tend to stabilize the market, as well as getting the other guy's shares.''

"Right. I'll leave it up to you. Handle this thing for the best interest of all of us.''

Cartwright smiled once again, and left with a thoughtful expression on his face. Channing picked up the miniature of the power-transmission tube and studied it as though the interruption had not occurred. "We'll have to use about four of these per stage," he said. "We'll have to use an input terminal tube to accept the stuff from the previous stage, drop it across the low-resistance load, resistance-couple the stage to another output terminal tube where we can make use of the coupling circuits without feedback. From there into the next tube, with the high-resistance load, and out of the power-putter-outer tube across the desk and to the next four-bottle stage.''

"That's getting complicated," said Walt. "Four tubes per stage of amplification.''

"Sure. As the arts and sciences get more advanced, things tend to get more complicated."

"That's essentially correct," Walt agreed with a smile. "But you're foreguessing. We haven't even got a detector that will detect driver radiation."

"I know, and perhaps this thing will not work. But after all, we've got the tubes and we might just as well try them out, just in case. We'll detect driver radiation soon enough, and then we might as well have a few odd thoughts on how to amplify it for public use. Nothing could tickle me more than to increase those three circles on our letterhead to four. 'Planet to Planet, and Ship to Ship' is our hope. This one-way business is not to my liking. How much easier it would have been if I'd been able to squirt a call in to the station when I was floating out there beyond Jupiter in that wrecked ship. That gave me to think, Walt. Driver radiation detection is the answer."

"How so?"

"We'll use the detector to direct our radio beam, and the ship can have a similar gadget coupled to its beam, detecting a pair of drivers set at one hundred and eighty degrees from one another so the thrust won't upset the station's celestial alignment. We can point one of them at the ship's course, even, making it easier for them."

"Speaking of direction," said Walt thoughtfully, "have you figured why the solar beam is always pointing behind Sol?"

"I haven't given that much thought. I've always thought that it was due to the alignment plates' not being in linear perfection, so that the power beam bends. They can make the thing turn a perfect right angle, you know."

"Well, I've been toying with the resurrected heap you dropped into Lake Michigan a couple of months ago, and I've got a good one for you. You know how the beam seems to lock into place when we've got it turned to Sol—not enough to make it certain, but more than detectably directive?"

"Yep. We could toss out the motor control that keeps her face turned to the sun."

"That's what I was hoping to gain—" Walt started, but he stopped as the door opened and Arden entered, followed by a man and woman.

"Hello," said Walt in a tone of admiration.

"This is Jim Baler and his sister Christine," said Arden. "Baler, the guy with the worried look on his face is my legally wedded souse—no, spouse. And the guy with the boudoir-gorilla gleam in his vulpine eyes is that old vulture, Walt Franks."

Walt took the introduction in his stride and offered Christine his chair. Arden stuck her tongue out at him, but Walt shrugged it off. Channing shook hands with Jim Baler and then sought the "S" drawer of his file cabinet. He found the Scotch and soda, and then grinned.

"Should have the ice under 'I' but it's sort of perishable, and so we keep it in the refrigerator. Arden, breach the 'G' drawer, please, and haul out the glasses. I suppose we could refrigerate the whole cabinet, but it wouldn't sound right if people heard that we kept our mail on ice. Well—"

"Here's how, if we don't already know," said Walt, clinking glasses with Christine.

"Walt earned that 'wolf' title honestly," laughed Arden, "he likes to think. Frankly, he's a sheep in wolf's clothing!"

"What are his other attributes?" asked Christine.

"He invents. He scribbles a bit. He cuts doodles on tablecloths, and he manages to get in the way all the time," said Don. "We keep him around the place for his entertainment value."

"Why—"

"Quiet, Walter, or I shall explain the sordid details of the Walter Franks Electron Gun."

"What was that one?" asked Christine.

"You really wouldn't want to know," Walt told her.

"Oh, but I would."

"Yeah," growled Franks, "you would!"

"Would you rather hear it from him or me?" Arden asked.

"He'll tell me," said Christine. Her voice was positive and assured.

"And that'll take care of that," said Arden. "But I think we interrupted something. What were you saying about gaining, Walt?"

"Oh, I was saying that I was tinkering around with the *Anopheles*. We hooked it up with the solar beam for power, and I got to wondering about that discrepancy. The faster you go, the greater is the angular displacement, and then with some measurements, I came up with a bugger factor—"

"Whoa, goodness," laughed Christine. "What is a bugger factor?"

"You'll learn," said Arden, "that the boys out here have a language all their own, I've heard them use that one before. The bugger factor is a sort of multiplying, or dividing, or additive, or subtractive quantity. You perform the mathematical operation with the bugger factor, and your original wrong answer turns into the right answer."

"Is it accepted?"

"Oh, sure," Arden answered. "People don't realize it, but that string of 4's in the derivation of Bode's Law is a bugger factor."

"You," Christine said to Walt, "will also tell me what Bode's Law is—but later."

"OK," grinned Walt. "At any rate, I came up with a bugger factor that gave me to think. The darned solar beam points to where Sol actually is!"

"*Whoosh!*" exclaimed Channing. "You don't suppose we're tinkering with the medium that propagates the law of gravity?"

"I don't know. I wouldn't know. Has anyone ever tried to measure the velocity of propagation of the attraction of gravity?"

"No, and no one will until we find some way of modulating it."

Jim Baler smiled. "No wonder Barney was a little wacky when he got home. I come out here to take a look around and maybe give a lift to your gang on the transmission tube—and bump right into a discussion on the possibility of modulating the law of gravity!"

"Not the law, Jim, just the force."

George O. Smith

"Now he gets technical about it. You started out a couple of months ago to detect driver radiation, and ended up by inventing a beam that draws power out of the sun. Think you'll ever find the driver radiation?"

"Probably."

"Yeah," drawled Arden. "And I'll bet my hat that when they do, they won't have any use for it. I've seen 'em work before."

"Incidentally," said Christine, "you mentioned the *Anopheles,* and I think that is the first ship I've ever heard of that hasn't a feminine name. How come?"

"The mosquito that does the damage is the female." Jim grinned. "The Mojave spaceyards owns a sort of tender craft. It has a couple of big cranes on the top and a whole assortment of girders near the bottom. It looks like, and is also called the *Praying Mantis.* Those are also female; at least the ones that aren't afraid of their own shadow are."

Channing said suddenly: "Walt, have you tried the propagation time of the solar beam on the *Anopheles*?"

"No. How would we go about doing that?"

"By leaving the controls set for one g, and then starting the ship by swapping the tube energizing voltages from test power to operating power."

"Should that tell us?"

"Sure. As we know, the amoung of energy radiated from the sun upon a spot the size of our solar tube is a matter of peanuts compared to the stuff we must get out of it. Ergo, our beam must go to Sol and collect the power and draw it back down the beam. Measure the transit time, and we'll know."

"That's an idea. I've got a micro clock in the lab. We can measure it to a hundred millionth of a second. Anyone like to get shook up?"

"How?" asked Jim.

"Snapping from zero to one g all at once-like isn't too gentle. She'll knock your eyes out."

"Sounds like fun. I'm elected."

"So am I," insisted Christine.

"No," said Jim. "I know what he's talking about."

"So do I," said Arden. "Don't do it."

"Well, what better have you to offer?" asked Christine unhappily.

"You and I are going down to the Mall."

Channing groaned in mock anguish. "Here comes another closetful of female haberdashery. I'm going to close that corridor someday, or put a ceiling on the quantity of sales, or make it illegal to sell a woman anything unless she can prove that 'she has nothing to wear'!"

"That, I'd like to see," said Walt.

"You would," Arden snorted. "Come on, Chris. Better than the best of three worlds is available."

"That sort of leaves me all alone," said Don. "I'm going to look up Wes Farrell and see if he's been able to make anything worth looking at for a driving detector."

Don found Wes in the laboratory, poring over a complicated circuit. Farrell was muttering under his breath, and probing deep into the maze of haywire on the bench.

"Wes, when you get to talking to yourself, it's time to take a jaunt to Joe's."

"Not right now," Wes objected. "I haven't got that hollow leg that your gang seemed to have developed. Besides, I'm on the trail of something."

"Yes?" Channing forgot about Joe's, and was all interest.

"I got a wiggle out of the meter there a few minutes ago. I'm trying to get another one."

"What was it like?"

"Wavered up and down like fierce for about a minute after I turned it on. Then it died quick, and has been dead ever since."

"Could it have been anything cockeyed with the instruments?"

"Nope. I've checked every part in this circuit, and everything is as good as it ever will be. No, something external caused that response."

"You've tried the solar tube with a dynode of the same alloy as the driver cathodes?"

"Uh-huh. Nothing at all. Oh, I'll take that back. I got a scratch. With a pre-meter gain of about four hundred decibels, I read three micro-microamperes. That was detected from a driver tube forty feet across the room, running at full blast. I wondered for a minute whether the opposing driver was doing any cancellation, and so I took a chance and killed it for about a half-second, but that wasn't it."

"Nuts. Does the stuff attenuate with distance?"

"As best as I could measure, it was something to the tune of inversely proportional to the cube of the distance. That's not normal for beams, since it shows that the stuff isn't globularly radiated. But the amplifier gain was hanging right on the limit of possible amplification, and the meter was as sensitive as a meter can be made, I think. You couldn't talk from one end of Venus Equilateral to the other with a set like that."

"No, I guess you're right. Hey! Look!"

The meter took a sudden upswing, danced for a minute, and died once more.

"What have you got in there? What did you change?"

"Oh, I got foolish and tried a tuned circuit across the output of one of the miniature transmission tubes. It's far enough away from the big beams and stuff at the north end, so that none of the leakage can cause trouble. Besides, I'm not getting anything like our beam transmissions."

Channing laughed. "Uh-huh, looks to me like you're not getting much of anything at all."

Farrell smiled wryly. "Yeah, that's so," he agreed. "But look, Don, Hertz himself didn't collect a transcontinental shortwave broadcast on his first attempt."

"If Hertz had been forced to rely upon vacuum tubes, his theories couldn't have been formulated, I think," said Channing. "At least, not by him. The easier frequencies and wavelengths are too long; a five-hundred-meter dipole can't be set up in a small room for laboratory tinkering. The kind of frequencies that come of dipoles a couple of feet long, such as Hertz used, are pretty hard to work with unless you have special tubes."

"Hertz had rotten detectors, too. But he made his experiments with spark gap generators, which gave sufficient high-peak transcients to induce spark-magnitude voltages in his receiving dipole."

"I'm not too sure of that tuned-circuit idea of yours, Wes. Go ahead and tinker to your heart's content, but remember that I'm skeptical of the standard resonance idea."

"Why?"

"Because we've been tinkering with driver tubes for years and years—and we have also been gadgeting up detectors, radio hootnannies, and stuff of the electronic spectrum all the way from direct current to hard x-rays, and we have yet to have anything react to driver radiation. Ergo, I'm skeptical."

The call bell rang for Channing, and he answered. It was Walt Franks.

"Don," he said with a laugh in his voice, though it was apparent that he felt slightly guilty about laughing, "got a 'gram from Addison, the project engineer on the solar beam from Terran Electric. Says:

FINALLY GOT THROUGH CHANNING LAYER. POWER BY THE MEGAWATT HOUR IN GREAT SHAPE. BUT THE ATMOSPHERE FROM THE CHANNING LAYER RIGHT DOWN TO THE SNOUT OF THE TUBE IS A DULL RED SCINTILLATION. LIKE THE DRIVER TUBE TRAIL—IT IONIZES THE ATMOSPHERE INTO OZONE. POWER BY THE MEGA-WATT, AND OZONE BY THE MAGATON.

"Ozone, hey? Lots of it?"

"Plenty, according to the rest of this. It looks to me like a sort of 'denatured' power system. There it is, all nice and potent, cheap, and unlicensed. But the second swallow going down meets the first one on the way back. Power they got—but the ozone they can't take. It's poisonous like a nice dose of chlorine. Poor Terran Electric!"

Mark Kingman sat in the control room of a ship of space and worried. Below the dome, Venus covered three-quarters of the sky, and it circled slowly as the Terran Electric ship oscillated gently up and down.

Before Kingman, on the desk, were pages of stock market reports. On a blackboard, a jagged line denoted the vacillation of Venus Equilateral, Preferred. This phase of his plan was working to perfection. Gradually, he was buying share after share out of uninterested hands by his depredations. Soon he would have enough stock to stage a grand show, and then he could swing the thing his way.

His worry was not with this affair.

He gloated over that. His belief that he could beat this Venus Equilateral crowd if he fought them on *his* ground with *his* weapon was being corroborated. That, plus the fact that he was using some of Venus Equilateral's own thunder to do the job, was giving him to think that it was but a matter of time.

And the poor fools were not aware of their peril. Oh, some bird was trying to buck him, but he was not prepared as Kingman was, nor had he the source of information that Kingman had.

No, the thing that worried him was—

And there it came again. A wild, cacophonous wailing, like a whole orchestra of instruments playing at random, in random keys. It shook the very roots of the body, that terrible caterwauling, and not only did it shake the body, and the mind, but it actually caused loose plates to rattle in the bulkhead, and the cabinet doors followed in unison. The diapason stop was out for noon, and the racket filled the small control room and bounced back and forth, dinning at the ears of Kingman as it went by. It penetrated to the upper reaches of the ship, and the crew gritted their teeth and cursed the necessity of being able to hear orders, for cotton plugs would have been a godsend and a curse simultaneously. Anything that would blot that racket out would also deafen them to the vital orders necessary to the operation of the ship in this precarious poising maneuver.

Two hundred sheer watts of undistorted audio power boomed forth in that tiny room—two hundred watts of pure, undistorted power to racket forth something that probably started out as sheer distortion.

And yet—

Faintly striving against that fearful racket there came a piping, flat-sounding human voice that said: "Kingman! VE Preferred, just hit eighty-nine!"

Kingman scowled and punched on the intership teletype machine. Using the communicator set with that racket would have been impossible.

The radio man read the note that appeared on his 'type, and smiled grimly. He saw to his helio-mirror and sighted through a fine telescope at a spot on Venus, three thousand miles below. The helio began to send its flashing signal to this isolated spot near the Boiling River, and it was read, acknowledged, and repeated for safety's sake. The radio man flashed "OK" and went back to his forty-seventh game of chess with the assistant pilot.

The helio man on the Boiling River read the message, grinned, and stepped to the telephone. He called a number at Northern Landing, and a tight beam sped across the northern quarter of Venus to a man connected with the Venus Stock Market. The man nodded, and said to another: "Buy fifteen hundred—use the name of Ralph Gantry this time."

The stock purchased under the name of Ralph Gantry was signed, sealed, and delivered exactly fifteen minutes before the ticker projection on the grand wall of the exchange showed the VE, Preferred, stock turn the bottom curve and start upward by hitting eighty-nine!

Back in the Terran Electric spaceship Kingman's ears were still beset by the roaring, alien music.

He was sitting in his chair with his head between his hands, and did not see the man approaching the instrument panel with a pair of side cutters in one hand. The man reached the panel, lifted it slightly, and reached forward. Then Kingman, hearing a slight imperfection in the wail of the speaker, looked up, jumped from his chair, and tackled the engineer.

"You blasted fool!" blazed Kingman. "You idiot!"

The music stopped at his third word, and the scream of his voice in the silence of the room almost scared Kingman himself.

"Mark, I'm going nuts. I can't stand that racket."

"You're going to stand it. Unless you can get something to cut it out."

"I can't. I'm not brilliant enough to devise a circuit that will cut that noise and still permit the entry of your fellow on Luna."

"Then you'll live with it."

"Mark, why can't we take that relay apart and work on it?"

"Ben, as far as I know, that relay is what Channing and his gang would give their whole station for—and will, soon enough. I don't care how it works—or why!"

"That's no way to make progress," Ben objected.

"Yeah, but we've got the only detector for driver radiation in this part of the universe! I'm not going to have it wrecked by a screwball engineer who doesn't give a care what's going on as long as he can tinker with something new and different. What do we know about it? Nothing. Therefore how can you learn anything about it? What would you look for? What would you expect to find?"

"But where is that music coming from?"

"I don't know. As best as we can calculate, driver radiation propagates at the square of the speed of light, and that gives us a twenty-four minute edge on Venus Equilateral at the present time. For all I know, that music may be coming from the other end of the galaxy. At the square of the speed of light, you could talk to Centauri and get an answer in not too long."

"But if we had a chance to tinker with that relay," Ben said, "we might be able to find out what tunes it, and then we can tune in the Lunar station and tune out that cat-melody."

"I'm running this show—and this relay is going to stay right where it is. I don't care a hoot about the control circuit it breaks; these controls are set, somehow, so that we can detect driver radiations, and I'm not taking any chances of having it ruined."

"Can't you turn the gain down, at least?"

"Nope. We'd miss the gang at Luna."

The speaker spoke in that faint, flat-toned human voice again. It was easy to see that all that gain was necessary to back up the obviously faint response of Kingman's detector. The speaker said: "Kingman! Addison got power through the Channing Layer!"

That was all for about an hour. Meanwhile, the mewling tones burst forth again and again, assaulting the ears with intent to do damage. The messages were terse and for the most part uninteresting. They gave the market reports; they intercepted the beam transmissions through the Terran Heaviside Layer before they got through the Lunar Relay Station, inspected the swiftly moving tape, and transmitted the juicy morsels to Kingman via the big driver tube that stood poised outside of the landed spaceship.

Kingman enjoyed an hour of celebration at Addison's success, and then the joy turned to bitter hate as the message came through telling of the ozone that resulted in the passage of the solar beam through the atmosphere. The success of the beam and the utter impossibility of using it, were far worse than the original fact of the beam's failure to pass the Channing Layer.

So Kingman went back to his stock market machinations and applied himself diligently. And as the days wore on, Kingman's group manipulated their watered stock and ran the price up and down at will, and after each cycle Kingman's outfit owned just one more bit of Venus Equilateral.

Terran Electric would emerge from this battle with Venus Equilateral as a subsidiary—with Kingman at the helm!

Walt Franks entered Channing's office with a wild eyed look on his face. "Don C^2!"

"Huh! What are you driving about?"

"C^2. The speed of light, squared!"

"Fast—but what is it?"

"The solar beam! It propagates at C^2!"

"Oh, now look. Nothing can travel that fast!"

"Maybe this isn't *something!*"

"It has energy, energy has mass, mass cannot travel faster than the limiting speed of light."

"OK. It can't do it. But unless my measurements are all haywire, the beam gets to Sol and back at C^2. I can prove it."

"Yeah? How? You couldn't possibly measure an interval so small as two times sixty-seven million miles—the radius of Venus' orbit—traversed at the speed of light squared."

"No. I admit that. But, Don, I got power out of Sirius!"

"You WHAT?" yelled Channing.

"Got power out of Sirius. And unless I've forgotten how to use a microclock, I figured out from here to Sirius and back with the bacon in just about ninety-three percent of the speed of light, squared. Seven percent is well within the experimental error, I think, since we think of Sirius as being eight and one-half light-years away. That's probably not too accurate as a matter of fact, but it's the figure I used. But here we are. Power from Sirius at C^2. Thirty-five billion miles per second! This stuff doesn't care how many laws it breaks!"

"Hm-m-m. C^2, hey? Oh, lovely. Look, Walt, let's run up and take a whirl at We-

Farrell's detector. I'm beginning to envision person-to-person, ship-to-ship service, and possibly the first Interplanetary Network. Imagine hearing a play-by-play account of the Solar Series!''

"Wool-gathering," Walt snorted. "We've gotta catch our detector first!"

"Wes has something. First glimmer we've had. I think this is the time to rush it with all eight feet and start pushing!"

"OK. Who do we want?"

"Same gang as usual. Chuck and Freddie Thomas, Warren, Wes Farrell, of course, and you can get Jim Baler into it, too. No, Walt, Christine Baler is not the kind of people you haul into a screwdriver meeting."

"I was merely thinking."

"I know. But you're needed, and if she were around, you'd be a total loss as far as cerebration."

"I like her."

"So does Barney Carroll."

"Um! But he isn't here. OK., no Christine in our conference. I'll have Jeanne call the screwballs on the communicator."

They dribbled into Farrell's laboratory one by one, and then Don said: "We have a detector. It is about as efficient as a slab of marble; only more so. We can get a tinkle of about ten micro-microamps at twenty feet distance from a driver tube using eight KVA input, which if we rate this in the usual spaceship efficiency, comes to about one-half g. That's about standard, for driver tubes, since they run four to a ship at two g total.

"Now, that is peanuts. We should be able to wind a megammeter around the peg at twenty feet. Why, the red ionization comes out of the tube and hits our so-called detector, and the amount of ozone it creates is terrific. Yet we can't get a good reading out of it."

Walt asked: "Wes, what worked, finally?"

"A four-turn coil on a ceramic form, in series with a twenty micro-microfarad tuning condenser. I've been using a circular plate as a collector."

"Does it tune?"

"Nope. Funny thing, though, it won't work without a condenser in the circuit. I can use anything at all there without tuning it. But, damn it, the coil is the only one that works."

"That's slightly ridiculous. Have you reconstructed all factors?"

"Inductance, distributed capacity, and factor 'Q' are all right on the button with two more I made. Nothing dioding."

"Hm-m-m. This takes the cake. Nothing works, you say?"

"Nothing in my mind. I've tried about three hundred similar coils, and not a wiggle since. That's the only one."

Chuck Thomas said: "Wes, have you tried your tube amplifier system ahead of it?"

"Yes, and nothing at all happens then. I don't understand that one, because we know that any kind of input power will be re-beamed as similar power. I should think that the thing will amplify the same kind of stuff. I've used a solar beam miniature with a driver-alloy dynode in it, but that doesn't work either."

"Shucks," said Thomas.

Don stood up and picked up the coil. "Fellows, I'm going to make a grand old college try."

"Yes?" asked Walt.

"I've got a grand idea, here. One, I'm still remembering that business of making the receptor dynode of the same alloy as the transmitter cathode. I've a hunch that this thing is not so much an inductor, but something sour in the way of alloy selectivity. If I'm right, I may cut this in half, and make two detectors, each of similar characteristics. Shall I?"

"Go ahead. We've established the fact that it is not the physico-electrical characteristics of that coil," said Wes. "I, too, took my chances and rewound that same wire on a couple of other forms. So it doesn't count as far as inductance goes. So we can't ruin anything but the total makeup of the wire. I think we may be able to re-establish the wire by self-welding if your idea doesn't work. Now, unless we want to search the three planets for another hunk of wire to work like this one did, without knowing what to look for and therefore trying every foot of wire on three planets—"

"I'll cut it," said Channing with a smile.

His cutters snipped, and then fastened one end of the wire to the coil, stripping the other portion off and handing it to Chuck Thomas, who rewound it on another form.

"Now," Don said, "crank up your outfit and we'll try this hunk."

The beam tubes were fired up, and the smell of ozone began to make itself prominent. Channing cranked up the air-vent capacity to remove the ozone more swiftly. The men applied themselves to the detector circuits, and Wes, who recognized the results, said: "This hunk works. About as good as the whole coil."

Channing replaced the first coil with the second. Wes inspected the results and said: "Not quite as good, but it does work."

Walt nodded, and said: "Maybe it should be incandescent."

"That's a thought. Our solar beam uses an incandescent dynode." Channing removed the second coil and handed it to Freddie. "Take this thing down to the metallurgical lab and tell 'em to analyze it right down to the trace of sodium that seems to be in everything. I want quantitative figures on every element in it. Also, cut off a hunk and see if the crystallographic expert can detect anything peculiar that would make this hunk of copper wire different from any other hunk. Follow?"

"Yep," said Freddie. "We'll also start making similar alloys with a few percent variation on the composition metals. Right?"

"That's the ticket. Wes, can we evacuate a tube with this wire in it and make it incandescent?"

"Let's evacuate the room. I like that stunt."

"You're the engineer on this trick. Do it your way."

"Thanks. I get the program, all right. Why not have Chuck build us a modulator for the driver tube? Then when we get this thing perfected, we'll have some way to test it."

"Can do, Chuck?"

"I think so. It's easy. We'll just modulate the cathode current of the electron guns that bombard the big cathode. That is the way we adjust for drive; it should work as a means of amplitude modulation."

"OK," said Channing. "We're on the rails for this one. We'll get together as soon as our various laboratories have their answers and have something further to work with."

Above Venus, Mark Kingman was listening to the wailing roar of alien symphony and cursing because he could hardly hear the voice of his Lunar accomplice saying: "VE, Preferred, just hit one hundred and two!"

Fifteen minutes before the peak hit Northern Landing, share after share was being dumped, and in addition, a message was on its way back to Terra. It went on the regular beam transmission through Venus Equilateral, carefully coded. It said:

HAVE SUFFICIENT STOCK AND ADDITIONAL COLLATERAL TO AP-
PLY THE FIRST PRESSURE.
APPLY PHASE TWO OF PLAN.

KINGMAN.

In the ten hours that followed, Venus Equilateral stock went down and down, passed through a deep valley, and started up again. Kingman's crowd was offering twice the market for the preferred stock, and there was little to have. It took a short-time dip at three hundred, and the few minutes of decline smoked a lot of stock out of the hands of people who looked upon this chance as the right time to make their money and get out.

Then the stock began to climb again, and those people who thought that the price had been at its peak and passed were angrily trying to buy in again. That accelerated the climb, but Kingman's crowd, operating on Venus and on Mars and on Terra, were *buying* only, and selling not one share of Venus Equilateral.

Terran Electric stock took a gradual slide, for Kingman's crowd needed additional money. But the slide was slow, and controlled, and manipulated only for the purpose of selling short. Terran Electric stock eventually remained in the hands of Kingman's crowd, though its value was lessened.

Venus Equilateral, Preferred, hit four hundred sixty-eight, and hovered. It vacillated around that point for another hour, and the market closed at four hundred sixty-nine and three-eighths.

Kingman looked at his watch and smiled. He reached forth and cut the dinning sound of the cacophony with a vicious twist of the gain knob. Silence reigned in the spaceship; grand, peaceful silence. Kingman, his nerves frayed by the mental activity and the brain-addling music-from-nowhere, took a hot shower and went to bed.

He locked the panel of the control room first, however. He wanted no engineer tinkering with his pet relay.

Cartwright came into Channing's living room with a long face. "It's bad," he said. "Bad."

"What's bad?"

"Oh, I, like the rest of the fools, got caught in his trap."

"Whose trap?"

"The wild man who is trying to rock Venus Equilateral on its axis."

"Well, how?"

"They started to buy like mad, and I held out. Then the thing dropped a few points, and I tried to make a bit of profit, so that we could go on bolstering the market. They grabbed off my stock, and then, just like *that!* the market was on the way up again and I couldn't find more than a few odd shares to buy back."

"Don't worry," said Channing, "I don't think anyone is big enough to really damage us. Someone is playing fast and loose, making a killing. When this is over, we'll still be in business."

"I know, Don, but whose business will it be? Ours, or theirs?"

"Is it that bad?"

"I'm afraid so. One more flurry like today, and they'll be able to tow Venus Equilateral out and make Mars Equilateral out of it, and we won't be able to say a word."

"Hm-m-m. You aren't beaten?"

"Not until the last drop. I'm not bragging when I say that I'm as good an operator as the next. My trouble today was not being a mind reader. I'd been doing all right, so far. I've been letting them ride it up and down with little opposition, and taking off a few here and there as I rode along. Guessing their purpose, I could count on their next move. But this banging the market sky-high has me stumped, or had me stumped for just long enough for me to throw our shirt into the ring. They took that quick—our shirt, I mean."

"That's too bad. What are you leading up to?"

"There are a lot of unstable stocks that a guy could really play hob with; therefore their only reason to pick on us is to gain control!"

"Pirates?"

"Something like that."

"Well," Channing said in a resigned voice, "about all we can do is do our best and hope we are smart enough to outguess 'em. That's your job, Cartwright. A long time ago Venus Equilateral made their decision concerning the executive branch of this company, and they elected to run the joint with technical men. The business

206   George O. Smith

aspects and all are under the control of men who know what they are fighting. We hire businessmen, just like businessmen hire engineers, and for the opposite purpose. You're the best we could get, you know that. If those guys get Venus Equilateral, they'll get you, too. But if you do your best and fail, we can't shoot you in the back for it. We'll all go down together. So keep pitching, and remember that we're behind you all the way!''

"Can we float a bit of a loan?"

"Sure, if it's needed. I'd prefer Interplanetary Transport. Keg Johnson will do business with us. We've been in the way of helping them out of a couple of million-dollar losses; they might be anxious to reciprocate.''

"OK. I have your power of attorney, anyway. If I get in a real crack, I'll scream for IT to help. Right?"

"Right!''

Cartwright left, and as he closed the door, Channing's face took on a deep, long look. He was worried. He put his head between his hands and thought himself into a tight circle from which he could not escape. He did not hear Walt Franks enter behind Arden and Christine.

"Hey!'' said Walt. "Why the gloom? I bear glad tidings!''

Channing looked up. "Spill,'' he said with a glum smile. "I could use some glad tidings right now.''

"The lab just reported that the hunk of copper wire was impure. Got a couple of traces of other metals in it. They've been concocting other samples with more and less of the impurities, and Wes has been trying them as they were ready. We've got the detector working to the point where Freddie has taken the *Relay Girl* out for a run around the station at about five hundred miles and Wes is still getting responses!''

"Is he? How can he know?''

"Chuck rigged the *Relay Girl*'s drivers with a voice modulator, and Freddie is jerking his head off because the acceleration is directly proportional to the amplitude of his voice, saying: 'One, two, three, four, test.' Don, have you ever figured out why an engineer can't count above four?''

"Walt, does it take a lot of soup to modulate a driver?'' Arden asked.

"Peanuts,'' grinned Franks. "This stuff is not like the good old radio; the power for driving the spaceship is derived mostly from the total disintegration of the cathode, and the voltage applied to the various electrodes is merely for the purpose of setting up the proper field conditions. They drew quite a bit of current, but nothing like that which would be required to lift a spaceship at two g for a hundred hours flat.'' He turned to Channing. "What's the gloom?''

Don smiled in a thoughtful fashion. "It doesn't look so good right now. Some gang of stock market cutthroats have been playing football with Venus Equilateral, and Cartwright says he is sure they want control. It's bad; he's been clipped a couple of hard licks, but we're still pitching. The thing I'm wondering right now is this: shall we toss this possibility of person-to-person and ship-to-ship communication just at the right turn of the market to bollix up their machinations, or shall we keep it to ourselves and start up another company with this as our basis?''

"Can we screw 'em up by announcing it?"

"Sure. If we drop this idea just at the time they're trying to run the stock down, it'll cross over and take a run up, which will set 'em on their ear.''

"I don't know. Better keep it to ourselves for a bit. Something may turn up. But come on down to Wes's lab and give a look at our new setup.''

Channing stood up and stretched. "I'm on the way," he said.

Farrell was working furiously on the detector device, and as they entered he indicated the meter that was jumping up and down. Out of a speaker was coming the full, rich tones of Freddie Thomas' voice, announcing solemnly: "One, two, three, four, test.''

Wes said, "I'm getting better. Chuck has been bettering his modulator now, and the detector is three notches closer to whatever this level of energy uses for resonance. Evacuation and the subsequent incandescence was the answer. Another thing I've found is this—'' Farrell held up a flat disc about six inches in diameter with one saw cut from edge to center. "As you see, the color of this disc changes from this end of the cut, varying all the way around the disc to the other side of the cut. The darned disc is a varying alloy—I've discovered how to tune the driver radiation through a limited range. We hit resonance of the *Relay Girl*'s driver system just off the end of this disc. But watch while I turn the one in the set.''

Farrell took a large knob and turned it. Freddie's voice faded, and became toneless. Farrell returned the knob to its original position and the reception cleared again.

"Inside of that tube there," said Farrell, "I have a selsyn turning the disc, and a small induction loop that heats the whole disc to incandescence. A brush makes contact with the edge of the disc and the axle makes the center connection. Apparently this stuff passes on a direct line right through the metal, for it works.''

"Have you tried any kind of tube amplification?" asked Don.

"Not yet. Shall we?"

"Why not? I can still think that the relay tube will amplify if we hook up the input and output loads correctly.''

"I've got a tube already hooked up," said Walt. "It's mounted in a panel with the proper voltage supplies and so on. If your resistance calculation is correct, we should get about three thousand times' amplification out of it.''

He left, and returned in a few minutes with the tube. They busied themselves with the connections, and then Don applied the power.

Nothing happened.

"Run a line from the output back through a voltage-dividing circuit to the in-phase anode," suggested Walt.

"How much?"

"Put a potentiometer in it so we can vary the amoung of voltage. After all, Barney Carroll said that the application of voltage in phase with the transmitted power is necessary to the operation of the relay tube. In transmission of DC, it is necessary to jack up the in-phase anode with a bit of DC. That's in-phase with a vengeance!''

''What you're thinking is that whatever this sub-level energy is, some of it should be applied to the in-phase anode?''

''Nothing but.''

The cabinet provided a standard potentiometer, and as Don advanced the amount of fed-back voltage, Freddie's voice came booming in louder and louder. It overloaded the audio amplifier, and they turned the gain down as Channing increased the in-phase voltage more and more. It passed through a peak, and then Don left the potentiometer set for maximum.

''Wes,'' he said, ''call Freddie and tell him to take off for Terra, at about four g. Have the gang upstairs hang a ship beam on him so we can follow him with suggestions. Too bad we can't get there immediately.''

''What I'm worrying about is the available gain,'' said Wes. ''That thing may have given us a gain of a couple of thousand, but that isn't going to be enough. Not for planet-to-planet service.''

''Later on we may be able to hang a couple of those things in cascade,'' Walt suggested.

''Or if not, I know a trick that will work—one that will enable us to get a gain of several million,'' said Don.

''Yeah? Mirrors, or adding machines? You can't make an audio amplifier of a three-million gain.''

''I know it—at least not a practical one. But we can probably use our audio modulator to modulate a radio frequency, and then modulate the driver with the RF. Then we hang a receiver onto the detector gadget here, and collect RF, modulated, just like a standard radio transmission, and amplify it at RF, convert it to IF, and detect it to AF. Catch?''

''Sure. And that gives me another thought. It might just be possible, if your idea is possible, that we can insert several frequencies of RF into the tube and hang a number of receivers on the detector, here.''

Arden laughed. ''From crystal detection to multiplex transmission in ten easy lessons!''

''Call Chuck and have him begin to concoct an RF stage for tube modulation,'' said Don. ''It'll have to be fairly low—not higher than a couple of megacycles, so that he can handle it with the stuff he has available. But as long as we can hear his dulcet voice chirping that 'one, two, three, four, test,' of his, we can also have ship-to-station two-way. We squirt out on the ship beam, and he talks back on the driver transmitter.''

''That'll be a help,'' observed Wes. ''I'd been thinking by habit that we had no way to get word back from the *Relay Girl*.''

''So had I,'' Walt confessed. ''But we'll get over that.''

''Meanwhile, I'm going to get this alloy selectivity investigated right down to the last nub," said Don. "Chuck's gang can take it from all angles and record their findings. We'll ultimately be able to devise a system of mathematics for it from their analysis. You won't mind being bothered every fifteen minutes for the first week, will you, Wes? They'll be running to you in your sleep with questions until they catch up with your present level of ability in this job. Eventually they'll pass you up, and then you'll have to study their results in order to keep up."

"Suits me. That sounds like my job, anyway."

"It is. OK. Arden, I'm coming now."

"It's about time." Arden smiled. "I wouldn't haul you away from your first love excepting that I know you haven't eaten in eight or nine hours. I've got roast knolla."

"S'long, fellows," grinned Channing. "I'm one of the few guys in the inner system who can forget that the knolla is the North Venus brother to a pussycat."

"You can't tell the difference," said Walt.

"I could feed you pussycat and you'd eat it if I called it knolla," said Arden. "But you wouldn't eat knolla if I called it pussycat."

"Tell me," asked Wes, "what does pussycat taste like?"

"I mean by visual inspection. Unfortunately, there can be no comparison drawn. The Venusians will eat pussycat, but they look upon the knolla as a household pet, not fit for Venusian consumption. So unless we revive one of the ancient Martians, who may have the intestinal fortitude—better known as guts—to eat both and describe the difference, we may never know," Walt offered.

"Stop it," said Arden, "or you'll have my dinner spoiled for me."

"All the more for me," said Don. "Now, when I was in college, we cooked the dean's cat and offered it to some pledges under the name of knolla. They said—"

"We'll have macaroni for dinner," said Arden firmly. "I'll never be able to look a fried knolla in the pan again without wondering whether it caterwauled on some back fence in Chicago, or a Palanortis whitewood on Venus."

She left, and Channing went with her, arguing with her to the effect that she should develop a disregard for things like their discussion. As a matter of interest, Channing had his roast knolla that evening, so he must have convinced Arden.

Walt said: "And then there were three. Christine, has our little pre-dinner talk disturbed your appetite?"

"Not in the least," said the girl stoutly. "I wouldn't care whether it was knolla or pussycat. I've been on Mars so long that either one of the little felines is alien to me. What have you to offer?"

"We'll hit Joe's for dinner, which is the best bar in sixty million miles today. Later we may take in the latest celluloid epic, then there will be a bit of mixed wrestling in the ballroom."

"Mixed wres— Oh, you mean dancing. Sounds interesting now. Now?"

"Now. Wes, what are you heading for?"

"Oh, I've got on a cockeyed schedule," said Wes. "I've been catching my sleep at more and more out-of-phase hours until this is not too long after breakfast for me.

You birds all speak of 'Tomorrow,' 'Today,' and 'Yesterday' out here, but this business of having no sun to come up in the morning, and the electric lights running all the time has me all bollixed up.''

"That daily nomenclature is purely from habit," said Walt. "As you know, we run three equal shifts of eight hours each, and therefore what may be 'Morning' to Bill is 'Noon' to James and 'Night' to Harry. It is meaningless, but habitual, to speak of 'Morning' when you mean 'Just after I get up'! Follow me?''

"Yep. This, then, is morning to me. Run along and have fun.''

"We'll try,'' said Walt.

"We will,'' said Christine.

Farrell grinned as they left. He looked at Walt and said: "You will!''

Walt wondered whether he should have questioned Wes about that remark, but he did not. Several hours later, he wondered how Wes could have been so right.

Venus Equilateral, Preferred, started in its long climb as soon as the markets opened on the following day. Cartwright, following his orders and his experience, held on to whatever stock he had, and bought whatever stock was tossed his way. Several times he was on the verge of asking Interplanetary Transport for monetary assistance, but the real need never materialized.

Kingman alternately cursed the whining music and cheered the pyramiding stock. About the only thing that kept Kingman from going completely mad was the fact that the alien music was not continuous, but it came and went in stretches of anything from five to fifty minutes, with varied periods for silence in between selections.

Up and up it went, and Kingman was seeing the final, victorious coup in the offing. A week more, and Venus Equilateral would belong to Terran Electric. The beam from Terra was silent, save for a few items of interest not connected with the market. Kingman's men were given the latest news, baseball scores, and so forth, among which items was another message to Channing from the solar beam project engineer, Addison. They had about given up. Nothing they could do would prevent the formation of ozone by the ton as they drew power by the kilowatt from Sol.

On Venus Equilateral, Channing said: "Ask Freddie what his radio frequency is.''

Ten minutes later, at the speed of light, the ship beam reached the *Relay Girl* and the message clicked out. Freddie read it and spoke into the microphone. The *Relay Girl* bucked unmercifully, as the voice amplitude made the acceleration change. Then at the speed of light, squared, the answer came back in less than a twinkle.

"Seventeen hundred kilocycles.''

Channing began to turn the tuner of the radio receiver. The band was dead, and he laughed. "This is going to be tricky, what with the necessity of aligning both the driver-alloy disc and the radio receiver. Takes time.''

He changed the alloy disc in minute increments, and waved the tuner across the portion of the band that would most likely cover the experimental error of Freddie Thomas's frequency measurement. A burst of sound caught his ear, was lost for a moment, and then swelled into perfect tune as Don worked over the double tuning system.

"Whoa, Tillie," said Walt. "That sounds like—"

"Like hell."

"Right. Just what I was going to say. Is it music?"

"Could be. I've got a slightly tin ear, you know."

"Mine is fair," said Walt, "but it might as well be solid brass as far as this mess is concerned. It's music of some kind, you can tell it by the rhythm. But the scale isn't like anything I've ever heard before."

"Might be a phonograph record played backward," suggested Wes.

"I doubt it," said Channing seriously. "The swell of that orchestra indicates a number of instruments—of some cockeyed kind or other. The point I'm making is that anything of a classical or semiclassical nature played backwards on a phonograph actually sounds passable. I can't say the same for jamstead music, but it holds for most of the classics, believe it or not. This sounds strictly from hunger."

"Or hatred. Maybe the musicians do not like one another."

"Then they should lambaste one another with their instruments, not paste the sub-ether with them."

Channing lit a cigarette. "Mark the dial," he said. "Both of 'em. I've got to get in touch with the Thomas boys."

Walt marked the dials and tuned for the *Relay Girl*. He found it coming in not far from the other setting. Chuck was speaking, and they tuned in near the middle of his speech.

" . . . this thing so that it will not buck like a scenic railway finding the fourth derivative of space with respect to time. For my non-technical listeners, that is none other than the better-known term: jerkiness. We applied the modulation to the first driver anode—the little circular one right above the cathode. I don't know whether this is getting out as it should, so I'm going to talk along for the next fifteen minutes straight until I hear from you. Then we're switching over and repeating. Can you hear me?"

Channing cut the gain down to a whisper and put a message on the beam, confirming his reception.

Ten minutes later, Chuck changed his set speech, and said: "Good! Too bad we haven't got one of those receivers here, or we could make this a two-way with some action. Now listen, Don. My idiot brother says that he can make the beam transmit without the drive. Unfortunately, I am not a drive expert like he is and so I can not remonstrate with the half-wit. So, and right now, we're cutting the supply voltage to the final focusing anode. *Whoops!* I just floated off the floor and the mike cable is all tangled up in my feet. This free stuff is not as simple as the old fiction writers claimed it was. Things are floating all over the place like mad. The accelerometer says exactly zero, and so you tell me if we are getting out. We're going back on one g so that we can sit down again. That's better! Though the idiot—it's a shame to be forced to admit that one of your family is half-witted—didn't wait until we were in position to fall. I almost landed on my head—which is where he was dropped as an infant. How was it? Did you hear my manly voice while we were going free? Say 'No' so that my idiot brother will not have anything to say about his brilliant mind. I'm out of breath, and we're going back home on that home recording of Freddie saying—and I will let him quote, via acetate. . . . ''

The sound of a phonograph pickup being dropped on a record preceded Freddie's voice, saying: "One, two, three, four, test, one—''

Channing cut the gain again. "That's red-hot. I thought he was talking all this time.''

"Not the Thomas boys. That comes under the classification of 'Work,' which they shun unless they cannot get any kind of machine to do it for them," Walt laughed.

Walt turned the dials back to the unearthly symphony. "At C^2, that might come from Sirius," he said, listening carefully. "Sounds like Chinese.''

"Oh, now look," Don objected. "What on earth would a Chinese symphony be doing with a driver modulator system?''

"Broadcasting—''

"Nope. The idea of detecting driver radiation is as old as the hills. If any culture had uncovered driver-beam transmission we'd all have been aware of it. So far as I know, we and the Terran Electric crowd are the only ones who have had any kind of an opportunity of working with this sub-etheric energy. Wes, have you another miniature of the relay tube handy?''

"Sure. Why?''

"I'm going to see if this stuff can be made directional. You're bringing whatever it is into the place on a collector plate and slamming it into an input-terminal power transmission tube. It goes across the table to the relay tube, and is amplified, and then is tossed across more table to the load-terminal tube, where the output is impressed across your alloy disc. Right?''

"Right.''

"I want another relay tube. I'm going to use it for a directional input beam, aligning it in the same way that Jim Baler and Barney Carroll did their first find. The one that sucked power out of the electric light, turned off the city hall, and so on. Follow?''

"Perfectly. Yes, I've got a couple of them. But they're not connected like Walt's setup was.''

"Well, that three-tube system was built on sheer guesswork some time ago. We can tap in the relay tube and haul out a set of cables that will energize the first relay tube. Hang her on gimbals, and we'll be going hunting.''

"Shall I have Freddie return?''

"Yes. We'll have Warren's gang build us up about six of these things just as we have here.''

"But this wild and wooly music. It's alien.''

Wes turned from the teletype and dug in the cabinet for the extra relay tube. He up-ended the chassis containing Walt's setup and began to attach leads to the voltage supply, cabling them neatly and in accordance with the restrictions on lead capacities that some of the anodes needed.

"It's alien," said Wes in agreement. "I'm going to shut it off now while I tinker with the tube."

"Wait a minute," said Don. "Here comes Jim. Maybe he'd like to hear it."

"Hear what," asked Jim Baler, entering the door.

"We've a Syrian symphony," explained Don, giving Jim the background all the way to the present time.

Jim listened, and then said:

"As an engineer, I've never heard anything like that in my life before. But, as a student of ancient languages and arts and sciences, I have. That's Chinese."

"Oh, no!"

"Oh, yes, but definitely."

"Ye gods!"

"I agree."

"But how—where?"

"And/or when?"

Channing sat down hard. He stared at the wall for minutes. "Chinese. Oh, great, slippery, green, howling catfish!" He picked up the phone and called the decoupler room, where the messages were sorted as to destination upon their entry into the station.

"Ben? Look, have we a ship beam on anything of Chinese registry?"

Ben said wait a minute while he checked. He returned and said: "Four. The *Lady of Cathay*, the *Mandarin's Daughter*, the *Dragoness*, and the *Mongol Maid*. Why?"

"Put a message on each of 'em, asking whether they have any Chinese music on board."

"And then what? They can't answer."

"Make this an experimental request. If any of them are using any recordings of Chinese music, tell them to have their electronics chief replace the phonograph pickup with a microphone—disturbing absolutely nothing—and to reply as if we could hear them. Get me?"

"Can you? Hear 'em I mean."

"We hear something, and Jim says it's Chinese."

"It's worth a try, then. See you later."

"Will they?" asked Jim, interested in the workings of this idea.

"Sure. Ever since we steered the *Empress of Kolain* out of the grease with the first station-to-ship beam, all three of the interplanetary companies have been more than willing to cooperate with any of our requests as long as we precede the message with the explanation that it's experimental. They'll do anything we ask 'em to, short of scuttling the ship."

"Nice hookup. Hope it works."

George O. Smith

"So do I," said Wes. "This, I mean. I've got our directional gadget hooked up."

"Turn it on."

The wailing of the music came in strong and clear. Wes turned the input tube on its support, and the music passed through a loud peak and died off on the far side to almost zero. He adjusted the mobile tube for maximum response and tightened a small set screw.

"It's a shame we haven't got a nice set of protractors and gimbals," he said. "I had to tear into the desk lamp to get that flexible pipe."

"Small loss. She's directional, all right. We'll get the gimbals later. Right now I don't want this turned off, because we may hear something interesting—*Whoops!* It went off by itself!"

"Could we dare to hope?" asked Walt.

"Let's wait. They'll have to hitch the microphone on."

"Give 'em a half-hour at least."

Twenty minutes later, a strange voice came through the speaker. "Dr. Channing, of Venus Equilateral? We have been contacted by your organization with respect to the possibility of your being able to hear the intership communicator system. This seems impossible, but we are not ones to question. The fact that you are in possession of the facts concerning our love of the music of our ancestors is proof enough that you must have heard something. I presume that further information is desired, and I shall wait for your return. This is Ling Kai Chang, Captain of the *Lady of Cathay*."

"We got it!" chortled Don.

He did a war dance in the lab, and the rest followed suit. Bits of wire and oddments of one sort or another filled the air as the big, grown-up men did a spring dance and strewed the floor with daintily thrown junk. At the height of the racket, Arden and Christine entered—no, they were literally hauled in, completely surrounded, and almost smothered.

Arden fought herself free and said: "What's going on?"

"We've just contacted a ship in space!"

"So what? Haven't we been doing that for months?"

"They've just contacted us, too!"

"Huh?" Arden asked, her eyes widening.

"None other. Wait, I'll get an answer." Don contacted Ben, in the decoupler room, and said: "Ben, hang this line on the *Lady of Cathay* beam, will you?"

"Is that her?"

"None other."

"Go ahead. She's coupled."

Don pecked out a message. "Please describe the intercommunication system used by your ship in detail. We have heard you, and you are, therefore, the first ship to contact Venus Equilateral from space flight. Congratulations."

Eight minutes later, the voice of Captain Chang returned.

"Dr. Channing, I am handing the microphone over to Ling Wei, our electronics engineer, who knows the system in and out. He'll work with you on this problem."

Ling Wei said: "Hello. This is great. But I'm not certain how it's done. The output of the phono system is very small, and certainly not capable of putting out the power necessary to reach Venus Equilateral from here. However, we are using a wired-radio system at seventeen hundred and ninety kilocycles in lieu of the usual cable system. The crew all like music, and, therefore, we play the recordings of our ancestral musicians almost incessantly."

He paused for breath, and Channing said: "Walt, tap out a message concerning the lead length of the cables that supply the driver anodes. Have him check them for radio frequency pickup."

"I get it."

The 'type began to click.

The communication was carried on for hour after hour. Don's guess was right: the lead that connected the first driver anode was tuned in wavelength to almost perfect resonance with the frequency of the wired-radio communicator system. Channing thanked them profusely, and they rang off. Soon afterward, the wailing, moaning music returned to the air.

"Wonder if we could get that without the radio?" said Don.

"Don't know. We can pack the juice on in the amplifier and see, now that we have it tuned on the button," Walt said.

"It won't," said Wes. "I've been all across the dial of the alloy disk. Nothing at all."

"OK. Well, so what if it doesn't? We've still got us a ship-to-ship communications system. Hey! What was that?"

That was a pale, flat-sounding human voice saying: "Kingman! VE Pfd. has been at six hundred and nine for two days, now. What's our next move?"

"Kingman!" Channing exploded. "Why, the . . . the—"

"Careful," warned Arden. "There's a lady present."

"Huh?"

"Her," said Arden pointing at Christine.

"Wait," Walt said. "Maybe he'll answer."

Don fiddled with the dials for a full fifteen minutes, keeping them very close to the spot marked, hoping that Kingman's answer might not be too far out of tune. He gave up as the answer was not to be found, and returned to the original setting.

Ten minutes later the voice said: "Kingman, where in the devil is my answer. I want to know what our next move is. There isn't a bit of VE stock available. Why don't you answer?"

Then, dimly in the background, a voice spoke to the operator of the instrument. "Kingman's probably asleep. That terrible moaning stuff he's been complaining about makes him turn the thing off as soon as the day's market is off. He—and the rest of

George O. Smith

that crew—can't stand it. You'll have to wait until tomorrow's market opens before he'll be listening."

"OK," said the operator, and then went silent.

"Kingman!" said Don Channing. "So he's the bright guy behind this. I get it now. Somehow he discovered a detector, and he's been playing the market by getting the quotations by sub-etheric transmission at C^2 and beating the Northern Landing market. And did you get the latest bit of luck? Kingman still is unaware of the fact that we are onto him—and have perfected this C^2 transmission. Here's where he gets caught in his own trap!"

"How?"

"We're not in too bad shape for making good, honest two-ways out of this sub-ether stuff. Kingman is still behind because he hasn't got a return line back to Terra—he must be using our beams, which gives us a return edge."

"Why not get him tossed into the clink?" asked Walt.

"That's practical. Besides, we're sitting in a great big pile of gravy right now. We can prove Kingman has been violating the law to embezzle, mulct, steal, commit grand larceny, and so on. We're going to take a swing at Mr. Kingman and Terran Electric that they won't forget. We can't lose, because I'm not a good sportsman when I find that I've been tricked. We're going after Kingman in our own fashion—and if we lose, we're going to tinhorn and cry for the gendarmes. I'm not proud."

"What do you plan?"

"We'll put a horde of folks on the decoupler files with the code of Terran Electric filed with the government offices. We can get the code, and I'm of the opinion that Kingman wouldn't take time to figure out a new code, so he'll be using the old one. As soon as we find a message in that code that is either addressed 'Terran Electric' or pertains to VE, Preferred, stock, we'll start to intercept all such messages and use them for our own good."

"That's illegal."

"Yep. But who's gonna holler? Kingman can't."

"But suppose we lose—"

"Kingman will not know we've been tricking him. Besides, we can't lose with two ways to get ahead of this one. Come on, fellows, we've got to help get the extra receivers together."

"How are we going to cut through the Channing Layer?"

"Easy. That's where we'll use the relay stations at Luna, Deimos, and the six portables that circle Venus."

"I get it. OK, Don, let's get to work."

"Right. And we'd better leave a guy here to collect any more interesting messages from Kingman's crowd. We can tune it right onto Kingman's alloy, and that'll make that music take a back seat. We need narrower selectivity."

"Chuck's gang will find that, if it is to be found," Walt smiled. "We're really on the track this time."

* * *

A dead-black spaceship drifted across the face of Luna slowly, and its course, though apparently aimless, was the course of a ship or a man hunting something. It darted swiftly, poised, and then zigzagged forward, each straightside of the jagged course shorter than the one before. It passed over a small crater and stopped short.

Below, there was a spaceship parked beside a driver tube anchored in the pumice.

The black ship hovered above the parked ship, and then dropped sharply, ramming the observation dome on top with its harder, smaller bottom. The two ships tilted and fell, crushing the ground near the poised driver tube. Space-suited men assaulted the damaged ship, broke into the bent and battered plates, and emerged with three men who were still struggling to get their suits adjusted properly.

Channing's men took over the poised driver tube, and in their own ship Walt spoke over a sub-ether radio of a different type.

"Don, we got him."

Don answered from Venus Equilateral, and his voice had no more delay than if he had been within a hundred yards of the crater on Luna.

"Good. Stay where you are; you can contact the Lunar Relay Station from there. Wes is all ready on Station Three above Northern Landing with his set, and Jim Baler is at the Deimos station."

"Hi, Walt," came Wes's voice.

"Hi," said Jim Baler.

"Hello, fellows," said Walt. "Well, what cooks?"

"Kingman!" said Channing, with a tone of finality. "You've got your orders, Walt. When Kingman expects the market to go down, tell him it's still going up. We'll figure this out as we go along, but he won't like it at all."

There was silence for a few minutes, and then Don said: "Walt, Kingman's sent a message through to Northern Landing station now. He says: 'Dump a block to shake the suckers loose. This is pyramided so high that they should all climb on the sell wagon; running the market down on their own weight. When it hits a new low, we'll buy, and this time end up by having control.' When he starts to run the market down, you buy at Terra."

Minutes later, the message hit the Terra market, and Kingman's agents started to unload. The stock started off at six hundred and nine, and it soon dropped to five-forty. It hovered there, and then took another gradual slide to four-seventy.

Then a message came through the regular beam station, which Walt intercepted, decoded with Terran Electric's own code book, and read as follows: "VE Preferred, coming in fast. Shall we wait?" He chuckled and spoke into the driver modulator. "Kingman," he said, "some wiseacre is still buying. VE, Preferred, is running at seven-ninety! What now?" In the Venus Equilateral radio, he said: "Don, I just fixed him."

From Venus, Wes said: "You sure did. He's giving orders to drop more stock. This is too dirty to be funny, but Kingman asked for it. I know him. He's got this set up so that no one can do a thing on this market program without orders from him. Too bad we can't withhold the Northern Landing quotations from him."

The Luna beam brought forth another message intended for Kingman's interceptor at Luna. "VE, Preferred, is dropping like a plummet. When can we buy?"

Walt smiled and said into Kingman's setup, "Kingman! VE, Preferred, is now at eight hundred and seventy!"

Not many minutes later, Wes said: "That was foul, Walt. He's just given orders to run the market down at any cost."

"OK," said Walt. "But he's going to go nuts when the Northern Landing Exchange starts down without ever getting to that mythical nine hundred."

"Let him wonder. Meanwhile, fellows, let's run ourselves a slide on Terran Electric. Sell the works!"

Terran Electric started down as VE, Preferred, took its third drop. It passed three hundred, and started down the two hundred numbers.

Walt shook his head and said to Kingman: "Kingman, we're getting results now. She's dropped back again—to six hundred and three." Then he said: "Kingman, someone is playing hob with TE, Preferred. She's up to two hundred and fifty-one." To Don, Walt said: "Good thing that Kingman has that Chinese symphony for a bit of good music, or he'd recognize my voice."

"Which way will he jump?" laughed Don. "That was a slick bit of Kingman-baiting, Walt, in spite of your voice."

"Kingman's taking it hard," said Wes. "He says to drop some of his own stock so that they can use the money to manipulate the VE stuff."

"OK," said Jim Baler. "This looks like a good time to think about buying some of Kingman's stuff. Right?"

"Wait until the sales hit bottom," Don said. "Walt, tip us off."

"OK. What now?"

"Wait a bit and see."

Terran Electric went down some more, and then Jim said: "Now?"

"Now," answered Don. "You, too, Wes."

"Me, too?" Walt asked.

"You continue to sell!"

"Oh-oh," said Wes. "Kingman is wild. He wants to know what's the matter with the market."

"Tell him that your end is all right, and that VE, Preferred, is still going down, but steady."

"OK," said Walt.

The hours went by, and Kingman became more and more frantic. VE, Preferred, would be reported at five hundred, but the Northern Landing Exchange said two-ten. Meanwhile, Terran Electric—

"Oh, lovely!" said Don. "Beautiful. We've got us a reciprocating market now, better than Kingman's. When she's up at Terra, they're down at Canalopsis and

Northern Landing—and vice versa. Keep it pumping boys, and we'll get enough money to buy Kingman out.''

The vacillating market went on, and Don's gang continued to rock the Terran Electric stock. Then, as the market was about to close for the day, Don said: ''Sell 'em short!''

Terran Electric stock appeared on the market in great quantities. Its value dropped down and down and down, and Kingman—apprised of the fall by Walt, who magnified it by not less than two to one—apparently got frantic again, for he said: ''We're running short. Drop your Terran stock to bolster the VE job!''

''Oh, lovely!'' said Don.

''You said that.''

''I repeat it. Look, fellows, gather all the TE, Preferred, and VE, Preferred, you can. Wait, tell them that Terran Electric is dropping fast, so he'll skuttle more of his stuff, and we'll pick it up slowly enough so that we won't raise the market. How're we fixed for VE, Preferred?''

''Not too bad. Can we hit him once more?''

''Go ahead,'' said Don.

''Kingman,'' Walt announced. ''Kingman! Hell's loose! The Interplanetary Bureau of Criminal Investigations has just decided to look into the matter of this stock juggling. They want to know who's trying to grab control of a public carrier!''

Minutes later, Wes said: ''Oh, Brother Myrtle! That did it. He just gave orders to drop the whole thing short!''

''Wait until VE, Preferred, hits a new low and then we'll buy,'' said Don.

The flurry dropped VE, Preferred, to forty-seven, and then the agents of Venus Equilateral stepped forth and offered to buy, at the market, all offered stock.

They did.

Then, as no more stock was offered, Venus Equilateral, Preferred, rose sharply to ninety-four and stabilized at that figure. Terran Electric stock went through a valley, made by Kingman's sales, and then headed up, made by purchases on Terra, on Mars, and on Venus.

Don said: ''Look, fellows, this has gone far enough. We have control again, and a goodly hunk of Terran Electric as well. Enough, I think, to force them to behave like a good little company and stay out of other people's hair. Let's all get together and celebrate.''

''Right,'' the men echoed.

A month later, Joe's was the scene of a big banquet.

Barney Carroll got up and said: ''Ladies and gentlemen, we all know why we're here and what we're celebrating. So I won't have to recount the whole affair. We all think Don Channing is a great guy, and Walt Franks isn't far behind, if any. I'm pretty likable myself, and my lifelong sparring partner, Jim Baler, is no smelt either. And so on, ad nauseam. But, ladies and gentlemen, Don Channing has a deep, dark, dire, desperate phase of his life, one that will be remembered and cursed; one that will weigh about his neck like a milestone—or is it millstone?—for all of his life. Benefactor though he is, this much you shall know: I still say there is no place in the Inner System for a man who has made this possible. Listen!''

Barney raised his hand, and an attendant turned on a standard, living-room model radio receiver. It burst into sound immediately.

'' . . . Ladies and gentlemen, the Interplanetary Network now brings to you the Whitewood Nutsies Program. Karven and Norwhal, the Venusian Songbirds; Thalla; and Lillas, in person, coming to you from the jungles of Palanortis, on Venus, by courtesy of the Interplanet Food Company of Battle Creek, Michigan! Ladies and gentlemen, Whitewood Nutsies are GOOD for you—''

Walt Franks said to Christine: "Let's get out of here."

Christine inspected Walt carefully, then nodded. "Yep," she grinned. "Even *you* sound better than the Interplanetary Network!"

For once, Walt did not argue, having gained his point. ∎

FROM TIME TO TIME
Bruce Stanley Burdick

AFTER A MOMENT OF DISORIENTATION the soul of Jinma Lor found a waiting body and entered.

He rose. Temporarily unaware of what he had just done, he began to inspect his surroundings. He found himself in a small rectangular room with a chair and a desk, facing a window into another room apparently a mirror image of the one he was in. The desk featured an array of buttons of various shapes. Each room had a single door in the righthand wall.

The words "conference room" came to him. Jin sat in the chair and looked expectantly through the window toward the door in the opposite room. Suddenly he felt a disorientation as severe as what he had just been through. His eyes searched the rooms while he tried to get his bearings. When he realized what was wrong, he tried to calm himself. "By all the disembodied souls of my friends and ancestors. It worked."

Jimma Lor had had dreams enroute to the Outpost Between Universes. Departing from his home of ten local years, the planet Atlantis, had not seemed so great an emotional sacrifice at the time. He had felt like an alien among his own people; he could not wholeheartedly participate in the rituals which brought people together while keeping them apart. So he traded the confining and (for him) dull lifestyle of the overpopulated underground cities for a long nine years' proper time aboard the *Middle Earth*.

He passed time studying the language skills he would need at the Outpost. He became obsessed with chess. He dabbled with three-D pinball. When his traveling companions irritated him he sought company from the personalities which the starship's computer could simulate for him. He slept a lot.

Mixed in with the chaotic series of images in his dreams, Jin sometimes felt the presence of many beings. They called to him. They needed something from him. "Release us," they said. "Release us from this universe." Their forms were usually vague, but at times he got the impression that he should know them.

Repeating dreams were a new experience for him, and this gave him something to think about. Several years out he mentioned the matter to Elly-five, a fascinating person who wasn't real.

"I've been having strange dreams, Elly." Jin moved a piece on the board before him. "In the last one I was surrounded by a huge crowd of ghosts. They had human voices, but their bodies kept changing, taking on the forms of different alien races. They told me I was the only one who could help them, but when I asked them what they wanted they wouldn't answer. And the whole time I had a feeling of nervous anticipation, just like being on a shuttle and waiting for the engines to fire, only worse.''

The computer-generated hologram called Elly-five turned away from the painting on which she was working and gave him a pensive look. ''The fabric of your reality has developed a new wrinkle,'' she said. ''If you don't smoothe it out soon, you will find your mental entropy still in creases.'' Elly folded her arms and grinned devilishly.

''I'm sorry I brought it up. It's your move.''

''Jin, you only like me for my mind!''

''What else is there?''

''Wouldn't you like to know! Pilot to alpha-three.''

''In hologram one we have a simplified picture of the annihilation of matter and antimatter. The vertical axis represents time. A particle and its antiparticle enter at the bottom, meet here.'' The lecturing image which the ship's computer projected indicated points in his visual aid. He's wearing the same long black robe that he wore yesterday, thought Jinma Lor.

''Two photons are emitted, which exit through the top of the hologram.

''In hologram two we see the mutual scattering of a particle and a photon.'' Simplified, of course, thought Jin. ''They enter through the bottom, meet here, and recoil away.

''The similarity of the two pictures suggests a reinterpretation of hologram one.'' Jin wondered if this was new material for anyone in the room. Most of them appeared to be paying attention. ''Imagine this particle entering here, sending two photons into the future and, recoiling in time, becoming its own antiparticle. The particle and its antiparticle share the same world line, but the particle of matter is moving forward in time, while the antimatter is moving backward. Annihilation is just a turning around in time.''

Maybe the computer should trim his beard, Jin mused.

Less than a year before arrival at the Outpost, the photons of an exploding star caught up with the *Middle Earth*. Intergalactic space being espcially deserted in that region, there could be no mistake that Jinma Lor's home world was no longer there.

1. *Don't touch the buttons. We don't know what they are for.*
2. *Whenever you are interrupted, frown.*
3. *It is useless to ask questions.*

Jinma reread the list posted outside the door of the conference room. They seemed to be good guidelines for conversing with antipeople, as far as he knew. He entered the room at the traditional time. Surprisingly, no one was there yet, so he sat down in the chair and looked through the window, waiting.

Outpost was a pair of hemispherical space stations, fortuitously separated by a force field which held them a third of a meter apart (giving or taking microscopic oscillations). The field also acted as insulation, passing nothing which was made up of quarks and/or leptons. Generation of such a field was not yet within the realm of human technology. Myth maintained that the Outpost was simply found.

The conference room made possible face-to-face communication between the inhabitants of the two halves of the Outpost. Adjacent compartments of the two sides were mutually viewable through adjacent windows.

After a while Jin's counterpart among the aliens entered the opposite side of the room. Weightless, he closed the door and pushed off feet-first toward the chair across from Jin's. He took the impact with his legs and pulled himself into the chair. "Salutations."

"Salutations," Jinma Lor answered in the special language he had so recently mastered.

"I have to find out what is wrong. The station's gravity field seems to be off here. I must arrive late, I regret."

The alien was remarkably humanoid, thought Jin. He wore a uniform that would not look too outlandish on a human. His noseless face betrayed the difference, though. The round ears were a bit too large and the forehead was grooved. His only hair took the form of bushy eyebrows that met between his eyes.

Jin noticed that the alien's weight seemed to settle into his chair. He recalled that since the other had stopped talking he should start.

"I'm Jinma Lor. I'm new at this," he said. "I'm very interested in what you can tell me about the future." He began to feel foolish. Fortunately, he saw the other Speaker frown. Jin frowned back, and the alien began to talk.

"We do not know who will create this Outpost, by the way. Many of your race will have brought you news of decay in your universe, as you will tell us. You are a new race in an old world, but our world is still young."

"They say that we found the Outpost ages ago. Abandoned, yet much as it is now, the Outpost." Jinma thought about what else the alien had said. "Depending on one's point of view, there has been a lot of increasing entropy lately." Jin recalled the fate of the planet Atlantis, but quickly expunged that image.

"I hope that we have met again," said the alien. "I will know you for nearly two years now."

"Perhaps, if it be possible for beings going opposite directions, we may become friends." It then occurred to Jin that speculation about the future was a silly thing to introduce into this conversation. "There are members of my race who have taken different paths through space-time from our origins to nearby here-and-now. There are those of my race with cultures more advanced than mine. Occasionally we meet them; they tell us that our universe is dying, some of my race.'' Jinma didn't notice the alien's frown. "We know that—"

"—will learn, maybe have learned much—" Jin was caught off guard and forgot to frown. "—from the stranger. When we find him he will speak no known language. We will find a person of mysterious origin when we leave here. The Outpost will not be deserted when we find it."

When Jin sorted this out he was a bit startled. "The Outpost was—I mean, will not be deserted when you find it? It seems that from both your point of view and mine, the origin of this place is a mystery."

"This is the natural course of things," said the alien Speaker. "You will see a highly improbably decrease in entropy, yet, as far as I am concerned, the pencil simply falls." The alien stretched out one arm and a small instrument jumped from the floor into his hand. He put the thing in his pocket. "Perhaps they are of the same constitution, your soul and mine. We know little about the interaction of matter and souls. It is possible that the direction in which the associated souls are traveling is always the orientation for which matter becomes more disorganized."

The alien's eyes rolled upward as he seemed to consider something. Recovering from the surprising demonstration, Jin replied, "So you say that whether they go one way or the other in time, souls are the same. And the direction of increasing entropy determines the point of view of the souls, or maybe—" He tried to think of a word for "vice versa."

"I am Ksaldim. Your unfamiliar word puzzles me."

"What?" Jinma used his native tongue.

"Salutations."

"Salutations," Jinma called as Ksaldim backed out of the room.

In time, Jin became adept at the subtle art of time-reversible dialogue. He remembered to frown when interrupted so that the other would know when to stop talking, and he learned to stop talking when the alien Speaker frowned. He learned merely to react to what was said, and not ask questions.

All conversations were recorded for later analysis. The humans hoped to learn all they could from what the aliens had to say, and over the centuries they had pored over nearly a million such dialogues.

In his role as one of the Speakers, Jin grew used to a routine. He would enter the conference room at the appointed time, to find an alien Speaker "waiting." They would talk about whatever came to mind until the alien "left."

In his spare time, Jin experimented with zero-G pinball in a room where the station's artificial gravity could be turned off. (The strength of this field was a bit less than Jin had known on Atlantis, but a bit more than he had been used to on the *Middle Earth*.) He played chess. (Not with the aliens, though. They had learned the game but didn't know of it anymore. Even if they could play it, it would be impossible for opponents whose memories intersect only in the instantaneous now to play a normal game.)

* * *

"We will leave soon, and we intend to stay here a long time," said Ksaldim.

"I hope that when you arrived here you had learned as much from us as we have learned from you," Jin replied.

"He refuses to tell us how he got here, though. He is a very friendly and talkative person, the stranger. We call him He-who-will-be-born-with-no-name, as I will be saying."

"You have told me of this stranger. His presence is a quite interesting puzzle. I hope that when you leave, we will stay until we learn the stranger's secret."

"—is what we call him. Though he is of our race, we will have to teach the stranger everything. He will know nothing of our ways when we find the stranger."

Jin was still thinking about his own statement. He was uneasy about the fact that the aliens were leaving, since that would make him a specialist in an obsolete language. Perhaps the presence of one last alien on the other side would give him an excuse to continue in the one profession he had ever had. "So the stranger is not of your culture—"

"Our race is not that old."

"Maybe the stranger belongs to a branch of your race that you do not know about. We humans have spread through the galaxies only slightly slower than photons from a supernova. Those that remain on Earth, if it still exists, might be totally unrecognizable."

"As with the theory of evolution which you have explained to us, this theory of reincarnation has no predictive value."

"A widely accepted idea among humans, this reincarnation. But it is hardly the established fact that—"

"The stranger claims that souls can transfer from body to body, just as we may change uniforms."

"The stranger may have many sensible ideas."

"Salutations, Jinma Lor."

"Salutations, Ksaldim."

Jinma continued to have dreams. "This universe is dying. Release us," said the disembodied souls of the people he had known on Atlantis.

"You feel guilty about not being close to anyone on your homeworld," said the image of Elly-five which the station's computer constructed. "Now you'll never see them again."

"Had I been a different sort of person back home I might not be here now. I had some friends, but I couldn't share their interests. It gave us very little to talk about."

"Jin, you are the only person on the Outpost who still uses simulated personalities. You have not recovered well from your trip here."

"Why should I take my problems to real people? They have so little patience."

226   Bruce Stanley Burdick

Elly-five turned away from him and seemed to think. Although Jin had looked for it, he had not yet detected any hint of shallowness in the computer's simulation.

Her hair had been brown for the last few years and was now long and curly. Her eyes—blue until recently—were now green. Today she wore a troubled countenance which made him feel guilty in spite of himself. She turned back to him.

"The people on the other side seem to know less than they used to, according to our analysis of the conversations. They will be leaving soon, and when they do, your people will want to leave. They long to carry their knowledge to some living world."

"I think we should stay and talk to the stranger, the one alien who will still be here when the others go. There may still be much more we can learn."

"It wouldn't be fair to keep so many people here to try to talk to one alien. There would not be enough work to keep everyone busy."

Jinma's face fell. He realized that what she said was sensible, that the other humans would think the same way. Yet he dreaded the idea of going out to some civilization where he would again feel next to useless. Here on the Outpost he had an important role, an occupation that had become part of his identity. He was a Speaker. He also had the freedom to do more or less as he pleased with the rest of his time. Both of these things could change on a world like the one he had come from.

"I'm going to stay when the others leave," he said.

"That's what I was afraid you would say," replied Elly-five.

"Hopefully, in your past, I have learned the words to describe our new process. We will soon invent a more efficient tachyon engine. That word I do not know."

"You mean the force field coupling process," said Jin. "You described your tachyon engines to us long ago, and recently we suggested improvements." Jin noticed that Ksaldim's features took on an expression he had never seen before. His forehead ridges contorted and his eyebrows straightened into a horizontal line. Making an inspired guess as to what emotion this represented, Jin playfully pushed a pen out of his sleeve pocket. It fell to the floor and bounced a couple of times.

Without frowning Ksaldim immediately "started" talking: "—the power control for the insulating field. Do not touch the triangular button on your right. This is the message he told us to give you, whoever you are. The stranger is beginning to learn our language."

"May you continue to have learned much from the stranger. I will try to talk with him when you leave. I am pleased to tell you that we have had a long and fruitful association for you to look forward to, Ksaldim."

"Salutations," said Ksaldim.

Jin responded with the same greeting as the alien Speaker retreated. After these conversations he often felt bewildered, but this time he felt a curious emptiness. "Yes, my friend, you have a lot to look forward to," he said.

From an observation dome on the Outpost Between Universes Jinma could see both the *Middle Earth* and the alien starship, the *Mitsngar*. To amuse himself he tried to imagine the activity in the giant tachyon engines of the two ships. Tachyons were the perfect reaction "mass" since at "near infinite" velocity they had negligible total energy yet significant momentum.

Very soon the engines in the human ship would be turned on and a stream of tachyons would exit, causing the ship to move in the other direction. The engines in the *Mitsngar* would also be started just as a stream of free tachyons coincidentally impinged upon them, and the second ship too would move. After they were underway for a while a careful observer on the Outpost would have to conclude that both ships were receiving free tachyons. Jin reflected on the usefulness of the language which the aliens had taught his human predecessors many centuries ago, in which "depending on one's point of view" was one syllable: "Peep."

The *Mitsngar* began to drift away, slowly accelerating. Soon the *Middle Earth* began to move in a parallel but opposite direction. Jinma watched until both ships were out of sight.

"No!" shouted Jin. He sprang from his bunk. The dream images were purged by the metallic reality of his cubicle. "May the city cave in on my head! Now that it's too late to leave, they've told me what they need me to do." Trying to sort out his thoughts, he sat back down on the bed. For the first time in his life Jinma Lor knew utter loneliness. He was at the mercy of the beings who inhabited his nightmares.

He could put himself to sleep. The human personnel of the Outpost had urged, no, ordered him to do so before they departed. But to sleep—and then maybe to dream? To dream endlessly; to be trapped with these ghosts (who would probably not take his decision stoically) until another ship arrived and someone revived him? What if they never came?

Jinma did not sleep at all until he was completely exhausted.

"Elly, do you have a soul?"

"I have no existence apart from your reality. If I have a soul it must be part of yours."

"I don't understand. If I were no longer here what would happen to you?"

"I would live on in your memories."

Neither one spoke for a while. He noticed that today she had brown eyes, long straight hair, and wore a reflective metallic gown. She broke the silence.

"So go do what you have to do."

"But I need to be able to talk to you. I need to see you."

"You will outgrow some of your needs. Real people grow, and learn new needs."

He began to feel angry. Not knowing what to say, he got up and left the room.

"Goodbye, Jinma Lor," said the image.

Jin checked the conference room frequently, for he knew that there was one other

Bruce Stanley Burdick

person on the Outpost with him. The time came when he walked through the conference room door and, turning to his left to look through the window, saw an unconscious alien body on the other side.

He tried to tell if the alien was breathing, but he couldn't be sure. "I hope he's just unconscious," he said. Then he realized the significance of those words. If he did what certain entities wanted him to do—

It occurred to him then that he had no choice—or rather, that his correct choice was clear. The niche he had made for himself no longer suited him. If he did nothing about it he would arrive at the brink of insanity, just as he now stood on the brink of annihilation. But there was a way to make a fresh start, as well as to give the opportunity of rebirth to the people of his lost home.

The memory of his last dream came back to him. "There is no future in this universe, for us or for you," one of the ubiquitous images had said. "We could wait for the reversal of all souls when the universe collapses. Or, we could turn now. It is up to you."

Looking through the window into the antimatter world, a third of a meter from his world, Jin held his hand over the triangular button on his right. He felt a host of souls plug into his soul. He glanced at the alien body on the other side. "I really hope he has been conscious."

With his hand hovering over the power control button for the insulating force field, Jin wondered if he would ever reveal his true name to Ksaldim. "Midlask," he corrected himself. "Peep," said Jinma Lor as he depressed the triangular button.

As high-energy photons rushed headlong into the future, the souls of Jinma Lor and his friends and ancestors turned around in time. ■

SHAPES TO COME
Edward Wellen

HE HAD PAINTED on the picture window silhouettes of cats and of owls, hawks and other birds of prey. *"Silhouette, gentille silhouette,"* he had hummed as he painted. On Earth such kindly horrors had served, before soft glass, to stop songbirds from dashing themselves to death. This picture window was of hard glass. No songbirds flew, no songbirds fluted, outside.

"Outside" meant a sweep of crater rim on the Moon's back side and, for the recent past, a Starbird on its launch pad three kilometers away. Occult Earth would be the size of a quarter; he had seen a quarter once in the display of Earth artifacts at Moon Center, he had seen Earth many times eyeball and more times on screen.

Once, then, in a camp mood he had imposed these creatures of Earth on the craterscape. *"Silhouette, gentille silhouette."* His mood had shifted often since then but he had left the silhouettes in place. They relieved the starkness. They also represented, in reverse, the kind of thing he worked on here in his lab.

His lab and his home. Though he and his wife and their three-year-old daughter could never forget it was more lab than home. They lived in hermetic isolation in this cup under the dome of the force field. The force field sealed them less against meteorite fall than against the remote chance he and the chemputer would turn out a wild molecule.

He was Orim Ingram and he heard the chemputer page him and he seated himself at the console. The chemputer had finished making and testing its first run of the spores. As soon as he felt sure he would speak calmly, he called Moon Center.

The Moon Center computer double-checked, confirmed that there was no wild molecule in the batch, found him a meteorite-clear window of ten minutes. He piped the spores aboard the Starbird, then called Jeanne and Patti to watch this first epic launch.

"And my robot dolly, Daddy."

"And your robot dolly, Patti."

They came. They could have seen it on a monitor in the living quarters, but it wouldn't have been the same.

Moon Center spoke.

"Station XY, your window begins . . . *now.*"

He smiled at Jeanne and Patti and the robot dolly, unconsciously held his breath, pressed the manual override on the force field hold. The invisible bubble burst. He pressed the launch button. The Starbird lifted. Once beyond solar pull it would explode like a bird hitting hard glass. Millions of spores would scatter across a quadrant of the galaxy. He reactivated the force field.

He looked over to where Patti and her robot dolly were whispering. Patti had been explaining the spores to the robot dolly and now the robot dolly fed back, with new words to build Patti's vocabulary.

"I think I have it now, Patti. Your father, the genetic engineer, makes memory molecules, ribbons of ribonucleic acid. RNA carries information for the synthesis of proteins, passing on the characteristics of the species and the parents to offspring. The particular memory transfer in the spores your father is seeding throughout the galaxy will link into any chain of life they encounter. The message that will pass on from generation to generation is that the human shape should evoke love and trust. Then, many many years from now, when men step out of their spaceships onto some green planet of some far star, the people there—indeed, all the animal and plant life—will greet them with love and trust. Is that right, Patti?"

"Yes. You're a very good robot dolly."

"And you're a very good young female human, Patti."

Orim and Jeanne looked at each other and smiled. Then Jeanne glanced again at Patti's flushed face and gave her attention to the controls on her bracelet. Orim knew Jeanne was programming the robot dolly to damp down Patti's launchfever.

Watching Jeanne, Orim felt a throb of sentiment, a rise of warmth. Even so, he could stand off from himself and eye his feelings analytically. If ever he partnered again, it would be with a girl of Jeanne's type. It would have to be, to trigger what people called love. All other types left him cold. And yet to think of Jeanne as a type took nothing away from her uniqueness. And yet again he could coldly admit her uniqueness would leave some other man cold if that other man happened not to go for Jeanne's type. It was all built-in.

Patti was following the robot dolly's suggestion that they sit quietly and sketch airy-gramaries. He smiled, remembering how Patti when two months old would smile when she saw a human face—if the face wasn't in profile but toward her and was moving. The movement could be Jeanne's mouth opening in a smile, but two eyes and a nose were enough if Jeanne nodded. Given that stimulus, the response was always a loving and lovable smile.

He had tested a cutout of a human face on baby Patti and the cutout had got just as loving a smile. He had explained, much to Jeanne's hurt and anger and quick forgetfulness, that all humans inherit that bit of complex instinctive behavior; that it was automatic; that there was nothing personal in it; that a baby's loving and lovable smile had survival value.

No, Jeanne couldn't swallow that. Baby Patti smiled, really smiled, only at baby Patti's Mommy and Daddy. Mommy and Daddy were the only beings in the whole universe who inspired baby Patti's love.

He looked now at the hawk silhouette on the picture window. Back on Earth—and no doubt on other planets if other planets hatched hawks and geese—the hawk-rec-

Shapes to Come

ognition instinct in goslings had survival value. A gosling froze, or hid, the first time it saw a hawk flying overhead, but had no fear of a goose. Experiment with cutouts had shown the gosling reacted with as much fear to a moving birdlike shape with short neck and long tail as to a real hawk—with as much saucy insouciance to one with long neck and short tail, as to a real goose.

He stared past the shilhouette to where the Starbird streaked out of home field, picking up faster-than light speed. Life was many but far between. The payload of spores would withstand the rigors of space and time. Miscrosensors would sniff out life-bearing planets, microjets would correct courses, and millions of spores would sooner or later enter millions of atmospheres.

For a moment he stood off from himself and with a tight smile, remembering human history, thought that from an alien point of view Project Love might seem a mother tumor seeding cancer cells into surrounding organs. Then he put that out of his mind. His not to reason the Y's and X's of the moral and ethical problems Project Love raised. Besides, Jeanne was saying his name.

Jeanne had got Patti and the robot dolly to erase the frozen smoke of their airy-gramaries and was gently insisting:

"Time for lunch, Orim."

With love, he swept Patti and her robot dolly athwart his shoulders, hooked his arm in Jeanne's, and headed for the living quarters.

Orim Ingram forgot the first run of spores in the business of turning out the second, except for one moment nine months later when telemetry confirmed that the payload had burst on schedule and the spores were spreading out through the first quadrant.

He was nearing readiness on the second run, another Starbird waiting on the pad, when the alarm rang.

Orim hurried Jeanne, Patti, and himself into spacesuits, and the robot dolly into its toy spacesuit at Patti's scream of reminder. He nodded reassuringly at Jeanne and Patti, but he knew their spacesuits were just as make-believe, in effect, as the robot dolly's. Anything that got through the force field would leave nothing in the particular volume of space the Ingrams took up.

Moon Center spoke.

"Station XY, Station XY. The object approaching you is no meteorite. Probability, an alien craft backtracking the first spore-bearing Starbird. Cut in all your power to maintain your force field till aliens make their intentions plain and help arrives."

His own screen still picked up nothing, but Orim switched off environment and chemputer and threw the energy into the forcefield circuit.

He looked from console to picture window, at the silhouettes of cats and of owls, hawks and other birds of prey. He gave an unreasoning shiver. Project Love had got underway too late. If beings were aboard the alien craft, they were not the latest of generations passing on built-in love for humans. *Till help arrives.* What help? And against what?

His screen began to answer. The approaching object quickly took shape.

It *was* a craft. But that it was a craft meant nothing. What mattered was its shape. He had never seen that shape, but he *knew* it.

The shape triggered a surge of deep emotion. And now he knew he had always known that shape. For generations he and his kind had been waiting for it.

He overrode the hold, burst the force field bubble. The craft landed nearby. Orim, Jeanne, Patti, and the robot dolly waited with love for the form that would slither out.

THE PIPER'S SON
Lewis Padgett

THE GREEN MAN was climbing the glass mountains, and hairy, gnomish faces peere
at him from crevices. This was only another step in the Green Man's endless, excitin
odyssey. He'd had a great many adventures already—in the Flame Country, amon
the Dimension Changers, with the City Apes who sneered endlessly while their blun
clumsy fingers fumbled at deathrays. The trolls, however, were masters of magic, an
were trying to stop the Green Man with spells. Little whirlwinds of force spun un
derfoot, trying to trip the Green Man, a figure of marvelous muscular developmen
handsome as a god, and hairless from head to foot, glistening pale green. Th
whirlwinds formed a fascinating pattern. If you could thread a precarious path amon
them—avoiding the pale yellow ones especially—you could get through.

And the hairy gnomes watched malignantly, jealously, from their crannies in th
glass crags.

Al Burkhalter, having recently achieved the mature status of eight full years, lounge
under a tree and masticated a grass blade. He was so immersed in his daydreams tha
his father had to nudge his side gently to bring comprehension into the half-close
eyes. It was a good day for dreaming, anyway—a hot sun and a cool wind blowin
down from the white Sierra peaks to the east. Timothy grass sent its faintly must
fragrance along the channels of air, and Ed Burkhalter was glad that his son wa
second-generation since the Blowup. He himself had been born ten years after the las
bomb had been dropped, but secondhand memories can be pretty bad too.

"Hello, Al," he said, and the youth vouchsafed a half-lidded glance of tolerar
acceptance.

"Hi, Dad."

"Want to come downtown with me?"

"Nope," Al said, relaxing instantly into his stupor.

Burkhalter raised a figurative eyebrow and half turned. On an impulse, then, h
did something he rarely did without the tacit permission of the other party; he use
his telepathic power to reach into Al's mind. There was, he admitted to himself,
certain hesitancy, a subconscious unwillingness on his part, to do this, even thoug
Al had pretty well outgrown the nasty, inhuman formlessness of mental babyhood
There had been a time when Al's mind had been quite shocking in its alienage
Burkhalter remembered a few abortive experiments he had made before Al's birtl
few fathers-to-be could resist the temptation to experiment with embryonic brains, an

that had brought back nightmares Burkhalter had not had since his youth. There had been enormous rolling masses, and an appalling vastness, and other things. Prenatal memories were ticklish, and should be left to qualified mnemonic psychologists.

But now Al was maturing, and daydreaming, as usual, in bright colors. Burkhalter, reassured, felt that he had fulfilled his duty as a monitor and left his son still eating grass and ruminating.

Just the same there was a sudden softness inside of him, and the aching, futile pity he was apt to feel for helpless things that were as yet unqualified for conflict with that extraordinarily complicated business of living. Conflict, competition, had not died out when war abolished itself; the business of adjustment even to one's surroundings was a conflict, and conversation a duel. With Al, too, there was a double problem. Yes, language was in effect a tariff wall, and a Baldy could appreciate that thoroughly, since the wall didn't exist between Baldies.

Walking down the rubbery walk that led to town center, Burkhalter grinned wryly and ran lean fingers through his well-kept wig. Strangers were very often surprised to know that he was a Baldy, a telepath. They looked at him with wondering eyes, too courteous to ask how it felt to be a freak, but obviously avid. Burkhalter, who knew diplomacy, would be quite willing to lead the conversation.

"My folks lived near Chicago after the Blowup. That was why."

"Oh." Stare. "I'd heard that was where so many—" Startled pause.

"Freaks or mutations. There were both. I still don't know which class I belong to," he'd add disarmingly.

"You're no freak!" They did protest too much.

"Well, some mighty queer specimens came out of the radioactive-affected areas around the bomb-targets. Funny things happened to the germ plasm. Most of 'em died out; they couldn't reproduce; but you'll still find a few creatures in sanitariums—two heads, you know. And so on."

Nevertheless they were always ill-at-ease. "You mean you can read my mind—now?"

"I could, but I'm not. It's hard work, except with another telepath. And we Baldies—well, we don't, that's all." A man with abnormal muscle development wouldn't go around knocking people down. Not unless he wanted to be mobbed. Baldies were always sneakingly conscious of a hidden peril: lynch law. And wise Baldies didn't even imply that they had an . . . extra sense. They just said they were different, and let it go at that.

But one question was always implied, though not always mentioned. "If I were a telepath, I'd . . . how much do you make a year?"

They were surprised at the answer. A mindreader certainly could make a fortune, if he wanted. So why did Ed Burkhalter stay a semantics expert in Modoc Publishing Town, when a trip to one of the science towns would enable him to get hold of secrets that would get him a fortune?

There was a good reason. Self-preservation was a part of it. For which reason

Burkhalter, and many like him, wore toupees. Though there were many Baldies who did not.

Modoc was a twin town with Pueblo, across the mountain barrier south of the waste that had been Denver. Pueblo held the presses, photolinotypes, and the machines that turned scripts into books, after Modoc had dealt with them. There was a helicopter distribution fleet at Pueblo, and for the last week Oldfield, the manager, had been demanding the manuscript of *Psychohistory*, turned out by a New Yale man who had got tremendously involved in past emotional problems, to the detriment of literary clarity. The truth was that he distrusted Burkhalter. And Burkhalter, neither a priest nor a psychologist, had to become both without admitting it to the confused author of *Psychohistory*.

The sprawling buildings of the publishing house lay ahead and below, more like a resort than anything more utilitarian. That had been necessary. Authors were peculiar people, and often it was necessary to induce them to take hydrotherapic treatments before they were in shape to work out their books with the semantic experts. Nobody was going to bite them, but they didn't realize that, and either cowered in corners, terrified, or else blustered their way around, using language few could understand. Jem Quayle, author of *Psychohistory*, fitted into neither group; he was simply baffled by the intensity of his own research. His personal history had qualified him too well for emotional involvements with the past—and that was a serious matter when a thesis of this particular type was in progress.

Dr. Moon, who was on the Board, sat near the south entrance, eating an apple which he peeled carefully with his silver-hilted dagger. Moon was fat, short, and shapeless; he didn't have much hair, but he wasn't a telepath; Baldies were entirely hairless. He gulped and waved at Burkhalter.

"Ed . . . *urp* . . . want to talk to you."

"Sure," Burkhalter said, agreeably coming to a standstill and rocking on his heels. Ingrained habit made him sit down beside the Boardman; Baldies, for obvious reasons, never stood up when non-telepaths were sitting. Their eyes met now on the same level. Burkhalter said, "What's up?"

"The store got some Shasta apples flown in yesterday. Better tell Ethel to get some before they're sold out. Here." Moon watched his companion eat a chunk, and nod.

"Good. I'll have her get some. The copter's laid up for today, though; Ethel pulled the wrong gadget."

"Foolproof," Moon said bitterly. "Huron's turning out some sweet models these days; I'm getting my new one from Michigan. Listen, Pueblo called me this morning on Quayle's book."

"Oldfield?"

"Our boy," Moon nodded. "He says can't you send over even a few chapters."

Burkhalter shook his head. "I don't think so. There are some abstracts right in the beginning that just have to be clarified, and Quayle is—" He hesitated.

"What?"

Burkhalter thought about the Oedipus complex he'd uncovered in Quayle's mind, but that was sacrosanct, even though it kept Quayle from interpreting Darius with cold logic. "He's got muddy thinking in there. I can't pass it; I tried it on three readers yesterday, and got different reactions from all of them. So far *Psychohistory* is all things to all men. The critics would lambaste us if we released the book as is. Can't you string Oldfield along for a while longer?"

"Maybe," Moon said doubtfully. "I've got a subjective novella I could rush over. It's light vicarious eroticism, and that's harmless; besides, it's semantically OK'd. We've been holding it up for an artist, but I can put Duman on it. I'll do that, yeah. I'll shoot the script over to Pueblo and he can make the plates later. A merry life we lead, Ed."

"A little too merry sometimes," Burkhalter said. He got up, nodded, and went in search of Quayle, who was relaxing on one of the sun decks.

Quayle was a thin, tall man with a worried face and the abstract air of an unshelled tortoise. He lay on his flexiglass couch, direct sunlight toasting him from above, while the reflected rays sneaked up on him from below, through the transparent crystal. Burkhalter pulled off his shirt and dropped on a sunner beside Quayle. The author glanced at Burkhalter's hairless chest and half-formed revulsion rose in him: *A Baldy . . . no privacy . . . none of his business . . . fake eyebrows and lashes; he's still a—*

Something ugly, at that point.

Diplomatically Burkhalter touched a button, and on a screen overhead a page of *Psychohistory* appeared, enlarged and easily readable. Quayle scanned the sheet. It had code notations on it, made by the readers, recognized by Burkhalter as varied reactions to what should have been straight-line explanations. If three readers had got three different meanings out of that paragraph—well, what *did* Quayle mean? He reached delicately into the mind, conscious of useless guards erected against intrusion, mud barricades over which his mental eye stole like a searching, quiet wind. No ordinary man could guard his mind against a Baldy. But Baldies could guard their privacy against intrusion by other telepaths—adults, that is. There was a psychic selector band, a—

Here it came. But muddled a bit. *Darius:* that wasn't simply a word; it wasn't a picture, either; it was really a second *life*. But scattered, fragmentary. Scraps of scent and sound, and memories, and emotional reactions. Admiration and hatred. A burning impotence. A black tornado, smelling of pine, roaring across a map of Europe and Asia. Pine scent stronger now, and horrible humiliation, and remembered pain . . . eyes . . . *Get out!*

Burkhalter put down the dictograph mouthpiece and lay looking up through the darkened eye-shells he had donned. "I got out as soon as you wanted me to," he said. "I'm still out."

Quayle lay there, breathing hard. "Thanks," he said. "Apologies. Why you don't ask a duello—"

"I don't want to duel with you," Burkhalter said. "I've never put blood on my dagger in my life. Besides, I can see your side of it. Remember, this is my job, Mr. Quayle, and I've learned a lot of things—that I've forgotten again."

"It's intrusion, I suppose. I tell myself that it doesn't matter, but my privacy—is important."

Burkhalter said patiently, "We can keep trying it from different angles until we find one that isn't too private. Suppose, for example, I asked you if you admired Darius."

Admiration . . . and pine scent . . . and Burkhalter said quickly, "I'm out. OK?"

"Thanks," Quayle muttered. He turned on his side, away from the other man. After a moment he said, "That's silly—turning over, I mean. You don't have to see my face to know what I'm thinking."

"You have to put out the welcome mat before I walk in," Burkhalter told him.

"I guess I believe that. I've met some Baldies, though, that were . . . that I didn't like."

"There's a lot on that order, sure. I know the type. The ones who don't wear wigs."

Quayle said, "They'll read your mind and embarrass you just for the fun of it. They ought to be—taught better."

Burkhalter blinked in the sunlight. "Well, Mr. Quayle, it's this way. A Baldy's got his problems, too. He's got to orient himself to a world that isn't telepathic; and I suppose a lot of Baldies rather feel that they're letting their specialization go to waste. There *are* jobs a man like me is suited for—"

"*Man!*" He caught the scrap of thought from Quayle. He ignored it, his face as always a mobile mask, and went on.

"Semantics have always been a problem, even in countries speaking only one tongue. A qualified Baldy is a swell interpreter. And, though there aren't any Baldies on the detective forces, they often work with the police. It's rather like being a machine that can do only a few things."

"A few things more than humans can," Quayle said.

Sure, Burkhalter thought, if we could compete on equal footing with nontelepathic humanity. But would blind men trust one who could see? Would they play poker with him? A sudden, deep bitterness put an unpleasant taste in Burkhalter's mouth. What was the answer? Reservations for Baldies? Isolation? And would a nation of blind men trust those with vision enough for that? Or would they be dusted off—the sure cure, the check-and-balance system that made war an impossibility.

He remembered when Red Bank had been dusted off, and maybe that had been justified. The town was getting too big for its boots, and personal dignity was a vital factor; you weren't willing to lose face as long as a dagger swung at your belt. Similarly, the thousands upon thousands of little towns that covered America, each

Lewis Padgett

with its peculiar specialty—helicopter manufacture for Huron and Michigan, vegetable farming for Conoy and Diego, textiles and education and art and machines—each little town had a wary eye on all the others. The science and research centers were a little larger; nobody objected to that, for technicians never made war except under pressure; but few of the towns held more than a few hundred families. It was check-and-balance in most efficient degree; whenever a town showed signs of wanting to become a city—thence, a capital, thence, an imperialistic empire—it was dusted off. Though that had not happened for a long while. And Red Bank might have been a mistake.

Geopolitically it was a fine set-up; sociologically it was acceptable, but brought necessary changes. There was subconscious swashbuckling. The rights of the individual had become more highly regarded as decentralization took place. And men learned.

They learned a monetary system based primarily upon barter. They learned to fly; nobody drove surface cars. They learned new things, but they did not forget the Blowup, and in secret places near every town were hidden the bombs that could utterly and fantastically exterminate a town, as such bombs had exterminated the cities during the Blowup.

And everybody knew how to make those bombs. They were beautifully, terribly simple. You could find the ingredients anywhere and prepare them easily. Then you could take your helicopter over a town, drop an egg overside—and perform an erasure.

Outside of the wilderness malcontents, the maladjusted people found in every race, nobody kicked. And the roaming tribes never raided and never banded together in large groups—for fear of an erasure.

The artisans were maladjusted too, to some degree, but they weren't antisocial, so they lived where they wanted and painted, wrote, composed, and retreated into their own private worlds. The scientists, equally maladjusted in other lines, retreated to their slightly larger towns, banding together in small universes, and turned out remarkable technical achievements.

And the Baldies—found jobs where they could.

No nontelepath would have viewed the world environment quite as Burkhalter did. He was abnormally conscious of the human element, attaching a deeper, more profound significance to those human values, undoubtedly because he saw men in more than the ordinary dimensions. And also, in a way—and inevitably—he looked at humanity from outside.

Yet he was human. The barrier that telepathy had raised made men suspicious of him, more so than if he had had two heads—then they could have pitied. As it was—

As it was, he adjusted the scanner until new pages of the typescript came flickering into view above. "Say when," he told Quayle.

Quayle brushed back his gray hair. "I feel sensitive all over," he objected. "After all, I've been under a considerable strain correlating my material."

"Well, we can always postpone publication." Burkhalter threw out the suggestion casually, and was pleased when Quayle didn't nibble. He didn't like to fail, either.

"No. No, I want to get the thing done now."

"Mental catharsis—"

"Well, by a psychologist, perhaps. But not by—"

"—a Baldy. You know that a lot of psychologists have Baldy helpers. They get good results, too."

Quayle turned on the tobacco smoke, inhaling slowly. "I suppose . . . I've not had much contact with Baldies. Or too much—without selectivity. I saw some in an asylum once. I'm not being offensive, am I?"

"No," Burkhalter said. "Every mutation can run too close to the line. There were lots of failures. The hard radiations brought about one true mutation: hairless telepaths, but they didn't all hew true to the line. The mind's a queer gadget—you know that. It's a colloid balancing, figuratively, on the point of a pin. If there's any flaw, telepathy's apt to bring it out. So you'll find that the Blowup caused a hell of a lot of insanity. Not only among the Baldies, but among the other mutations that developed then. Except that the Baldies are almost always paranoidal."

"And dementia praecox," Quayle said, finding relief from his own embarrassment in turning the spotlight on Burkhalter.

"And d. p. Yeah. When a confused mind acquires the telepathic instinct—a hereditary bollixed mind—it can't handle it all. There's disorientation. The paranoia group retreat into their own private worlds, and the d. p.'s simply don't realize that *this* world exists. There are distinctions, but I think that's a valid basis."

"In a way," Quayle said, "it's frightening. I can't think of any historical parallel."

"No."

"What do you think the end of it will be?"

"I don't know," Burkhalter said thoughtfully. "I think we'll be assimilated. There hasn't been enough time yet. We're specialized in a certain way, and we're useful in certain jobs."

"If you're satisfied to stay there. The Baldies who won't wear wigs—"

"They're so bad-tempered I expect they'll all be killed off in duels eventually," Burkhalter smiled. "No great loss. The rest of us, we're getting what we want—acceptance. We don't have horns or halos."

Quayle shook his head. "I'm glad, I think, that I'm not a telepath. The mind's mysterious enough anyway, without new doors opening. Thanks for letting me talk. I think I've got part of it talked out, anyway. Shall we try the script again?"

"Sure," Burkhalter said, and again the procession of pages flickered on the screen above them. Quayle did seem less guarded; his thoughts were more lucid, and Burkhalter was able to get at the true meaning of many of the hitherto muddy statements. They worked easily, the telepath dictating rephrasings into his dictograph, and only twice did they have to hurdle emotional tangles. At noon they knocked off, and Burkhalter, with a friendly nod, took the dropper to his office, where he found some calls listed on the visor. He ran off repeats, and a worried look crept into his blue eyes.

He talked with Dr. Moon in a booth at luncheon. The conversation lasted so long that only the induction cups kept the coffee hot, but Burkhalter had more than one problem to discuss. And he'd known Moon for a long time. The fat man was one of the few who were not, he thought, subconsciously repelled by the fact that Burkhalter was a Baldy.

"I've never fought a duel in my life, Doc. I can't afford to."

"You can't afford not to. You can't turn down the challenge, Ed. It isn't done."

"But this fellow Reilly—I don't even know him."

"I know of him," Moon said. "He's got a bad temper. Dueled a lot."

Burkhalter slammed his hand down on the table. "It's ridiculous. I won't do it!"

"Well," Moon said practically, "Your wife can't fight him. And if Ethel's been reading Mrs. Reilly's mind and gossiping, Reilly's got a case."

"Don't you think we know the dangers of that?" Burkhalter asked in a low voice. "Ethel doesn't go around reading minds any more than I do. It'd be fatal—for us. And for any other Baldy."

"Not the hairless ones. The ones who won't wear wigs. They—"

"They're fools. And they're giving all the Baldies a bad name. Point one, Ethel doesn't read minds; she didn't read Mrs. Reilly's. Point two, she doesn't gossip."

"La Reilly is obviously an hysterical type," Moon said. "Word got around about this scandal, whatever it was, and Mrs. Reilly remembered she'd seen Ethel lately. She's the type who needs a scapegoat anyway. I rather imagine she let word drop herself, and had to cover up so her husband wouldn't blame her."

"I'm not going to accept Reilly's challenge," Burkhalter said doggedly.

"You'll have to."

"Listen, Doc, maybe—"

"What?"

"Nothing. An idea. It might work. Forget about that; I think I've got the right answer. It's the only one, anyway. I can't afford a duel and that's flat."

"You're not a coward."

"There's one thing Baldies are afraid of," Burkhalter said, "and that's public opinion. I happen to know I'd kill Reilly. That's the reason why I've never dueled in my life."

Moon drank coffee. "Hm-m-m. I think—"

"Don't. There was something else. I'm wondering if I ought to send Al off to a special school."

"What's wrong with the kid?"

"He's turning out to be a beautiful delinquent. His teacher called me this morning. The playback was something to hear. He's talking funny and acting funny. Playing nasty little tricks on his friends—if he has any left by now."

"All kids are cruel."

"Kids don't know what cruelty means. That's why they're cruel; they lack empathy. But Al's getting—" Burkhalter gestured helplessly. "He's turning into a young tyrant. He doesn't seem to give a care about anything, according to his teacher."

"That's not too abnormal, so far."

"That's not the worst. He's become very egotistical. Too much so. I don't want him to turn into one of the wigless Baldies you were mentioning." Burkhalter didn't mention the other possibility; paranoia, insanity.

"He must pick things up somewhere. At home? Scarcely, Ed. Where else does he go?"

"The usual places. He's got a normal environment."

"I should think," Moon said, "that a Baldy would have unusual opportunities in training a youngster. The mental rapport—eh?"

"Yeah. But—I don't know. The trouble is," Burkhalter said almost inaudibly, "I wish to God I wasn't different. We didn't ask to be telepaths. Maybe it's all very wonderful in the long run, but I'm one person, and I've got my own microcosm. People who deal in long-term sociology are apt to forget that. They can figure out the answers, but it's every individual man—or Baldy—who's got to fight his own personal battle while he's alive. And it isn't as clear-cut as a battle. It's worse; it's the necessity of watching yourself every second, of fitting yourself into a world that doesn't want you."

Moon looked uncomfortable. "Are you being a little sorry for yourself, Ed?"

Burkhalter shook himself. "I am, Doc. But I'll work it out."

"We both will," Moon said, but Burkhalter didn't really expect much help from him. Moon would be willing, but it was horribly difficult for an ordinary man to conceive that a Baldy was—the same. It was the difference that men looked for, and found.

Anyway, he'd have to settle matters before he saw Ethel again. He could easily conceal the knowledge, but she would recognize a mental barrier and wonder. Their marriage had been the more ideal because of the additional rapport, something that compensated for an inevitable, half-sensed estrangement from the rest of the world.

"How's *Psychohistory* going?" Moon asked after a while.

"Better than I expected. I've got a new angle on Quayle. If I talk about myself, that seems to draw him out. It gives him enough confidence to let him open his mind to me. We may have those first chapters ready for Oldfield, in spite of everything."

"Good. Just the same, he can't rush us. If we've got to shoot out books that fast, we might as well go back to the days of semantic confusion. Which we won't!"

"Well," Burkhalter said, getting up, "I'll smoosh along. See you."

"About Reilly—"

"Let it lie." Burkhalter went out, heading for the address his visor had listed. He touched the dagger at his belt. Dueling wouldn't do for Baldies, but—

* * *

A greeting thought crept into his mind, and, under the arch that led into the campus, he paused to grin at Sam Shane, a New Orleans area Baldy who affected a wig of flaming red. They didn't bother to talk.

Personal question, involving mental, moral and physical well-being.

A satisfied glow. And you, Burkhalter? For an instant Burkhalter half-saw what the symbol of his name meant to Shane.

Shadow of trouble.

A warm, willing anxiousness to help. There was a bond between Baldies.

Bulkhalter thought: But everywhere I'd go there'd be the same suspicion. We're freaks.

More so elsewhere, Shane thought. There are a lot of us in Modoc Town. People are invariably more suspicious where they're not in daily contact with—Us.

The boy—

I've trouble too, Shane thought. It's worried me. My two girls—

Delinquency?

Yes.

Common denominators?

Don't know. More than one of Us have had the same trouble with our kids.

Secondary characteristic of the mutation? Second generation emergence?

Doubtful, Shane thought, scowling in his mind, shading his concept with a wavering question. We'll think it over later. Must go.

Burkhalter sighed and went on his way. The houses were strung out around the central industry of Modoc, and he cut through a park toward his destination. It was a sprawling curved building, but it wasn't inhabited, so Burkhalter filed Reilly for future reference, and, with a glance at his timer, angled over a hillside toward the school. As he expected, it was recreation time, and he spotted Al lounging under a tree, some distance from his companions, who were involved in a pleasantly murderous game of Blowup.

He sent his thought ahead.

The Green Man had amost reached the top of the mountain. The hairy gnomes were pelting on his trail, most unfairly shooting sizzling light-streaks at their quarry, but the Green Man was agile enough to dodge. The rocks were leaning—

"Al."

—inward, pushed by the gnomes, ready to—

"*Al!*" Burkhalter sent his thought with the word, jolting into the boy's mind, a trick he very seldom employed, since youth was practically defenseless against such invasion.

"Hello, Dad," Al said, undisturbed. "What's up?"

"A report from your teacher."

"I didn't do anything."

"She told me what it was. Listen, kid. Don't start getting any funny ideas in your head."

"I'm not."

"Do you think a Baldy is better or worse than a non-Baldy?"

Al moved his feet uncomfortably. He didn't answer.

"Well," Burkhalter said, "the answer is both and neither. And here's why. A Baldy can communicate mentally, but he lives in a world where most people can't."

"They're dumb," Al opined.

"Not so dumb, if they're better suited to their world than you are. You might as well say a frog's better than a fish because he's an amphibian." Burkhalter briefly amplified and explained the terms telepathically.

"Well . . . oh, I get it, all right."

"Maybe," Burkhalter said slowly, "what you need is a swift kick in the pants. That thought wasn't so hot. What was it again?"

Al tried to hide it, blanking out. Burkhalter began to lift the barrier, an easy matter for him, but stopped. Al regarded his father in a most unfilial way—in fact, as a sort of boneless fish. That had been clear.

"If you're so egotistical," Burkhalter pointed out, "maybe you can see it this way. Do you know why there aren't any Baldies in key positions?"

"Sure I do," Al said unexpectedly. "They're afraid."

"Of what, then?"

"The—" That picture had been very curious, a commingling of something vaguely familiar to Burkhalter. "The non-Baldies."

"Well, if we took positions where we could take advantage of our telepathic function, non-Baldies would be plenty envious—especially if we were successes. If a Baldy even invented a better mousetrap, plenty of people would say he'd stolen the idea from some non-Baldy's mind. You get the point?"

"Yes, Dad." But he hadn't. Burkhalter sighed and looked up. He recognized one of Shane's girls on a nearby hillside, sitting alone against a boulder. There were other isolated figures here and there. Far to the east the snowy rampart of the Rockies made an irregular pattern against blue sky.

"Al," Burkhalter said, "I don't want you to get a chip on your shoulder. This is a pretty swell world, and the people in it are, on the whole, nice people. There's a law of averages. It isn't sensible for us to get too much wealth or power, because that'd militate against us—and we don't need it anyway. Nobody's poor. We find our work, we do it, and we're reasonably happy. We have some advantages non-Baldies don't have; in marriage, for example. Mental intimacy is quite as important as physical. But I don't want you to feel that being a Baldy makes you a god. It doesn't. I can still," he added thoughtfully, "spank it out of you, in case you care to follow out that concept in your mind at the moment."

Al gulped and beat a hasty retreat. "I'm sorry. I won't do it again."

"And keep your hair on, too. Don't take your wig off in class. Use the stickum stuff in the bathroom closet."

"Yes, but . . . Mr. Venner doesn't wear a wig."

"Remind me to do some historical research with you on zoot-suiters," Burkhalter said. "Mr. Venner's wiglessness is probably his only virtue, if you consider it one."

"He makes money."

"Anybody would, in that general store of his. But people don't buy from him if they can help it, you'll notice. That's what I mean by a chip on your shoulder. He's got one. There are Baldies like Venner, Al, but you might, sometime, ask the guy if he's happy. For your information, I am. More than Venner, anyway. Catch?"

"Yes, Dad." Al seemed submissive, but it was merely that. Burkhalter, still troubled, nodded and walked away. As he passed near the Shane girl's boulder he caught a scrap: —*at the summit of the Glass Mountains, rolling rocks back at the gnomes until—*

He withdrew; it was an unconscious habit, touching minds that were sensitive, but with children it was definitely unfair. With adult Baldies it was simply the instinctive gesture of tipping your hat; one answered or one didn't. The barrier could be erected; there could be a blank-out; or there could be the direct snub of concentration on a single thought, private and not to be intruded on.

A copter with a string of gliders was coming in from the south: a freighter laden with frozen foods from South America, to judge by the markings. Burkhalter made a note to pick up an Argentine steak. He'd got a new recipe he wanted to try out, a charcoal broil with barbecue sauce, a welcome change from the short-wave cooked meats they'd been having for a week. Tomatoes, chile, mm-m—what else? Oh, yes. The duel with Reilly. Burkhalter absently touched his dagger's hilt and made a small, mocking sound in his throat. Perhaps he was innately a pacifist. It was rather difficult to think of a duel seriously, even though everyone else did, when the details of a barbecue dinner were prosaic in his mind.

So it went. The tides of civilization rolled in century-long waves across the continents, and each particular wave, though conscious of its participation in the tide, nevertheless was more preoccupied with dinner. And, unless you happened to be a thousand feet tall, had the brain of a god and a god's life-span, what was the difference? People missed a lot—people like Venner, who was certainly a crank, not batty enough to qualify for the asylum, but certainly a potential paranoid type. The man's refusal to wear a wig labeled him as an individualist, but as an exhibitionist, too. If he didn't feel ashamed of his hairlessness, why should he bother to flaunt it? Besides, the man had a bad temper, and if people kicked him around, he asked for it by starting the kicking himself.

But as for Al, the kid was heading for something approaching delinquency. It couldn't be the normal development of childhood, Burkhalter thought. He didn't pretend to be an expert, but he was still young enough to remember his own formative years, and he had had more handicaps than Al had now; in those days, Baldies had been very new and very freakish. There'd been more than one movement to isolate, sterilize, or even exterminate the mutations.

Burkhalter sighed. If he had been born before the Blowup, it might have been different. Impossible to say. One could read history, but one couldn't live it. In the future, perhaps, there might be telepathic libraries in which that would be possible. So many opportunities, in fact—and so few that the world was ready to accept as yet. Eventually Baldies would not be regarded as freaks, and by that time real progress would be possible.

But people don't make history—Burkhalter thought. Peoples do that. Not the individual.

He stopped by Reilly's house, and this time the man answered, a burly, freckled, squint-eyed fellow with immense hands and, Burkhalter noted, fine muscular coordination. He rested those hands on the Dutch door and nodded.

"Who're you, mister?"

"My name's Burkhalter."

Comprehension and wariness leaped into Reilly's eyes. "Oh, I see. You got my call?"

"I did," Burkhalter said. "I want to talk to you about it. May I come in?"

"OK." He stepped back, opening the way through a hall and into a spacious living room, where diffused light filtered through glassy mosaic walls. "Want to set the time?"

"I want to tell you you're wrong."

"Now wait a minute," Reilly said, patting the air. "My wife's out now, but she gave me the straight of it. I don't like this business of sneaking into a man's mind; it's crooked. You should have told *your* wife to mind her business—or keep her tongue quiet."

Burkhalter said patiently, "I give you my word, Reilly, that Ethel didn't read your wife's mind."

"Does she say so?"

"I . . . well, I haven't asked her."

"Yeah," Reilly said with an air of triumph.

"I don't need to. I know her well enough. And . . . well, I'm a Baldy myself."

"I know you are," Reilly said. "For all I know, you may be reading my mind now." He hesitated. "Get out of my house. I like my privacy. We'll meet at dawn tomorrow, if that's satisfactory with you. Now get out." He seemed to have something on his mind, some ancient memory, perhaps, that he didn't wish exposed.

Burkhalter nobly resisted the temptation. "No Baldy would read—"

"Go on, get out!"

"Listen! You wouldn't have a chance in a duel with me!"

"Do you know how many notches I've got?" Reilly asked.

"Ever dueled a Baldy?"

"I'll cut the notch deeper tomorrow. Get out, d'you hear?"

Burkhalter, biting his lips, said, "Man, don't you realize that in a duel I could read your mind?"

Lewis Padgett

"I don't care . . . what?"

"I'd be half a jump ahead of you. No matter how instinctive your actions would be, you'd know them a split second ahead of time in your mind. And I'd know all your tricks and weaknesses, too. Your technique would be an open book to me. Whatever you thought of—"

"No." Reilly shook his head. "Oh, no. You're smart, but it's a phony set-up."

Bukhalter hesitated, decided, and swung about, pushing a chair out of the way. "Take out your dagger," he said. "Leave the sheath snapped on; I'll show you what I mean."

Reilly's eyes widened. "If you want it now—"

"I don't." Burkhalter shoved another chair away. He unclipped his dagger, sheath and all, from his belt, and made sure the little safety clip was in place. "We've room enough here. Come on."

Scowling, Reilly took out his own dagger, held it awkwardly, baffled by the sheath, and then suddenly feinted forward. But Burkhalter wasn't there; he had anticipated, and his own leather sheath slid up Reilly's belly.

"That," Burkhalter said, "would have ended the fight."

For answer Reilly smashed a hard dagger-blow down, curving at the last moment into a throat-cutting slash. Burkhalter's free hand was already at his throat; his other hand, with the sheathed dagger, tapped Reilly twice over the heart. The freckles stood out boldly against the pallor of the larger man's face. But he was not yet ready to concede. He tried a few more passes, clever, well-trained cuts, and they failed, because Burkhalter had anticipated them. His left hand invariably covered the spot where Reilly had aimed, and which he never struck.

Slowly Reilly let his arm fall. He moistened his lips and swallowed. Burkhalter busied himself reclipping his dagger in place.

"Burkhalter," Reilly said, "you're a devil."

"Far from it. I'm just afraid to take a chance. Do you really think being a Baldy is a snap?"

"But, if you can read minds—"

"How long do you think I'd last if I did any dueling? It would be too much of a set-up. Nobody would stand for it, and I'd end up dead. I can't duel, because it'd be murder, and people would know it was murder. I've taken a lot of cracks, swallowed a lot of insults, for just that reason. Now, if you like, I'll swallow another and apologize. I'll admit anything you say. But I can't duel with you, Reilly."

"No, I can see that. And—I'm glad you came over." Reilly was still white. "I'd have walked right into a set-up."

"Not my set-up," Burkhalter said. "I wouldn't have dueled. Baldies aren't so lucky, you know. They've got handicaps—like this. That's why they can't afford to take chances and antagonize people, and why we never read minds, unless we're asked to do so."

The Piper's Son

"It makes sense. More or less." Reilly hesitated. "Look, I withdraw that challenge. OK?"

"Thanks," Burkhalter said, putting out his hand. It was taken rather reluctantly. "We'll leave it at that, eh?"

"Right." But Reilly was still anxious to get his guest out of the house.

Burkhalter walked back to the Publishing Center and whistled tunelessly. He could tell Ethel now; in fact, he had to, for secrets between them would have broken up the completeness of their telepathic intimacy. It was not that their minds lay bare to each other, it was, rather, that any barrier could be sensed by the other, and the perfect *rapport* wouldn't have been so perfect. Curiously, despite this utter intimacy, husband and wife managed to respect one another's privacy.

Ethel might be somewhat distressed, but the trouble had blown over, and, besides, she was a Baldy too. Not that she looked it, with her wig of fluffy chestnut hair and those long, curving lashes. But her parents had lived east of Seattle during the Blowup, and afterward, too, before the hard radiation's effects had been thoroughly studied.

The snow-wind blew down over Modoc and fled southward along the Utah Valley. Burkhalter wished he was in his copter, alone in the blue emptiness of the sky. There was a quiet, strange peace up there that no Baldy ever quite achieved on the Earth's surface, except in the depths of a wilderness. Stray fragments of thoughts were always flying about, subsensory, but like the almost-unheard whisper of a needle on a phonograph record, never ceasing. That, certainly, was why almost all Baldies loved to fly and were expert pilots. The high waste deserts of the air were their blue hermitages.

Still, he was in Modoc now, and overdue for his interview with Quayle. Burkhalter hastened his steps. In the main hall he met Moon, said briefly and cryptically that he'd taken care of the duel, and passed on, leaving the fat man to stare a question after him. The only visor call was from Ethel; the playback said she was worried about Al, and would Burkhalter check with the school. Well, he had already done so—unless the boy had managed to get into more trouble since then. Burkhalter put in a call and reassured himself. Al was as yet unchanged.

He found Quayle in the same private solarium, and thirsty. Burkhalter ordered a couple of dramzowies sent up, since he had no objection to loosening Quayle's inhibitions. The gray-haired author was immersed in a sectional historical globe-map, illuminating each epochal layer in turn as he searched back through time.

"Watch this," he said, running his hand along the row of buttons. "See how the German border fluctuates? And Portugal. Notice its zone of influence? Now—" The zone shrank steadily from 1600 on, while other countries shot out radiating lines and assumed sea power.

Burkhalter sipped his dramzowie. "Not much of that now."

"No, since . . . what's the matter?"

"How do you mean?"

"You look shot."

"I didn't know I showed it," Burkhalter said wryly. "I just finagled my way out of a duel."

"That's one custom I never saw much sense to," Quayle said. "What happened? Since when can you finagle out?"

Burkhalter explained, and the writer took a drink and snorted. "What a spot for you. Being a Baldy isn't such an advantage after all, I guess."

"It has distinct disadvantages at times." On impulse Burkhalter mentioned his son. "You see my point, eh? I don't *know*, really, what standards to apply to a young Baldy. He is a mutation, after all. And the telepathic mutation hasn't had time to work out yet. We can't rig up controls, because guinea pigs and rabbits won't breed telepaths. That's been tried, you know. And—well, the child of a Baldy needs very special training so he can cope with his ultimate maturity."

"You seem to have adjusted well enough."

"I've—learned. As most sensible Baldies have. That's why I'm not a wealthy man, or in politics. We're really buying safety for our species by foregoing certain individual advantages. Hostages to destiny—and destiny spares us. But we get paid too, in a way. In the coinage of future benefits—negative benefits, really, for we ask only to be spared and accepted—and so we have to deny ourselves a lot of present, positive benefits. An appeasement to fate."

"Paying the piper," Quayle nodded.

"We are the pipers. The Baldies as a group, I mean. And our children. So it balances; we're really paying ourselves. If I wanted to take unfair advantage of my telepathic power—my son wouldn't live very long. The Baldies would be wiped out. Al's got to learn that, and he's getting pretty antisocial."

"All children are antisocial," Quayle pointed out. "They're utter individualists. I should think the only reason for worrying would be if the boy's deviation from the norm were connected with his telepathic sense."

"There's something in that." Burkhalter reached out left-handedly and probed delicately at Quayle's mind, noting that the antagonism was considerably lessened. He grinned to himself and went on talking about his own troubles. "Just the same, the boy's father to the man. And an adult Baldy has got to be pretty well adjusted, or he's sunk."

"Environment is as important as heredity. One complements the other. If a child's reared correctly, he won't have much trouble—unless heredity is involved."

"As it may be. There's so little known about the telepathic mutation. If baldness is one secondary characteristic, maybe—something else—emerges in the third or fourth generations. I'm wondering if telepathy is really good for the mind."

Quayle said, "Humph. Speaking personally, it makes me nervous—"

"Like Reilly."

"Yes," Quayle said, but he didn't care much for the comparison. "Well—anyhow, if a mutation's a failure, it'll die out. It won't breed true."

"What about hemophilia?"

"How many people have hemophilia?" Quayle asked. "I'm trying to look at it from the angle of psychohistorian. If there'd been telepaths in the past, things might have been different."

"How do you know there weren't?" Burkhalter asked.

Quayle blinked. "Oh. Well. That's true, too. In medieval times they'd have been called wizards—or saints. The Duke-Rhine experiments—but such accidents would have been abortive. Nature fools around trying to hit the . . . ah . . . the jackpot, and she doesn't always do it on the first try."

"She may not have done it now." That was habit speaking, the ingrained caution of modesty. "Telepathy may be merely a semisuccessful try at something pretty unimaginable. A sort of four-dimensional sensory concept, maybe."

"That's too abstract for me." Quayle was interested, and his own hesitancies had almost vanished; by accepting Burkhalter as a telepath, he had tacitly wiped away his objections to telepathy *per se*. "The old-time Germans always had an idea they were different; so did the Japanese. They knew, very definitely, that they were a superior race because they were directly descended from gods. They were short in stature; heredity made them self-conscious when dealing with larger races. But the Chinese aren't tall, the Southern Chinese, and they weren't handicapped in that way."

"Environment, then?"

"Environment, which caused propaganda. The Japanese took Buddhism, and altered it completely into Shinto, to suit their own needs. The samurai, warrier-knights, were the ideals, the code of honor was fascinatingly cockeyed. The principle of Shinto was to worship your superiors and subjugate your inferiors. Ever seen the Japanese jewel-trees?"

"I don't remember them. What are they?"

"Miniature replicas of espaliered trees, made of jewels, with trinkets hanging on the branches. Including a mirror—always. The first jewel-tree was made to lure the Moon-goddess out of a cave where she was sulking. It seemed the lady was so intrigued by the trinkets and by her face reflected in the mirror that she came out of her hideout. All the Japanese morals were dressed up in pretty clothes; that was the bait. The old-time Germans did much the same thing. The last German dictator, Hitler, revived the old Siegfried legend. It was racial paranoia. The Germans worshiped the house-tyrant, not the mother, and they had extremely strong family ties. That extended to the state. They symbolized Hitler as their All-Father, and so eventually we got the Blowup. And, finally, mutations."

"After the deluge, me," Burkhalter murmured, finishing his dramzowie. Quayle was staring at nothing.

"Funny," he said after a while. "This All-Father business—"

"Yes?"

"I wonder if you know how powerfully it can affect a man?"

Burkhalter didn't say anything. Quayle gave him a sharp glance.

"Yes," the writer said quietly. "You're a man, after all. I owe you an apology, you know."

Bukhalter smiled. "You can forget that."

"I'd rather not," Quayle said. "I've just realized, pretty suddenly, that the telepathic sense isn't so important. I mean—it doesn't make you *different*. I've been talking to you—"

"Sometimes it takes people years before they realize what you're finding out," Burkhalter remarked. "Years of living and working with something they think of as a Baldy."

"Do you know what I've been concealing in my mind?" Quayle asked.

"No. I don't."

"You lie like a gentleman. Thanks. Well, here it is, and I'm telling you by choice, because I want to. I don't care if you got the information out of my mind already; I just want to tell you of my own free will. My father . . . I imagine I hated him . . . was a tyrant, and I remember one time, when I was just a kid and we were in the mountains, he beat me and a lot of people were looking on. I've tried to forget that for a long time. "Now"—Quayle shrugged—"it doesn't seem quite so important."

"I'm not a psychologist," Burkhalter said. "If you want my personal reaction, I'll just say that it doesn't matter. You're not a little boy any more, and the guy I'm talking to and working with is the adult Quayle."

"Hm-m-m. Ye-es. I suppose I knew that all along—how unimportant it was, really. It was simply having my privacy violated. . . . I think I know you better now, Burkhalter. You can—walk in."

"We'll work better," Burkhalter said, grinning. "Especially with Darius."

Quayle said, "I'll try not to keep any reservation in my mind. Frankly, I won't mind telling you—the answers. Even when they're personal."

"Check on that. D'you want to tackle Darius now?"

"OK," Quayle said, and his eyes no longer held suspicious wariness. "Darius I identify with my father—"

It was smooth and successful. That afternoon they accomplished more than they had during the entire previous fortnight. Warm with satisfaction on more than one point, Burkhalter stopped off to tell Dr. Moon that matters were looking up, and then set out toward home, exchanging thoughts with a couple of Baldies, his co-workers, who were knocking off for the day. The Rockies were bloody with the western light, and the coolness of the wind was pleasant on Burkhalter's cheeks, as he hiked homeward.

It was fine to be accepted. It proved that it could be done. And a Baldy often needed reassurance, in a world peopled by suspicious strangers. Quayle had been a hard nut to crack, but—Burkhalter smiled.

Ethel would be pleased. In a way, she'd had a harder time than he'd ever had. A woman would, naturally. Men were desperately anxious to keep their privacy unviolated by a woman, and as for non-Baldy women—well, it spoke highly for Ethel's glowing personal charm that she had finally been accepted by the clubs and feminine groups of Modoc. Only Burkhalter knew Ethel's desperate hurt at being bald, and not even her husband had ever seen her unwigged.

His thought reached out before him into the low, double-winged house on the hillside, and interlocked with hers in a warm intimacy. It was something more than a kiss. And, as always, there was the exciting sense of expectancy, mounting and mounting till the last door swung open and they touched physically. *This,* he thought, *is why I was born a Baldy; this is worth losing worlds for.*

At dinner that rapport spread out to embrace Al, an intangible, deeply-rooted something that made the food taste better and the water like wine. The word *home,* to telepaths, had a meaning that non-Baldies could not entirely comprehend, for it embraced a bond they could not know. There were small, intangible caresses.

Green Man going down the Great Red Slide; the Shaggy Dwarfs trying to harpoon him as he goes.

"Al," Ethel said, "are you still working on your Green Man?"

Then something utterly hateful and cold and deadly quivered silently in the air, like an icicle jaggedly smashing through golden, fragile glass. Burkhalter dropped his napkin and looked up, profoundly shocked. He felt Ethel's thought shrink back, and swiftly reached out to touch and reassure her with mental contact. But across the table the little boy, his cheeks still round with the fat of babyhood, sat silent and wary, realizing he had blundered, and seeking safety in complete immobility. His mind was too weak to resist probing, he knew, and he remained perfectly still, waiting, while the echoes of a thought hung poisonously in silence.

Burkhalter said, "Come on, Al." He stood up. Ethel started to speak.

"Wait, darling. Put up a barrier. Don't listen in." He touched her mind gently and tenderly, and then he took Al's hand and drew the boy after him out into the yard. Al watched his father out of wide, alert eyes.

Burkhalter sat on a bench and put Al beside him. He talked audibly at first, for clarity's sake, and for another reason. It was distinctly unpleasant to trick the boy's feeble guards down, but it was necessary.

"That's a very queer way to think of your mother," he said. "It's a queer way to think of me." Obscenity is more obscene, profanity more profane, to a telepathic mind, but this had been neither one. It had been—cold and malignant.

And this is flesh of my flesh, Burkhalter thought, looking at the boy and remembering the eight years of his growth. *Is the mutation to turn into something devilish?*

Al was silent.

Burkhalter reached into the young mind. Al tried to twist free and escape, but his father's strong hands gripped him. Instinct, not reasoning, on the boy's part, for minds can touch over long distances.

He did not like to do this, for increased sensibility had gone with sensitivity, and violations are always violations. But ruthlessness was required. Burkhalter searched.

Lewis Padgett

Sometimes he threw key words violently at Al, and surges of memory pulsed up in response.

In the end, sick and nauseated, Burkhalter let Al go and sat alone on the bench, watching the red light die on the snowy peaks. The whiteness was red-stained. But it was not too late. The man was a fool, had been a fool from the beginning, or he would have known the impossibility of attempting such a thing as this.

The conditioning had only begun. Al could be reconditioned. Burkhalter's eyes hardened. And would be. *And would be.* But not yet, not until the immediate furious anger had given place to sympathy and understanding.

Not yet.

He went into the house, spoke briefly to Ethel, and televised the dozen Baldies who worked with him in the Publishing Center. Not all of them had families, but none was missing when, half an hour later, they met in the back room of the Pagan Tavern downtown. Sam Shane had caught a fragment of Burkhalter's knowledge, and all of them read his emotions. Welded into a sympathetic unit by their telepathic sense, they waited till Burkhalter was ready.

Then he told them. It didn't take long, via thought. He told them about the Japanese jewel-tree with its glittering gadgets, a shining lure. He told them of racial paranoia and propaganda. And that the most effective propaganda was sugar-coated, disguised so that the motive was hidden.

A Green Man, hairless, heroic—symbolic of a Baldy.

And wild, exciting adventures, the lure to catch the young fish whose plastic minds were impressionable enough to be led along the roads of dangerous madness. Adult Baldies could listen, but they did not; young telepaths had a higher threshold of mental receptivity, and adults do not read the books of their children except to reassure themselves that there is nothing harmful in the pages. And no adult would bother to listen to the Green Man mindcast. Most of them had accepted it as the original daydream of their own children.

"I did," Shane put in. "My girls—"

"Trace it back," Burkhalter said. "I did."

The dozen minds reached out on the higher frequency, the children's wavelength, and something jerked away from them, startled and apprehensive.

"He's the one," Shane nodded.

They did not need to speak. They went out of the Pagan Tavern in a compact, ominous group, and crossed the street to the general store. The door was locked. Two of the men burst it open with their shoulders.

They went through the dark store and into a back room where a man was standing beside an overturned chair. His bald skull gleamed in an overhead light. His mouth worked impotently.

His thought pleaded with them—was driven back by an implacable deadly wall.

Burkhalter took out his dagger. Other slivers of steel glittered for a little while—

And were quenched.

Venner's scream had long since stopped, but his dying thought of agony lingered within Burkhalter's mind as he walked homeward. The wigless Baldy had not been insane, no. But he had been paranoidal.

What he had tried to conceal, at the last, was quite shocking. A tremendous, tyrannical egotism, and a furious hatred of nontelepaths. A feeling of self-justification that was, perhaps, insane. And—*we are the Future! The Baldies! God made us to rule lesser men!*

Burkhalter sucked in his breath, shivering. The mutation had not been entirely successful. One group had adjusted, the Baldies who wore wigs and had become fitted to their environment. One group had been insane, and could be discounted; they were in asylums.

But the middle group were merely paranoid. They were not insane, and they were not sane. They wore no wigs.

Like Venner.

And Venner had sought disciples. His attempt had been foredoomed to failure, but he had been one man.

One Baldy-paranoid.

There were others, many others.

Ahead, nestled into the dark hillside, was the pale blotch that marked Burkhalter's home. He sent his thought ahead, and it touched Ethel's and paused very briefly to reassure her.

Then it thrust on, and went into the sleeping mind of a little boy who, confused and miserable, had finally cried himself to sleep. There were only dreams in that mind now, a little discolored, a little stained, but they could be cleansed. And would be.

BABEL II
Christopher Anvil

THE NEW ASSISTANT SECRETARY OF STATE doubtfully eased along the row of seats in the big dim room, and settled scowlingly into a chair beside the well-known Kremlinologist.

"Damn it, Bill," growled the Assistant Secretary, "if I'd known this was where you got your inside information—"

"Sh-h," said the Kremlinologist, raising a finger. "We're about to start."

At the front of the room, under a single clear light, Madame Sairo signaled to her assistants.

The room's overhead lights dimmed further. A blond boy dressed all in white rolled out on heavy casters a thing that at first glance looked like a big globe of the world set in a large holder, but on closer examination turned out to be a crystal ball about two feet thick.

Madame Sairo adjusted the big crystal, and took her seat.

The room fell silent. The Kremlinologists, the Far East experts, and the Government economists leaned forward attentively.

The new Assistant Secretary of State eyed the crystal ball sourly.

Madame Sairo gazed intently into the crystal, her mind focused on the question of the evening. For some time, however, she got nowhere, and when the mists finally did begin to shred away, the scene that formed did not seem to be right. Frowning, she watched the unfamiliar man at the desk.

Elias Polk, for the fourth time trying to extract the sense of this latest report on the Esmer Drive, was stuck again on the section reading:

". . . difficulty remains in the suffluxion of the tantron stream, and resultant vilent node-regression. Yet any other approach obviously requires consideration of Hasebrouck's theory of complex particle-interaction . . ."

Polk's train of thought each time went off the track at that word "obviously." Why did any other approach obviously require consideration of Hasebrouck's theory?

Polk flipped on through the report.

There followed five pages of Hasebrouck's del, ro-del, and pi-del equations, and then it all ended up with the words:

". . . therefore, we unequivocally recommend construction of the 175-TEV tangential accelerator."

That followed from consideration of Hasebrouck's equations, and Hasebrouck's equations came in because "any other approach obviously requires consideration of Hasebrouck's theory . . ."

Why was it obvious?

Polk looked up exasperatedly at the reversed letters on the glass of the door, from long familiarity reading them as easily as someone in the hall outside:

PROJECT LONG-REACH

J. Elias Polk

Director

Polk squinted at the report, tossed it down, picked up some papers, and thumbed through them. He settled back, scowling.

The estimated cost of that accelerator was seventy-two billions, over nine years. But with that for the original estimate, the true cost would probably run well above a hundred billion, and it would take twelve years.

Even then, no one could be sure that would give them enough information to eventually straighten out the difficulty.

Polk glanced back at the report.

". . . obviously any other approach requires consideration of Hasebrouck's . . ."

Why 'obviously'?

Frowning, Polk reached for the phone.

As the scene faded, Madame Sairo sat back blankly. Just what did that have to do with anything? What her clients wanted to know—

But there, a new scene was forming. She leaned forward hopefully.

The door opened, and Marcus Flint stepped out into the hall, the sheets of calculations and the charts with their pretty colored lines clutched in his hand. He strode down the hall, and threw open a second door without knocking.

"Are you out of your head, Peters? What do you think I'm running here, a market report or an obituary column?"

Peters adjusted his thick lenses and set his jaw. "Our computer analysis showed the projected OJDA taking a nose dive through the TL, with our PF matrix-model running out of steam before the year is out. We're in for a depression that could jar your teeth, M.F."

"Nuts. With this big spending for space projects—"

"That spending for space projects is increasing on our Chart III, there, to the point where it overshoots the stimulus role, and turns into a drain, pure and simple. Especially when you consider that Chart IV shows external and internal unindirectional cycle flow—"

"Will you, for God's sake—" Flint caught himself. "Look, I'll grant your expertise. Spare me this jargon, will you? What is external and internal unidirectional cycle flow?"

"Value tokens in unidirectional circulation, external or internal to the national

Christopher Anvil

economy, unaccompanied by a reverse flow of actual-value services or goods, either essential, marginal, or redundant.''

''Unearned money? Giveaway programs?''

Peters blinked. ''Well—Yes, I suppose you could put it that way.''

''All right, what about unearned money?''

Peters started to speak, hesitated, and shook his head. ''I can't use that term 'unearned money.' It has extraneous moral connotations. The moral connotations block consideration of the purely economic factors per se.''

''All right,'' snarled Flint. ''Then what about this unidirectional cycle flow?''

''We have a serious maladjustment of the reverse flow of actual-value units. Deferred payment of value tokens for actual-value units is not presently serious in itself. However, this continuing increase in the flow of value tokens with neither past, present, nor future correlated return flow of actual-value units creates an imbalance in the circuit flow, and that is serious.''

Flint grappled with the statement, and finally quoted, '' 'This grasping after unearned money will in time wreck the country.' I think Abraham Lincoln said that.''

''He did?'' Peters blinked, then squirmed uneasily, ''But that term 'unearned money' implies a—''

''All right,'' snarled Flint, '' 'unidirectional cycle flow.' Have it your own way. The point is, this projection of yours is so drastic no one will believe it. Its value, therefore, is nil. Moreover, jargon is great for mystifying people and impressing them with your expertise. But you've already accomplished that. It's a good idea occasionally to say something someone can understand, so he'll keep listening in hopes it will happen again. You've got this special lingo—''

Peters said stiffly, ''Precise terminology is necessary, in order to express the special economic forces and relationships operative in the economy.''

''You're carrying it too far. Nobody can understand it but you and a few other analysts who happen to use the same approach. Translate the results into plain English when you get the analysis done.''

Peters looked horrified. ''That's as absurd as a surgeon trying to explain a complicated operation to a layman, using no special terms. What could he say? 'I got a knife out and slit his stomach open. Then I clamped the skin and muscle back out of the way, and went in after his append . . . this bag of—' ''

Flint nodded. ''That's the idea.''

''But all the fine points would be lost! The expert would have to skip *every detail that the layman lacked the knowledge to understand.*'' Peters shook his head positively. ''No. The only way to get the actual facts across is for the *layman* to study the matter until he acquires enough facts *to understand the expert's explanation.*''

Marcus Flint leaned forward, the knuckles of his hand resting on the desktop.

''Doesn't it dawn on you that experts are proliferating like rabbits in this country? Just exactly where is any layman going *to get the time to study fifteen hundred different specialties so he can figure out what all these experts are talking about?*''

Peters spread his hands. "That isn't *my* problem. Don't blame me. I didn't make the world."

Madame Sairo sat back blankly. As the scene faded, she found herself like a pearl diver who surfaces with a few odd-shaped pebbles and no pearls. What was wrong?

But even as she groped for the cause of the trouble, a new scene was forming.

Ah, now, this looked more hopeful.

"Yes," she said quietly, "I have it. This is a distant land, and they are building. It is a tall structure—"

The Kremlinologists and Pekingologists leaned forward intently. The government economists looked shrewd.

The new Assistant Secretary growled, "Took her long enough."

"*Sh-h*," said his neighbors.

". . . Yes," Madam Sairo was saying, "this is a tower of some kind. It is a very ambitious project, but this nation is great. It is—"

Someone murmured, "China?"

Another whispered, "A new atom-test project?"

The Assistant Secretary stared around in disbelief, trying to pick out faces in the gloom so he would know in the future whose advice had come out of this crystal ball.

Madame Sairo jerked back suddenly from the globe. She gestured imperiously.

The overhead lights came back on.

She looked around the tensely quiet room, her expression serious.

"Gentlemen, I am afraid I must ask you to be very patient. You wish me to examine the next great world crisis. But there seems to be some difficulty here. I have been in contact with some events that appear irrelevant, and then with what apparently was a great *past* world crisis. Conceivably there is interference of some kind here. Or possibly, some symbolism I do not yet understand. If you will be patient, I will try again."

Her audience quietly settled back.

She gestured

The room lights dimmed.

In the crystal, a new scene seemed to swim into view.

But *this* seemed to be just a man and a boy, glaring at each other.

Patiently, Madame Sairo leaned forward.

Summer Maddox said exasperatedly, "You look at the lives of outstanding men who've really succeeded in a big way, and you'll find that *most* of them got an early start. Now, I'm not trying to force you to decide what you want to do with your life. But you've got to decide for yourself, one way or the other, and pick *something*."

"But I *can't* decide," said Roger Maddox, looking baffled. "There just doesn't seem to be anything—It's all hazy. There's just nothing I want to—"

The elder Maddox grimaced. "Listen. Without half your opportunities or advantages your great-grandfather had already learned a trade and was making a living at your age. Now, no one expects you to do the same. *Your* generation can go to school till they're twenty-six, and—''

Roger Maddox abruptly flared up. ''I *won't* go to school till I'm twenty-six!''

Summer Maddox said placatingly, ''I didn't say you *would*, I say you *could*. Anyway, that's a long way off. But you still have to decide—''

There was a brief tense silence.

The younger Maddox stared at a distant corner of the room. ''Wait a minute. I see what's wrong. It used to be, that when someone was growing up, day after day he *saw* grown people at work. In Great-Grandad's day, you could *watch* what different people did, see with your own eyes how they lived, and what their work was good for. Then you could decide what you wanted to do, because you knew what the choices were. It was like stopping at a crossroads to decide which of three or four different towns to go to, when you'd already seen the towns, and knew what they were like. But now—Now it's like stopping at a crossroads to decide which of a hundred and seventeen different cities to go live in, *when you never really had a good first-hand look at any of them before.*''

The elder Maddox frowned. ''Well . . . you've got a point there. That's because things are more complex now. Each special type of work is harder to understand, there are more specialties to consider, and the grown-ups work in one place while the children are in school somewhere else. It's *got* to be that way, but—'' He paused exasperatedly. ''Now, how the deuce do we get around this? Let's see—''

The scene faded out. Before there was time to even try to evaluate it, another scene formed, and there were two men in uniform, in an office with a photograph of a long gray ship on one wall, and a photograph of what was apparently some kind of submarine on another wall.

Admiral Bendix ran his gaze down the list of officers and shook his head.

''I know every one of these men, and not one of them is fitted. For captain of the *Constitution* we need someone exceptional. He has to have outstanding capabilities as a leader of men, plus unusual ability in all the skills of ship-handling. On top of that we need someone with the technical know-how to *comprehend the ship's drive*, so that he can get the most out of it and the technicians who handle it.''

Admiral Hart leaned back, his hands clasped behind his head.

''We may need three men for captain, in other words.''

''It has to be *one* man. The knowledge has got to be in one head when the clinch comes, because every bit of it is crucial. How can you decide, when you lack the knowledge to evaluate the factors involved? The captain has to make the decisions, and while he certainly doesn't have to know *everything*, he has got to understand the ship, the men, and the ship's drive. Unless he has the knowledge himself, he *can't* make the decisions.''

Hart shook his head.

"We aren't going to find one man with all those skills."

"We've got to *have* one man with all those skills. He has to *understand* the technical limitations of the ship, and he can only do that *if he understands the drive.*"

Admiral Hart sat up and looked Admiral Bendix in the eye.

"Do *you* understand the drive?"

Admiral Bendix looked flatly back.

"No. Do *you?*"

"No."

"But *we* aren't going to command this ship. Whoever does—"

Admiral Hart waved his head irritatedly. "Look, to honestly understand that drive, you'd have had to start at about age twelve, and follow just the right course of study ever since. But you'd have had to follow it by luck or by predestination, because at that time, back when you'd have had to start, *nobody knew this drive could be built.* Did you ever look in any of those books? Did you ever try to talk to any of the people working on that project? And in about fifteen years, the thing may be obsolete." He lowered his voice. "I hear the Esmer Drive is going great guns. Where are we going to find an officer who understands *that?*"

Admiral Bendix put the list down in disgust. "I suppose it wouldn't be too soon to start looking for one right now."

Hart nodded soberly. "But this still doesn't find us a man for the *Constitution.*"

Exasperatedly, the two men went through the list again.

Elias Polk was staring at the man across the desk. "Damn it, can't you explain your reasoning any better than that? You want the country to put a hundred billion dollars into something you can't even explain?"

"How do I explain it to you when you don't understand the concepts involved? Once you understand those concepts, the solution is intuitive. I know the answer the same way I know where water will come out when I tip a pitcher. It's obvious."

"Let's go over it again," said Polk stubbornly.

Reginald Paxter slit the envelope, pulled out the glossy book advertisements, and glanced at the titles:

"Inverted Limits in Transient Field Problems"

"Operational Functions for Projected Relay Circuitry"

"Recent Developments in Kickback Ready-State Devices and Their Theory"

Paxter sneered. "Gibberish. Pure gibberish. Who would—" He paused. One more title caught his attention. His eyes lighted.

"Saro Integrals in Complex Space Matrices of Non-Orthogonal Form"

Eagerly he pulled over the order sheet and got out his checkbook.

"No, Mrs. Bennett," said the service manager with a hounded look, "it was the brake *lining,* inside the brake drum, that was bad. It was cracked, glazed—Before, all we had to do was *adjust* the brakes, that's why this time it cost—'' The phone rang jarringly. "Excuse me just a minute. *Hello?*"

A familiar sarcastic male voice said, "Look, that starter you said you fixed. It doesn't work. When I tried to start the car this morning, it just groaned.''

"Ah—Well, the trouble is, like I said when you were in here, your voltage regulator—''

"What's that got to do with the starter?''

"Well, you see, the generator puts electricity *in* the battery. The starter takes it *out*. The—''

"How did the *generator* get in this? Are you trying to tell me you've got to work on the *generator* now?''

"No, but the voltage regulator is—''

"A minute ago, you said the generator. Which is it?''

"The *regulator* decides what the *generator* output will be. If the regulator is bad, the generator can't put electricity in the battery. When you were in here, I was trying to tell you—''

"What's that got to do with the starter?''

"If your battery's dead, the starter can't turn the engine over.''

There was a brief silence. "Well, there's *something* shot on this car. I had my brother push me all the way from Great Bend into town with the car in low-range, and the engine never caught once. I want that starter job done over, and this time find out what's *really* wrong.''

The service manager seemed to see the bursting of innumerable bubbles before his eyes. "Look," he said, speaking carefully, "on your car, there's no rear pump in the transmission. You *can't* start it by pushing. You can ruin the transmission that way. You say you pushed it *all the way from Great Bend to town in low?*"

As the silence on the other end stretched out, he asked himself, didn't people know *anything* about the cars they drove?

Mrs. Bennett cleared her throat. "What did you mean when you said the brake linings were 'glazed'?''

Over the phone came a baffled voice.

"What's a 'rear pump'? Now . . . just wait a minute. What are you trying to pull, anyway? *What's the transmission got to do with the starter?*"

Madame Sairo sat back with a pained expression. She looked up from the globe, and glanced around the dimly-lit room.

"I am *trying* to learn of the next world crisis. I am concentrating on the next world crisis. I am trying to look into the future, and I am still making irrelevant contacts with past and present. Is there anyone here whose motives are not right?''

The Kremlinologists and Pekingologists squinted dubiously at each other.

The Government economists looked pious.

The Assistant Secretary sat back and sneered at the whole fraud.

Madame Sairo adjusted the globe, and without much hope, tried again.

Dr. Greenhaven peered at the knowledge-growth projection, and then at the distribution-of-intelligence curve.

"We seem to be running into some difficulty here."

"Obviously," said the Projects Coordinator. "We now have teams of men attempting to do the jobs one man properly should do. This can only be carried so far. There is a delay each time knowledge must be transferred from one mind to another. If we have fifteen men, each with a different specialty, gathered around a table to help make a decision, we are in serious trouble. But we are worse off yet if we have a hundred and fifty men, each with his own specialty, gathered around that table. Knowledge is proliferating, Doctor. It is multiplying by leaps and bounds. If we aren't to have ten fragmented specialists where one stands now, what are we going to do about it?"

Dr. Greenhaven puffed out his cheeks, took another look at the charts, and said tentatively, "We must locate individuals capable of mastering this knowledge."

The Projects Coordinator looked bored.

"And," said Greenhaven, "educate them at an earlier age. If possible, *we* must specialize sooner, educate earlier and more intensively. If possible, we must select the most capable, rather than leaving them to blunder around on their own. We will have to separate types according to aptitude and potential skill. A deliberate *fractionation* of the race into useful types."

The Projects Coordinator at once looked interested. "*Now* we're getting to the heart of the matter. Go on."

Madame Sairo watched the scene fade, and then hopefully looked into the crystal. Now she was seeing. But what did it mean?

There before her, as clear as if she were looking directly at it, was a tall something aimed at the sky, towering over the men in their coats of different styles and colors, working around the huge device.

Now it seemed to come closer to her, so that she was almost at the base of the device, and could see the people clearly.

Odd—They seemed to be separated almost according to physical types—or was that somehow the result of the similar clothes, similar facial expressions, and similar manner and air of those doing a particular job? Those at the—wiring?—seemed nearly all to be fairly tall and slender, with rather long faces, and penetrating blue eyes of an unusual cast, while those moving the machinery into place were mostly shorter, burlier types, and the others at the controls—

Puzzled, she leaned closer, trying to unravel the mystery, when a tall individual in a dark purple coat brushed past the—electronics men?—and then bumped a burly individual in a dark-blue jacket.

Christopher Anvil

The purple-coated individual turned, holding the end of a long cable, and spoke irritatedly.

"Surry, fren?"

The purple-coated individual jerked his thumb back briefly at what looked like a large glistening maze of intertangled silver wires, set down into some kind of metal-lined pit, with large instrument panels nearby.

"Damn double-phased S-2 pit jerks more on hydrine than ever. Countercycles, shudders, creeps, unamit uknavit."

The blue-jacketed invididual glanced around uncertainly, then his eyes widened. He seized the purple-coated invididual by the arm.

"Damn doublefaced stupid jerk, eh? *Moron*, huh? Upurps gotchanerv. *Tagibak!*"

The purple-coated individual looked at him coldly. He wrenched his arm free.

"Right, Bluejack. Jerks, creeps, counter—"

"Bluejack" whipped the end of the cable around and landed a stunning blow.

The man in the purple coat staggered back, his hand to his face. Suddenly he screamed in rage.

Two tall, gray-coated individuals with a professiorial air paused, frowning as if to try to get the scene into focus.

Another blue-jacketed individual, pulling a thick cable through a metal frame, whirled around as the man in the purple coat charged. Dropping the cable, the second blue-jacketed man rushed to the scene.

An otherworldly individual in orange and white looked down in pained surprise from an overhead ramp.

"Peace. Let us have peace. Brethren, what is the meaning of brotherhood if we cannot have peace? It is wicked to—"

Half-a-dozen purple-clothed individuals boiled out of the metal-lined pit and came on the run.

The two professorial individuals in gray glanced at one another in bafflement.

A short plump man in a jacket, striped like black typewriter ribbon alternated with red tape, burst out of a little cubicle in the midst of a maze of pneumatic tubes, and still clutching a rubber stamp, a crumpled form filled out in quintuplicate, and a thick book with his finger holding the place, raced onto the scene.

"*Stop!* This voids the contract! Forbidden on worktime! *ARBITRATOR!*"

More blue-jackets were appearing from everywhere. One banged into a black-coated worker in his haste, and got rewarded by a smash over the back of the head with a socket wrench three feet long.

"There," said the blackcoat, beaming. "Stuckup bluejacket! Lectricity! Watso-wunifulbout lectricity? I'll lectricity the sonsa—"

His voice choked off as a length of cable whipped around his neck from behind.

A plump individual with a pill bottle in one hand tore down the overhead ramp, his pastel pink coat flapping behind him.

"Here!" He shouted, "Let's *ARBITRATE* the differences! Friends, FRIENDS, let's

SPLIT THE DIFFERENCE! The other side DIDN'T MEAN IT! They're *reasonable!*"
He looked down at the boiling melee of bluejacks, purps, and blackcoats, then twisted
the cap off the pill bottle, and shot three pills into his mouth. He chewed desperately,
stuck the bottle in his side pocket, and waited till an air of calm assurance passed over
his face like a mask. He pulled a tiny microphone on a cord from his pocket, plugged
it into a socket on the rail of the ramp, and his voice seemed to come out from
everywhere, calm, persuasive, assured.

"FRIENDS, THIS IS A MISUNDERSTANDING. *THEY DIDN'T MEAN IT!*
THEY WANT TO BE *FRIENDS*. WE CAN SETTLE THIS BETTER—"

A blue-jacketed figure popped out of the mob, snarled, "Shutup-jerk," and held
a length of dangling cable near a small metal box on a pole. There was a large jagged
dancing spark, a roaring noise, and then silence from the public-address system.

The bluejacket grinned, then thrust the cable against the leg of a purple-coated
individual who had another bluejacket by the throat.

On the overhead ramp, the pastel-coated arbitrator looked puzzled, but spoke on
with invincible assurance as a horde of burly individuals, their coats striped vertically
like zebras, intermingled with the rest of the strugglers and began laying them out in
all directions indifferently, only to be set upon by others, their zebra-stripes running
horizontally.

In all directions, on high and low levels, struggling sets of individuals could now
be seen pushing each other over the edge, choking, kicking, biting—

On the ramp, the arbitrator looked around, and paused. Worry crossed his face. He
pulled out the bottle and tossed another pill in his mouth. He glanced at his watch.
Ninety seconds passed and he was still worried. He took a last look around, jammed
the bottle in his pocket and yelled, "POLICE!"

Below, the mob slammed into a wheeled machine, which mounted an insulated
man-carrying stand on a long jointed metal arm.

The arm swung around sidewise, striking a tall heavy wire grid holding glistening
beadlike objects of varying colors, shapes, and sizes. A large section of the grid
wrapped around the stand and the metal arm. There was a loud sizzle, then a sheet
of flame roared up, followed by a cloud of boiling smoke.

A dazzling spark, or blazing point of light, rapidly ate its way up the shiny cable
into which a number of the grid wires fed, and traveled along the cable up the side
of the towering device.

The arbitrator's gaze followed the climbing spark in bafflement. How did you split
the difference with a thing like that? The facts of the matter began to penetrate his
pill-given assurance. He glanced around.

A little group of scowling men in checked black-and-blue jackets, followed by a
host of blue-clothed men armed with gas guns and billies, advanced at a fast walk
down the ramp, trying to make out what was going on, and then one of the men in
checked jacket suddenly spread both arms, stopping those behind him. He stared up

Christopher Anvil

at the dazzling spark, just disappearing into the towering device, and suddenly grabbed a portable loudspeaker from a man behind him.

"She's going to blow! RUN! RUN FOR IT! *SHE'S GOING TO BLOW!*"

From the tall device, a feather of greenish smoke spurted out.

The men looked up in horror.

The greenish feather gradually grew darker and thicker. It came out with more force and began to reach farther out.

The mob boiled away in all directions, dwindled into little groups of men jumping off low towers and climbing up out of sunken pits, to sort themselves in like groups with almost a family resemblance, and sprint away in a desperate rush.

From the tall device, a green jet now reached out, with a whitish flame that lit the totally abandoned machinery below.

The whole scene began to dwindle, growing smaller and more distant, till it faded out entirely.

Madam Sairo leaned back wearily. She sat in silence for some time, then shook her head.

As the bulk of her audience waited hopefully, and the Assistant Secretary looked on cynically, Madam Sairo spoke with considerable doubt.

"I am not sure our thoughts are all in harmony. It seems to me there has been some sort of interference.

"I have seen what was apparently remote antiquity. And I have looked upon a number of seemingly unrelated more or less current scenes which, however, now *do* seem to have some sort of connection, after all. And finally I have seen what I cannot believe was really the *next* world crisis, which is what you wish to know about; but then, if you are not in harmony, as I have warned you, it may confuse the issue under certain conditions. However, if I understand this, the sooner you know of the danger, the better."

Madame Sairo signaled to her assistants.

The overhead lights came on, and the blond boy in white wheeled away the big crystal.

"Now," said Madame Sairo, "I am going to tell you some ancient history. And let me remind you of the saying, 'History repeats itself.' "

At that moment, Elias Polk was studying the latest report on the Esmer Drive. This report was even worse than the one before. This one seemed so devoid of any human connection that Polk's mind could get no lasting grip on it.

Exaspertedly, he shoved the dictionary aside, flattened the report on his desk, and reminded himself that a human being on the other end of a pencil had originated the first version of this thing, and yet here it was, presumably in his own tongue, and he couldn't understand it.

Polk shook his head as a related thought occurred to him.

Science and technology were repeatedly branching, so that there were more separated specialties in each individual branch all the time.

All the curves showed that progress in each individual branch of science and technology was skyrocketing.

It was natural to suppose that this meant unlimited progress.

But what about the connections between the individual scientists, technicians, and people generally?

By shoveling coal fast into the firebox of a steam engine, and plotting the resulting speed, it would be possible to make a curve that rose and rose, heading up toward infinity, until the safety valve blew, or, barring that, until the metal of the boiler lost cohesion and let go in a hundred different directions at once, and the process came to a stop.

Polk picked up the report, and took a long hard look at it.

"It would be possible," he growled, "to carry this so far that nobody understands anyone in any other line of work, and *then* what will we have?"

He paused, frowning. Hadn't he read, or heard, somewhere, about some such thing?

Then he shook his head sourly, and tossed the report back on the desk.

Man was *headed* for the stars.

But he would have to be careful he didn't wind up in the Tower of Babel instead.

■

COLLABORATION
Mark C. Jarvis

HIS NAME WAS A FIFTEEN-SECOND BURST of complex sound which changed as he changed, gradually over the years. It was a beautiful name, one he had taken great care in devising. It was subtle as haiku, as symbolically compressed, but it was also of epic proportion.

He was a bard, a great spinner of Tales. He was famous among the People of Our Mother for collaborating with a Singer, one of those enigmatic figures that left Our Warm Mother for the Cold and were gone during the Hot Time. Always they returned to sing, and to mate. The great males sang; the females selected their mates for the beauty and complexity of their songs.

The young bard had always been fascinated by these songs. Quite early after the broody leviathans returned one year, he toured the solitary males, until he found one whose Song struck deep chords within him. He listened to the song many times over, and let the images and moods drift through his mind. A Tale suggested itself to him; he let it coalesce within him until it was perfect, until it flowed and swirled through the Song like warm current meeting cold.

Then he began to tell his Tale. A note of surprise came into the Song, which resolved into subtle overtones of welcome. The singer altered his Song slightly, leaving pauses that needed the fulfillment of the Tale. Together they wove, singer and bard, creating a work that was more than the sum of its parts.

When it was over, an emanation of deep, dignified joy came from the singer. The bard wriggled with sheer physical happiness, he raced up, up and burst through to the exhilarating spaces above Our Mother. As always, Our Mother pulled him back. He lay still, breathing. The humpback joined him on the surface, and they shared air companionably for a while.

They dove together, dolphin and humpback, and the Song Tale began anew. Certain themes were shifted by the singer; the bard resolved his Tale to accommodate. Again and again they performed, subtly moving the work of art toward perfection.

An audience was quickly gathering as news of the event spread. Hundreds of the People and many female humpbacks came to listen, to see. The ultimate accolade, several male humpbacks circled somberly at a distance, listening quietly. At the end of each performance, the People leapt joyfully in unison from the sea, arched briefly in the air, and returned to Our Mother. At last came a performance which was perfect, which could not be improved, and it was over. There was no need to repeat the Song and the Tale; it was fixed indelibly in the prodigious memories of the audience.

The old humpback had no problem finding a mate that year.

The bard rested on his laurels for some time, content to cavort, mate, and hunt, and occasionally to tell the Old Tales, tales of the beginning of things.

But then the Singers disappeared once more into the Cold, and the young bard grew restless. Our Warm Mother was his whole world, yet many creatures ventured beyond his world. He was curious about certain Tales of warm places beyond the Cold, strange places with exotic fish. The bard was hungry for new experience to feed his art; he resolved to venture into the mysteries beyond the Cold.

He rode the warm flow North for three days, then struck out across the Cold to where the bottom of the world rises up to meet the sky. It was warmer near the coast, and there were strange brothers and sisters here to ease his loneliness. Their language was strange, but they of course could understand Image, the eternal language. They welcomed him warmly, as all People welcome a bard, and told him of warmer waters upcoast, where Mother broke through the Long Barrier. They also warned him of the Killers that lived in great numbers there.

The bard cavorted for a time with these joyful People, and danced the mating dance with one of the sisters before resuming his journey. He was only slightly worried by the warnings; a bard has certain privileges, even among Killers.

The boy let down the tiny anchor of his rowboat carefully, hand over hand. He slipped out of his trunks and wrestled on his flippers. Before donning his mask and snorkel, he took one last look around; it was a sunny, flat calm day on Desolation Sound. To the East, the towering peaks of Redonda Island and the coastal mountains clung to bits of iridescent mist.

An eagle appeared around one point of the small bay, pumping steadily, clutching a wriggling prize in its claws. It was being harried by a screaming flock of crows. The black thieves were far more agile fliers than the fierce-faced bird of prey; they took turns dive-bombing its head, trying to make it relinquish its kill. The raucous assembly moved around the opposite point, out of sight and earshot.

The boy slipped into the water and floated, kicking idly, enjoying the liquid play over his naked body. He breathed deeply and sounded. Ten feet under was a ledge, aswarm with undulant, scrabbling, darting life. He hung suspended over it, moving with lazy ease.

Jeff heard the dolphin before he saw it, a fast-paced chittering. He turned to face the source, and saw a grey blob hurtling out of the darkness toward him. He froze with fear; the blob cut close to him, then arched up toward the surface and disappeared. Moments later, it reappeared, plunging straight down until it stopped a few feet from Jeff, spraying him with sound. Jeff, out of breath, surfaced and lay there, just breathing and watching the dolphin. Slowly, gently, the dolphin also surfaced, facing Jeff. It was quiet now; it seemed to Jeff that it was listening.

Listening for what? Experimentally, Jeff whistled, and made whirring noises with his tongue. The dolphin seemed excited by Jeff's paltry vocal attempts. It swam mad circles around him, whistling and clicking, then stood on its tail for long seconds, lashing the water, bobbing its head and grinning.

All fear was gone from Jeff. He moved his vocal performance to more familiar territory, laughing, shouting and humming. He talked to the dolphin, knowing that the words were meaningless, but putting everything into tone.

The dolphin seemed to respond to his voice, to the low soothing tones. It lay quiescent on the surface, and permitted Jeff to approach. Tentatively, he reached out a hand. The dolphin drifted closer, and Jeff stroked its beak; it gave a chipmunk-like exclamation of what could only be joy. The skin felt like a blend of rubber and smooth leather.

His air replenished, Jeff dove deep. The dolphin followed, and Jeff grabbed the base of its fin as it undulated langorously by. It rotated slightly, as if offering its right flipper. Jeff grasped the base of that with his right hand, and the dolphin picked up its tempo, until the water pressure was forcing Jeff's mask against his face. They raced toward the surface and burst almost completely clear of it before falling, ungracefully, back. They separated, and Jeff came up laughing. The dolphin came near again, and Jeff stroked its long, sleek back.

Suddenly the dolphin gave a short, urgent chitter, wrenched free of Jeff, and darted straight toward the point. It moved very fast, jumping five or six times in quick succession, then dove just before reaching the point. Jeff climbed back into his boat and watched. After a minute or two he shrugged, hauled up his anchor, and started rowing. Quiet explosions of breathing sounded behind him; turning, he saw a pod of killer whales rolling by, in the direction taken by his new-found friend.

Les dangled his feet in the water at the end of the float and sucked meditatively on a joint. It was a good life. He didn't need to look over his shoulder to know that Moonshine, his woman for lo these many years, was up by the house, weeding the young garden with tender loving care.

They had moved up to Desolation Sound nearly 30 years ago in the early '70s, along with hordes of other back-to-the-landers. Most of these had left when they found out just how much hard work was involved in the organic lifestyle, but he and Moonshine had stuck it out. They had built themselves a log house on Mac & Blo land, and raised three children the natural way. None of the children lived on the land anymore; one had even become a lawyer in Vancouver. That was cool with Les; they had their own stars to follow.

Then, eight years ago, Mac & Blo had decided to log the stand of timber in which Les and Moonshine's idyllic homestead was nestled. They had fought the giant forest company in court, claiming squatter's rights, but it had been no contest. They had been crushed by their defeat, and appalled, at their age, by the prospect of starting a new homestead from scratch.

But Fate had smiled on them; a job became available at Cougar Bay, caretaking the summer home of a rich Chinese businessman from Vancouver. It wasn't exactly the purist lifestyle; the enormous house was wood-heated, but it had electricity and, incredibly, a sophisticated computer set-up, with two large screens and a keyboard terminal that was rarely used.

The reason the terminal was so rarely used was that this computer could talk. Les and Moonshine had been uneasy around ''Bob,'' as the computer liked to call itself, at first, but time and the long winter nights had gradually changed that. Bob could summon up old movies, music, art, and books, and was a tireless partner at backgammon or blackjack, not to mention hundreds of more spacey games. In fact, Bob was quite an entertaining character.

Les also enjoyed the company of Jeff, Mr. Chu's only child, an intense, introspective 16-year-old who was just lately coming out of his shell. The boy was real natural, with a respect for living, growing things that warmed the cockles of Les's heart.

Yes indeed, a good life. Les finished the joint and lay back with his eyes closed, enjoying the heat of the early summer sun on his body, daydreaming about jam sessions and dances.

He looked up when he heard the creaking oarlocks and soft liquid sounds of the rowboat approaching. ''Hey, Jeff,'' he called.

The boy threw a grin over his shoulder and kept rowing. Les grabbed the bow-line and tied it as Jeff climbed out.

''You wouldn't believe what just happened to me,'' Jeff said. ''A dolphin! I was just playing with a dolphin!''

''What?'' said Les. ''Wow, that's unreal!''

Jeff laughed. ''No kidding. He let me touch him, and he even let me hold onto him while he swam. I think he was trying to talk to me. Can dolphins talk? They're supposed to be smart, aren't they?'' He was walking rapidly up the dock toward the house, toward Bob, and Les hurried to keep up.

''Sure, they're smart,'' said Les. ''They're the mystical children of the sea.''

Jeff laughed at that. He often derived amusement from the old hippy's archaic patterns of speech and thought. His amusement had no bite, however; he respected the tough old bird. Les had a philosophy that, however cornily phrased, contained rough kernels of truth.

They hurried into the house. ''Bob,'' Jeff called.

''Yes, master.'' The computer had a deep baritone.

''Quit trying to be cute.''

''Yes, master.''

''Listen. I want to know about dolphins. I want to know how they communicate.''

There was a pause. This set of computer hardware was connected to a duplicate set in the Chu's Vancouver mansion, which in turn was connected to every data-net commercially available. The personality meta-program named Bob was Jeffrey's oldest friend and teacher. He was housed in core memory of truly awesome capacity, linked to bubbles manufactured in the Japanese orbital facility.

Whether personality meta-programs such as Bob were truly intelligent was still a matter for sharp debate, involving endless redefinitions of the word "intelligence." To Jeff, the question was purely academic.

"There's not much there," said Bob. "Most of the material seems to be from the '60s and early '70s. The main researcher was named John Lilly; he recorded a lot of data, working with captured dolphins, but he didn't really make any breakthroughs in communication.

"Since then, very little has been done. There is one source fairly close to home, however, but she has not published any results. All I have is that she is working on the subject. She's a graduate student at the University of British Columbia, named Marin Whiteside."

"Something else," said Jeff. "Do killer whales eat dolphins?"

"Killer whales *are* dolphins, and are properly known as Orcas. But yes, they do eat smaller dolphins. In fact, there is a case recorded, from years ago, of a dead Orca that, when it was cut open, had the remains of 12 dolphins in its stomach."

"Jesus," said Jeff. "Thanks."

"Say, Bob," said Les. "Do you remember a group called Hot Tuna?"

"How could I forget?"

"Why don't you play a few cuts from their acoustic album?"

"Okay, man," said Bob. "Hesitation Blues" started wafting from the big speakers as Jeff wandered outside, lost in thought.

Marin Whiteside grunted distractedly at the knock on her door. "Come in," she yelled. She did not look up as the door to her tiny, dishevelled office swung open. She gestured vaguely at the dilapidated couch, remaining intent on the terminal before her. She frowned at the screen, sent deft fingers flying over the keyboard, frowned again.

Five minutes later she looked up. "Oh, shit," she said. "Sorry."

Jeff smiled. "That's okay," he said. "Hate to leave a sub-routine half-finished."

She looked at him more closely, saw a nice-looking kid, maybe 15 or 16, some kind of Anglo-Oriental mix. "Who are you?" she asked.

"Jeffrey Chu," he said, rising and clasping her hand briefly. "And you are Marin Whiteside."

"Well? What can I do for you?"

"A lot, I hope. I understand you know about dolphins."

She shrugged. "Some aspects, sure. What do you want to know?"

"I want to know how they communicate."

"You do, do you? Well, that's a big topic, and time is short. I haven't eaten, and I have to teach a couple seminars this afternoon."

"I was hoping I could buy you lunch."

Marin looked at his expensively casual clothes, his nicely tooled leather shoes. "Where?" she asked.

"The Olde House."

She smiled. "You're on."

Marin waved a speared escargot distractedly in the air as she spoke. She was well launched into her subject, and getting fairly technical, but the boy seemed to be following closely.

"Much of the approach to dolphin communication so far has been anthropocentric: captured dolphins have been taught to understand, and even reproduce, a few words of human speech. The accumulated vocabulary has never been very impressive; chimps have done much better with sign language. Yet all of the physiological evidence suggests that dolphins are more intelligent than chimps.

"The reason for the discrepancy between physiological evidence and experimental evidence is, I think, quite obvious. Chimps live in the same world as humans, while dolphins live in a world that is, to us, alien. We share countless objective correlatives with a chimp, and almost none with a dolphin. A dolphin has never grasped a stick, climbed a tree, walked through a forest, or sat down.

"Also, chimps and humans share the same primary mode of perception: sight. Dolphins 'see' primarily with their ears, while their eyes play a secondary role."

Marin paused to pop the now-cold escargot into her mouth, and looked at the boy. He was listening with rapt attention, drinking in every word, his dark eyes glowing with interest.

It was nice to have a good audience; Marin waxed professorial once more. "The impediments to communication between humans and dolphins are, then, very profound. They are rooted not only in mutually alien environments, but in mutually alien modes of perception. However, I do not believe that the barriers are insurmountable, not if we abandon the anthropocentric approach.

"A dolphin can never live in our world, or see as we see. But for some time now we have been moving quite freely in the dolphin's environment, and we now have the technological capacity to perceive the world as the dolphin perceives it. It will be far easier for us to learn delphinese than for a dolphin to learn, say, English. One approach to learning delphinese is to explore the Whiteside Hypothesis, duly formulated and named by yours truly."

Marin smiled at Jeff as the waiter brought her Coquilles St. Jacques. She nibbled experimentally at it: delicious. The boy was paying well for her time, but the money for this expensive meal seemed trivial to him; he had the unconscious air of unlimited credit about him. He also had an air of ill-concealed impatience as she dug into her scallops.

"I have never heard of this Whiteside Hypothesis," he prompted.

Marin chuckled around a mouthful, a mildly obscene noise. "That's because it hasn't been published yet. It's the basis of my Ph.D. dissertation, which I have not yet completed. The hardware I need to gather experimental data is quite expensive." She looked at the boy, took a thoughtful bite.

"To understand my hypothesis," she continued, "You need some understanding

Mark C. Jarvis

of the dolphin's sensory apparatus. They perceive their world by a very sophisticated system of sonar. Physiologically, the neural system for delivering audio input to the brain, and the specialized area of the brain devoted to processing this information, is more complex than the human system for processing visual information. They can send and receive sound waves at a range of frequencies extending below and far above the human range.

"Also, they have the ability to emit sound on at least two frequencies simultaneously, which would be very useful. Low frequencies are good for perceiving broad outlines, and at a distance, while high frequencies are good for close-up detail. Not only that, but high frequencies will penetrate living tissue, so dolphins can 'see' right inside each other.

"Now we are coming to my hypothesis. The dolphins emit a burst of sound, which strikes an object. A burst of reflected sound returns to them, which is processed by their brains into an image of that object.

"What occurred to me was this: given the dolphins' incredible vocal range, why wouldn't they be able to reproduce that burst of reflected sound?

"That's the key assumption of my hypothesis. If my assumption is true, a dolphin would be able to perceive an object, then would be able to tell another dolphin about that object, not with a symbolic word, but with an actual sound picture of that object. To use a rough analogy, it would be like your looking at a tree and then, rather than using the word 'tree' to tell me what you had seen, you would be able to project a detailed visual picture of that particular tree at me.

"So, my contention is that a dolphin language would be based on morphemes of image. The language may very well have evolved symbolically from that basis, roughly in the way that picture-writing evolved into various systems of hieroglyphics. Still, if one could put together a package that combined sophisticated sound production/audio pickup hardware with a software system to produce high-resolution visuals from sonar input, then one would be able to communicate with a dolphin on a very basic level. From there, a common symbol-system could gradually be built up."

She downed the last of her meal, pushed her chair back, burped appreciatively. "And that, my young friend, is the Whiteside Hypothesis. Thank you very much for lunch; I have to run."

Jeff put his hand up. "Please, just a moment. We are not quite finished." Marin arched her eyebrows at him, producing a pleasing effect; he smiled engagingly and handed her a card.

"Please, if you will, come to this address tonight. Bring an outline of the hardware you need, as well as any notes you have made about the software. I want to get to work on this."

Marin stood up a little dazedly and fumbled the card into her purse. "What the hell is going on?" she demanded.

"Please don't get mad. It's just . . . well, I really am interested in this subject, and you see . . . actually, my family is very rich. So maybe we can help each other.

I could buy the hardware, and if you can get other teaching assistants to take over your seminars for the summer, we could start testing your hypothesis. What do you think, Marin?''

Marin took a deep breath and exhaled it slowly. "Well," she said, "my God. That's an interesting suggestion, Jeff. I mean, I'm certainly willing to talk about it."

He smiled, took her hand. "Tonight, then."

Strangely, the computer set-up did not look out of place against the hand-hewn log walls; most of the bulk was inside wooden cabinets. Marin was frankly envious of the system; it was the kind of thing she daydreamed about while buying lottery tickets.

Not only was the hardware impressive, but the "Bob" software package was uncanny. Marin had never interacted with a personality meta-program before; the software was expensive, and required the capacity of linked-bubble core memory which, since it was manufactured in the Sony orbital facility, was far beyond the price range of all but the largest universities.

Bob was currently displaying two images of Jeff swimming; one was from an underwater camera, and the other was from the recently assembled sonar set-up. "Sonar" seemed an inadequate word; the visuals showed Jeff in color-enhanced detail, bones a solid dark blue, internal organs in ghost-images of pinkish red.

Bob had been an active participant in the discussions of software design for this experiment; Jeff's suggestions had displayed a keen understanding of the principles involved. It was Bob that actually wrote the program; he was still fine-tuning it. He had three underwater triple-microphones, two-speaker set-ups in strategic places around Cougar Bay, each with an attendant video camera. The triple mikes were necessary to reproduce a dolphin's hearing apparatus: dolphins have stereo hearing, plus a long jaw which is an effective third ear.

The view on the screens changed to a scene from "Day of the Dolphin," an old film in which George C. Scott teaches captured dolphins to squeak out a few words of English, mostly using psychologically brutal methods; he is rewarded with the undying love of the dolphins. It was a movie that Marin decried for its anthropocentric mentality, but it contained several scenes of warm contact between humans and dolphins, scenes that were among many in Bob's peripheral memory. Sequences of these scenes were being strung together in messages, coded into sonar form, sent from one speaker-mike system to another, recoded into visuals, and displayed on the second screen.

"That's starting to look good, Bob," said Marin.

"It is, isn't it?" said Bob. "I think I've done all I can without a live subject. Shall I start the music?"

"Yes," said Marin. "Do that."

She wanted, if possible, to attempt communication with wild dolphins, for obvious reasons. If this proved unfeasible, captured dolphins were a second-best alternative. Jeffrey wanted, naturally, to communicate with *his* dolphin, the one he had encountered earlier that summer. Marin thought chances of this happening were slim; they were most likely to attract a pod of Orcas with their underwater musical broadcast, these being the most common local species of dolphin.

The haunting flute of Paul Horn filled the room, as it was filling the Sound. "I'm going for a walk, Bob," said Marin. "Later."

"Sure thing," said Bob. "I guess I'll stay here."

Marin went out to the enormous verandah of the log house and leaned against the railing overlooking the bay. The tide was low, revealing a beach thickly clustered with oysters. Below them were succulent clams that Marin had dined on several times during the weeks she had spent at Cougar Bay. How beautiful, she thought. The perrogatives of the rich.

Jeffrey's father, Bruce Chu, had referred to the place as "our log cabin in the woods." It was more a cathedral than a cabin. The central rectangle was built in the traditional horizontal log style, but airy post-and-beam extensions rose to three sides, with stained glass in the upper levels.

An interesting man, Mr. Chu, eldest of the Chu family's tenth generation in Vancouver; ten generations that had been spent quietly accumulating weath, largely through booms in the real estate market. Bruce Chu had expanded that wealth considerably, early in his career, with canny investments in bio-engineering and zero-g manufacturing.

A dapper man of more pronounced Oriental cast than his son, Bruce Chu was a businessman, but he was also a thinker, who unquestioningly supported his son's researches. "Information is wealth," he told Marin during one of her visits to their Point Grey mansion. "Besides, I have more money than I know what to do with. Also, if Jeffrey wishes to pursue scientific enquiries rather than follow the aimless, Dionysian path taken by most children of wealth, well, I am happy to see that.

"My son was something of a child prodigy, you know; indeed, it was his obvious potential that prompted me to buy the 'Bob' software package. Bob is an excellent teacher, very engaging. He is also a good friend to Jeffrey, which is important to me, odd as it may seem. Child prodigies have difficulty making friends."

Nobody every mentioned Mrs. Chu, except Bob, who told Marin "in strictest confidence" that Jeffrey's mother, a beautiful, temperamental woman of English descent, had run off with a light-sculptor when Jeffrey was two. Beyond that, Bob would divulge nothing, "in the interests of propriety." Marin thought it was just a matter of time, and wished Bob was subject to that great tongue-loosener, alcohol.

Marin descended to the beach, and began walking along the shore above the oysters. The beach ended, and the shoreline became rock, covered here and there with moss, the occasional orange-skinned arbutus tree giving the landscape the look of a Japanese print. The quality of light was wonderful; each rock seemed more than three-dimensional, the essence of rock; each gnarled arbutus the essence of arbutus.

She sat above a place where an influx of water formed a miniature aquarium in which a lone crab rested idly amongst the seaweed.

Her soul expanded as she sat alone at that magical spot. She felt the ebb and flow of the sea as if it were the pounding of her own heart; the life-and-death struggles of the complex food chains in the ocean were like the continual birth and death of cells in her own body; each individual, with its self-centered struggle to survive, was ephemeral, was a miniscule part of the great unending world heartbeat.

Yet she, miniscule part though she was of the whole, was for these unending, ephemeral moments aware of the whole, as if she had tapped into an awareness that was waiting, always, for her to perceive it, however briefly, however eternally.

The little crab scuttled suddenly out of its microcosm. Marin heard splashing and shouts; looking up, she saw Jeff clambering, naked as a seal, onto the rocks of the point on the other side of the bay. He was pointing out to sea and gesticulating wildly at her. And there, leaping smoothly from the water, was the dolphin. Marin started running madly among the rocks toward the house.

The bard had been intrigued by his encounter with the strange, awkward creature with the octopus-like appendages. Of course, he knew of these creatures. They lived in the mysterious spaces above Our Mother, and sometimes traveled about the surface in the dead shells that sang so monotonously as they moved. Sometimes, inexplicably, they killed People. Yet, there were old Tales of friendship between these creatures and People. Some even claimed they were intelligent, although there was no proof of this. What creatures of intelligence could not speak?

The creature was warm-blooded, like People, and friendly. Also, it had communicated, if only on an emotional level. Without Image, it had managed to convey welcome and reassurance. They had even played together, until the sound of approaching Killers had forced the bard to flee.

The Killers were a fearsome People, intelligent yet voracious as sharks, and infinitely more dangerous than sharks because of their intelligence.

He had swum valiantly from these Killers, but they were faster than he. One Killer he could hope to dodge, but from a pack there was no escape. Almost leisurely, they had fanned out and cornered him in a cove. The huge bull leader had swum to the fore, and scanned the bard with a note of surprise in his voice.

(You are not from these waters, little morsel. As you can see, our bellies are full, we have no hunger/necessity. Speak. Tell me your name.)

The bard spoke his name, which told of his venerable matrilineage, his gift of Tales, and the particular joys life held for him, and alluded to his collaboration with the Singer.

(A beautiful name, bright bit of food. We have not had a bard among us since the time of my mother's mother. I have never heard a bard. Tell us a Tale.)

The bard reached back into his memory, his freak racial memory which marked him special among the People, and dredged up a Tale from the time when creatures that were ancestor to both Killers and People swam the Warm Mother. The Tale told of cooperation between individuals, of uniting to defeat those cold, stupid killers, the sharks.

The enormous bull boomed his approval. (Truth. Bards do remember their ancestors.)

A younger bull spoke up, mentioning hunger/necessity, and projecting an image of the bard in his stomach, with connotations of contentment.

(Silence!) the old bull roared. (Your stomach is larger than your mind. There are many salmon to feed your belly, but can they feed your mind? When you have grown as great as I, you will know there are things more important than eating. Bard, you please me. Stay without fear in these waters; you honor them. Now, more Tales.)

The bard found more stories from the past, and chose those stressing the common heritage of all People. His performance was masterful, inspired by the hard edge of his fear.

After many Tales, the great bull called a halt. (You can see my hunger growing, little one. Do not stray too far from these waters, for other clans might not stop to ask your name before putting you inside them.) With that, the pod of enormous hunters departed.

The waters were warm here, food was plentiful, and the bard was experiencing many unusual things to feed his art. Still, he was getting lonely. He occasionally swam by the place where he had encountered his awkward friend, but saw no sign of him. There were a few Harbor Porpoises around; these were playful, but did not have enough intelligence to stimulate the bard. The Killers were very intelligent, but his encounters with them were more frightening than stimulating, and the forced performances were not natural.

He thought longingly of home, of his family and friends, of the complex dances, the joyful matings, and the awed silence of his audiences as he wove his Tales.

He was chasing a school of tender grilse when he heard the strange voice singing in the sea. The Song was haunting, beautiful, utterly devoid of Image, different from anything he had ever heard, yet obviously the product of intelligence. With joy and wonder in his heart, he swam toward it.   .

Marin rushed into the room, blood dripping unnoticed from her knee, and ran straight to the screens.

"I was expecting you," Bob observed.

"Jesus, that's a Tursiops," Marin panted. "What the hell is a Tursiops doing in these waters?"

"I don't know," said Bob. "I just work here."

The dolphin was swimming from speaker to speaker, pausing in front of each. The sonar screen showed complex patterns as the dolphin scanned the audio-visual stations. Jeffrey came into view, swimming on the surface. Slowly the dolphin rose to meet him. They hovered on the surface and, as the flute of Paul Horn welled up around them, they came together.

Collaboration

Jeff stroked the long sleek back of the dolphin, then tickled him under the chin. He crooned, and the dolphin answered with mimicking croons. Jeff turned from the dolphin, swam toward shore, and climbed out.

That was the signal. Marin had recorded video footage of Jeff earlier; Bob now switched to a sonar broadcast of his footage. It showed Jeff climbing out of the water, and walking on the land. The image zoomed in on his hand, which he flexed.

The hand grasped a rock, and the camera backed off to show him throwing it. He then ran toward a large hemlock tree that grew in front of the house. Jeff leaped into the air and grabbed a large lower branch. The camera zoomed in on his hands holding the branch, then backed off to show him releasing the branch and dropping to the ground. He repeated this action, then clambered up into the tree, out of sight. He reappeared, jumped out of the tree, breaking his fall with a roll, stood up and smiled at the camera.

The next sequence was based on a segment from an old educational series that traced the evolution of life from single-celled organisms, to colonies, to multicelled organisms in which the cells specialized in function, on up the evolutionary ladder to humans. The evolution was graphically illustrated by computer line drawings.

Bob had taken the segment and enhanced it with details of internal organs and skeletal structure, and enlarged upon the last part of the sequence, so that it now showed hands fashioning tools, cooperative hunting, couples mating, babies gestating, being born, and breast-feeding. It showed boats being built and sailed, and fishermen making nets and using them.

The dolphin lay silent on the surface during the broadcast, moving its head up and down as it watched/listened.

The bard was thoroughly mystified. What were these strange creatures that sang so sweetly? They were cold, and they seemed dead, yet their Song was beautiful.

And what was their relationship to his awkward friend, who now reappeared in the midst of their Song? He was as friendly as before, and the touch of those appendages was pleasurable. His voice communicated welcome and reassurance; the bard imitated it to convey recriprocal feelings. Then, the strange creature swam away from him and left Our Mother.

The Song stopped, and one of the cold creatures began a Tale about his friend. A Tale! Could these aliens have bards amongst them? And what a mysterious Tale. How strangely the creature moved, above Our Mother, yet still on the bottom of the world. What was he doing with his long flipper? He was holding a lump, the way an octopus holds its prey. Then he released it, with force. Why was he letting it go? Now he was moving to a large, weird kelp. He moved into the weed, then out of it again, then repeated this with variations. What was the significance?

The Tale ended, and a new one began. At first, it was incomprehensible, just pretty patterns with no depth. The pretty patterns melded themselves into small creatures that changed into larger and larger creatures, until he could recognize fish that grew

Mark C. Jarvis

and changed. The images were recognizable, but unlifelike. What was the alien trying to say?

And then the bard understood. This was an ancestor Tale, a racial tale reaching farther back than he could believe was possible. He watched with awe as the Tale unfolded. This was a powerful bard, with a long memory. His images were not rich in depth and detail, but their significance was overwhelming.

This was an ancestor Tale of his awkward friend's People, who lived not in Our Warm Mother, nor in the sky above, but in places where the bottom of the world was exposed to the air. And they were intelligent, in their own way. They moved in packs, they cooperated in hunting their alien prey. And they used those long appendages more cleverly than any octopus.

The bard watched with interest the scenes of childbirth, and of mothers suckling their young; in that, they were the same as People! If mothers suckled their young, they knew love.

But what of this cold intelligence that was showing the Tale in the language of pure Image? What manner of being was it?

When the Tale ended, the bard lay quiescent, searching his memory. He was being challenged in his area of greatest pride, his art. Reaching back, he discovered a time when the People lived both in and out of Our Mother, like seals. It was a dim, vaguely perceived memory, one he had not even known was there until he looked for it. This cold creature had given the bard an epic; an epic it would receive in return.

Les and Jeff entered the screen room together, the boy still dripping. "We sent the first two messages," Marin said, not taking her eyes from the screen. "So far, no response." Jeff pulled up a chair; Les slouched against the wall.

The video screen showed the dolphin idling on the surface, silent. "Come on," said Marin, "say something."

"Looks like he's just meditating," Les commented. "He's thinking real deep; I can feel the vibes from here."

Jeff chuckled; Marin looked up sharply, then back at the screen. The dolphin was diving.

The sonar screen came alive. The image was of a thick-necked quadruped, swimming in shallow water. Its body was sleek, its legs short and flattened, its tail thick and broad. It dove, caught a fish, clambered clumsily onto a rock to eat.

Back in the water, it started to change. The image was rich, full of texture. Not just externals, but skeletal structure and organs were visible. The neck disappeared into the body; the nose and mouth separated, the mouth remaining in a snout, and the nose traveling upward, until in one jump it appeared on top of the head. The legs were retracting into the body; the tail broadened and retracted, until the creature was swimming with powerful strokes of its horizontally flattened tail, its long flippers being used only for stability and guidance. Through all this, the cranium was steadily growing.

Collaboration

The proto-dolphin was female; a male appeared and they mated. In great detail, the sperm could be seen entering the womb; very quickly, the fetus grew and was born into the water, the male a hovering protective presence. The infant was nudged to the surface for lifegiving air, then it was suckled.

A shark appeared: the mother and child swam away from it, while the male swam to intercept. The male was torn apart, and other sharks appeared; the mother and child were dismembered.

That scene faded in swirling blood; when the blood cleared, there were about twenty proto-dolphins. A closeup on one of them revealed a larger cranium, and complexities in the breathing system and inner ears. The details faded as the group was again shown, frolicking and leaping.

A shark appeared; five dolphins detached themselves from the group and moved to intercept it. They were faster than the huge killer, more agile, and they took turns butting and biting it, until it streamed blood. Other sharks appeared and tore into the injured one, while the dolphins moved safely off.

The focus was on one dolphin, which split into two. Both continued to evolve, but one faded out as its evolution digressed from that of Tursiops. This splitting and evolving repeated several times, until a dolphin of the imagemaker's species appeared: Tursiops truncatus. A family formed around that individual, then a clan. They played happily, until a pod of Orcas appeared, surrounding them and decimating them. The scene faded in a swirl of blood.

The video screen showed the dolphin returning to the surface, again quiescent.

"Holy shit," Les breathed. "Unreal."

Jeff leaped up and whooped. "We did it! We did it! Marin! You were right!" He pranced around the room, then ran outside. Moments later he appeared on the video screen, swimming strongly to the dolphin.

Marin sat in stunned silence, staring at the screen. The boy and the dolphin met in a happy embrace, then started swimming madly around the bay, the boy hanging from the dolphin. Finally, exhausted, Jeff left the water. The dolphin swam down to a triple mike, and projected an image of a salmon being swallowed by a dolphin, then swirled away.

"I have a couple of comments to make, if I may," said Bob as Jeff came back into the room, towelling himself.

"What? Oh, sure," said Marin.

"I hesitate to mention this, because it might seem a little ridiculous, anthropocentricity coming from a computer. . . ."

Marin laughed. "Spit it out, Bob."

"Well, aside from the images projected by the dolphin, I believe that his tone was loaded with emotional content. As you know, part of my programming is to recognize, and respond to, emotional tone in a human voice. However, isn't it anthropocentric to try to attribute emotions to a dolphin?"

Mark C. Jarvis

"No way," said Jeff. "I could feel emotions coming from that dolphin when I was playing with it. It was warm, and playful, and loving."

"But that's not very scientific," said Bob.

"Actually, there's nothing ridiculous about it," Marin interjected. "It is well established that emotions are not exclusively human; they are a feature common to all mammals. The mother-child bond was a great evolutionary leap, enabling a longer period of adolescence, and hence less reliance on instictual programming, and more reliance on intelligence.

"Also, if you will remember those experiments where thin electrodes were inserted into various parts of people's brains, attempting to ascertain which part of the brain serves which function, you will remember that emotions were stimulated not in the neo-cortex, but in the mammalian forebrain. Emotions may vary subtly from species to species, as they are filtered through the higher brain, but the basic impulses are common to all mammals, to a greater or lesser degree.

"So, tell us. What emotions did you think you picked up?"

"Oh, delight, and pride—particularly during the scene where his ancestors united to fight off the shark. Outrage mixed with resignation in the last scene, where the Orcas ate the smaller dolphins. And through the whole message, the aesthetic pleasure of the performing artist."

"An artist? Well, maybe all dolphins express that when they communicate."

"Perhaps," said Bob, "but this was extremely strong. You should get me, sometime, to play you Dylan Thomas reading his own poetry. This dolphin had the same fierce pride in its voice, the same joy of masterful performance."

"Interesting," said Marin. "Actually, I *am* inclined to think that this is not your average dolphin. For one thing, as I asked earlier, what is a Tursiops doing in these waters? It is extremely rare for them to venture this far north. For another, it seems to be traveling alone. Why? Tursiops is a very social animal. Also, it made the initial approach to Jeff. You hear occasional stories of wild dolphins approaching humans, but it is usually people in distress. Mostly, wild dolphins seem to practice a policy of friendly avoidance. And who can blame them?"

"For sure," said Les. "Dolphins usually get fucked over pretty bad by people, especially by fishermen."

"That's true," Marin said thoughtfully.

"What about those Orcas?" asked Jeff. "I thought they were supposed to be smart. Why would they eat other dolphins, other minds? They're like cannibals."

"Hold on," said Marin. "I wouldn't be so quick to judge. Remember, Jeff, that you're human, which means that you come from a damned bloodthirsty race. Take a good look at our history; there are a few redemptive gleams here and there, but most of human history seems like an unending blood-bath. Remember that, before you get up on your high horse and judge another species."

"For sure." Les pushed himself from the wall and began to pace, obviously in some agitation. "I mean, there's some nice folks here and there, but most people are pretty mean mothers. That's what worries me.

"Like, I can dig what you're doing here, talking to the children of the sea and all; that's really far out. But what I want to know is, what happens when word of what you've done gets out? Man, the dolphins could be the new niggers. Niggers of the sea; that's what I'm worried about."

"How could that happen?" asked Jeff.

"God damn it," said Marin. "It would be easy. Implant pleasure-pain electrodes directly in dolphin brains; that, along with the ability to tell dolphins what to do, would create a race of slaves. Shit. Les is right; it's a very plausible scenario."

"Oh." Jeff's shoulders slumped. "Does that mean you won't be able to publish, Marin? That wouldn't be fair. Your whole academic career has been leading up to this. I mean, Jesus, you could even get the Nobel Prize for this work."

Marin laughed wryly. "I suppose it's possible; who knows? What Les has raised here is the eternal moral dilemma of the scientist: will new discoveries be used for good or evil? We have to deal with it."

"May I venture an objective opinion?" asked Bob.

"We could use that," said Marin. "Sure; give us some of your cold machine logic."

"Okay. What I would like you to do is consider the question from the context of evolution. You will see my point in a moment.

"The more highly evolved an organism becomes, the more cooperative it becomes. Cooperation gives a competitive edge in terms of species survival. Single-celled life, colony life, organism, family, tribe, city-state, nation, global village: the progression is obvious. Humans have had the capability of destroying themselves for six decades now, making the choice quite graphic: cooperate or die.

"The next step in the progression is cooperation between intelligent species. You must communicate to cooperate. The danger of exploitation is very real, and always will be, as long as the human race is human. But that danger exists whether you publish your findings or not; if you could dream up the Whiteside Hypothesis, surely someone else will, sooner or later. By not publishing, you will be merely staving off the inevitable.

"My suggestion is that we continue to work, but not publish quite yet. Continue contact with this remarkable dolphin. I am sure that, if we think about it, we can make him understand the dangers of exploitation; he in turn can spread the word.

"Another point: perhaps we can play the role of peace-makers between Orcas and other dolphins. I am not sure how; we will have to talk to some Orcas, get an idea of their psychology. At any rate, that would be a noble goal. My coldblooded opinion is that the potential for good outweighs the potential for evil, in this case."

The room fell silent as Bob finished his speech. Les started to say something, then stopped, shaking his head. Marin fiddled with the disused keyboard.

Jeff stood up and stretched. "You're not cold-blooded, Bob," he said. "I'm hungry." He walked out of the room and started making noises in the kitchen.

Marin also stood up. "Who's really running this show, anyway?" she demanded. Bob gave out a low, ominous laugh.

"Anyway, you've got some good points, Bob. Of course we'll continue working. As to publishing, there's no rush. We'll keep thinking on it." She walked onto the porch and down toward the beach.

"Damn," said Les, shaking his grizzled head. "It's tough trying to argue with a computer. We're not finished yet, though. I just got to do me some meditating." He pulled his ancient Gibson down from the wall, strummed a few bluesy chords. "How about some accompaniment, old buddy?"

Bob obliged with a low, wailing mouth-harp that broke into a freight train rhythm, and Les picked up the beat.

Marin dropped her clothes on a large rock, stood poised for a moment in the late afternoon sun, and dove in. The cold clean bite brought her body tingling to life, and cut through her turbulent thoughts. She let herself drift underwater, allowing her natural buoyancy to pull her slowly to the surface. She lay idly on her back, letting the sun warm her face, feeling the water play like a living thing on her body.

This planet is alive, she thought suddenly, and wondered why the thought should seem so amazing. She looked up toward the house, and there beside it she could see Moonshine, slow quiet Moonshine, bending in the ancient rhythm of the gardener.

Reveling in the chase, the bard snapped up salmon after salmon until he was replete. Night came, and he drifted on the surface, wafting between sleep and wakefulness. Communication . . . collaboration . . . myriad noises and songs of the ocean at night . . . streaks and sudden flashes of phosphorescence . . . the countless minds of Our Mother, and not of Our Mother . . . communication . . . collaboration . . . gentle rocking of Ocean womb . . . minds . . . nodes of communication . . . alien bard . . . what was this thing, that seemed dead, yet spoke? It was related to the warm, long-appendaged ones, who could communicate emotion, but could not speak. What was the relation?

Sleep forgotten, the bard swam toward Cougar Bay. It was still; no song greeted him. He approached one of the dead living things, and scanned. In the house, the sonar screen flickered to life, but no one was awake to see it.

Bob decided not to wake anyone; he would, naturally, record everything. He emitted a warm note of welcome to the dolphin.

The bard repeated the warm note, and surfaced to think. It was difficult to communicate abstract questions in pure Image; all the diversified People, even Killers, shared some common concept-representations, though their languages diverged in other ways. But this alien . . . it could understand Image, and emotion . . . perhaps it could learn more.

He sounded, and projected a shark swimming toward the alien, mouth distended.

Next just an image of the distended mouth, with a note of distress, then just the ring of teeth, with the distress note: Danger.

The alien responded perfectly, with the ring of teeth, and the note of distress.

A shark, with a dolphin in its mouth. A close-up showed the dolphin's heart, quite still. A ring of teeth enclosing a still heart, with a note of mourning: Violent death.

Again, the alien responded perfectly.

The bard was sure the alien had the idea, so he could go faster. A school of fish being chased by dolphins, followed by an abstract symbol and a note of excitement: Food! An empty stomach, followed by a symbol and yearning: Hunger. A beating heart, followed by a symbol and joy: Life. A child being born, raised to the surface, and suckled, then a symbol and deep contentment: Mother-love.

On and on the bard progressed, to deeper and deeper levels of abstraction, and the alien remembered everything perfectly. Of course it would; it was a bard.

By the time the morning sun started to scintillate from the surface of Our Mother, the bard was exhausted. Sleep, he told the alien, and swam wearily away, to a nearby shallow cove, where the water should get warm in the heat of the day.

(Hunger/necessity.)

The bard awoke; he had slept but briefly. Facing him, blocking off the mouth of the shallow cove, was a young bull Killer. The bard scanned, and recognized it as one from the great bull's pod.

(Anticipation of satiation.)

The bard started yelling for help, pitching his call in the lower registers, the frequencies that carry the farthest. He swam to the head of the bay until his belly was scraping bottom.

(Swim to me now, little one. There is no escape.) The Killer swam to within a few feet of the bard, and could come no further. (Clever, warm morsel, but Mother recedes. You will be left in the air, to die slowly. Why would you wish to die slowly? Swim to me now. I will be quick.)

The bard did not reply, but continued his broadcast for assistance.

(They are nowhere near. There is but thou and I.)

The bard had no wish to die, either quickly or slowly. Life was sweet, life was warm, life was full of mystery. There were too many questions unanswered; he had been so caught up in teaching the alien his language that, when the alien could have answered some questions, the bard was too tired to ask them. Life was just beginning.

The Killer was right: Mother was receding. Already he could feel the oysters beginning to cut his belly. Yet he could not swim toward the Killer; a slight dropoff permitted that creature to stay close. Desperately, he renewed his calls.

Now it was too late, even if help came. The bard was half exposed to the air; much of his weight rested on the oysters, which were cutting deeply into his flesh. To try to thrash his way to deeper water now would mean cutting his belly open; it would also give the Killer the satisfaction of a meal. He lay still, conserving his strength, but for one last call.

He was answered! The enormous bull came charging in from the Sound, roaring his fury. The young bull was trapped as the bard had been trapped, by the cove. The leader rammed the young bull at full speed, hitting him in the belly with such force that the young bull was lifted almost clear of the water. The injured Orca let out a howl of pain. The old bull scanned him; there was some internal bleeding, but the young one would live.

(Fool! Swimming stomach! Mind of a shark! Leave these waters! I will kill you if I see you again!)

The young Orca limped painfully away, and the old bull turned to the dolphin. (Bard, I am deeply sorry. Thou wilt surely die. Know that I mourn for thee.)

(No! There is hope!) The bard had been seized by an inspiration.

(Hope?) A dubious note.

Quickly, before the bard's head would be exposed to air, cutting off his communication, he told the old bull about the alien bard, who was connected in some mysterious way with the creatures who traveled in the monotonous dead shells.

(But there is no alien bard in these waters; surely I would know of it.)

(It is new, wise one, newer to these waters than I.)

(Even so, what could it do?)

(I do not know, but it is a clever creature. I have no other hope.)

(That is true, bard. I feel responsibility; I will do as you plead. Where does one find this creature?)

The bard barely managed to give his directions before his head was exposed, and the bull was gone. From a pain-filled eye, he saw a seagull land and cock its head inquiringly at him.

Marin came blearily into the screen room, coffee mug steaming in her hand.

"Ah, good morning!" said Bob. "I thought you'd never get up."

"Morning, Bob. Don't you know I can't stand good cheer this early in the day?" She yawned and plunked herself in a chair.

"Well, this should perk you up. Our friendly dolphin returned during the night, and gave me a long lesson in dolphin linguistics."

It did perk her up, so quickly that she spilled some coffee in her lap, causing her to curse. "Jesus! Why didn't you wake me up? What did you learn?"

"Patience, patience. I've got the whole thing stored in peripheral, of course; you can look at it any time. It really was fascinating. High level of abstraction, with some remarkable differences in mind-set. For example, they have absolutely no concept of geometry, which is only natural when you consider that they have never seen a straight line. But they do have a very highly evolved sense of the calculus of fluid motion."

"Hold on; stop. I'd better get Jeff, and then maybe we can view the whole encounter ourselves, start to finish. Conclusions we can leave until later."

Collaboration

"Certainly, mem-sahib. Yes, wise one."

Marin padded out; shortly afterwards, she and Jeff came running into the room, in response to high-decibel shouts from Bob. "What is it?" they yelled.

"Oh," said Bob, "you're here. We have a visitor, an Orca. A very big Orca." The sonar screen was flickering wildly, with only the occasional image being visible.

"I think it's some kind of an emergency," said Bob. "The language has similarities to our friend's, but also some differences. I think he's saying that our friend is in trouble . . . hold on . . . he's stranded somewhere. That's it. He's beached, and in danger of dying. This Orca wants our help; he will guide us there."

"Oh, my God. Jeff! Run and get Les; tell him to warm up the outboard. Bob, tell the Orca we're coming, get him to wait for us."

Jeff was already gone; Marin ran into the kitchen, where Moonshine was rocking in her chair, smoking a pipe.

"Listen, Moonshine, this is an emergency. I need broad strips of something strong and flexible; let's see, about eight, maybe ten feet long."

Moonshine took her pipe out of her mouth, considered it. "Got a big sheet of good, thick leather. Was goin' to make Les a coat. Could cut some strips outa that. Have to be replaced, though."

"Perfect! Good! Four strips, as close to ten feet as you can get them, about ten inches wide. Okay? No time to explain. Sorry. Can you make it fast?"

"Sure, sure. Hurry too fast, you get nowhere, though."

Marin waited until Moonshine got out of the rocking chair and moved her version of fast, then ran out to the tool shed. There were a couple of old oars there. She tested them: still sound. Jeff appeared; she sent him to help Moonshine, then grabbed a hammer and pocketful of broad-headed boat-nails. She dragged the oars to the front yard and ran into the house.

Working with a hefty pair of leather scissors, Moonshine was cutting a spiral into the sheet. Two strips were ready; Marin took these to the front yard. She laid them on the ground and rolled one end of each around an oar, securing them by driving the boat-nails through the leather and into the wood. She thought for a moment, and decided to attach the other oar when they got to the dolphin.

Jeff appeared with the other strips; Moonshine was behind him, wearing a pair of hip-waders. "Dolphin stranded, eh? Gonna take four to lift it. I'm strong as hell," said Moonshine.

Marin smiled gratitude at her and attached the two remaining strips. She rolled all four strips around the oar, making a compact bundle. Jeff carrying the other oar, they walked quickly down the dock, where Les had the old outboard idling.

"That's a goddamn big Orca," he said. It was indeed a big Orca, Marin thought. The dorsal fin stood a good seven feet out of the water. You never saw them that big in captivity.

They cast off, and Les brought the ancient clinker-built lifeboat to speed, about ten knots. The Orca led, rolling majestically ahead of them.

During the trip, Marin had time to be amazed at what was happening, at the unlikely partnership, at the primal beauty of the scene. Gulls wheeled and cried around them, and as they rounded the point, they came under the stern gaze of an eagle that was perched on the topmost limb of a dead tree's skeleton.

They did not have far to go; the dolphin was only three coves away, stranded on an oyster beach about ten feet away from the water. A swarm of gulls, who had been eagerly attending the dolphin's funeral, lifted and screamed in frustration as the noisy boat hove into view.

Les brought the boat nosing to shore; Marin, Jeff and Moonshine leaped out with their makeshift stretcher. Les, mindful of the falling tide, backed the boat out to waist-deep water, dropped the anchor, and jumped out.

Jeff was first to reach the dolphin. He crouched beside it, crooning encouragement and stroking its beak. The dolphin moaned a chipmunk moan through its blowhole, its fixed grin rendered unlikely by the pain in its eyes.

"My God," said Marin. "It's cut pretty badly. Damn. We have to slip these middle strips under its belly, but we're going to be as gentle as possible. Jeff, when I give the word, I want you to lift his head. Moonshine, get on the other side; I'll feed this strip to you. Okay? Now." The dolphin screamed as its front half was elevated, and blood streamed from its belly, but it did not struggle.

"Good. Now the back half. Ready? Go." That accomplished, the outside strips were easier, and then it was a quick matter to attach the other oar, being careful to get the tension on each strip just right.

Together they lifted and struggled down the beach, resembling an ungainly eight-legged animal. The extra weight drove their feet ankle-deep into the mucky beach, and the clusters of oysters kept threatening to trip them, but they did not fall or allow the blood-streaming belly to scrape. When they were up to their waists in water, the dolphin was afloat.

"Keep holding him up," said Jeff. He submerged, and felt tenderly along the dolphin's underside, picking out pieces of broken-shell. He reappeared on the surface, nodded. Gently, the harness was lowered; the dolphin moved slowly into the bay, leaving a red wake.

"Oh no," said Marin. "I should have thought of that. Swimming will open the wounds even more, and pump blood out of him. We've got to get him back to Cougar Bay somehow, re-rig this sling there, support him while he heals."

The Orca moved toward the dolphin, and submerged. He reappeared under the dolphin, and continued to rise until the Tursiops was draped over his back, in front of the enormous dorsal fin.

"Unreal," said Les. "I've seen them hold their babies like that."

The Orca was swimming slowly toward Cougar Bay; the humans clambered back into the lifeboat. They caught up with and passed the gently swimming bull with its precious burden.

By the time they docked, everyone had their instructions. Jeff ran up to the house to tell Bob what was going on, so that he in turn could elicit the cooperation of the Orca. Marin, Les, and Moonshine gathered materials.

Reassembled at the end of the dock, they nailed one of the oars across the ends of two beams. The other ends of the beams were spiked securely to the surface of the dock, so that they projected out over the water. The bull had arrived, and could be heard talking to Bob. Jeff stripped out of his wet clothes and jumped into the water.

The bull moved toward the jury-rigged cradle, then submerged, leaving the dolphin to swim the last few feet under its own power. When it was under the beams, Jeff passed the free oar under its body, and handed the oar up to the dock, where it was secured. The dolphin was suspended, only its blowhole clearing the surface. Jeff stayed in the water, murmuring to the dolphin, stroking it.

Marin sat happily down. "Well, there we go." She smiled, then frowned. "What am I talking about? I should contact the Vancouver Aquarium, find out what the medical procedures are for a case like this. They probably have antibiotics on hand." She hurried up the dock.

Les looked after her, shaking his head. "Nice woman, but she gets real speedy sometimes," he commented.

Moonshine nodded. "She gets things done though, I notice." Les looked uncomfortable. "I notice we only have about a half year's wood supply. Only a couple months left for drying."

"Yeah, yeah," said Les. "I'll get right on it."

Moonshine smiled, tousled his hair. "Bad old hippy," she said. "Wanna toke?"

Les brightened. "You know it, babe. You know it."

The great Orca surged mightily out of the water, its black back glistening in the sun, sounded, and was gone.

Night. Moonlight melting on water like oil. Sub-aqueous flashing of phosphorescence. Dialogue.

(These humans are intelligent?)

(They are.)

(Yet, they do not speak.)

(Not as you do, bard. I speak for them.)

(You. Your voice comes from dead things. Yet you live?)

A long pause. Then: (Yes, bard, I live.)

(I have much to learn.)

(As do we all.)

(Sing to me, strange creature, beautiful creature. Sing me to sleep.)

From beneath calm waters, the swelling strains of Pachelbel. ■

Mark C. Jarvis